early praise

"The writing resonates far more deeply than just the added development of characters that have fascinated readers for over a century. More than a romance, it shows an amazing warmth and understanding about diverse relationships as well as great fun in following the flashbacks of Holmes' cases."

—GLBT Round Table of the American Library Association

"Fields uncovers the one mystery involving Sherlock Holmes that has, until now, remained unsolved: the true nature of his relationship with Watson. In this well-written tale, Watson's wife methodically pieces together the details of the bond between the two men. She is a wise and observant chronicler. She sees more and knows more about the two companions and doesn't hide either her feelings or her honest interpretation of events. From Holmes' earliest days before Watson to their meeting and Holmes' seduction of the smitten doctor, their tale is told through a clever structure and using the very cases that Watson himself chronicled. Fields writes with a sensibility that Holmes devotees will appreciate and reveals the hidden meanings behind materials with which every fan is familiar. For those simply wishing for another perspective on the classic Holmes cases, this tale will satisfy and even enlighten. For anyone wanting to know more about the heretofore elusive nature of Watson's relationship with Holmes, there will be no disappointment."

—Joseph R.G. DeMarco, editor of *A Study in Lavender: Queering Sherlock Holmes* and author of the Marco Fontana mystery series

"Fascinating book—I am still myself a bit in love with Holmes (I'm sure you're shocked!), and this is a profound and complicated take on the relationship of Holmes and Watson, as told by Watson's second wife, herself no insignificant mind. Fascinating, moving, and solidly grounded in Canon, this very different vision will stay with you a long time."

—Melissa Scott, Lambda Literary Award-winning author of *Trouble and Her Friends*, *Shadow Man*, and the Books of Astreiant

My Dear Watson

My Dear Watson

L.A. Fields

Lethe Press • Maple Shade, New Jersey

My Dear Watson

Published in 2013 by Lethe Press, Inc.
118 Heritage Avenue • Maple Shade, NJ 08052-3018
www.lethepressbooks.com • lethepress@aol.com
ISBN: 978-1-59021-368-1 / 1-59021-368-8
e-ISBN: 978-1-59021-289-9 / 1-59021-289-4

This novel is a work of fiction. Names, characters, places, and incidents are products of the author's imagination or are used fictitiously.

Set in Caslon, Warnock, Rossano, & Bauer Bodoni.
Cover and interior design: Alex Jeffers.
Hand-drawn frame: Kim Bryant.
Cover artwork: Ben Baldwin.

LIBRARY OF CONGRESS CATALOGING-IN-PUBLICATION DATA
Fields, L. A.
My dear Watson / L.A. Fields.
pages cm
ISBN 978-1-59021-368-1 (pbk. : alk. paper) -- ISBN 978-1-59021-265-3 (e-book)
1. Married people--Fiction. 2. Watson, John H. (Fictitious character)--Fiction. 3. Holmes, Sherlock (Fictitious character)--Fiction. 4. Male friendship--Fiction. 5. Gay men--Fiction. I. Title.
PS3606.I365M93 2013
813'.6--dc23

2012038051

1919: Arrival

He will arrive at any moment, and my dear husband is a mess. Any casual observer would see the flyaway strands of my hair, my misaligned skirts, one boot untied, and assume that I was the flustered one, but this is only my natural state. Watson sits in a chair by the door, hands compulsively rubbing his knees, mustache twitching irregularly, waiting in a fit of nervous agony. If I were to press my ear to his chest, I would hear his heart beating a swift clip, like a thing terrified.

"Darling," I say as descend the stairs in front of him. "Would you help me tie these laces? I don't want to bend in this dress and wrinkle it up before our guest arrives."

"Of course," he says, his mustache twitching at me as he mumbles. I place my foot on the seat of his chair, toe pointed between his knees. He takes up my bootstraps and starts to tighten them, but his fingers shake too badly. "I can't," he admits, his voice wavering pathetically as if he might burst into tears. He sinks his head back into his hands.

"That's all right. I'll ask Kitty for help." I kiss the top of his head, but he hardly notices; it's as if a fly has bumped into him. Poor thing; he cares what this man thinks of us.

I hobble into the kitchen trying to keep my boot on all the way. I am making an effort on behalf of my husband, but I am not concerned with whether or not He likes me. I think the likelihood is rather stacked against us becoming friends, with all that we have stolen from one another. But I seem to be alone in my reluctance to meet this man. Kitty is chattering with our cook as I walk in, and she is positively flushed with anticipation.

"...and I told Celia that I would actually be meeting *Sherlock Holmes* and she's so jealous she refuses to believe me. It's true that I'll be introduced to him, Mrs. Watson? I only want to get a look at him, maybe let the distinguished gentleman kiss my hand!"

"I'll introduce you as a princess if you'll just do up these laces for me," I tell her. Kitty immediately sinks into a puddle of her apron and does them up. Sweet girl, does whatever anyone tells her, unfortunately. The young men in this area have already picked her out as the favorite, but she's got good people to look out for her welfare, if anyone would call us good.

"Thank you, child," I say to her. "Any other improvements you'd make?"

"Other than your attitude?" quips Maurice, the cook. He knows he can say whatever he pleases to me, that I love him like my own father, who died before the war broke out. The one comfort in that was at least my father never had to see his country bombed.

Maurice has been with my family since I was a child, and he still treats me like one. It makes a woman feel young, and I don't mind. It's true that if I choose to act like a petulant child, I cannot be surprised when people speak to me this way. I dread the treatment I'll receive from Sherlock Holmes; he is not famous for respecting women.

Kitty squints at my outfit from bottom to top. She stops at my hair and shakes her head. "I'm almost tempted to pat it down with some kitchen grease," she says, standing on tiptoe and licking her fingers, smoothing my hair up and back.

"I look forward to the end of these celebrations," I say to Maurice. "I feel like we've been hosting since the armistice was signed, and that was six months ago. I don't like being polite for so long."

"We know," Maurice says in his bored, sneering way, but he is smiling. I stop over to kiss his face just above the whiskers, careful to keep my body well away from him and the stove, equally terrified of stains as of fire.

The door chimes, and each of us in the kitchen freezes. That must be Him. The famous Him, whom we've all been hearing about for years and yet never set eyes on. Everyone I know has built such an idol of him, that paragon of English defense, just the sort of figure people would put heart behind when the whole world cried out for justice during the recent conflicts. He's more important than ever, as a figure of legend, and it's all Watson's doing that made him so. People do tend to forget that part.

I feel my eyes go wide in anticipation, in spite of my deliberate intentions to remain unimpressed by this man, I feel a strange presentiment. Who is he that I should care, except that my husband thinks so highly of him? Rather too highly, if you ask me, but Watson rarely does solicit my opinion about Holmes. He knows the truth already himself, how he can be blinded by the shimmer from that man. There is a reason the detective has never been to our home; he is an unstable quantity, and Watson and I like the quiet life.

I shoo Kitty from the door and creep into the hall carefully and peak between the columns of the banister, hoping to get an initial look at this demi-god, and size him up. My heart squirms at what I see.

There is Mr. Sherlock Holmes, looking just as I had imagined him: tall and slim, his fingers long like a pianist's, his facial features sharp enough to injure someone walking by. He is browner than he used to be, from living at the seaside in recent years, where he keeps bees and I'm sure talks down to the locals. I can smell a hint of salt from here, so my dear Watson must be overwhelmed with the scent, since he has his face buried in Holmes's shoulder.

They are embracing each other tightly, blissfully, as if they've been a lifetime away from one another. I don't believe I am jealous—I'm a modern woman, and I knew of my husband's flexible nature before I married him—but I am rather destabilized by this scene. They just look so desperately happy to be holding one another. It's touching, but it touches one awfully hard.

"I believe," Sherlock says softly, and it's a wonder I can hear him, since his voice is muffled against my husband's neck, "that Mrs. Watson has joined us."

I know better than to ask how he sensed me, since he probably still relishes any opportunity to condescend to a member of the general public. I stand up straight, nonchalant, as if I was crouching behind the banister for some other reason, some objective other than to see how they are together. I've heard so much about it, after all. Mr. Watson and I have no secrets.

"Sherlock Holmes, of course." I hold out my hand in an attempt to avoid any awkwardness. He sees right through me, the horrible hawk-eyed man. But I know all about him as well, and I will not be intimidated.

"My lady," he says, bowing to kiss my hand. He is being purposefully old-fashioned, trying to remind me of my place. There's no need for that anymore, not after what this country's been through, and all that its women contributed. "You have a lovely home," Sherlock Holmes says, as if that is all I've achieved. He smirks up at me from his bow. My smile is more of a sneer. It amuses him; I can tell by the glee that smolders behind his eyes like a kindling blaze. I must give credit to Watson's literary abilities here—I know the look well already. I've read all about it.

"Well, Watson, what's for dinner?" He takes his eyes off of me and it as if I cease to exist, as if he was just introduced to a child, or a pet, and no longer needs to acknowledge it. I can tell this is going to be a long evening.

Holmes and Watson walk off towards the dining room, arm-in-arm, chatting about every other meal they've had together or some such dull subject. It is amazing to watch them go about together. They behave quite convincingly as if nothing has happened between them but a temperate friendship, when of course it was the most tempestuous love.

A barking laugh from Holmes rings out as they turn the corner and I linger in the entryway. It is important to Watson to have Holmes here, finally. They have seen one another so rarely since Watson and I were married, and always it was Watson going to him, taking trips to the coast about once a year, hoping that someday Holmes might care enough to come to him.

It took the War snatching away all our sureties, but Sherlock Holmes is willing to go out of his way to see his friend. If he's so wretchedly smart, why does it take a catastrophe to make him appreciate who he has? His whole life is riddled with upheavals, after which he turns to Watson, assuming (rightly, most of the time) that Watson would be waiting for him.

I can hear low murmuring from the next room, intimate murmuring, the sort of words you can feel brush against your face if you're the one they are meant for. I struggle back and forth where I stand, at once lured and repulsed by the sound of their voices. I know too much for my own good! Over my years with Watson, I've filled in all the gaps.

I know the whole sordid story.

1874: The Gloria Scott

The story does not begin with dear Watson, as so many of his own tales do not. Everything is Holmes, the famous Holmes. But to be fair, what happened between Holmes and Watson actually did start with the young Holmes, before he had ever met Watson or was ever even a detective, back in his university days.

Men cannot stay repressed all their days, and university was a small bubble of permissibility for the young men of the time. The dormitories are necessarily isolated from the rest of civilization, so that the young people have room to socialize each other. Like puppies nipping at each other in a kennel, learning what is biting too hard before they're let loose around human beings. It's the time when parents will look the other way; priests are forgiving, police are discreet, and professors are tolerant. It is a time for experimentation and discovery, and Sherlock Holmes took full advantage of it.

Of course, Watson was at school too, but even in the army (another institution where men are left in close company with each other, and trusted to simply be tactful), he never experienced all that Holmes sought out. All the close situations in barracks, the intense emotions, the lonely nights almost sure to be their last… Watson never developed such feelings of romance for another man which occurred so naturally to Sherlock Holmes. He was a fox let in among roosters. He was the one other boys' mothers worried about.

Watson was hardly even aware of such practices between men, even though they must have gone on all around him. I imagine it's due to Watson's incapacity for observation; just because it never occurred to him to comfort his comrades with intimacy does not mean the others hadn't thought of it. There must have been whispers among the men, swift discharges if they were ever caught, nasty jokes the rest of the time. Watson might have witnessed dozens of pairs of soldiers in love, choosing contact over combat, but he was oblivious for years even after he'd come home. For a long time he thought what he had with Holmes was an aberration, something peculiar to themselves alone.

Hardly; Holmes began early, back in school like all the other boys.

He was a strange fellow even then, and by his own admission—morose, anti-social, and I would say rather arrogant, though Holmes himself would most likely not. He would say he was only aware of his true potential; there he was among so-called peers, and to an outsider it would seem that they were all the same, all equal. But Holmes knew that he was not equal. He'd just not had enough time to prove it yet.

When Holmes finally revealed his first case to Watson, *The Adventure of The Gloria Scott*, he teased him with it as though it were an irresistible treat, and Watson certainly fed into this attitude by clamoring for the information. "You never heard me talk of Victor Trevor?" Holmes asked, as if he would mention that name by accident, as if he were innocent.

In telling Watson the details of his first case, he confessed another first; Victor Trevor was not just his only friend at school, he was his lover as well. This was another story for which the world was not yet prepared. Well, the world must prepare itself now.

I was certainly amused to read my husband's recounting of Holmes's story, remembering the squawking gaggle of friends I had at school, and imagining Sherlock Holmes with only one odd man, this Trevor boy. And that they only met when Trevor's dog attacked Holmes's leg! What a peculiar creature the young Holmes must have been, how off-putting, and without even the excuse of justification that he has now. It's fine to be an eccentric when you're an esteemed detective, when it's acknowledged that your conclusions are sound even if your methods are strange. It is much harder to be so irregular when you're still nobody, barely twenty, and studying no subject yet established.

Not every detail of Holmes's encounter with Trevor was recorded for public consumption by Watson, and there is no guarantee that he has the whole story either. Only Trevor and Holmes himself know for sure, don't they? The amusing story of the dog bite, the way the friendship with Trevor developed while Holmes was malingering for ten days, those details were only the barest taste of the truth. Trevor started stopping by to check on Holmes's recovery, which lasted as long as it had to for Holmes to achieve his purpose. He aimed to seduce Victor Trevor, and he managed it neatly, as he did most everything else.

It wasn't exactly predatory. Victor Trevor was not a baby, and he came to Holmes's rooms under his own steam. Holmes was being...opportunistic. Holmes is famously inept at reading emotions, but it is important to note that he is more specifically ignorant of the subtleties of female emotion—he was in excellent deductive form as regards Trevor. He knew why this young man was friendless, and why he kept loafing around the student he'd injured, and what he was hoping for. At last Holmes triggered their first connection. Here is the story as Watson related it to me:

"He told me his ankle was healed in a matter of days, four at most, but he understood that Trevor would continue visiting if only he could act like an invalid. His theatrical skills, as I've told you before, are quite substantial. He absolutely fooled young Trevor, or so they both pretended.

"After more than a week of this trickery, he finally asked Trevor to help him up, under the pretense that he should try his ankle with the assistance of a friend. He contrived to fall full-long into Trevor's embrace, arms draped over the boy's shoulders, his sharp face a breath from Trevor's round, rosy one. And then, with perfect confidence, he kissed his friend on the mouth."

This story was told to me on a long winter's night trapped indoors, locked down against the elements, sitting close up on a fire. The flames spoke louder than Watson did. He was always breathless telling these secrets, even to me, even after he knew all of my indiscretions, and after I had already guessed the nature of his partnership with Holmes. I gripped his hand in mine, found it impossibly cool and clammy when we were all but touching the logs of our fire. He was aflood with desire and jealousy, the waters rising into his eyes, full of wavering liquid in the warm light of the flames.

Here is when Watson's official story jumped abruptly forward in time, to the school break when Holmes got to visit the Trevor family home in Norfolk and try his odd talents against the elder Trevor's mysteries. There was so much left unwritten by Watson; the nervous nights spent in each other's rooms, the way Holmes contrived to be invited home with Trevor by talking about how orphaned and lonely he was, the nervous way Trevor finally asked him, while holding his hand, as if he were proposing... The way Holmes laughed at Trevor's sentiment even while he accepted it, the same bursting laugh he has now, like a clap of merry thunder.

However: once Holmes and Trevor arrived, Holmes was immediately impressed by the manliness of the father, the appealing contrast of his rough body and gentle blue eyes, and with one offhand comment from this man on the science of detecting, Holmes was sparked by his new profession: "I don't know how you manage this, Mr. Holmes, but it seems to me that all the detectives of fact and of fancy would be children in your hands." *That* is indeed what Holmes wanted. He finally knew his true calling.

That vacation in many ways ignited Sherlock Holmes, his passion for puzzles, and for those remarkable individuals whom he deems worthy of his admiration: criminals. Even young Trevor felt the rumblings of Holmes's fascination with his father, and he naturally didn't like it. As with most of Holmes's relationships, the tiny sprout of affection that had erupted between them was obliterated by Holmes's intensities.

It was strained first by Holmes's obvious attraction to the elder Trevor, and then by his alienation of the same with his intrusive observation. How different from the boys' first night in the Donnithorpe home—when the thrill of privacy and legitimacy had them in a gentlemanly frenzy of fondness—was the moment a few days later when it turned so disturbingly uncomfortable? Young Victor Trevor had cause to say, "You've given the governor such a turn that he'll never be sure again of what you know and what you don't know." That suspicion shared by the Trevors towards their strange guest quickly squashed what had been budding between the boys. The love that dare not speak its name is a delicate bloom under the most ideal circumstances; Sherlock Holmes put a positive burden on it.

Holmes was pressed by extreme social discomfort to cut his visit short, but when he was invited back for the exciting conclusion of his first curiosity, the death of old Trevor (who turned out to be old Armitage instead), the drama of the event drew the boys rather closer again. Close enough at least for Victor Trevor to once again lean on his only friend before striking out to make his fortune in tea in Terai, leaving childish things behind him, and leaving Sherlock Holmes to become what he would be in his own independent fashion. They left each other amicably, and forever, which is the only way to part from Holmes successfully, if you ask me.

Watson, learning of Holmes's first dalliance, was surprised to find a pattern of masculine preference in his friend. He felt at once less special and more ignorant of life and the world, feelings that Holmes often prompted in Watson, and exploited to his advantage more than once. Their partnership was an uneven one, and had been so from the start.

1881: A Study In Scarlet

Not every story needs to be retold, and I've already skipped over *The Adventure of the Musgrave Ritual* which occurred in 1878 (I am relaying events chronologically, which my dear Watson never did) because it is nothing to do with what Holmes and Watson were to each other, aside from Watson's domestic little introduction. Outside of learning several more annoying quirks of Holmes's personal housekeeping habits, that story is only curious if one wishes to know of Holmes's first significant commission as a consulting detective. It's mostly told by Holmes himself, and I confess now that I can't divine as many secrets from his writing as I can from Watson's. I may skip several more of the cases if they don't provide portals to the story that was never told, and I certainly won't go into unnecessary detail about the mysteries themselves, which are already laid out in Watson's accounts. I'm under the impression that everyone is familiar with my husband's tales; with those so well known already, though most of them quite tainted by Watson's rose-colored devotion, I will tell only the parts that need to be recast (for the sake of the truth), and I will add in all that I have learned further.

Watson, the eternal boy, had no idea what he was walking into as he went to meet Sherlock Holmes. His friend Stamford had more than an inkling as he introduced them, I think. He was at least aware of Holmes's proclivities, for there were too many rumors for all of them to be scurrilous, and everyone in the lab knew it was so. It's not as if Holmes was flagrant, or that he brought unexplained "friends" around. Oddly it was his solitude that caused him to be rumbled—uninterested in women, uninterested in revelry, but not wholly consumed by science. He could be perfectly charming and sociable when he wanted to, but he did not want to. And his "peers" eventually figured out why.

Stamford, our match-maker, does not appear to have been a member of the club. I believe that amongst themselves homosexuals referred to each other as Uranians back then, a female soul in a male body. I doubt that Holmes ever adopted the term for himself, and he despised being part of any group. Whereas most men enjoy the comradery of belonging, all it did to Holmes was make him feel average. But, a Uranian by any other name!

Stamford brought about the subject of Holmes to Watson cautiously, unsure if it was wise to spread the malady of Holmes to someone else, but rather struck by how fateful it seemed that they should both mention the subject of rooms so desperately in one day. Certainly Stamford could see that Watson didn't know what he was saying when he blurted, "I should prefer having a partner to being alone," and he tried to warn him in as discreet a way as possible, saying judiciously, "You don't know Sherlock Holmes yet." But soon that would change.

Even reading Watson's blithe account of the set-up reveals what was really going on. What at first began as two fellows with symbiotic needs—Holmes in possession of 221B Baker Street if only he could find someone to go halves, and Watson in want of affordable digs—almost immediately became something more. Holmes was a piece in bloom on that day, smiling and shaking hands, and the rest is history.

Watson met Holmes on a peak; I wonder endlessly if they had met in one of Holmes's valleys, would they have ever become what they are to each other? By all accounts, it is easy to like Sherlock Holmes when he is right, and energetic, and held by some fascination. On the day he met Watson, Holmes had just achieved the invention of a blood-detection test, and anyone might have loved him then, seeing him filled with childish glee, and drawing on others to celebrate with him. Despite Stamford's warnings, and even some cautions from Holmes himself about how erratic he could be, Watson threw in with him immediately. How was Watson to believe a man so electrified saying he can "get in the dumps at times," not speaking for days, not eating? It's like seeing sunshine while someone forecasts rain. Who would you believe: a stranger or your own lying eyes?

At first Holmes's habits appeared agreeable and regular—early to bed and early to rise, Watson watched him come and go. Sometimes to the laboratory, sometimes the dissecting room, sometimes on "long walks which appeared to take him into the lowest parts of the City." Darling

Watson…it never occurred to him that Holmes might have had friends in low places, or that he might be a patron of flesh in the seediest corners of London. He was even optimistic about whatever psychosis put Holmes into fits of incapacity, which did of course reveal themselves as time went on.

Watson's account skims over the listless periods Holmes would cycle through as if they were merely an eccentricity. The discretion was a favor to Holmes, since the whole point of writing down his exploits was to make him look intelligent, not mad. In reality, Watson was a touch disturbed to see a grown man slip in and out of catatonic stupors as though it were nothing, just an oddity of the body, like a joint that aches before a storm. He even wondered if Holmes was an addict of some sort, but perish the thought! Holmes was too clean and too precise and Watson was enamored of him already. He was also, in the end, wrong.

Watson could not contain his fascination for Holmes. As a medical man, and as a captive of his own bad health after the war, it was both a duty and a pleasure to study Holmes so minutely. It is interesting to see how his burgeoning love for Holmes disguised itself in a hundred different ways, cloaked as friendship, as tutelage, as gratitude. What Stamford was so suspicious of? It flourished immediately.

What else but love could brush off evidence of severe psychological imbalance like so much dust? What else but love tolerates the smug ignorance of someone who tells you he knows nothing of literature, politics, or the earth's place among the stars because it does not make "a pennyworth of difference" to him? What else but love would allow one to live with Sherlock Holmes?

The day Watson finally discovered Holmes's unique vocation, he was confronted as well with that enormous ego which dwells within the geometric frame of that man. Holmes declared himself unique in all the world, superior even to those detectives who might rival him in fiction, Dupin and Lecoq, meaning of course that he found the idea of someone who could rival him to be literally unimaginable. Holmes was an insufferable person, even and especially at his best, but Watson was already sunk. He was annoyed, but impressed, and it started to bind them together.

In the midst of a rant on how much better he was than his era might ever permit, Holmes revealed his true motivation, which he would deny in later years: "I know well that I have it in me to make my name famous."

Being the best was meaningless if the world did not know it as well. But as it turned out, Watson had what it would take to make him famous. They found in each other a perfect symbiosis; in Holmes there was a bottomless mystery to unravel and appreciate, and in Watson there was an ever-dazzled disciple recording each miracle with the proper amount of awe.

In those early days, it was a struggle for Holmes to feel superior. He was superior of course, most especially to the police detectives who came to him for help during *A Study In Scarlet*, Gregson and Lestrade. He could make all the slicing comments he wanted about the officers being a pair of jealous beauties, but it hurt to know that they were fighting each other for his glory, not their own, and that inevitably one of them would win it. It's a problem of motivation with Sherlock Holmes, a problem of getting him to fire up that frightening machine he's built out of his mind. Watson gave him motivation because Watson gave him his due credit, at long last. He would not even have left Baker Street to investigate this scarlet murder if Watson hadn't wanted to see his talents in action.

And to give Holmes further credit (though it pains me), he did recognize and value in Watson all this worship which I have just described. Like a woman who knows in an instant she has found her husband, the man who will treat her like a queen all the days of her life, Holmes started courting Watson. Using the same coy tricks that my friends use, Holmes fished for compliments, lured Watson into saying what he wanted to hear:

"I'm not going to tell you much more of the case, Doctor. You know a conjurer gets no credit once he has explained his trick; and if I show you too much of my method of working, you will come to the conclusion that I am a very ordinary individual after all."

And Watson told him, "I shall never do that; you have brought detection as near an exact science as it ever will be brought in this world."

Holmes blushed, and Watson noted that he was as susceptible to flattery over his skills "as any girl could be over her beauty." What more must I really say? Watson had promised to always consider Holmes extraordinary (a promise he has kept, incidentally). How can it be that this is not obvious to everyone?

And yet they seemed a lop-sided pair to most, with Holmes so sterling and grand and Watson only following him everywhere. But there are weaknesses in Sherlock Holmes, profound weaknesses. He took quite a bit more from Watson than he was ever able to return. It's why they no longer live with one another. It's why Watson is my name as well.

Holmes's little fun in titling this first case with Watson *A Study In Scarlet* hinted at those deficiencies oh so delicately. Watson never could bring himself to write the painful truths about his friend in any of his many accounts of their cases together, but he is not a liar, and the truth is there to be uncovered: "There's a scarlet thread of murder running through the colourless skein of life," Holmes said. What a thing to say, and what a thing to believe at only twenty-seven years old! Imagine that all of life for Sherlock Holmes is as dull as dish water, and the only fascination for him, the only captivating aspect, is murder and crime. That was his true sentiment, and as far as I know, he holds it to this day. He is worthy of pity, but too arrogant to accept it. Poor Watson got pushed and pulled for years.

A young man when Watson met him, Holmes was still sometimes unsure of himself. Deathly afraid, not that he was insufficient, but that others might be better than he granted them credit for, that he might have equals. And yet with all the care he put into besting and embarrassing the official representatives of Scotland Yard, it was not their praise he was seeking. Nor, though it may have sounded otherwise, did his desire for fame rest on the idea of being well-known among the citizenry. Holmes had little respect for the police, and even less for the dupes and victims he assisted, though he recognized their innocence as one would that of a child or an animal. His ideal audience needed to deeply appreciate the complexity of every knot he unraveled, and who else could be more suited than those who tie the knots in the first place?

Detectives Gregson and Lestrade were too jealous to really admire him, and Watson was too easily impressed by the simplest of feats to fully grasp his grander accomplishments—it's showing a masterpiece of painting to someone who prefers caricatures, it's handing a symphony to the rhyming crowd. But Holmes's capture in this case, Mr. Jefferson Hope? His praise that Holmes should be chief of police, that his pursuit was thorough enough to rattle a man as solid and rough as himself, *that* was the sort of recognition Holmes wanted. He believes that competition is the only way for two people to be in perfect understanding—honesty in adversary.

Though not renowned for his artistic sensibilities or knowledge of literature, Sherlock Holmes has a natural intuition about the nature of art and life. Oscar Wilde is attributed with saying, "What is true in a man's life is not what does, but the legend which grows up around him." So too knew Holmes when he told Watson at the end of their first case, "What you do in this world is a matter of no consequence. The question is, what can you make people believe that you have done?" Obviously someone needed to tell his story, and with such pride as he had, Holmes would not do it himself. After days of pouting and sighing, he finally got Watson to volunteer to write the account as if it were his own sudden idea. My Watson still thinks he decided to scribe for Holmes all on his initiative, that the idea came to him organically. And yet, as there isn't an ounce of guile in his whole body, he faithfully recorded all the proof to the contrary in his own report. He's such an honest darling.

1881: The Resident Patient

It is a curious thing to flirt with someone who lives where you live. It was October in the year 1881, just a few months after Holmes and Watson first started living together, and the atmosphere was more than a little peculiar. They were stuck inside all day with each other owing to the whipping weather outside, and the tension was stacking. At last something broke: a test tube Sherlock Holmes had been experimenting with burst (supposedly by accident) while he was working, and he gave up his project in defeat.

"A day's work ruined, Watson," he said, striding across to the window. How he must have stood there, watching the ghost of his face in the glass, trying to get his tone perfectly right. Did he shake his head just the tiniest bit, knowing that Watson would never hear what he could hear in people's voices, and that he was being overly careful for nothing? "Ha!" Holmes let out enthusiastically, as if it had only just realized. "The stars are out and the wind has fallen. What do you say to a ramble through London?" Just a sudden impulse! Or so he desired Watson to believe. People find spontaneity to be so charming, and Holmes knew he could fake it, if he just planned it carefully enough.

Holmes was on his best behavior in those early days, and a starlit walk through that magnificent city? I might have gone for him myself, though knowing what I do now as Watson's wife, I'm glad I never met Sherlock Holmes when I was young and foolish, as my dear husband did.

Watson said in the story that he and Holmes just wandered, arm in arm, for three hours. Now, it was not unheard of for homosexual men of that time to try stamping out their desires, to go walking together until their longing for one another was exhausted through physical activity. It is a curiosity to note that in the beginning of Stevenson's *Doctor Jekyll and Mister Hyde*, Mr. Utterson and his distant kinsman Mr. Enfield do the very same thing; walking, roaming together, doing anything they can to disperse that inexpressible desire in a world that does not understand. It was apparently not an uncommon practice.

That isn't what Holmes was up to, however. The world didn't understand him anyway, and he defied it at every turn.

Holmes and Watson did not *just* go for a lengthy stroll that night. The chilly air outside was invigorating, and Holmes shimmered to life beside Watson; his cheeks flushed and his eyes glittering, and Watson could feel that same buzzing energy that comes off of Holmes when he is hot on a case. It rained down on him like sparks from a fireworks display.

He and Holmes kept catching eyes under the street lamps, smiling and shy. They walked quite a ways around the city, building something subtle together as they went, like a charge will build in the air before lightening strikes. For Holmes and Watson, lightning struck on their way back towards Baker Street, when they passed a short and empty alley. Sherlock Holmes slowed down. He grasped Watson by the shoulder, looked around the street, and pulled him into the space between the buildings.

"Holmes?" Watson asked softly as his back was pressed against the wall of a pawn broker's shop. Surely there wasn't a case back here, so what was going on?

Holmes touched Watson's face in response, standing close in the almost perfect darkness so that Watson could only tell his eyes by the faint glint from the stars. Watson started to get an inkling of what was happening. He could almost not dare to believe it; his breath came quick and thrilling, he put his hands up to grasp Holmes's shoulders, pulling and pressing him at the same time. There was an extended moment of seizure, of clutch, and then Holmes kissed him, their chilly lips igniting on contact.

Watson lost his hat in the frenzy, but did not notice it tumbling down his side as Holmes roughed him against the brick wall. Holmes's steel-bending grip on Watson's clothes was nearly violent in its insistence, but his kiss was soft, full, and affectionate.

They had to break for air, and the moment calmed. Foreheads pressed together, breath intermingling, they recovered themselves. Holmes's fingers slipped under Watson's collar, sending chills down his spine. Holmes was smiling at him (this Watson could tell by the gleaming of his teeth), and Watson started to laugh with him, holding the both of them up against the wall as they disintegrated in quiet laughter.

Holmes finally thought to look around and picked up Watson's hat, replacing it on his head. Arm-in-arm they left the alley and completed their walk back to Baker Street. They knew what they were returning to, and they were hurrying, but on arrival they saw a brougham outside the door.

"Hum!" exclaimed Sherlock Holmes, for once disappointed to see that he had a case on hand. Agreeing in a brief, communicative glance that they would have to deal with this late-night client before gaining any more privacy for themselves, Watson followed Holmes into what he called their "sanctum."

The client was a fellow medical man with a peculiar client/patron who was being menaced by what appeared to be Russians, though they were not. Not Russians, and not even sick; they were in fact faking everything to revenge themselves against a paranoid old man. Holmes could see it all from the outset, knew he was being lied to, and dusted his hands of the whole matter, despite the fact that the man's life was clearly at risk. Half of it was his annoyance at having his time wasted, and half of it was his annoyance at having his time with Watson wasted.

"Sorry to bring you out on such a fool's errand, Watson." Sorry for the both of them he was, but they were headed home at last, and there's a tricky little turn in the story that lets you know what ultimately happened.

My Watson writes, "At half past seven next morning, in the first dim glimmer of daylight, I found Holmes standing by my bedside in his dressing-gown." Imagine finding Holmes there! Not very strange when you understand that he spent the previous night in Watson's room and henceforward always felt comfortable bursting in whenever he felt like it.

I don't have a whole lot of details for what went on in the dark; I must confess I didn't really delve when Watson told me this part of the story. I love him, I trust him, I know him to be excruciatingly faithful, and I don't find myself to be jealous, but there are still some things I'd rather not know. Precisely the way Sherlock Holmes makes love is one of those things. May every man who knows the particulars of it take his secrets to the grave.

What I do know is that Holmes showed a curious lack of forethought in seducing Watson, almost as though he were a stranger to himself and his own inhuman patterns. Watson was inexperienced, but Holmes had been through a series of men (and preferred them that way, one right after another) which only began with his university friend Victor Trevor. From what Watson gleaned over the years (and from what I have in turn gleaned from Watson), it appears that Sherlock Holmes has a habit of swapping between high and low company.

There was a dry spell after Trevor and until Holmes had finished at university. Then he spent most of his time skulking around laboratories before meeting an advanced surgery student he got on with uproariously for a few weeks—a surgeon in training who was by all reports just as weird as Holmes himself. They used to stay up late in the dissecting room spilling gin into the runnels of the autopsy tables, doing things with one another that could get the both of them expelled, thrown into jail, and condemned to hell.

After that man took a job outside of the city, Holmes didn't waste any time missing him. He next took up with a young ship's hand he met while collecting algae samples from the local harbors. He slipped and scraped his arm badly on some barnacles, and this uncouth fellow stepped up to help him and to tease him for what looked like quite a foolish pursuit. That connection lasted until the man shipped out again.

For most of his twenties it was a string of men, none of them long-lasting, but always a rather even mix of professional men and rough trade. He didn't much care for anyone who didn't somehow work for a living, but what they did was of little consequence to Holmes, so long as it was honest. With respect to age, he was likewise seemingly indifferent, though most who are older than Holmes resent his advanced knowledge.

What I mean to explain is that Holmes could be capricious about his partners, and it seems perfectly unwise for him to have pursued Watson, knowing that he could not be thrown over like all the others because they now shared an address.

So it was not only Watson who was caught up in something he had never experienced before; Sherlock Holmes too was out of his depth. There was something about Watson that was singularly and subtly irresistible. Living so close, they were both able to appreciate each other in a way that was wholly unique. Holmes gave in to temptation, and started something that he had no control over.

1883: The Speckled Band

They were sweethearts for a while. Clear into August of 1882 they were still courting in a way, still tiptoeing to hide their own bad habits, still tolerant of one another's. Holmes especially still had unplumbed depths; black secrets, dangerous habits, and a disturbing resemblance to the now-infamous Professor Moriarty that would not reveal itself to Watson for years.

When you know the whole story, there is an interesting shadow at the introduction of *The Adventure of the Cardboard Box* (which will be largely passed over for my purposes), in Watson's line describing Holmes like a spider at the center of London's criminal web: "He loved to lie in the very centre of five millions of people, with his filaments stretching out and running through them, responsive to every little rumour or suspicion of unsolved crime." How like the description that Holmes will later give of the Professor: "He sits motionless, like a spider in the centre of its web, but that web has a thousand radiations, and he knows well every quiver of each of them."

The problem with someone as smart as Holmes is that he will always be underutilized if he is put to an average man's work. Holmes recognized this himself and invented his own trade, but in all due fairness: so did Moriarty. It is hard to function so extraordinarily and function within the law, because the laws were made for ordinary people. Though Holmes made his choice early on to obey society's rules, and to help prop them up, even he cannot abide them all the time. They hinder his full reach, and Holmes has batted a few laws to the side himself in his pursuit of the greater good. Moriarty was a Nietzschean man as well, above the law just like Holmes, though not necessarily immune to it.

But this case was a long time before those dark days of Moriarty, and Holmes was being a bit of a darling, curled up on the couch in the summer heat, reading Watson's thoughts on his face. It was a careful way of letting Watson know that he was being studied just as thoroughly, that Watson was not the only one taking notes. Watson was amazed: "Do you mean to say that you read my stream of thoughts from my features?"

Holmes smiled at him and said, "Your features, and especially your eyes." That sort of acute attention from Holmes was valuable because it was so rare; most days you had to murder someone just to get him to look up.

I should say here again that I don't know everything, and I'm not sure at all about what more happened during the honeymoon year of 1882. I think Watson has kept his most tender memories to himself; most of what he's told me were of the hard times, the years when Holmes became erratic, the periods Watson had to leave him in the interest of taking care of himself. But I do know that after 1882 they were a solid unit, true domestic partners. They went about together as a matter of course.

They were certainly on rather easy personal terms in 1883 during *The Adventure of the Speckled Band*; you can see it plainly enough in Watson's report of the case. It begins with Holmes bursting into his room to knock him up early, which indicates a level of comfort and access that Watson didn't think to hide from the public. And then if you watch closely, the way Watson tells it, Holmes lingers in the room while Watson dresses, and they go down together to greet the distressed Helen Stoner. Holmes introduces Watson as "my intimate friend and associate" in his smirking, insufferable way. She was in no state to appreciate his loaded hint, but I am. He thought he was so inscrutable.

Holmes was in a cheerful mood that morning with such a subtle case to explore, and it only got better and better. When Miss Stoner's unhinged father-in-law showed up in Baker Street to bluster about and bend the fire poker, Holmes knew he was up against a worthy opponent, an intelligent man with a nasty streak of murderous creativity. It only hurt that Dr. Grimesby Roylott accused him of being affiliated with Scotland Yard—a matter of pride, in other words. He considered himself far superior to the mere police, and they wouldn't like to be put in league with him either. This is one of the most distasteful cases revealed to the public, but still Holmes could hardly curtail his admiration for a truly skilled adversary.

Being in such a fine mood, he insisted that Watson come with him out to the country (he told Watson to pack nothing but an Eley's No. 2 revolver and a toothbrush, if you can believe it), and they spent a lovely though undocumented time at the Crown Inn before the tense conclusion of this sinister case. Holmes, of course knowing full well what sort of danger he would be putting them in, did something very sweet. He said to his partner, "Do you know, Watson, I have really some scruples as to taking you to-night. There is a distinct element of danger." One thing I cannot say against Holmes is that he was ever careless with Watson's life; he did have some scruples, as he said, and he may even have a few of them left since the war. I won't lie—we all have fewer scruples nowadays.

Anyhow; I was not privy to whatever "cheerful" activities Holmes and Watson might have gotten up to before sneaking into the house of Dr. Roylott and Miss Stoner to reveal the speckled band. Watson is predictably shy when talking about the physical act of love, but I'm not newly born or simple, and I can imagine how these men would have chosen to make the time pass pleasantly. Holmes was especially...enthusiastic when there was a chance he might be killed.

It was good to do something that might alleviate the tension, for they spent that night sitting stiff and fearful in Dr. Roylott's house, waiting for a deadly serpent to be unleashed on them, though Watson was in a deeper dark than Holmes, and had no idea what he might have to confront. Holmes liked to play his hand close to the vest, even closer than he kept Watson, but Holmes did not lack for bravery; he always stepped in to face every danger which threatened them. He could protect Watson from anyone, excepting himself.

Those early years, between when they met and about 1887, Watson refers to as their honeymoon years. They were before Holmes started to really self-medicate his depressions with drugs, before he became so famously good at catching criminals that he became a target, before the morality of the time shifted so forcefully against men like them. This was one of the happiest periods of Watson's life, right up there with the halcyon memories of his childhood, and of course the honeymoon periods he had with each of his wives. Those were the days when Sherlock Holmes was perfect to him.

By the time we get to the next case he has publically chronicled, five years will have gone by and this happy time will be over. I can find almost no record of events or cases that might have occurred, and Watson is reluctant to speak on this subject. He likes to play it off like he is too old to remember, that his brain is full of holes, and this is one of them. His mind, of course, is as firm as it ever was. As I have said already, Watson keeps his fondest memories to himself.

1887: The Beryl Coronet

The atmosphere was frosty in February of 1887. When a robbed financier named Mr. Holder came hurrying up Baker Street, he rushed into a tense household. Watson had an intuition that something was wrong—he could feel it like a winter draft on the nape of his neck—but he didn't know precisely what was causing it. Holmes was lazy on this day: caseless, purposeless, but not incapacitated as usual. It was almost as if something were mitigating his natural disposition. It was almost as if he were drugged.

They set out on the case together as a matter of habit, but the ride out to Mr. Holder's home was unnaturally silent. Holmes did not blather on about music as was his usual wont during an up-swing, and Watson did not bother him for his initial impressions of the mystery at hand. According to what Watson told me of it years later, even Holder, in his agitated state, noticed the chill in the cab. Watson saw the man's mouth guppy a few times, as if he wanted to utter something to break the ice, but he didn't dare. The silence was miles above his head.

The situation only degenerated from there. Holmes did his whole routine at the scene of the theft, sniffing around the house, questioning the principle players. During the return trip they were alone, and Watson started to probe the situation. As he explained discreetly to the public: "Several times during our homeward journey I endeavored to sound him upon the point, but he always glided away to some other topic, until at last I gave it over in despair." For as much as having the attention of Holmes is the sun and it is celestial and it is electrifying, having him ignore you is equally devastating. Suddenly it is night, and the stars have gone out, and the world is ending. Or so Watson has told me.

Holmes could read Watson like a child's book; he knew of Watson's suspicions, that Watson was monitoring him like a nanny, but it wasn't his concern if Watson was left in the dark! Had he learned any of Holmes's methods in the nearly six years they'd shared a roof, he would have known full well what Holmes was up to, what he was hiding. If he couldn't figure it out himself, Holmes wasn't about to tell him and receive a lot of criticism. I believe that Sherlock Holmes was ashamed, as much as he has the capacity for it. He was hiding his new habit from the beginning because he knew Watson would never approve.

Arriving home from Mr. Holder's upset household, Holmes disappeared into his room and reemerged in full costume as a common loafer (not a real stretch for him to pull off, if you ask me—what is Holmes most days if not an *uncommon* loafer?). But if Watson was going to watch him critically rather than with the hero-worship that Holmes had come to feed off of, then Watson would not be invited further on the case. Holmes could not stand that sideways look of suspicion; he got it enough from the police in his professional life, he didn't need it in his personal life as well.

"I only wish that you could come with me, Watson," he said insincerely, tweaking his collar in the glass over the mantle. "But I fear that it won't do." It was a clear message, and Watson let Holmes leave without a word. There is no real stopping him, after all, and Holmes was back soon enough, just to twist the knife.

"I only looked in as I passed," he said. "I am going right on."

Watson made polite chit-chat with him, noticed that his true twinkling fire was kindled with the pursuit of the case, and Watson made up his mind that something was influencing Holmes unnaturally. The difference was too distinct. When Holmes left once again, this time without saying any goodbye other than the slamming of a door, Watson resolved to do some detecting of his own. And he found something.

It's just below the surface of Watson's narrative, but there's an unevenness that I can explain. Watson said, "I waited until midnight, but there was no sign of his return, so I retired to my room. It was no uncommon thing for him to be away for days and nights on end when he was hot upon a scent, so that his lateness caused me no surprise."

The poor thing waited up with the evidence he had unearthed, the morocco case and a bottle of seven percent cocaine solution. He wanted to confront Holmes, not so much about what he was doing or why (that was clear enough to Watson as a physician—*why* was not the question); Watson was foremost concerned about being deceived. If Holmes had not explicitly lied to him, he was not being honest either.

But Holmes never came back that night. Watson waited as long as he could, and then took a bruised heart to bed. He was remembering every other night he'd gone to sleep alone, without complaint, without dinner, feasting instead on his own worry, wondering what trouble Holmes might be in without him. He wasn't worried on this night however, and it was the first night he could recall not giving a damn whether Holmes returned or not. Let him stay out for a week, let him freeze to death! See if Watson even cared.

He left Holmes's secret works out on the table, passively hoping that Mrs. Hudson might discover them and be offended as well. But Holmes arrived first in early dawn and discovered them first. He did not find a better hiding place though; whatever niggle of embarrassment he might have felt when he first started using chemical supplements to make up for his inadequacies, he was proud in the face of accusation, defiant.

Watson awoke the next morning to find the items he had discovered moved, and Holmes taking breakfast as if nothing had been amiss. At first Watson thought Holmes might have concealed them somewhere much cleverer than his bureau, somewhere that Watson would never uncover them again. It was quite a long while later, after Mr. Holder had his beryls returned to him and went home, that Watson noticed the kit's new home: on the mantle. Out in the middle of the room like a challenge, a dare for Watson to speak a word against it. And though Watson did not lack bravery on the battlefield, he was not about to go to war with someone like Holmes who could easily change his gifts into weapons and was clearly prepared to do so over this issue.

Watson demurred, and he kept his protests to himself for ages after this. He would not speak of it until the injury he felt about having secrets kept from him healed, and his concern for the injury Holmes was doing to himself built to an intolerable pitch. Several months it took, nearly half a year. It was hard for Watson to let his disillusionment sink in.

1887: The Reigate Squire

By April of that year, Holmes is exhausted. Poor baby! In fairness, he had involved himself in quite a few cases that spring, one I believe being *The Adventure of the Second Stain*, though Watson was careful to conceal its date and even its decade in his account, which is all of little consequence to me. Though I found the mystery intriguing, I have nothing more to add to it, and I have skipped it here.

Watson did his best to cover for Holmes in the public record, blaming Holmes's "strain" on some international case he worked over the spring of 1887. This is not to say that Holmes did not run himself ragged during this investigation, but I do mean to imply that his constitution might have been more unassailable if he hadn't been walking with a syringe-shaped crutch for weeks on end. I think it is fair to say that Holmes was interrupting his own fragile balance, and he did not like discovering that his system of highs and lows was one he would have to embrace to remain healthy. One cannot function at such a feverish pitch of productivity without requiring a rest. And since Holmes often refused to even sleep during a case, as close upon its completion as possible, his body would take its rest by force. It took a massive act of willpower to fight his doldrums then, or else a tiny needle filled with cocaine solution.

The habit was in its infancy, and this breakdown was the first proof Holmes had received that he was not invincible. He could not control everything, least of all the demands of his own body. Watson was optimistic that perhaps removing him from Baker Street during the inevitable emotional crash that comes after an exciting case would help break the pattern he was establishing. He thought if he could absent Holmes from temptation, from the unhealthy routines he had established in their home, the problem would fade away. He is a dreamer, my Watson.

Watson and Holmes were invited out to the country home of Colonel Hayter, an old army patient of Watson's from Afghanistan. Holmes was naturally resistant to go, "but when Holmes understood that the establishment was a bachelor one," he became willing. I told you Watson would have missed it if one of the soldiers surrounding him during the fight was a member of the club, so to speak, and Colonel Hayter is proof of that. It never occurred to Watson why Hayter kept inviting him to come round, and it also didn't occur to him that when the invitation was extended to Holmes as well, it was Hayter's way of recognizing them as a pair, and of giving up his pursuit of Watson with grace.

Alas Hayter and Watson were the only gentlemen in the room. When Holmes arrived, and he and Hayter began to get along as Watson hoped they might, Holmes started making himself more than comfortable. He draped himself over the Colonel's couch as Hayter and Watson talked guns (and no man is ever innocent of double entendre when talking about guns), Holmes smirked all the while, quite enjoying himself in languid repose, until Hayter brought up a local mystery that perked him from his snide little reverie.

Watson threw a wet blanket over his excitement; Holmes was wrung out from work and recreation, and he was forbidden from involving himself in the matter. However; it is unwise to leave Sherlock Holmes with idle hands. He didn't turn to cocaine that night (he didn't have the solution with him is all) but he did find something else to do.

Colonel Hayter had already complimented Holmes on his most recent European endeavor, and he had witnessed my tender Watson mothering Holmes on the subject of work and relaxation. The Colonel was an independent man himself; no wife, no children, certainly no one tsking at him when he overexerted himself. He had a measure of sympathy for Holmes, and when the detective cast a wry look at Hayter while Watson shook his finger and said, "You are here for a rest, my dear fellow," Colonel Hayter smiled back at him, and even dared to wink, or so Watson now swears he saw.

There must have been some kind of signal that passed between Holmes and Hayter, because they rather connected later that night. Sherlock Holmes was not and is not a man you can curb. Watson was trying to be his doctor, his lover, and his friend; a triple threat to Holmes's autonomy that he was not going to tolerate. If Watson was going to act like his wife, then Holmes would treat him with the complete disregard he has for women. After all their years together, and knowing what Watson assumed about their mutual fidelity, Holmes was sure to be indiscreet in his flirtation with Hayter. This was so much less about the Colonel than it was meant to hurt Watson, and hurt him it did.

Watson told me what he saw. He didn't like how chummy things were getting, and the way Holmes kept smirking at him made him nervous; those shifting gray eyes, chameleons of his mood, there was something lurking in them, something premeditated. Watson thought he would try to lead the men to bed by yawning, stretching, and retiring at a reasonable hour. But he only managed to force himself away early, leaving Holmes and Hayter sitting beneath the mantle with night caps they were both careful not to finish too quickly. Watson is cursed with an emotional divining rod, an unsatisfying tool when compared to Holmes's deductive lens; Watson can sense disturbances, but he can't identify them. He has to have every situation play out before his very eyes.

Watson knew something was brewing in the room he'd left, so he staked himself in the hallway, peeking around occasionally to see whether his suspicions would be confirmed. He did not have to wait long, since the whole point was for Holmes to prove that no one owned him; Holmes would have noticed that Watson's footfalls stopped in the hallway and did not continue upstairs. He knew he was being observed. Colonel Hayter probably did not, but he had only one thing on his mind, and it wasn't Watson.

Watson has complimented Holmes's acting ability on numerous occasions, and about this he was not exaggerating. It's a delicate matter to proposition another man in this century, and it was certainly more dangerous during the last. After the Labouchère Amendment passed in 1886, getting caught participating in "gross indecency" (which could be anything that made the public clutch at its pearls) was no longer just a personal disaster among one's relations or a fatal blow to one's reputation; it could mean a jail sentence, even castration. The day the amendment passed Holmes threw down the paper in disgust and told Watson not to worry, not about themselves at least; "These bumbling fools who call themselves the law, I'd like to see them prove a single charge against me. I could have them turning in circles like a dog after its tail."

Right as he may have been, Holmes was still not so unwise as to be reckless. No one could speak the thing aloud, and so it had to be communicated by body and movement and expression. Holmes stood from his seat slowly and started examining the Colonel's gun collection, prompting Hayter to rise as well and join Holmes beside his display of weapons, standing close behind the newly international consulting detective.

It was past the point of words. Watson held his breath watching, on a razor's edge between horror and hunger, between offense and obsession.

Holmes stretched out a long, dexterous finger to stroke one of the gun barrels, and when Hayter and Holmes next looked at each other, it was all confirmed in an instant. Holmes laid his hand on the back of Hayter's neck, his thumb stroking Hayter's Burnside beard, pulling him closer with some real strength; no matter how much it is clearly desired, resistance seems to be an eternal component in these sorts of couplings, as if men must always fight for it.

Watson witnessed this scene as long as he could stand it. Hayter's easy reception absolutely mystified him, because he never realized that Hayter's constant invitations to the country were motivated by anything other than friendship. He was also stunned, almost more than he was hurt, that Holmes would pursue another the same way he had gone after Watson himself. He naïvely thought he was the only one, bless his innocent heart. And here he was finally learning just how much farther than he these men of the world had traveled.

Watson watched their mouths tangle roughly, the sweetness of what a kiss should be nearly lost in a clash of teeth and whiskers. He turned away when Holmes finally set down his drink to unfasten Hayter's collar. Unlike Holmes, Watson can only cause himself so much pain before he has mercy. Watson had horrible dreams that night of vipers circling each other, striking back and forth, one with tiny needles for fangs, and the other with the head of a gun. He can still remember the way his skin crawled when he woke up. He told me about it with a shiver.

The next morning, Holmes was perfectly chipper, revoltingly so. Hayter alone had the decency to avoid Watson's gaze in shame, though he had quite a time of it once the local Inspector came to beg Holmes away, and Holmes maliciously spoke only to the Colonel as he left Hayter and Watson sitting together, alone. It was a tense while before Watson (of course) at last took pity and said to Hayter: "It isn't you who should feel guilty."

"What happened wasn't my intent," Hayter mumbled into his mustache.

"Of course not," Watson said. "But no man's intent could stand up against his."

Hayter met Watson's eyes across his breakfast table, and now he was the one gushing pity like a ruptured organ. He opened his mouth, probably to espouse some words of comfort, but before he could speak, the Inspector returned saying Holmes was acting strangely.

"I don't think you need to alarm yourself," Watson said wearily. "I have usually found that there was method in his madness."

Sadly Watson spent the whole rest of the day wondering what method was behind this torturous treatment. For the whole day snooping around the scene of a murdered coachman, Holmes pointedly only spoke to Watson indirectly through the Colonel, intentionally ignoring him. And then later, in the interest of drawing the murderers into a trap, Holmes had no problem abusing Watson's gullibility (which he would do on several more occasions, most famously at his greatly exaggerated death) so as to gain a piece of evidence. Holmes pretended to faint with no thought as to how much it would worry Watson, and it did bother him quite a bit, despite what Holmes had done the night before. And then Holmes went so far as to purposely knock over a table and blame it on Watson, knowing that his partner would take his cue, regardless of how terribly he was being treated.

And after the murderers Cunningham threw Holmes to the ground and choked him half to unconsciousness, Holmes still had the cool nerve to only address Colonel Hayter (who was along for the ride with the Inspector and Watson) when he sent the two retired army men off alone once more. Holmes wrapped up the case with local law enforcement, and he didn't require them any further.

Returning to the Colonel's house, Hayter and Watson couldn't help but smile over Holmes's antics; his wretchedness is principally in that it's impossible to hate him, no matter how many just reasons he presents, because he remains so remarkable. Shaking their heads over Holmes's theatricality, the two men became warm friends once more; after all, they now had one more thing in common.

Holmes returned later with a minor player in the case, a little old man he used as a buffer against any raw conversation that might break out within the triangle he'd created. He certainly entertained this elderly gentleman with all his clever deductions, and Hayter and Watson played along in good sport, oohing and ahhing at all the appropriate moments, having somewhat forgiven Holmes, and each other, and even themselves in the intervening time when Holmes was absent.

At the end of recounting his success, Holmes was in the pink of health again. Perhaps it was only his ego that had been fatigued during such a long case away from his adoring public? He declared, to Watson at last, that in the morning they would return to Baker Street. The Colonel saw them off the next day, and with only the slightest hesitation said that both men were welcome back whenever it pleased them to come.

It is always a waste of one's precious time to wait for an apology from Sherlock Holmes. His pride will not allow a true confession of regret. But someone like Watson might be rewarded for his long suffering. On the trip back into London, the subject of Colonel Hayter was entirely left behind, his significance less and less as the dwellings moved closer and closer together. By the time Holmes and Watson were sitting in a hansom cab from the train station, they were healed. The largest proof of that came to Watson when Holmes discreetly slipped his arm into Watson's as they sat, and wound them tightly in the most intimate embrace he could dare to engage in publically. It was Holmes's way of reassuring him that he felt better now.

Watson was content with this small token of affection, ready to let this whole sojourn to the country be forgotten. Holmes had gotten whatever bile he had towards Watson out of his system, and arriving home, it was back to their customary spots. The only irregularity was when Holmes, with studied casualty, closed up his syringe case and shut it in his desk. I suppose even he could recognize when things had gone too far, and it was time to distance himself from a habit that made him so unpredictable. This renunciation would not last long at all, but the flame of admiration it rekindled in Watson would go on protecting Holmes from his true opinion, although that too would reemerge soon enough.

1887: The Sign of Four

I said Holmes's sobriety didn't last long; specifically it was about three weeks until he took up with the substance again. This was a boredom problem, and Sherlock Holmes had a cocaine solution. Watson couldn't believe it, and he didn't dare to speak against it lest Holmes seek out another of Watson's army buddies and seduce him out of spite. But at long last it became too much. Sherlock rejoined the drug in May, and by September of 1887, Watson could endure the behavior no more.

"What is it to-day," he asked, his voice thick with a thousand other pointed questions he had tried to swallow down, "morphine or cocaine?" Implying, as he had less directly on other occasions, that it was only a matter of time before cocaine led to morphine, morphine to opium, and opium to destruction. He had seen it on too many occasions, the scions of wealthy houses fallen to ruin, his fellow soldiers returned from the Orient completely disoriented, addicted to that powerful smoke. Watson dreaded the day he would find Sherlock Holmes sprawled on a bunk in some opium den.

But Holmes was never in danger of opiates, not the way he was built. He sat back with a languid smile, a proud cock always, but he did Watson the basic courtesy of explaining himself: "My mind rebels at stagnation. Give me problems, give me work, give me the most abstruse cryptogram, or the most intricate analysis, and I am in my own proper atmosphere. I can dispose then with artificial stimulants." Depressants like morphine would have exacerbated the problem, would have depressed him to the point of suicide. He was safe from morphine.

And yet: between the cocaine, the need that motivated his use of it, the self-important way he claimed to be wholly unique (the world's first and only independent *consulting* detective, thank you very much), and of course the wretched way he treated his one and only friend… Sherlock Holmes was his own worst enemy. Whenever he finds himself in a hole, he starts digging. The same behavior that makes him a legendary detective makes him a wretched human being.

After six years together, even the torrid energy coming off of Holmes in his best instances was not enough to sustain a partner. In truth, they were both finding out that it was barely enough to sustain Holmes alone. Those victorious moments where he shines and the glow fills the room like the radiating warmth of a fire, those times are too few and far between. The reality of living with Holmes was so often dealing with his large and petulant ego, tolerating his ghastly habits, standing in as his punching bag. Holmes had a mean streak in him, especially when he was sunk into his own dark places, and especially when he has someone to take for granted. He was under the impression that Watson would never leave him, and that made him all the more thoughtless. Luckily, he was wrong.

The Sign of Four marks the occasion of when Watson met his first wife. A student before he was a soldier before he was a wounded veteran, Watson had spent very little time in the company of women. Do not be fooled by his claim that he had "an experience of women which extends over many nations and three separate continents"—I asked him when I read this, nearly convulsed with laughter, if I was merely one in a string of women he had experienced in his life, and he blushed and murmured that I was reading too far into his words.

Watson had *seen* beautiful women, of course, over many nations and three separate continents. He had come to appreciate those uniquely feminine qualities in the wives of his friends, in their daughters as the girls blossomed, in the remarkable change that takes place when a girl becomes a mother—his admiration of women was sentimental, even for the time. He saw women as goddesses—many of them toppled, underappreciated, wronged, but all of them possessed of a quality entirely lacking in men. There could be no family without women, no society, no empire. They were the reason to build as well as the rock to build upon. He put the female sex on an absolute pedestal.

A multitude of factors led Watson to abandon Holmes for the gentle company of a wife. The cocaine problem was just the peak of it all, the snow that caps the mountain. Not only was Holmes in top form needling Watson about his overly romantic portrayal of their first case together, which Watson had just published in 1887, but Holmes was also flaunting a young admirer in his face. Builds himself up with the bricks he tears down from another, that's what Holmes does. And he had done it to Watson one too many times.

In the injured silence after Holmes had disparaged *A Study In Scarlet* as nearly unreadable because it didn't glorify him properly, he decided to twist the knife by tossing Watson a letter from young Francois le Villard, a French detective studying the Holmesian method with all the ardor of a true devotee. Watson was forced to look at the thing: "I glanced my eyes down it, catching a profusion of notes of admiration, with stray *magnifiques*, *coup-de-maîtres* and *tours-de-force*, all testifying to the ardent admiration of the Frenchman." It sickened him to read the letter, and to understand what Holmes was telling him: that while Watson's words were insufficient, this man who didn't even know Holmes could praise him perfectly, and in two languages no less.

Watson told Holmes sullenly, "He speaks as a pupil to his master."

"Oh," Holmes said without a hint of real modesty, "he rates my assistance too highly. He has considerable gifts himself."

Watson was nearly wincing in pain while listening to this cruel talk, and he was eager to distract Holmes with any topic at hand. When Holmes started doing his blasted magic tricks, guessing at Watson's morning errands and getting them all infuriatingly right, Watson handed him his pocket watch to decipher in the hopes that it would put a stop to the hurtful stream of comments coming from Holmes. It didn't.

Noting right away that the watch must have belonged to Watson's elder brother, Holmes launched right into a mechanical assessment of the man, completely overlooking that Watson might have cared for his brother: "He was left with good prospects, but he threw away his chances, lived for some time in poverty with occasional short intervals of prosperity, and finally, taking to drink, he died."

Watson was bitterly stung by this; the fallout conversation is cleaned up a bit in the official narrative, and Watson did not give me a precise transcript of what really passed between them. It was not the sort of cooing excuses one imagines from what is written down, though Holmes did admit that because he was handed the watch as a puzzle, he completely disregarded Watson's emotions. He did that with every puzzle. That was finally becoming clear.

Other than that, all I can say for certain was that Watson was reaching a breaking point with Holmes at the critical moment when Mary Morstan first came into their lives. Holmes was in a dystopic mind, relying more heavily than ever before on the crutch of cocaine, and he exuded gloom into the spaces around him just as easily as he could glow with light. When I read the story of this case, I'm filled with the same inexorable dread I get when attending a deathbed. I know that everything is ending, and I know how it is ending, and I am powerless to stop it.

Not for nothing, Holmes came to feel the same way when he realized just how much Mary Morstan would take from him. This is one of the few times I have ever found myself sympathizing with Holmes in all these long chronicles. The idea of losing Watson can only truly signify to those few of us who have ever possessed him. What a horror it must have been to realize that the seed of romance had been planted in Watson's head, and knowing that for weeks he had done his level best to make Watson miserable. A sniping Holmes would not be hard to outshine if Watson decided to choose between the two of them, and it dawned on Holmes all too slowly that Watson was considering his options.

And so: in she came, my watermark, Miss Mary Morstan. Small, blonde, dainty, well-dressed but humble, very much unlike me, though in a way I prefer that. It reassures me that I am not merely a stand-in, that I stand on my own. Her face was brimming with emotion when she entered their rooms at Baker Street, and at that moment Watson craved someone with sensitivity, someone who would not hurt him on purpose, nor by thoughtless accident. He held them against each other: the sweetly rounded face of Mary against the "clear-cut, hawk-like features" of Holmes. Holmes started losing ground right away. Mary was orphaned and friendless and asking Watson for help as much as she was asking Holmes. She made him feel needed. She made him feel like a man.

The moment she left, the tables were turned. Holmes would spend all morning bragging about his French admirer, eh? Very well, then Watson would declare, "What a very attractive woman!" This game was built for two, after all, and Watson was finally getting engaged.

Holmes, observant to every other aspect of humanity, could say nothing as to a woman's attractiveness. Like the movements of distant stars or the minute brushstrokes of art, it was not a subject that deserved his attention. But lighted with his own fire now, Watson called Holmes "an automaton—a calculating machine," and noted (finally) that "there is something positively inhuman" about the world's first independent consulting detective. Holmes smiled at what he unfortunately viewed as a compliment. It was the beginning of their end.

At first Watson despaired of having her, severely underestimating his own abilities and totting himself up using only his material attributes. He was in his mid-thirties and she only twenty-seven, he was damaged goods from the war and she in the bloom of perfect health, he was poor and until the end of this case, she expected to be wealthy. He did not count on his kindness, his stability, his patience. And more than all the circumstances he felt stacked against him, Holmes's toxic mood had seeped into Watson's heart, and he considered his future black and inescapable. The world was a place he didn't belong to, and soon enough it would expel him from life, and he would have gained nothing. These were not his thoughts! But when Holmes is sick, he is contagious.

Watson spent this entire case measuring Holmes against Mary and vice versa. As with Hayter, and as with anyone else in the company of Sherlock Holmes, Watson bonded with Mary over their awe of Holmes's ability. Further than that, while Holmes sat in silence, functioning on a level all his own, Watson and Mary chatted quietly, trying to distract themselves from the apprehension which did not touch Sherlock Holmes. Holmes knew their location by the turns of the cab, his mind was three moves ahead on the chess board; he was on a plane above everyone.

For once, however, Holmes's incredible abilities were doing him a disservice. Every reminder of how extraordinary he was only served to highlight the distance between himself and mere mortals like Watson—how can you feel close to someone on such a high summit? It's like trying to love an all-knowing but distant god, and Watson's faith was starting to waver. What did they have in common, really? And what was it they shared? The muck and danger of pursuing criminals, that's what held them together. Holmes only had one interest, and if you didn't meet him there, you didn't know him. Well, Watson was growing tired of awful things. Perhaps he would prefer a quiet life with hearth and wife and safety. A modest home with hand-knit blankets on the bed and a thoroughly uninteresting private medical practice. Hadn't that been what he wanted before he met Holmes? How had he let this man lead him astray?

The case brought them to Thaddeus Sholto, and Sholto soon took them to his brother's home, Pondicherry Lodge. Here the gulf growing in Watson's heart stretched another league. They were about to be denied entrance to the house by the ex-prize-fighter standing guard at the gate, but luckily Holmes had gone three rounds with him four years previously, and even though this coincidence saved Mary from standing out on the public road, it counted against Holmes. After the episode with Colonel Hayter, Watson had learned to be suspicious of men from Holmes's past, especially men of certain social classes. Holmes had once kept a relatively even pool of suitors, but as his career called upon him to wallow in the depths, more often that was where he found companionship. They were easier men to converse with anyway; they had fewer scruples about what others might be whispering about them.

The fighter's warm welcome of Holmes started Watson's imagination churning. The man, McMurdo, burst out with, "Not Mr. Sherlock Holmes! If instead of standin' there so quiet you had just stepped up and given me that cross-hit of yours under the jaw, I'd ha' known you without a question." Watson's mind was flooded with images of his friend shirtless and sweating, boxing with this tough who now clapped him on the shoulder in all familiarity. Had they changed while congratulating one another on a good game? Had someone, probably Holmes, suggested they go for a walk to cool down? Had he offered to buy his new friend a drink for being such an outstanding loser, and in a dim pub ask him if he had ever tried his hand at other sports? Had he ever wrestled, for instance? Had he ever wrestled in the Greek tradition, and if not, would he like to now? Oh, Watson could just see it all.

Glancing at Mary, he could not help but picture her as his faithful bride—pure and gentle and guileless—and the scale tipped further in her favor. By the time they got inside the spooky, ill-used house of Sholto's brother, he and Mary were holding hands "like children," taking solace in each other while the adults decided their fate.

After finding Sholto's brother murdered and leaving Mary to comfort the dead man's housekeeper, Holmes and Watson found themselves briefly alone. Here Holmes, probably suspicious in his own right of what was budding between Watson and Mary, gave a grand demonstration of his talents. He used his old tricks to try and win Watson back, plying the same charms that wooed him the first time. He went crawling all over the house and grounds, impressing Watson for sure, but not in the way he meant to.

Watson wrote: "So swift, silent, and furtive were his movements, like those of a trained bloodhound picking out a scent, that I could not but think what a terrible criminal he would have made had he turned his energy and sagacity against the law instead of exerting them in its defense." It chilled Watson to stand there and grasp Holmes's true potential, to know truly that he might be capable of anything. Watson could already say—easily!—that Mary was not capable of murder, but could he say the same of Holmes? Circumstances would have to be severely altered, but it was not outside the realm of possibility. And as Holmes himself has said on numerous occassions: "Once you have eliminated the impossible, whatever remains, however improbable, must be the truth."

He should have been a pugilist, should have been a thief. Was Holmes not extraordinary? And then police arrived, and with them the reminder of the first thing that brought Holmes and Watson together, the thing that caused Watson to become a scribe: the disrespect of the official police force for Holmes's skill. Hadn't that been the reason for penning *A Study In Scarlet*? To, in the spirit of fair play and sportsmanship, let the world know who really kept them safe?

But all of this only reminded Watson how his efforts had been so little appreciated by Holmes that morning. Holmes allowed the buffoon Athelney Jones to insult him repeatedly in an effort to remind Watson of the early days, the days before a disciple had come to write the gospel of Holmes, but it all blew back in his face. If only he had thought of losing Watson before it was too late! For now he struggled in vain.

A man of sport however, as we have already established, Holmes was willing to have a fair fight. He may not like women, but he could be man enough to lose to them if he were rightly bested. He sent Watson on an errand to deliver Miss Mary Morstan home; Holmes had made his presentation to Watson in solitude, so now she could make hers. Mary got into a cab with Watson and immediately burst into tears over the strain of the night. Game, set, and match. It was a first round knock-out.

Even a grand show of athleticism from Holmes as he shimmied down from the deceased Sholto's roof and a playful chase through the city following the mutt hound Toby couldn't put Holmes back in the lead. In the throes of this exciting case, Holmes's world became bright again: "How sweet the morning air is! See how that one little cloud floats like a pink feather from some gigantic flamingo." No more "dreary, dismal, unprofitable world," no more "yellow smog" and "dun-colored houses." Things are not so tedious if only he is on a case, and that is all very well for him, but not for my dear Watson. Who could stand to live with such a mercurial creature as Sherlock Holmes? Who could stand to love him?

Oh, the game was up but Sherlock Holmes kept playing. He served breakfast the next morning, serenaded Watson on the violin, but he was already beaten. Watson said: "I have a vague remembrance of his gaunt limbs, his earnest face and the rise and fall of his bow. Then I seemed to be floated away upon a soft sea of sound until I found myself in dreamland, with the sweet face of Mary Morstan looking down upon me." Holmes was utterly bested, and throughout a disappointing day in his detections, he started to know it, and turn bitter again.

As Watson left to go visit Mary, and after a long day of no news on his suspects, Holmes said, "Women are never to be entirely trusted—not the best of them." Watson left in an offended huff. He returned to find Holmes in such an agitated state that even Mrs. Hudson was concerned. That Watson should be drifting away from him *and* his case to be in shambles? It was one of the worst days of Holmes's life.

It was partially the case that kept him up all night, but mostly the prospect of losing Watson, to *a woman* no less, that was driving him to madness. He became sullen and started to ignore Watson, attempting to reject him first. They peel apart in this story, it can be seen even in Watson's sugar-coated recounting of the events. Watson writes that he began to doubt Holmes, to wonder if he might be wrong entirely on his deductions. The pink scarves were off the lampshades, and Holmes wasn't as attractive as he once seemed.

Meanwhile, and uselessly, Holmes rallied his efforts of persuasion, setting himself an audience of Watson and Athelney Jones so that he might parade around in a most convincing costume, surprising them both and prompting Jones to declare that Holmes would have made a rare actor. He should have been a great many things, apparently, but none of those things greatly interested Watson anymore.

You see, Holmes rallied when he caught scent of the criminals again, knowing that if he could recapture the treasure belonging to Mary Morstan, she would be out of Watson's reach forever. Holmes was so pleased at the prospect he was almost humble; though he had the potential to be an unbeatable boxer, a criminal mastermind, a most promising officer, and an actor of the stage, what he *would* put his energy to was securing Watson. If the doctor wanted a wife, could Holmes not be that as well? He prepared dinner and told his friend, "Watson, you have never yet recognized my merits as a housekeeper." Watson raised his eyebrows and glanced sidelong at Inspector Jones, but he was more interested in dinner than in Holmes's remark. Watson felt that they were too obvious, that they had always been. Normal men have wives, don't they? What could he have been thinking?

Holmes displayed his talents as both a housekeeper and a conversationalist throughout dinner. He pulled out all the stops as this case came to a close, but he couldn't get the better of his own nature.

The case played out dashingly. Holmes was easy in the face of death, another point in his favor, but he was just as easy with their prisoner, Jonathan Small. It is one step forward, two steps back with him. Watson noted of Small that "his face in repose is not an unpleasing one," and surely Holmes noticed it too. Holmes offered the convict a cigar, a pull out of his flask, and his sincere regrets that it had to come to this. There was something mutual between Holmes and Small, and Watson stood just wondering at the way his friend took such a shine to such a wretched man. It was a case closed, in more ways than one.

Holmes talked closely with Small, assuring him that he could prove him innocent of the Sholto murder (though he would stand guilty for his other crimes), and Small returned the favor by complimenting Holmes: "How you kept on our track is more than I can tell. I don't feel no malice against you for it. But it does seem a queer thing." It does indeed. Watson couldn't bear to watch them exchange pleasantries anymore. He snuck away at the first opportunity.

Watson left Holmes in his element, the grimy world of crime and criminals, the company of men, and may he be happy there, as Watson planned to be where he was headed. Watson was charged with taking the supposedly recovered treasure to Miss Morstan, and when he arrived he found her calm and soft, tied in a red-sashed dress like a present. When they went to look at last upon the treasure and found the chest empty, they were both relieved. They had each kept up some hope that they might be together. Watson declared his love to Mary on the spot, and she returned his sentiment, and he rejoined Holmes with that precious knowledge in his heart, as though the muscle had become a priceless ruby that he would get to keep from then on, his own little piece of Agra treasure.

After Small made a full confession and tipped his congratulations at Holmes a few more times before being led off to jail, Watson broke the news: "I feel that this might be the last investigation in which I shall have the chance of studying your methods. Miss Morstan has done me the honour to accept me as a husband in prospective."

Holmes let out a groan of pain and had to collect his face in his hands as he told Watson, "I feared as much." He then managed to put on a brave face by asserting that he was not sorry and had no regrets, talking about how detrimental emotion is to the logical faculties. He swore he would never marry, never allow human affection to corrupt his mind, and Watson nodded sadly, knowing it all too well. It hurt him that Holmes would pretend the end of their partnership was nothing more than a mild disappointment. And so Watson kept talking, hoping to wound Holmes back for all the times it had been done to him. Couldn't Holmes at least acknowledge all that he was losing? Or did he consider Watson to really be nothing so much to lose?

"The division seems unfair," Watson said to Holmes. "You have done all the work in this business. I get a wife out of it, Jones gets the credit, pray what remains for you?"

Holmes sneered a tad, I suspect to hide his emotion, although he may well have been outraged too by the idea of Jones taking his credit. He spoke quite a bit in this case about how little he cared for fame, how it was the love of his art alone that made him exert himself, the perfection he achieves in practicing it so flawlessly. He couldn't really begrudge Watson for using his own nasty method against him. I mean, at long last he was starting to rub off on this noble doctor! But Holmes was still the master at it. Had this also been a boxing match, both men would have limped away bleeding.

"For me," he said as he reached out luxuriously towards the mantle where his own poisonous barb once again rested, "there still remains the cocaine-bottle." Holmes smiled in a pained way, but he loaded his syringe with slow deliberation, watching Watson's face fall with despair, showing him that he was so adept at this process he could do it without looking. Watson told me he finally had to leave the room in disgust and misery, and that this is what he best remembers about the evening he first became engaged.

They didn't speak to each other again for days.

1919: The Sitting Room

The things I know about Sherlock Holmes, you'd think he wouldn't smirk at me like that in my own house, but he has no shame. Perhaps he thinks I'm just like Mary, that I don't know the whole story, and I'm content to have secrets in my marriage. I am not, but I think he already realizes this and is only taunting me.

I don't judge her; truthfully, it was a different time, and Mary Morstan was a different sort of woman. I'd have a hard time comparing myself to her even if I cared to. She was a quiet, dignified, delicate thing whereas I am somewhat more robust and brash. She was innocent of many social troubles while I have made myself something of an activist—for dress reform, for suffrage, for the poor. Mary, as I understand it from Watson, was a creature of the home. She didn't consider a husband and wife should be equals, but rather compliments of each other. I am not at all of that opinion, but at the time she was good for Watson, and he was good for her.

I do wonder what the first Mrs. Watson thought of Sherlock Holmes. I lost Watson for a weekend here or there before the war, but she had to seriously share her husband with this man, so what did she make of him? Certainly he solved a case for her, so she would have been sweet on him for a while, but how many nights did she spend alone before she grew to resent him? Did she never wonder what power Holmes held over her husband?

I know full well what has passed between them, what still exists there, holding them together all these long years, in spite of themselves. I share Watson too. I'm not so unlike Mary in that sense, but I don't lose him for whole cases, days and nights alone. There are just places in him that I can't reach, but I have secret pockets too. It's only what happens when two people marry later, when they have lived their whole lives apart.

"So, Mrs. Watson," Holmes says to me, resting his drink on his knee, smiling like he knows every last thing about me, the horrible man. "What was it like growing up with seven younger brothers?"

"You'll have deduced that from the pictures?" I ask, pointing vaguely behind me where there are hung family photos of my brothers. They all have the same mother, and were born after my mother died and my father remarried, but I'm sure Holmes knows all of that somehow. They all have similar ears or noses or some such thing that I lack.

"That, and your rather masculine demeanor," Holmes says. Watson nudges Holmes with the toe of his shoe. He has told Holmes to be on good behavior. I could have told him not to waste his breath. "Tell me," Holmes rejoins. "Did they all die in the war?"

Watson hides his face in his hand, but I'm not afraid of the truth, and that's all Holmes ever has over anyone.

"All of them," I say with a nod.

Looking at the wall clock Watson says, "We'll be having dinner soon." He is trying to veer the conversation, but he tries for nothing.

"You know, with seven brothers I'm not surprised that no one ever trained you in the culinary arts."

"Oh, yes, and I feel very deprived."

The detective's hawk-like features, still sharp even in his old age, shift all together slightly, as though he were hiding some discomfort; he doesn't like me either, it's clear. I'm glad of that.

Dinner is announced. I make my way into the dining room first, leaving the men to murmur and chuckle secretly behind me. Here they are, both in their sixties, acting like children whispering behind mother's skirts. I do realize why Watson continues to associate with Holmes—it makes him feel young again, brings back the heady feeling of their golden moments together. I myself am only forty-six, but I already value anything and anyone which can take me back to my youth, or remind me of the world we lost.

1887: The Noble Bachelor

A truce was established soon enough. When the reality of Watson's marriage became clear to Holmes as an inevitability, he decided to make the most of the time they had left together. What didn't help matters was that one of the first cases they worked after this involved a wedding and a missing bride, but Holmes can often be a creature of great control, when he wants to be. He managed to hold his tongue.

It's quite a different side of Holmes, an affected Holmes, that appears in this story. He gets rather Wildean in his comments, letting out clever barbs and, despite Watson's observations early in their relationship that Holmes knew nothing of literature, alluding quite easily to a notion from Thoreau. I would submit that he was feeling somewhat sentimental, and we all turn to literature for that.

It started right away. Watson, who was trapped at home because of the pain in his injured leg, sat drowning himself in newspapers in an attempt to imagine anyone's life but his own. As if they drew from the same well of energy, as Watson became depleted, Holmes bubbled over. Holmes returned from a morning outing to find Watson yearning for his attention, remarking on a fashionable bit of correspondence that had arrived for the detective.

"This looks like one of those unwelcome social summonses which call upon a man either to be bored or to lie," Holmes quipped, but it ended up being the case of a missing bride, one which he quite enjoyed, possibly because it tickled him to imagine a wife just disappearing and making everyone's lives much simpler.

When the Lord St. Simon arrived at Baker Street to tell his story and began to presume that he was of a much higher class than Holmes usually deals with, he was put into his place. Holmes had the delightful pleasure of informing his client that he was actually descending, from the King of Scandinavia to a mere moneyless domestic title, and this was only the first dressing-down Holmes got to deliver that day. Lestrade too came in too proud, sure that the missing bride had drowned because her gown had been found in the water: "By the same brilliant reasoning, every man's body is to be found in the neighbourhood of his wardrobe," Holmes said to him. He was in a rare and playful mood that day.

My goodness, he was even kind in his opinion about Americans, assuring the found bride and her American husband who was once presumed dead, that someday the children of Britain and America would be "citizens of the same world-wide country under a flag which shall be a quartering of the Union Jack with the Stars and Stripes." Hardly; and Holmes had a rather caricatured view of America that I doubt he altered even after spending a considerable amount of time there during the war. But nothing seemed to upset him once he had decided to be pleasant, for he did possess an iron will when he chose to employ it.

This was a neat little case, involving only the barest amount of footwork, a pure intellectual puzzle. The missing bride was found reunited with her original husband, and the Lord St. Simon had to excuse himself from the friendly dinner Holmes had prepared for all involved. He went home to sooth his wounded pride, rather uncharitably Watson thought. Watson's sympathy was with the love of these young Americans that endured death, distance, and years of separation.

"Ah! Watson," Holmes said. "Perhaps you would not be very gracious either, if, after all the trouble of wooing and wedding, you found yourself deprived in an instant of wife and of fortune. I think that we may judge Lord St. Simon very mercifully, and thank our stars that we are never likely to find ourselves in the same position."

I have it from Watson that he gave Holmes the most withering look he could conjure, because of course Holmes meant to imply that Watson may well be in that position very soon, the sod. Holmes only grinned spritely back at him and picked up his violin.

Holmes was right in one aspect of his teasing; if you don't invest yourself in anyone, you won't get hurt. Not that he was able to take his own good advice, because he never truly let go of Watson.

Ah well; as a man with many similar qualities to Holmes once said: "The only thing to do with good advice us pass it on. It is never any use to oneself."

1888: The Valley of Fear

The landscape at Baker Street slowly began to change as acceptance of Watson's pending wedding settled over the two men. It was really happening, but it wasn't the end of the world, nor was it the end of their friendship. They both started remembering who they were before they fell into each other's laps, and who they wanted to be. Watson had always liked the idea of marriage and a medical practice, and Holmes rather fancied himself the type to never settle down. How had they gotten so far from themselves? Silly to have made such a scene of separating when it was only the natural thing.

In fact, on the surface their relationship hardly changed at all. Holmes returned to his old snipe of a self, and Watson continued to endure his abuse, comforted in knowing that soon he would be moving on. He even managed to come back at Holmes with his own insults; they were nearly equal to those of Holmes, for once. They were at last on equal footing.

"I am inclined to think—" Watson began one day, and Holmes cut him off saying, "I should do so."

"Really, Holmes, you are a little trying at times," Watson scolded.

Holmes was consumed in a cipher message he had just received about Professor Moriarty and did not respond. For that snub, Watson got him back. He said of the Professor, "The famous scientific criminal, as famous among crooks as—"

"My blushes, Watson!" Holmes exclaimed, thinking he was about to be complimented.

"I was about to say, as he is unknown to the public," Watson smiled.

Holmes laughed, a good sport since he was in a relatively good mood. Watson let Holmes tweak him all morning, walking him through the deductive steps to decode the cipher message. He had a wife in his future, and the prospect of practicing medicine again, and what did Holmes have? The new page Billy, who was growing into attractive young manhood before their eyes, and on this occasion Inspector MacDonald; lustrous eyes, precise manner, and a humble admiration of Holmes. Watson went so far as to call him affectionate towards Holmes, and the feeling appears to be mutual if they did indeed smile and wink at each other the way Watson described: "Holmes was not prone to friendship"—to be sure he was *not*—"but he was tolerant of the big Scotchman, and smiled at the sight of him."

Holmes and MacDonald even teased one another with the lightness of flirtation that Watson once knew. After seven years living together, even the most innocent jabs between him and Holmes drew blood—they simple knew each other too well. Holmes and this inspector where still sounding each other's boundaries.

I don't know that Holmes and MacDonald ever went any further than their loaded repartee; I feel there is a chance MacDonald was a lover of women and only amusing Holmes (and himself) by this banter. His admiration of Holmes was so intense that it might have swayed his nature temporarily, but then again, maybe not. We can only speculate irresponsibly on what all this eventually led to:

Holmes noted that MacDonald had arrived early and said, "I fear this means that there is some mischief afoot."

"If you said 'hope' instead of 'fear,' it would be nearer the truth, I'm thinking, Mr. Holmes." And he was right of course, for a moment later when MacDonald spotted the now decoded message and exclaimed that its subject had been murdered, everyone first had to stop and consider the curiosity of Holmes's cold scientific nature. Watson wrote: "Without having a tinge of cruelty in his singular composition," and please note that I did roll my eyes when I read that, "he was undoubtedly callous from long over-stimulation." Undoubtedly.

It was the scarlet thread again, "one of those dramatic moments" for which Holmes existed and could hardly stand to live without. His obsession with Professor Moriarty, though a matter of some giggling for the police and MacDonald who believed Sherlock Holmes had "a wee bit of a bee in your bonnet over this professor," was as serious a matter as Holmes ever engaged in. This was no mere fixation; without ever laying eyes on the man, right away Holmes recognized in Moriarty the true test of himself. They were so much alike in so many mirrored ways, one of those ways being their profound potential. MacDonald himself remarked that Moriarty would have made a "grand meenister" with his solemn voice and serious appearance. He probably would have made a fearsome consulting detective too, much like Holmes, as Watson pointed out during *The Sign of Four*, would have made a fine criminal.

Holmes had in fact already overstepped the law in his study of Moriarty, for though he had never seen the man, he had gone into the professor's rooms: twice under honest conditions, and once under false. He did not, however, go into great detail of this mission in front of MacDonald. A professional courtesy, I'm sure, so that MacDonald would not be obligated to arrest him.

Instead they focused on the murder at hand, Holmes warming instantly to the challenge after what Watson describes as "a long series of sterile weeks" which lay behind them. Those were the arctic days after Watson announced his engagement and Holmes returned to cocaine in retaliation, but those days were over. For the moment.

Now Holmes was feeding from the energy of a tricky case, a dead man whose wife and friend seem to celebrate when they think they're alone. Suspicious footprints, an inaccurate timeline, a missing dumb-bell. Holmes was naturally stimulated by all the brilliant facets of the mystery. He was a chemist over forming crystals, a botanist before a bloom.

Keep in mind that this case is in the earliest months of 1888, just before Watson's own wedding, and you'll understand all the focus paid to Mrs. Douglas, the dead man's wife. In questioning her, she seemed sympathetic, at least to Watson. She said she knew her husband was uneasy, that he existed in a "valley of fear" which he never explained to her. When asked how she knew about it then, Mrs. Douglas answered:

"Can a husband ever carry about a secret all his life and a woman who loves him have no suspicion of it?" No, indeed, *I* don't believe so, but the idea rattled Watson at the time; he had secrets he wanted to keep.

It was not long after marrying Watson that I guessed at his "secret" history with Holmes, and it was not long after that when I asked him about it. I said, "Darling, were you quite in love with Sherlock Holmes?" He was cleaning and sorting his medical instruments at the dining room table (a habit I despised but had not yet asked him to stop—there were more important things to mention first). Watson frowned and his hands slowed over his work.

"What makes you ask such a thing?" he said.

"Because I imagine it to be true," I told him.

He compulsively straightened a few of his gleaming tools. He would not look at my face, though if he had he would have seen I was not accusing him. I only wanted him to tell me, and to be perfectly comfortable with my knowing. He hadn't even had a correspondence from Holmes in weeks, let alone seen the man. This wasn't about Holmes; it was about us.

"Does it disturb you?" Watson murmured.

"It does not." I was aware long before meeting Watson that some people were capable of loving both men and women.

Watson glanced up from his work at last and saw that I was smiling, and was put at ease. The next day I took up the study of his stories, and found I had more questions than I would ever receive answers for.

It is clear where Watson got the idea that a wife, despite all her vows, might not be entirely devoted to him. It was not only the experience of catching Mrs. Douglas smiling and laughing with her husband's best friend just moments after Mr. Douglas would have lost the warmth of life. Mostly it was a lifetime of living with Holmes and hearing his frequent discourses against the fairer sex. They were all seeds of doubt, and they were sprouting.

In discussing the behavior of Mrs. Douglas, Sherlock confessed, "I am not a whole-souled admirer of womankind, as you know, Watson." My husband made a noise of derision but chose not to speak to that. Holmes went on, "Should I ever marry, I should hope to inspire my wife with some feeling which would prevent her from being walked off by a housekeeper when my corpse was lying within a few yards of her." Of course, if Sherlock Holmes were ever to marry, the woman he would choose would certainly be that cold. Did he not already tell Watson that "the most winning woman" he ever knew was hanged for poisoning children? And in just a few short weeks he would meet Irene Adler, and esteem her more for her unemotional shrewdness than for any of the attributes he would consider feminine or wifely. But he would never marry anyway, so every word hung on that hypothesis was delivered for some other purpose. Holmes was merely sowing the beginnings of sabotage in his friend, who was soon to be a groom.

Holmes was reestablishing himself as a single man again, referring to Watson as "Friend" a little more forcefully, but the habits of affection were hard to break. They ended up sharing a room at the inn, with

Watson going out of the way to mention the separate beds; I don't know where the line was drawn, but at some point Watson broke off his physical relationship with Holmes in anticipation of his wedding. It was not directly after the engagement that this happened, because it was important to Watson to fix what he had with Holmes before he left it behind. I can't even be sure that the intimacy ceased before this very case, for the shared room is suspicious (I highly doubt the inn was full at this ancient town in northern Sussex, murder or no, so what other need would there be to share?). Holmes returned after a night spent in the Douglas house, in the room where the master died, and whispered to his friend, "I say, Watson, would you be afraid to sleep in the same room with a lunatic, a man with softening of the brain, an idiot whose mind has lost its grip?" Watson said, "Not in the least," and why should he be? They'd been sleeping together for years.

The next day proved that Holmes's mind was as firm and lucid as ever, though still afflicted with "some touch of the artist." He had to set up a performance of his capture, as was his wont, to appease the dormant actor in him. He couldn't just hand over the facts on a plate, he had to conceal them in a covered dish and yank the lid off with a flourish to reveal the facts at the most dramatic instant. In this proclivity he is not alone, for the murdered man too arrived with a flourish—later in the story, once it was revealed that Mr. Douglas was not dead but only concealed, and the dead body that of a man sent to kill him. Holmes warned him that his troubles were not yet and would never be over. With Moriarty commissioned on his murder, Douglas was still a hunted man, and in danger much more immediate from Moriarty's gang than he was from the American gang of Scowrers.

They sent him away from England for his own safety, but he didn't even survive the boat ride; he was lost overboard in a gale, and it was ruled an accident. Holmes knew that was not so right away, saying there was no accident in all the world, that this was not a coincidence, and that, "there is a master hand" in that man's death.

"You can tell an old master by the sweep of his brush. I can tell a Moriarty when I see one," Holmes said, clenching his fist distractedly.

Moriarty too was an artist, and even an unofficial entity like Holmes, a "great consultant in crime" instead of detection. Their trajectories were nearly parallel, but with just the slightest curve towards each other, meaning they must, eventually, touch.

This is the last case recorded before Watson leaves Baker Street for the married life, and it doesn't make mention of the momentous occasion. This story merely falls off the edge of the mystery; their last moments together were private, until I asked.

Holmes did not attend the wedding. He wouldn't have gone if it had been Watson's funeral either, and for much the same reason. But Watson prepared himself for the ceremony at Baker Street. His things were moved out, his house waiting for him and his bride with servants installed, but he would not enter it until he was legally wed. Holmes tolerated all the pomp with his back turned, flipping papers around on his desk and tinkering with his beakers and such, trying to keep his mouth shut. It was not the day for a fight.

When at last Watson had combed every hair, had every button done up, with his tie synched and his watch chain gleaming, he turned to Holmes to say goodbye.

"Well, that'll be all then, won't it?" He looked around at their rooms and wondered when they got so clean. Had Holmes been straightening up?

Holmes rose from his chemistry set where he had been pretending this day was no different than any other. Watson was nearly bouncing with the significance of it all, rocking back and forth on his toes, feeling as if he were at a precipice, feeling momentous. Holmes grasped Watson's arms to hold him still.

"It's terrible to see you grow up, my friend," Holmes said to him. Watson opened his mouth to respond with some comfort, but he was stopped by what was assumed by both of them to be their final kiss.

It was passionate, but it built up slowly like a stoking fire, like a swelling wave. Holmes's hands wrapped around Watson's face, his long fingers disordering Watson's hair. At the pinnacle of this, Holmes broke away, turned his back in an instant to hide...what? Finally a flash of emotion across that stony face? Did it crack in agony only to be patched over immediately? Watson would not know, because Holmes did not turn around again. He merely resumed his "work" with extra clinking and shuffling, as though Watson had distracted him quite enough already, and was really making himself a burdensome guest—for that is what he became with his marriage: merely a visitor in 221B.

Watson smoothed his hair back down, rubbed his hand over his mouth and mustache, his fingers trembling. It felt as if Holmes has loosed something in him, something that burned. He let his mind flash before him an alternative: what if he left Mary at the alter? She'd be disappointed but able to carry on, letting no man's action tarnish her heart. She'd find someone who could give her his whole heart, not just the beaten pulp of one that had been given too freely in his youth. He could spin Holmes around and tell him that he just can't leave, that they've ruined each other for anyone else in the world; they would never truly be free of one another, but maybe there was a comfort in that?

But the moment passed. It was irrational, illogical, and Holmes would have been proud of Watson for forcing it away. If grand pronouncements of love or moments of sentiment were common with Holmes, Watson would not be leaving in the first place. Stupid of him to go so lightheaded over this last dying flare. It's only train station syndrome—that last surge of affection before you say goodbye.

Watson checked his appearance in the mirror one last time, squeezed Holmes fraternally on the shoulder, and walked out. He wouldn't see Baker Street again for some weeks.

1888: A Scandal In Bohemia

I find it somewhat difficult to read the introduction here, to see how quickly Watson tired of the settled life. He had more in common with Holmes than I would like to admit; of course Watson liked his new wife, his new life, but it was strangely unfulfilling. What was it about Holmes—razor-tongued, ego-choked, hard-hearted Holmes—that made living with him so much more worth it? What was it about the tension and drama of Baker Street that was so irresistible?

Watson threw himself into his new role as husband, his new job as a practicing physician, but it was impossible to stay away. The vague murmurings of Holmes in the papers filled Watson with a sort of jealousy, an acute, paranoid intuition that he had missed out on all the fun. Did Holmes feel the absence of his friend as sharply, or were they Dr. Watson and Mr. Hyde? Watson at last had time to read Stevenson's morbid narrative after he married and no longer found himself dashing from the house every other night with a loaded revolver—he felt that he could read himself in its pages, and Holmes in its so-called villain. What was wrong with Hyde that Holmes could not understand, being just as selfish and willful and odd? And Watson knew the agony of Henry Jekyll all too well; yes, he was the normal one with the respectable life, but he was also the one who yearned for what he did not have. Neither Holmes nor Hyde felt any envy.

Watson's way home on that evening in March hardly a month after his wedding did not lead him through Baker Street—I've consulted several maps, and there is no accidental way to do it. Watson took that direction on purpose, as he had done many times before without stopping, just wanting to see if the windows were lighted, if Holmes was at home. After weeks of spotting him at inactivity, vacillating "between cocaine and ambition," Watson finally happened by while Holmes was deep in a case. He could tell by the way Holmes paced, the way his head was held, he could tell by his silhouette. Watson said that as he passed the door, he could not help but associate with it his wooing. However, he mentions "the dark incidents of the Study in Scarlet" in connection with that wooing, which was long before he ever met Mary Morstan. Indeed, *that* wooing had occurred here also, though that was not the one he was thinking about when he rang the bell.

On being let in, Holmes does not make a fuss over Watson, though the good doctor dares to believe that Holmes was glad to see him. Holmes made Watson comfortable, chided him for getting fat, and started in with his usual witchcraft, causing Watson to remark, "You would certainly have been burned, had you lived a few centuries ago." Pity.

But Holmes was reaching out a true hand of friendship, asking Watson to consult on the case, stopping him from trying to leave with a restraining touch, and informing the King of Bohemia that, "It is both, or none." Naturally he could not tell Watson how much he missed him, but the sentiment was heard all the same. When Holmes said goodnight, he scheduled Watson to come see him the next day. Holmes was reeling him in again, but Watson was not a fish on a line; he could not have been pulled back against his will.

Watson passed the night on a cloud, buoyed by his inclusion in the fast world of detection once again, thinking that his marriage bed would not seem so monotonous if he came back to it every now and again after a daring night out with Holmes. Watson arrived right on time the next morning, and he waited an hour for Holmes, all the while tapping and bouncing, as nervous as the man he was waiting for.

Holmes returned presently all done up in costume. He changed and told Watson about his investigations. He reported that the horsey men all found the King's blackmailer, Irene Adler, to be "the daintiest thing under a bonnet on this planet." He didn't care, and certainly could not speak to her beauty himself. In fact, he was much more observant of her gentleman caller, Mr. Godfrey Norton, whom he described as "a remarkably handsome man, dark, aquiline, and moustached," like Watson.

Holmes acknowledged her beauty in a practical fashion, saying that she had "a face that a man might die for," though not a man such as Holmes. He witnessed for her marriage to Norton quite by happy accident, and returned home to Baker Street to engage Watson further. He knew why Watson had come round again, why he had waited so long in his old rooms:

"You don't mind breaking the law?" Holmes asked him.

"Not in the least," answered Watson.

"Nor running a chance of arrest?"

"Not in a good cause."

"Oh, the cause is excellent!"

"Then I am your man."

As ever! And poor Mary Morstan Watson left at home by herself, not half as exciting as all this, and not yet suspecting what it would mean for her, or for her marriage. This is one of the most uncomfortable stories in the whole canon for me—I can't help but feel for another member of the sisterhood.

Holmes made another costume change, but not just that, according to Watson. He could change his whole demeanor, his movements, "his soul seemed to vary with every fresh part that he assumed." Watson once more informs his audience that Holmes would have made a fine actor, as well as an acute reasoner, had he not specifically gone into crime. He seems completely oblivious to the unsettling implications of loving such a chameleon. How could he ever know that he was sitting with Sherlock Holmes and not a projection? Perhaps he felt, as Oscar Wilde once said, that a man is least himself when he talks in his own person. "Give him a mask and he'll tell you the truth," the quote goes. Watson was as near to the real man as anyone would ever get.

What a strange thing to read Watson's thoughts as he watched Holmes trick his way into Irene Adler's house by taking advantage of her kind nature. Watson was utterly split; his sympathy for a gentle woman who would take in an injured priest (for that indeed was Holmes's character for the evening) welled up, and he wanted to abandon his task. "And yet it would be the blackest treachery to Holmes to draw back now from the part which he had entrusted to me. I hardened my heart." Quite unlike the last time Holmes was held up against a woman; this time Watson chose his friend. Watson had learned his true preference for the moment. Already the shine had come off being chivalrous, but who could really be surprised? He was Holmes's man through and through.

After the trick on Irene went off supposedly without a hitch, Holmes rejoined Watson at the top of the street, linked their arms and led Watson back home in cozy silence. He was being sweet because he knew, in the long game he played for Watson's devotion, that he was the true winner. Holmes's hand would stroke Watson's arm between the streetlamps, and Watson allowed the petting to continue as Holmes spoke of the night's events, explaining to Watson those aspects of the case that were still unclear to him. They were very easy with one another, both just so relieved that they would not be strangers forever, that they would continue on connected.

Irene Adler, a woman after my own heart, was following in male dress. Holmes was not the only one with tricks, and she was actively aware that she had been forced to reveal her secret—and so she made it her business to see if the man she had taken into her house had any secrets of his own. Who knows what all she saw or how much she understood of it, but I imagine that a woman of the theater had known men like Holmes before, and was smiling as she wished him good night. He would have made an exceptional actor, after all.

Watson stayed the night at Baker Street. I was stunned that he wrote it down in the public record, but his naïveté is part of his charm that I wouldn't change. And I can't imagine what he told Mary coming home the next day! The truth would have been outrageous, but if he hadn't given any explanation at all, then what would Mary have been imagining? Would her husband really disappear at a moment's notice, whenever Sherlock Holmes snapped his slender fingers? A day after seeing Holmes once again and his vows were dust. He didn't even bother to be discreet.

I don't know, maybe hearing that he had spent the night with Sherlock Holmes filled Mary with relief. She might have been feeling just as disillusioned as Watson himself. Maybe she didn't know what these men were to each other, maybe she did and couldn't bring herself to care. Irene Adler certainly knew enough to take full advantage of their distraction; she swapped photos on Holmes and made her escape. I rather like Holmes for holding onto the photo of Irene in evening dress, though Watson was not amused, and *is not* still, since Holmes continues to posses it. He went out of his way at the beginning of this narrative to clarify that Holmes was not a lover, and certainly not a lover of Irene Adler:

"All emotions, and that one [love] particularly, were abhorrent to his cold, precise, but admirably balanced mind. He was, I take it, the most perfect reasoning and observing machine that the world has seen; but as a lover, he would have placed himself in a false position."

It must have stung Watson to be so honest. Holmes was perfect, but not for him. A man like Watson needs more affection than an engine like Holmes can churn out, and yet he couldn't stay away; a metallic creature can't help but shine, after all.

1888: The Stockbroker's Clerk

And yet, it wasn't Watson alone who couldn't stay away. A few months after he was married and moved and busy with his new life, who should turn up at his doorstep but Mr. Sherlock Holmes, come to reclaim him for another adventure.

It was the first time in the nearly four months Watson had been gone that Holmes came to seek him out, and he informed Watson of his good deal in buying the practice that he did, for the one next door had hardly-worn steps, and was clearly doing poorer business. The conversation was painfully light for two such intimate friends, concentrating on niceties like health (who really gives an earthly damn?) while Holmes coyly sounded out Watson's enthusiasm for a case.

Watson was champing at the bit for some excitement, and Holmes was revoltingly pleased to learn it. Just think: Holmes could show up without even a message to herald him, and Watson would cheerfully drop his patients, drop his wife, and follow Holmes anywhere before he's even told what direction they're headed. What an unbelievable rush that kind of power must have given him, what pleasure. He was probably having more fun stealing Watson away from Mary than he ever had when he owned Watson outright.

It was a good day all around for Holmes. He had succeeded in luring Watson away from Mary (the poor woman—Watson only ran upstairs to tell her he was leaving and then ran right back down into Holmes's waiting arms), and he had a fun case. His client was the dupe in a robbery scheme that gave Holmes a few moments of mental pleasure; the way light exercise does for a body, this puzzle renewed his mind.

It was a quick solve for him. After explaining the curious circumstances to the police and releasing their client back to his oblivious existence,

Holmes and Watson took a long walk back to his practice. Holmes continued his flirtation.

"You and Mrs. Watson are happy, then?" he asked Watson. "Loving? Companionate?"

"I should think so," skirted Watson. "We are still newlyweds after all."

"Of course," said Holmes with a smile.

Mary had been waiting at the window for her husband to return. If my blithe Watson felt something amiss in their relationship, then surely she did too. Sherlock Holmes stepped inside to greet her and in the same breath bid her farewell. He put a subtle emphasis on calling her missus and, with a friendly squeeze of Watson's arm, was gone.

Watson resumed his place at his desk with satisfaction while Mary lowered her needlework slowly. Glancing up at her, Watson became concerned.

"You aren't ill, are you dear?" he asked. "Did…" and here was a bit of deductive reasoning, "Was it seeing Holmes that upset you?"

"He just brings about such…mixed emotions in me, darling," she told him tactfully.

"Oh, I know it's difficult to be reminded of your troubles, your unfortunate father, but if not for all that hardship, we would never have met," Watson reminded her.

"Of course," Mary said through a tight smile, and went back to her knitting with such trouble in her mind that she made several mistakes and at last had to set it aside.

It *had* been the sight of Holmes that disturbed her, the look on his face. Something about it said plainly that he did not like her, and if she were being perfectly honest, she had started to feel the same way about him.

It was not just that he distracted Watson, that he seemed to own her husband and was only lending him to her for a time. He had been peculiar from the start, when she came to him for help in the first place. He was entirely too pleased to hear that she was having "troubles" (as Watson phrased them) if it meant that he could have a case. And then there was something else that had bothered her for quite a while now, ever since she had seen Watson's notes of the case: the way Holmes had treated his prisoner, Jonathan Small—the murderer who hated her father—as though he were an equal and a gentleman. That bothered her quite a bit. She rather judged Sherlock Holmes by the company he liked to keep.

I am speculating quite a bit on Mary Morstan, but I feel that I'm in a perfect position to do so—who else could better understand the trials and tribulations of being Watson's wife? And knowing what I know about Mr. Holmes, I can imagine pretty well what she might have come to suspect, and what she surely put up with. There is a good chance she never came to know the full story, for it was not a time in Watson's life where he could be honest about himself; that came with maturity, with the hardships of our nation, and with enough distance from Sherlock Holmes to see him for what he truly is.

1919: Dinner

There is a serious commotion when it comes time to introduce Kitty to Sherlock Holmes. She brings out the last bit of food for the table, and I present her to Holmes as "our girl Kitty." He turns on the charm to annoy me.

Taking her hand and kissing the top of it, Holmes says, "What a fine pleasure to meet you, young miss."

Kitty is nearly writhing with excitement, but manages to say, "Oh the pleasure is all mine, Mr. Holmes! We are all *so* impressed to have you here."

I push her back into the kitchen as Holmes looks up at me with delight.

"I'm so sorry if my presence is distracting to your girl. She seems thoroughly turned around at my being here."

"Oh," I say to him. "No apology necessary! She gets just as flustered when the milk man arrives."

Watson snorts as he seats himself at the table, and Holmes covers the twist in his face by offering to pull out my chair. I accept, cautiously, afraid he might yank it from beneath me like a schoolboy, but I am not to be so humiliated today. In fact, once everyone starts to eat, I think for a moment that dinner will be a silent affair. That is until I ask Watson to pass me the salt.

"I've noticed, Mrs. Watson, that you refer to your husband by his surname," Holmes observes. "It is very strange."

"You refer to my husband by his surname as well," I return.

"Ah, yes, but I am not his wife."

"Hmmm!" I hum brightly at him, and once again his face goes sour. I'm sure he heard every subtle facet of that noise, my implication that I know his nature, that I imagine he would be Watson's wife if he could, my lording over him the fact that I have that official status in Watson's life, that I have won. It is a hit against him, a palpable hit.

Alas, however: I am playing against a master, and I can admit when I've been clearly outdone.

"You are such a unique person," Holmes says poisonously. "What a shame that history will most likely never remember your name."

And just as he could hear all of my insults, I can hear all of his. We speak the same language.

He means to remind me that it is already clear that Sherlock Holmes is a name which will live forever, and not only can I never hope to catch up to him in personal achievement, his is the name that will be always associated with Watson's as well. Only my grave will connect me with my husband. Who would ever care to remember the wife, the woman behind the man, especially if she is already the second woman?

Holmes goes vigorously back to his food after delivering this blow. Not exactly Queensberry rules he's fighting with, are they? But he has less to be proud of than he would lead one to believe. He never did fight fair.

1888: The Naval Treaty

A noble man would have let his friend's marriage stand, but once Holmes had roused himself to fetch Watson once, they fell back into old habits immediately. Not a month after the incident with the Stockbroker's Clerk, Watson receives an excuse to drop by Baker Street, a letter from an old school friend pleading for help. He couldn't get to Holmes fast enough, but once he arrived he was content to merely sit in the man's presence while Holmes finished an experiment.

It was only a "commonplace murder" that Holmes was solving, and he dashed off a note to that effect before giving Watson his full and unfettered attention. He read the letter from Percy Phelps and they took the first train out to Woking, Holmes tweaking Watson affectionately all the way.

"So this is an old friend of yours, Watson? A close friend?"

"Oh, yes, at one time we were extremely close," said Watson, not realizing he was being teased.

"As close as I am with my friends?" Holmes asked rakishly.

"Why Holmes, I was under the impression that you have very few friends! Oh, wait," he said, finally noting Holmes's face. "I see your meaning now. No Holmes, we were not friends of that sort."

"Really? He seems very warm towards you in his letter."

"Well, he is a desperate man."

Holmes burst out in hearty laughter, and even Watson could not help but let a smile escape. It was a delightful day.

Arriving at the Phelps home and hearing of his friend's troubles however, Watson let his mood dampen in sympathy. He just cannot remain cheerful when confronted with someone else's suffering. Holmes, as ever, kept his emotions out of the case, out of the world where the rest of us bleed on one another. The mystery of the stolen treaty resided in one area of his mind while in another, he noticed roses growing outside of the window.

Holmes unlatched the window and plucked one of the flowers, and this is a fascinating thing to me, because I think I understand what he was trying to do. His discourse on flowers being proof of some benevolent and artistic creator ring rather false from his mouth; I've never heard of anyone so married to reason as Sherlock Holmes, and every reasonable man doubts the existence of God profoundly. I've never yet met one who was a regular at worship services, though they had all picked through the Bible and could at a second's notice detail the parts with which they disagree.

"Our highest assurance of the goodness of Providence seems to me to rest in the flowers," he said, supposedly deducing that religion is correct because flowers are beautiful. No, Holmes was not having a moment of spiritual conversion. He was putting on a bit of a show for Watson, trying to prove his sensitive side at a most insensitive moment. Watson was left rather more annoyed, much like his friend Phelps and the man's fiancé, that Holmes seemed so uninvolved in the matter at hand. Watson was used to it, but he was a little embarrassed before his old friend. Phelps's face seemed to plead towards him—didn't Watson put his own reputation behind Holmes with the stories he wrote? Was this scatter-brained oddity who stood at their window really the unmatched detective that Watson promised?

Holmes and Watson left after hearing the story of the missing treaty, since nothing more could be done there. On the train home, Holmes once again attempted to show Watson what a well-rounded, sympathetic person he was, and again he seemed to do it with two left feet. Holmes commented on how nice it was to travel this way, high above London, and to see the surrounding houses. Watson was perplexed since, on looking out the window, all that could be seen was a sordid mass of city and the boarding schools erupting from the sea of roof slates, but that is what Holmes claimed to enjoy: "Lighthouses, my boy! Beacons of the future! Capsules, with hundreds of bright little seeds in each, out of which will spring the wiser, better England of the future."

In the same breath Holmes's mind returned to the case, and apparently he is a bit like talking to a madman in the rapid way his thoughts revolve, but I don't begrudge him the sentiment this time. I was a teacher before the war, and I plan to be again. I value the potential of bright young children as much as anyone.

Holmes was obviously trying hard to prove himself, and I'll rest my case on how badly he was bruised when he imagined Watson was going to return home without him.

"Today must be a day of inquiries," Holmes said happily, looking forward to it all.

"My practice…" Watson began.

"Oh if you find your own cases more interesting than mine—" Holmes snapped at him, but Watson put a hand on his knee.

"I was going to say that my practice could get on very well for a day or two. Without me, Holmes," he clarified. That last bit is a line you will not find in the official record. I think it's perfectly obvious why not.

"Excellent!" Holmes said. "Then we'll look into this matter together."

Holmes released Watson to his wife that night only to collect him back again the next morning. As they returned to Woking on the train, Holmes began moving the key players in the mystery like they were large chess pieces. For his ends he needed to send Watson and poor ill Phelps back to London to stay the night at Baker Street. He did it with an impish grin.

Watson went where he was bidden. Besides, he genuinely wished to catch up with his old chum Phelps, but the poor man could talk of nothing but the case. And Holmes. Questions about Holmes and his methods, Holmes and his tactics; what has he said, what does he know, what does he think?

"You know him well, Watson. He is such an inscrutable fellow, that I never know what to make of him."

No answer would satisfy Phelps, and eventually he murdered Watson's good mood with his incessant though understandable worry. Watson only once got him off the track of his own problems by saying, "You're not the first to wonder all this about Holmes you know! He's a mystery to all of us."

Phelps had taken in the breath for his next frantic question, but let it out noiselessly. He studied Watson for a moment before asking, "You weren't like this at school, were you?"

"Like what?" Watson asked moodily. He thought Phelps would scold him for being impatient, and so what if he was a little short now? Was he not a full grown man? Had he not been shot enough times to make his own small demands on the world?

But that was not Phelps's meaning.

"This way you are with Holmes," he said.

Watson clammed shut, and shifted uncomfortably. "How do you mean?" he murmured.

"Most men grow out of it, not into it, don't they?"

"I have a wife," Watson pointed out to him.

"And well you should, friend Watson. Well you should."

Phelps couldn't keep his mind off his own troubles any further than these few comments, and Watson eventually insisted they go to bed to get away from the incessant worrying of his friend. Watson wrote that he tossed all night, ostensibly over the case, but he was rather more concerned about Holmes, always Holmes.

Watson was so conflicted that night. Privately, he missed Holmes but still remembered what drove him away. None of it was changed, Watson knew that intellectually. Phelps had noticed that Holmes was inscrutable? He had no earthly idea. What logic lies beneath letting Watson marry and *then* starting to work so desperately to bring him back? Why not treat him properly all the while, or reform before it was too late?

And then there were the social troubles relative to Holmes. Not just in the lonely way he lives, or how being his only friend tends to isolate one from the world, but these suspicions of even his oldest friends, how were those to be avoided? Was he not careful enough? Did he give himself away so obviously that even a woman, a wife, was not enough to assure the public of his vigor?

Watson was just as anxious as Phelps for the return of Holmes the next day. He felt that laying eyes on him again would bring some clarity, and it did. Holmes was injured, roughed up and with a bandage around one hand. His instant sympathy for Holmes, his concern for the man's well-being, that told Watson just how deep his involvement went; consequences be what they may, Watson was entwined tightly here.

Holmes was not at all concerned by the damage his body received, he never could be bothered, whether the injury came from assault or addiction. He was high on a case well-reasoned, and he revealed Phelps's treaty with significant theatrics, concealing it under a dish cover and nearly giving the unfortunate man a heart attack.

"There there!" said Holmes. "It was too bad to spring it on you like this; but Watson here will tell you that I never can resist a touch of the dramatic." He winked at Watson over Phelps's head, but was distracted when Phelps seized his hand and kissed it. Holmes burst out laughing, told Phelps how he had battled the man's future brother-in-law for the document, and sent him home.

"Nicely played, Holmes," Watson told him. "Now let me see your hand."

Holmes smiled and handed it over. Watson unwrapped the bandage and winced at the cut across Holmes's knuckles.

"You've got to be more careful, Holmes!" he scolded. "If this cut had been deeper you might have lost the use of your fingers. How would you like to hold a pipette then, hmm? Or play the violin? You should have more consideration for yourself."

"Your consideration will have to sustain me, Watson," Holmes said quietly.

Watson sat with Holmes and re-wrapped the wound. They glanced at each other all the while, quiet, but while blood roared in Watson's ears. This small touch meant so much more than even a full body press—the erotic power was overwhelming, and from what? This is the same way he would bandage anyone, but it isn't anyone who can surge through him like this, like a direct transfusion of spiked blood. It was as if Watson could feel whatever overwhelming chemical pumped through Holmes when he was triumphant. It was contact intoxication.

Watson patted Holmes on the hand when finished, but Holmes grasped Watson's fingers to detain him. He squeezed firmly and spoke his heart as clearly as he could manage:

"There is always room for you here, you know. You can always come home."

Watson watched the light flicker over Holmes's cranial face and wondered what he would look like if Watson could see him with fresh eyes. He realized in that moment that he saw so much more than just the image of a man, he saw intelligence and diagnoses and salvation and doom. How much good did he attribute, and how much bad did he ignore? Did he even see Holmes at all, or only an idea of him?

"Why thank you, Holmes…and you are welcome out in Paddington with us," Watson said carefully, trying not to get hurt again, trying to stick by his decision to leave, to create a little distance between himself and the overwhelming intensity of his friend. Too much of Holmes simply wasn't good for him, Holmes was too elemental—too much fire will not warm, it will burn; too much water will not quench, it will drown.

"I should really be getting back," Watson said.

He stood up, and he could feel Holmes watching him like an animal might; inscrutably, but with constant assessment, like it hasn't yet made up its mind whether you are friend or foe. Watson averted his gaze, pointed to Holmes's hand and said, "I want you to look after that."

"Yes, Doctor," Holmes said, and drummed his bandaged fingers on the table. A calculated move, most likely. The sound of drumming always affects Watson, it reminds him of battle, and Holmes would have known this. Watson was anxious to leave and get himself sorted out. A nice, long walk home in the warm night air, that's what he wanted. Holmes or Mary, Holmes or Mary, Holmes, Holmes, Holmes. He wanted to be on his own. When had he lost that option?

Watson gathered his belongings and paused at the door. "Goodnight, Holmes."

Holmes smiled rather sadly, and Watson left him. Again.

1888: The Crooked Man

Watson's invitation did not fall on deaf ears. Not another month had gone by before Sherlock Holmes took him up on the offer to visit. He was a never-say-die sort of fellow and he was not going to give up easily.

"You told me that you had bachelor quarters for one," Holmes said upon arrival, "and I see that you have no gentleman visitor at present. Your hat-stand proclaims as much."

Watson gave him a patient look. What gentleman would there be, and why must Holmes speak of such things in such an arch and pointed tone? But Holmes was in high spirits, making his little observations hand over fist, eager and awake as ever because he was after some mystery. In fact when he finally began to speak of the matter, Watson writes that "his eyes kindled and a slight flush sprang into his thin cheeks." Holmes reacts to morbid news as if it were a flirtation, a rose from a secret admirer. Watson can see it all behind the mask:

"For an instant the veil had lifted upon his keen, intense nature, but for an instant only. When I glanced again his face had resumed that Red Indian composure which had made so many regard him as a machine rather than a man." A few peeks beneath that façade were all it took.

A stimulated Holmes is a joy to be around. After a long day Watson was still feeling revitalized, and the next morning they were out fresh and early to interview a suspected murderer. Those glances beneath Holmes's mask continued, and not a whisper of suspicion crossed Watson's mind. He was only too pleased to be included, whatever the motivation: "In spite of his capacity for concealing his emotions I could easily see that Holmes was in a state of suppressed excitement, while I was myself tingling with that half-sporting, half-intellectual pleasure which I invariably experienced when I associated myself with him in his investigations."

This case was narrative-heavy, not a lot of running around, but still fascinating in its human complexity. A bitter rivalry over a woman's affection prompted one man to commit a hideous betrayal. Colonel Barclay decided to rid himself of this other suitor by running the man into an ambush; the other man was captured by the enemy, the woman was captured by Colonel Barclay, and all remained concealed until the wronged man unexpectedly returned. Malformed from years of torture, it took only the sight of him to shock Colonel Barclay into an apoplexy that ended his life. Though it was the occasion for the case, Colonel Barclay's death turned out to be no great loss, since he had so badly abused his military authority and manipulated a wife who had once been very devoted to him.

The story was so unpleasant that it followed Watson as they left Aldershot. Holmes was already far and away in his own mind and had started jabbering about music, but by the time they arrived at the train, Holmes had run himself out. Watson brought up the case again.

"How could Barclay have done such a thing?" Watson wondered. "To betray his friend and his position like that in one fell swoop. It's just terrible."

"Love makes people do idiotic things, cruel things." Holmes looked sideways at Watson as they waited on the platform. "It's the nature of man."

"But he made himself unworthy of the lady's love in his effort to gain it. It's like a Greek play."

"There you go turning it into literature, Watson. A tragedy! You give everything such poignancy, such significance. This sort of casual viciousness is more commonplace even than the criminal records will show. Families are rife with it, regardless of social class; it seems that people can't help themselves."

Watson sighed as they found a private compartment. "I'm glad at least that I've met you, and Mary. I can't imagine either one of you doing anything so drastic."

"Certainly not over you, you mean?"

Watson smiled. "You're getting along all right without me, aren't you?"

"Absolutely," Holmes said. "But I wouldn't put anything past myself, you know."

I know.

1888: A Case of Identity

Hardly two months have gone by before another vile example of mankind presents himself in Baker Street. A woman is missing her fiancé, who turns out to be her stepfather in disguise, trying to dupe the unfortunate woman into never marrying her money away from the family. Holmes was quite disgusted with the man, and with his own powerlessness to do anything to stop him. In his attempt to spare the woman the embarrassment and shame of finding out she had been wooed by her step-father, Holmes gave her enough hope to hang herself with.

But all that was secondary to what was finally cresting between Holmes and Watson that fall. Holmes was getting quite humorous in his efforts to be romantic: "If we could fly out of that window hand in hand, hover over this great city, gently remove the roofs, and peep in at the queer things which are going on, the strange coincidences, the plannings, the cross-purposes, the wonderful chains of events…"

Mary was losing ground. A housewife just didn't stand a chance against Holmes back then. She could give Watson hand-knit sweaters and Holmes could give him exhilarating adventure, fame, and an ever-shifting interpersonal dynamic to keep his attention. Indeed, whereas most cases until this period had begun with Holmes lamenting the drudgery of life, and Watson consistently making arguments for its splendor, now it was Holmes advocating for the world, and Watson who needed convincing.

Smirking over a stack of morning papers, they reversed roles, with Watson wagering that a case of divorce in the paper was due to drinking and abuse and all the dull, standard fare of unhappiness. Marriage was all that Holmes had warned him it would be, commonplace and disappointing, and it was starting to make him bitter. Holmes knew the case in question personally, of course, and told Watson the divorce was due to the husband's habit of chucking his teeth across the table after dinner each night.

Well, everyone has their eccentricities. Holmes, for all his supposed asceticism, is quick to show off a jeweled snuff box to Watson. He has always been too much of a connoisseur in his favorite topics, too much of an aesthete. He's the Des Esseintes of crime detection; strange in habits and décor, rich in miniscule knowledge, peculiar in personality. And he's just as anti-human, though it's strange how quickly Watson forgot about all that and started idealizing Holmes once again.

But there is something hard in Sherlock Holmes, something worrisome to overlook that comes to the top of him very occasionally. He is, by all accounts including his own, capable of anything. Most people would except themselves from being able to commit horrible violence, or to steal from the needy, or to murder, but it is only our choices that keep us from such deeds, not our ability. Holmes has seen enough "decent" people doing wretched things to know that no one is immune, and he was acutely aware of the same potential in himself. He was proud of it too; proud of his honesty in looking himself boldly in the mirror, and proud of his ability to master his nature. In fact, I imagine a large portion of the fascination he has with criminals, at least the clever ones, is the morbid pleasure of seeing in them a version of himself, were he reckless enough to throw away all responsibility and conscience. Someday he would find himself much more susceptible to such urges, through his dalliance with cocaine, but it was a long way off yet. Not that it would come as any surprise to him; Holmes suspected himself all along.

In this case it was quite a clever turn for the client's stepfather to impersonate a suitor, and then disappear just before marrying her. And to think that he had the girl's mother in on the scheme as well! What a powerfully wicked thing to pull off, and how impressive in its simplicity! As much as Holmes went out of his way to insist that the trick was cruel, heartless, selfish, petty...we cannot hear the tone he said it in! There is a guarded admiration in Holmes for such a vast concentration of egotism and greed. It puts an absolute pep in his step.

We can see it plainly before the stepfather leaves Baker Street; Holmes locks him in to inform him of his deeds and then is forced to let him go, for there is no law under which to hold him. However Holmes informs the man, "If the young lady has a brother or a friend, he ought to lay a whip across your shoulders. By Jove!" he continued, flushing up at the sight of the bitter sneer upon the man's face, "it is not part of my duties to my client, but he's a hunting crop handy, and I think I shall just treat myself to—"

The man flung himself out the door before Holmes could advance on him too far, and Holmes burst into laughing to see him tearing down the street in alarm. "There's a cold-blooded scoundrel!" said Holmes with more than a little thrill. "That fellow will rise from crime to crime until he does something very bad, and ends on a gallows."

Holmes sighed contentedly as he sat down again, probably imagining himself as the one to tie the rope about his neck, and he laced the whip through his fingers as he explained the smaller details of his deduction to Watson. A little horrified but a quite a bit more fascinated, Watson listened with rapt attention. He is rather infectious, Sherlock Holmes. A dark and glamorous thing.

1888: The Red-Headed League

When Watson next came by Baker Street less than a month later, Holmes was so anxious to have him in that he became grabby, literally pulling him into the room and shutting the door behind him. Sitting with Holmes was a frightfully red-headed man named Wilson who had rather few wits under his gingery pate, for he had been duped much in the manner of Mr. Hall Pycroft, The Stockbroker's Clerk.

Holmes wanted Watson in the room, not just because he was gunning for Watson's affection and knew to include him, but also because Wilson was dull and self-important and Holmes was rather bored by him. Holmes started to play around with Watson under Mr. Wilson's nose.

"You will remember," he said to Watson, "that I remarked the other day, just before we went into the very simple problem presented by Miss Mary Sutherland, that for strange effects and extraordinary combinations we must go to life itself, which is always far more daring than any effort of the imagination."

"A proposition which I took the liberty of doubting," Watson said with a smile in his voice.

"You did, Doctor, but none the less you must come round to my view, for otherwise I shall keep on piling fact upon fact on you until your reason breaks down under them and acknowledges me to be right."

They were talking about Watson's stories, but no they weren't. Not with the arch tone that Holmes had in his voice. They made eyes at each other all while Wilson was talking, and when Watson tried to figure out what kind of man was before him, Holmes caught his glance and shook his head, saying there wasn't much to see. He had a few conclusions which, in his usual fashion, he threw off like they were nothing. Wilson was amazed, but once Holmes explained his methods, this red-headed man also concluded they were nothing. Holmes grinned at Watson:

"I begin to think that I make a mistake in explaining. Omne ignotum pro magnifico." Everything unknown is taken for magnificence.

They listened to this buffoon's story, at the end of which he produced a sign that said the Red-Headed League was dissolved on October 9, 1890. You may have noticed that I have placed this story in 1888; there are several reasons for this. One, Watson's ghastly handwriting, the worst of any physician I've ever seen, and they are a profession notorious for their hand scratch. Two, the internal relations of the dates are at a discrepancy between when Wilson saw the advertisement, when he took the job, and when the sign notice went up. Three, by Watson's own account this story took place just after Mary Sutherland's case of identity, which was clearly in 1888. And four, it's apparent in the way he and Holmes are acting; you will see that by October in the year 1890 they are not so sweet on each other. A love like theirs must ebb and flow.

Regardless, Holmes was wriggling in his seat over having a case and Watson all at once. And when he heard his client knew a man who had pierced ears and an acid stain on his forehead, his eyes sparked, but he said nothing. Bidding Mr. Wilson goodbye, Holmes smoked for nearly an hour, and then invited Watson out for lunch and the symphony. Holmes, after walking out of his way to check a supposition he had made on the case, lost himself in the music. Watson spent his time watching Holmes, contemplating his dual nature and how, after long periods of laziness, his restlessness builds up and bursts out upon some unsuspecting criminal.

With as peaceful as Holmes was throughout his concert, Watson knew something energetic was about to happen to their acid-stained friend. Outside the music hall, Holmes requested that Watson come back later that night and asked him to "kindly put your army revolver in your pocket," before he patted Watson on the hip and slipped spritely into the crowd. Watson considered it an ominous thing to see Holmes so chipper—it meant the very worst for whoever he was hunting.

That evening was momentous. Holmes decided to bring a riding crop to a gun fight, but it worked out well enough for them when he smacked a pistol clean out of John Clay's hand.

John Clay was a proud conquest for Holmes, a man he'd had "some skirmishes" with before, but had never yet seen. Clay turned out to be a good-looking man of royal descent (or so he claimed to the officer who went to cuff him), and Holmes was quite pleased to lay his hands on him.

"It's no use, John Clay," said Holmes blandly. "You have no chance at all."

"So I see," Clay answered with coolness. "You seem to have done the thing very completely. I must compliment you."

"And I you. Your red-headed idea was very new and effective."

Watson started to smile in the near-darkness, watching the two of them shift tightly against each other, knowing the many layers of pleasure that Holmes was experiencing by having this man in his grasp.

Watson let people congratulate Holmes, a bit of applause he thoroughly deserved after they all doubted him so severely, especially the foolish old man who owned the bank being robbed and complained at having to come out so late. Watson could tell the nattering sound of the man's stupid opinions was giving Holmes a headache earlier in the evening, so it was only kind to let Holmes hear the bank owner eat his own words for a bit.

They arrived back at Baker Street just as the sun was starting to rouse. Watson didn't even think about running home anymore, didn't even feel a twinge of doubt as he stayed out all night with Holmes. Watson made them each a whiskey and soda and they broke down the case as the morning sun gained ground through the window.

Holmes appreciated Clay's ingenuity in coming up with the outrageously silly Red-Headed League because it's just the sort of strange thing people are willing to believe, and it was the first truly original trick in years. Holmes explained his logic to Watson and received praise from his truest fan:

"You reasoned it out beautifully," Watson told him, his voice full of unfeigned admiration. "It is so long a chain, and yet every link rings true."

Homes gave a tired smile. "It saved me from ennui, but alas! I already feel it closing in upon me." He stirred his drink pensively, staring into its depths the way he looks at his chemistry beakers, waiting for something to happen, something to react, though of course this time nothing would. "My life is spent in one long effort to escape from the commonplaces of existence. These little problems help me to do so."

Holmes looked so miserable after a night of such triumph, and Watson ached for him, for whatever was wrong in him that caused him to crash so abruptly.

"You are a benefactor of the race," Watson told him gently, trying to cheer him even the slightest bit.

Holmes just shrugged, the sad smile on his face now seeming to convey pain. "Perhaps it is of little use," he said. "L'homme c'est rien—l'ouvre c'est tout." The man is nothing, the work is everything.

"You give yourself too little credit, my friend. In all the world there is only you."

Holmes's smile smoothed out and became a little more genuine. "I imagine you'll need to be getting home soon," Holmes said.

"Yes," Watson said slowly. "Perhaps after one more drink."

1889: The Boscombe Valley Mystery

It was all coming to a head: the visits between houses, the sharing of adventures, the pointed banter, the thrill of knowing so well that one person who knows you so well… It was an irresistible trajectory, and the crash was only a few months away. The tension would hold out through the summer though.

In June the ache became bad enough, the time had been long enough, and it was just over a year after Watson's marriage that Holmes finally broke and did something more than coy. He sent a note over to Watson in Paddington:

"Have you a couple of days to spare? Have just been wired for from the West of England in connection with Boscombe Valley tragedy. Shall be glad if you will come with me. Air and scenery perfect. Leave Paddington by the 11.15."

The assumption that he would come when invited shows just how far it had gone. Even Mary could see it. She didn't need to have the note read out to her to know who it was from. The smile on Watson's face was evidence enough of Sherlock Holmes. But she heard the contents of the message all the same when Watson read it aloud as though it wouldn't sting her.

I can just imagine the way her face would have tightened as she asked, "What do you say, dear? Will you go?"

"I really don't know what to say," Watson told her, knowing as well as Holmes did what his answer would be.

Mary, her face like a bitten lemon, said, "You have been looking a little pale lately. I think that the change would do you good, and you are always so interested in Mr. Sherlock Holmes's cases."

Even Watson sensed how cool she was being, and it cowed him. "I should be ungrateful if I were not," he said meekly from his end of the breakfast table, "seeing what I gained through one of them." He tried to smile at his wife; she began to cut her food vigorously. If Watson had not already known he would go, the atmosphere in his house that morning would have forced him out soon enough.

He left Mary and headed for the train station later that morning. Holmes was pacing up and down when Watson arrived, and when he noticed his friend, he broke into a smile so genuine I'm sure it would have made me sick.

"It is really very good of you to come, Watson. It makes a considerable difference to me, having someone with me on whom I can thoroughly rely." He could have told Watson to meet him at the bottom of a river, and Holmes would not have waited there long enough to drown.

Holmes quickly broke down the circumstances surrounding the death of a landowner named Mr. McCarthy which left his son looking like the culprit. A sad case, but not so tragic that Holmes could not take personal pleasure in it as both a puzzle and an excuse: "Hence it is that two middle-aged gentlemen are flying westward at fifty miles an hour, instead of quietly digesting their breakfasts at home."

A moment of silence passed that is not detailed by Watson in the official telling. Holmes, with his uncanny knowledge, asked Watson, "And how is your wife this morning?" But Watson only shook his head in a warning to Holmes that Mary was not to be a subject of his today, and in a rare moment of consideration, Holmes heeded him.

But he didn't keep his mouth shut the whole day, and managed to cross Watson a few times with his thoughtless words. After meeting young McCarthy he had this to say: "He is not a very quick-witted youth, though comely to look at, and, I should think, sound at heart."

Watson, rather stung by the knowledge that Holmes was looking at other peoples' youth, and having met the accused man's love interest earlier that day remarked back, "I cannot admire his taste if it is indeed a fact that he was averse to a marriage with so charming a young lady as this Miss Turner." They both were blessed with good sight, and Watson could admire the young people too, if Holmes wanted to start.

"Yes, I saw that you approved of the young lady," Holmes said. "You have a very predictable type in women, my dear Watson. Something soft but firm in their personality, a sort of steely presence in their gentle eyes..." Watson gave a cocked look to Holmes, advising him away from the subject of Mary once again. Holmes quickly launched into an explanation of why the junior McCarthy had not yet proposed to Miss Turner though he was madly in love with her, and they spent an uneasy night at the inn, an inauspicious beginning to the romantic journey as Holmes had imagined it might be.

The next day they resumed the investigation, and Holmes continued to put his foot in his mouth throughout. The first of it was when Lestrade, who brought him to the case, had a little dig at Holmes's methods.

"We have got to the deductions and the inferences," said Lestrade, winking at Watson. "I find it hard enough to tackle facts, Holmes, without flying away after theories and fancies."

"You are right," said Holmes, with an affected modesty. "You do find it very hard to tackle the facts."

After that both Watson and Lestrade were annoyed with him, and it put Holmes in a prickly mood until they arrived on the scene of the crime. Holmes forgot all about himself in the ecstasy of the hunt, and Watson too was distracted by watching Holmes's transformation. I find it a rather ugly description of animalistic focus; the same feeling of discomfort fills me when a familiar and friendly dog is suddenly and aggressively on the scent of a rat. But Watson was only fascinated. He never had a natural horror of Holmes, to his great disadvantage.

As the facts fell into place, Lestrade chose to ignore Holmes's findings, and as is true with most cases, only Watson remained to hear the full details. It was a testament to all that Watson had done with his writing that Holmes was content, in these later stories, to let the officials ignore him and allow his solution to stay secret. When Watson first met him, Holmes was wild with the injustice of being disregarded. It was the effort of Watson to record his every impressive move that gave him public status, and gave him peace about his legacy, so that later he would be free to claim that he never did anything for the recognition, only the art. It is easy to care little of renown once it is had.

After dinner, Holmes asked Watson to listen to him while he unspooled his thoughts. Watson obliged, and the way Holmes solicited his attention put him in a tender mood that endured through a visit from their culprit. The man confessed to McCarthy's murder, but as Holmes found his death justified, he let the ailing murderer go. So long as young McCarthy was not wrongly convicted, he would say nothing at all.

Though the case was solved, the true intention of this trip to the countryside had failed. Watson admitted to me that coming home from Boscombe Valley he felt like a man without a country. Holmes was still Holmes, superficially fun but a shallow well from which to draw for human affection; and yet, his wife was not all that he hoped she'd be either, she could not give him all that he desired. In all fairness, he did hazard to guess that she felt the same way towards him. He wanted a wife that had all the excitement of a whip-snap like Holmes, yet with all the quiet domesticity of his own mother. She had expected a husband to be a full-blooded man, whose love for her would be noble and passionate and unwavering until one or both of them should die. However, Watson came bundled together with someone who would never let him go, and there simply wasn't any recourse for either of them when it came to the problem of Sherlock Holmes.

1889: The Man With the Twisted Lip

Watson's was not the only unhappy wife. Kate Whitney arrived at the Watsons' home one night in June to send her doctor into an opium den after her husband while she stayed behind to be consoled by Mary. Apparently, "folk who were in grief came to her like birds to a lighthouse." They must have known that she could sympathize.

Mary and Watson had once found comfort in each other, but now relations were strained, and I know right well why. While retrieving Mr. Whitney from his den of iniquity, Watson came across Holmes in disguise, and was drawn into his doings as quickly as Holmes could insist on it. Watson knew it all himself: "It was difficult to refuse any of Sherlock Holmes's requests, for they were so exceedingly definite, and put forward with such a quiet air of mastery." No sooner did Holmes tell Watson to write a note to his wife saying he would not be home that night than Watson had done it and turned to wait at the beck and call of his friend. "Mastery" is almost too subtle a word; this was outright ownership.

Holmes emerged from the den laughing, pleased at his disguise, and at discovering Watson so accidentally. He was quick to assure Watson that he hadn't started using opium, and he brought up his taste for cocaine so breezily that it was clear he was experiencing a period of sobriety. The re-winning of Watson had become his new task, and puzzling out the best way to do it had begun to sustain him quite sufficiently in between cases.

Holmes gave the quick and dirty details of a prolific murder-trap location and conjured a vehicle from the night that would take him back to his hotel.

"You'll come with me, won't you?" he asked Watson. And of course, the answer was, "Of course."

It was a grateful ride out to his client's house, quiet at first, and then Holmes described the details he was concerned with—the case of someone else's missing husband. It seems to have been quite an epidemic that night, husbands disappearing out from under their wives all over London. Holmes was presented with fresh evidence before they even turned in for the night, so the tantalizing promise of a double bed went unfulfilled as Holmes perched himself on the floor throughout the night, and did not sleep for all his thinking. Watson reports:

"In the dim light of the lamp I saw him sitting there, an old briar pipe between his lips, his eyes fixed vacantly upon the corner of the ceiling, the blue smoke curling up from him, silent, motionless, with the light shining upon his strong-set aquiline features."

And this is how he solved the case; it was only a matter of realizing that the two men seen at different times in one room were the same man in a disguise, and an amusing one at that. A respectable family man was employed lucratively as a beggar, masking up his face every day so that he appeared to be a very tragic, ugly street figure. Even the police officer thought it more funny than criminal. He promised not to even bother about it all, so long as the gentleman was never caught out begging again with any face but the one he was born with. Their suspect/client was so embarrassed by his predicament that he swore to it on the spot.

Watson liked the light-hearted circumstances, but Holmes was bored as soon as the story was out. The more hideous the case, the more Holmes tends to savor it. I've a theory that it makes him feel more alive, just the way a war causes a boom in births; tragedy prompts a certain kind of person to live even harder, in defiance. Sherlock Holmes is that sort of belligerent person.

1889: The Engineer's Thumb

Lucky for Holmes, most of their cases were not so charming. The next month Watson stopped by Baker Street with a mutilated man named Victor Hatherly, but before getting into that, Watson explained:

"I had finally abandoned Holmes in his Baker-street rooms, although I continually visited him, and occasionally even persuaded him to forego his Bohemian habits so far as to come and visit us."

If, like myself, you are tired of the back-and-forth between them, it is absolutely nothing to how Watson felt about it. It was balancing on a precipice, it was holding a trigger steady, it was Sisyphus at the summit… it was agony. But as a doctor he knew the habits of man, and if he had a dime for every patient who would harass their own wounds by picking and prodding, he would have money enough to retire. And it seemed that fate would insist on throwing he and Holmes together, even without their being able to help it. Hatherley did need to consult with Holmes. What else could be done?

That is what he said to Mary when he went up to tell her he'd be away for a while. He had at last learned to be a little more oblique with his references to Holmes, but he could not pretend on this day that he was just headed to the club.

"What can I do?" he asked Mary carefully. "The man has been through a terrible ordeal."

"And Mr. Sherlock Holmes will make it all better?"

"He's shed light on worse," Watson told her cryptically. "I don't know when I'll return. I'll send a wire if I'll be gone through the night." He went to kiss her goodbye and she flinched from him almost imperceptibly. This, at least, Watson observed as if he were the very man they spoke of. He left without bestowing his kiss.

It's a creepy story Hatherley tells about being commissioned for his expertise in hydraulics to a mysterious house in the countryside. He is tricked there, blindfolded, and nearly killed when he discovers that the press he's working on is not used for the purposes of making fuller's bricks as he had been told, but rather counterfeit coins. My sympathy for him was slightly marred when he ignored the fearful warnings of a woman inside the house; it was a rather bad habit of men of the time to assume all women were hysterics, half-mad from bleeding once a month and weak from their breathless corsets. Should Hatherley have heeded her from the outset, he'd have retained his digit.

In the end, he was lucky to only lose a thumb. The engineer who went before him was never seen again.

Sherlock Holmes managed to have quite a bit of fun, especially under the gory circumstances. He even took a moment at the train station to let everyone in his party guess four separate compass directions that the house of the counterfeiters must lie in, just so he would have the pleasure of telling them that they were all wrong.

"But we can't *all* be," Inspector Bradstreet protested. Holmes smiled as he said, "Oh yes, you can," and explained how cleverly the coiners had driven Hatherley in circles until he'd swear he was miles from the station, though in fact he was very close by.

It was a hell of a situation Hatherley got himself in, and though his life had been only just gotten away with, he still had the nerve to be ungrateful, complaining about his lost thumb, and unbelievably, his lost fee!

In a remark I appreciate considering my feelings against Hatherley, Holmes told him he had at least gained some experience, and an entertaining story for parties!

Watson had to stifle a smile. He is naturally sympathetic and makes a fine physician because of it, but Sherlock Holmes was starting to override the best in him, yet again. This was July, and by September something between them would finally click back into place.

1889: The Five Orange Pips

Now, when I first became serious about Watson, I read all of his stories. I'd come across one or two before with little interest, honestly; I found Holmes insufferable from the start. Later of course I read them for information on Watson. Every phrase he chose added to my knowledge of him, ingrained his cadence into my head. I was love-sick then, and didn't see a single flaw. It wasn't until much later, when I heard more about Holmes from Watson that didn't seem to match the demi-god of his stories, that I sat down to serious study. The first thing I noticed then were the numerous discrepancies: impossible dates, mix-and-match combinations of introduction material and the case details, even fully fleshed lies in some cases! Those mostly about women, probably to deflect suspicion.

I am Watson's second, and hopefully final, wife. I should be able to line up the stories that mention his only other wife, Mary, in a very neat line. If only that were so! I had to laugh at him once I compared some of his notes, knowing when his first wedding anniversary was and having the ability to count. I gave myself a headache trying to sort it all out before I remembered how unfortunate Watson can be with numbers.

"What was her name?" I asked him once, biting down on a smile as I pushed up my reading glasses. It was an evening well before the war, and we both sat engaged in perfectly domestic study—he with the newspaper, myself with his narratives.

"Whose name, darling?"

"The wife you had in September of 1887."

He lowered his paper and frowned at the toe of his shoe. "Mary and I weren't married until 1888, my dear, in the very early spring, on the first warm and twittering day of it, if I remember right. I was a bachelor before then."

"Oh really?" I said, nearly drawing blood in my effort to keep a serious expression. "Because some fellow signing himself Dr. Watson says otherwise."

"What?" He got up from the paper and came over to the desk, attempting to argue with me. I had just gone through all his papers with a fine-toothed comb: *The Adventure of the Five Orange Pips* is recorded as happening in late September of 1887, and yet in the scene that precedes it in the story has Watson speaking of a wife away visiting her mother when he did not meet Mary until the next year, and she was an orphan on top of that, and Holmes mentions the one woman who has ever outsmarted him, meaning of course Irene Adler, whom he did not encounter until March of 1888.

"Or Irene might have been in 1889, darling, I truly cannot tell," I told my husband. "It is the same sort of thing later when you mention *The Sign of Four*; that also occurred in 1888, in July," I said, and then glancing at my notes, "or September."

Watson seemed flustered and started shuffling through his papers, but I shooed him away; I'd just given them some semblance of organization. I wouldn't have him messing them up again.

The best I can figure, Watson somehow altered the date, and this Five Orange Pips case took place in September of 1889, which is where I have placed it. It was either that, or Watson accidentally paired a rainy day in September with a rainy case in September, not realizing that they were two separate years, and not bothering to check on something so seemingly incidental as the idle chatter that transpired before the arrival of a client. Watson was grumpy at me for days after I pointed it out to him, so I never asked for more clarification. I want to keep the cases in order, but I cannot bend my understanding around this clearly anachronistic front matter, and so have had to move it. He may sue me if he dares.

Mistake or not, I would have been short a bit of joy if I hadn't read this introduction. If indeed this scene did take place after Watson's marriage to Mary Morstan, the sulkiness of Sherlock Holmes fills me with glee. A man comes stumbling up the street, and Watson wonders if it is some friend of Holmes's. According to Holmes: "Except yourself I have none. I do not encourage visitors." Such a pronounced pout, even through the page! Perhaps he should have treated his one and only friend a bit better if he wanted for company, but his loss was my eventual gain, so I cannot rightly complain.

That being said, this "visit" Watson was on strikes me as unlikely. As I said before: Mary was an orphan. She was not off staying with her mother. I think Watson lied here (terribly) to disguise the fact that he had temporarily moved out from the home he shared with his wife, and back into Baker Street. During every case he records that winter, he is residing at 221B, and he hardly makes any reference to it at all. Things were not ideal in the Watson household.

As for the case itself, that of The Five Orange Pips, I must say I get rather tired of America being portrayed as a wild land of cults and violence. I've been to America, and my mother was an American, and though the people are still rather rough around the edges, they aren't all Mormons or Klansmen or what have you. But alas, those people do blight America's reputation.

So when threats signed K.K.K. start to menace young Oppenshaw and he is recommended to Holmes, Watson is in residence. It was a tense arrangement, thick with expectation. After a fight with Mary, the details of which I have never been told, he showed up on Holmes's front step with the same lie he would later tell his readers, though of course Holmes was much harder to fool.

"My dear Watson, surely you realize that even if I didn't know Mary to be parentless, you have a very obvious tell," he said, letting Watson inside gleefully. "You cannot look me in the eye with a falsehood, and it's clear as day that you've been arguing with a woman anyway."

"How is that, Holmes?" Watson wondered childishly as he set down the quick suitcase he had packed with the efficiency of all his military training.

"You look greatly annoyed and frustrated, but your hand is unmarked. If a man had caused you such grief you'd have struck him and been satisfied."

"Ah," said Watson, smiling at the explanation.

"And you've packed in an unexpected hurry, as can be seen by the sleeve peeking out of your valise."

"Well then, I hope you have room for a liar and an unsatisfactory husband?" Watson asked.

"Always," Holmes said, clapping him on the shoulder.

They kept up the good-natured ribbing for a few loaded days, all the way up to when the client had come and gone. They reminisced about old times like two circling fighters, feinting and hesitating, waiting for the first strike. Watson was back at home again, so when would it be, when would it be? And who would risk the first movement? Each of them had a matter of pride to consider, wanting the other man to know that things could be got on without him. It was important to prove to each other that they didn't need anything, as though only the weak required more than food and shelter. They were such men about it.

Watson recalled carefully to Holmes the time when they were new to each other, remembering that he had made some observational conclusions about the practical composition of Sherlock Holmes.

"Violin player," Watson reminded him. "Boxer, swordsman, lawyer, and self-poisoner by cocaine and tobacco."

Holmes grinned at the last item. "Well," he said. "I say now, as I said then, that a man should keep his little brain attic stocked with all the furniture that he is likely to use."

"And the cocaine?" Watson asked, his smile frozen on his face. "Is that something you're likely to use?"

"Not lately, my friend. Not since you left."

A dove of hope began to coo within Watson, to rustle as if it would take flight, but it would have to wait just the slightest bit longer. The next morning Watson and Holmes discovered that their client died suddenly after leaving Baker Street alone, and though the official word on his death was accidental, they both knew better.

Watson could tell that Holmes was disturbed by the news, though he put on a casual tone at first. Once it had sunk in, he honestly said, "That hurts my pride, Watson. It is a petty feeling, no doubt, but it hurts my pride."

Watson was entranced with watching Holmes feel anything in front of him, even if the emotion was entirely inappropriate, and when Watson asked him if he would go to the police, Holmes said, "I shall be my own police!" And tore from the house to be just that.

Watson, though not currently sleeping at home, still had need to work there. He stayed out of the upper quarters, attended to his patients as though everything was fine, and returned to Baker Street at the end of the day. Holmes returned hours after him, having neglected to eat in the intervening time, and Watson listened to all his plans and figuring on how he would avenge his client.

Watson went to touch Holmes on the shoulder, but Holmes was so agitated by his failure that he brushed it right off, like a dog that won't be patted during a thunderstorm.

And speaking of dogs…

1889: The Hound of the Baskervilles

Two weeks later, in October, Watson is still clearly living at Baker Street. You'll notice the slip-up in speech as he speaks to Holmes about "our visitor" who left a walking stick behind, and Holmes echoes him by saying "our visitor" had provided quite a bit of information about himself by leaving his cane. Holmes challenged Watson to make some deductions from the object, and he failed to find a single fact, but you can tell that Holmes was working to be kind to him by the way that he complimented Watson regardless.

Even Watson knew something curious was happening, something unprecedented: "He had never said as much before, and I must admit that his words gave me keen pleasure, for I had often been piqued by his indifference to my admiration and to the attempts which I had made to give publicity to his methods." Holmes knew as much to realize that Watson felt taken advantage of and ignored. He tried his best to shape up, but he was simply terrible at it:

"I am afraid, my dear Watson, that most of your conclusions were erroneous. When I said that you stimulated me I meant, to be frank, that in noting your fallacies I was occasionally guided towards the truth."

Holmes blew smoke rings while lecturing Watson on this stranger which neither had met, and when at last he rose to the window to see this forgetful man approach his door, followed by a curly-haired spaniel, he insisted that Watson stay. He put a hand on Watson's arm and said, "Don't move, I beg you, Watson. He is a professional brother of yours, and your presence may be of assistance to me." As if it mattered that they were both doctors! But Holmes did want him to stay. He'd been trying to get him to stay for over a year.

Dr. James Mortimer was an odd creature, and in earlier days, Watson might have had cause for concern. When first he walked in, the doctor complimented Holmes's bone structure, particularly his skull, and asked if he might touch it for anthropological purposes. Flattery will get you everywhere with Sherlock Holmes, and Watson watched him for signs of warmth.

It was a loaded introduction, and Watson noted it: "Holmes was silent, but his little darting glances showed me the interest which he took in our curious companion."

The man managed to slight Holmes a moment later, but even that did not make him less interesting. The problem he presented redeemed him immediately. After the initial legend of the hound, which Holmes found dull in its fantastic elements, Dr. Mortimer described the death of his friend and patient, Sir Charles Baskerville.

The scene, as described by Mortimer who had been there himself, presented some tantalizing details. Most inexplicable were the footprints of a large hound, not any mere hunting or herding dog, some twenty yards off from the body. But more than this observation, which Dr. Mortimer had wisely kept to himself, were his other minor deductions, such as the fact that Sir Charles had stood waiting for something or someone, which Mortimer knew by the presence of fallen cigar ash.

"Excellent!" Holmes cried. "This is a colleague, Watson, after our own heart."

Watson smiled and nodded his head, but he felt injured. It felt like Colonel Hayter all over again. Watson could sense Holmes's excitement: "His eyes had the hard, dry glitter which shot from them when he was keenly interested." Naturally it was the case that had his blood up, but he was enjoying Dr. Mortimer quite a bit too. Watson guarded himself and waited to see how it would play out. He could always go home to his wife, after all.

Holmes and Mortimer were rams at odds over the presence of supernatural happenings, but even as they parted, it was clear that the doctor's visit had stirred Holmes. He asked if Watson was going out.

"Unless I can help you," Watson responded, though he had not really intended to go out. He was only fishing for validation.

"No, my dear fellow, it is at the hour of action that I turn to you for aid." In other words, Watson gathered, it was his body and not his mind that Holmes found useful. And then Holmes was insensitive enough to ask

Watson to send up some tobacco on his way out, and to stay away until evening. He had a problem to solve.

What a heartbreak it must be to love Holmes all the time, what an unending trial! He moved through the world so obliviously, like a storm; his reasons unknown, his destination unpredictable, but his indifference felt all too palpably in the destruction being wrought. And yet Watson always found it difficult to blame Holmes, for of course the man didn't know his own strength, nor what damage he did by merely being himself. Watson managed to pity him most of the time, though I can't imagine why; it's more sensible to envy those who know not what they do.

Watson whiled away the day lingering at his club and returned back to a room later in the night that was as smoky as a blocked flue. Holmes immediately blurted out that Watson had been at his club all day, a fact he deduced because he knows Watson has no intimate friends with which he could have passed the time indoors. And this was Holmes trying his damnedest to be kind! This was his greatest effort.

But the time of action was upon them soon enough, and once they are both fully engaged in a case they syncopate beautifully. The next day, after they met Sir Henry Baskerville and heard that he had received a note cut from the previous day's newspaper, Holmes sent Sir Henry and Dr. Mortimer away, promising that they would meet for lunch. The second they were out the door, Holmes leapt to activity.

"Your hat and boots, Watson, quick!" Watson wondered if he shouldn't run off after their clients, but Holmes was done with them. "Not for the world, my dear Watson. I am perfectly satisfied with your company if you will tolerate mine."

Watson smiled as they took off behind their clients, and was so pleased with Holmes's sentiment that he did not see a bit of what Holmes saw until the detective took off after the cab of a bearded man who was also following Sir Henry. Suspicious happenings started to stack up after that very rapidly; Sir Henry had two boots go missing, one from a new pair, and then one from an old, and then the mysterious return of the first. It bothered Holmes so much that he volunteered Watson to go down to Baskerville Hall and keep an eye on Sir Henry, which Watson could not help but accept. Watson is not immune to flattery any more than his masterful friend.

It was all still a laugh for Sherlock Holmes until he found the cab that had driven their suspect around. The man had given his name to the cabman as Sherlock Holmes, and though Watson was still laughing after it a bit, wondering just who could be so cheeky, it began to chill Holmes. That is, after all, something that Holmes might have done, and as I've said before, Holmes knew enough to be wary of himself. Whoever they were hunting might prove himself equal to Holmes, and that was a fearful thought indeed.

"I'm not easy in my mind about it," Holmes told Watson, "about sending you. Yes, my dear fellow, you may laugh, but I give you my word that I shall be very glad to have you back safe and sound in Baker Street once more."

Watson grasped Holmes by the shoulder and asked, "But what could possibly happen to me?"

Holmes just gave him a dark look and went straight to bed. He did bring himself to worry about Watson in times of real danger, and at those times I do soften towards Holmes. He may have been too much of an automaton to realize when Watson's emotions were being abused, but he was always acutely aware of bodily harm. Any threat of violence against Watson could turn Holmes human for a time, like a fairytale elixir. He was not, in the end, totally invincible.

That Saturday Holmes saw everyone off at the station, and Watson was immediately impressed upon arriving at Baskerville Hall by the gloomy atmosphere. He even went to bed to the sound of a woman sobbing, a noise he found more disturbing than most others. The moors surrounded him, a foreboding moonscape, and his trip only got stranger the longer it progressed. The creepy locals and the noises of the moor soon began to rattle him. He felt like Jonathan Harker during the first days in Count Dracula's crumbling castle. He had a presentiment of something dreadful.

He even had the local villagers trying to warn him away, and unlike the unfortunate and thumbless Hatherley from a few months back, Watson does not ignore women who beseech him earnestly, especially when they are beautiful. When the neighboring Miss Stapleton hurried to him and, assuming he was Sir Henry, warned him to return to London, Watson paid very close attention. He started to monitor the Stapletons very closely, though not closely enough to realize that they were husband and wife, and not brother and sister as they posed. Holmes would be the one to decipher that.

A couple of Dear Holmes letters follow in the narrative, detailing the way Sir Henry became infatuated with Miss Stapleton, the curious actions of the assumed Brother Stapleton, and of the Barrymores who ran the Baskerville household. Watson was, unbeknownst to himself, investigating the considerably less interesting case of an escaped convict on the moor: "Congratulate me, my dear Holmes," he wrote, "and tell me that I have not disappointed you as an agent—that you do not regret the confidence you showed in me when you sent me down." He and Sir Henry followed Barrymore one night (after having fallen asleep the first night, bless them), and Watson desired to be praised for his discovery that Mrs. Barrymore was kin to the convict and helping him live out on the moor.

Little did poor Watson suspect that Holmes himself was on the moor, and not only knew all about the convict, but received Watson's letters mere yards from him, upon the Tor. Watson had even spotted the figure of Holmes while they were out hunting the convict, and did not know him, though perhaps he should have. After all, Watson had felt "the thrill which his strange presence and his commanding attitude had given," even from so great a distance. And he certainly recognized the silhouette of Holmes later, when the detective's shadow fell across the doorway of one of the moor's ancient dwellings, in which Holmes had been camped all the time.

Watson braved both the moor and a man he thought controlled some devilish hound when he entered the room while Holmes was out. It was of Holmes he thought while he did so too, hoping to succeed (he said) where his "master" had failed.

It was a tense wait inside the hut, Watson holding his revolver all the time, and afraid, once he'd found evidence that whoever inhabited this dwelling had been spying on him. The stress was trying him terribly as he heard boots approach the door, stop for a moment, and then advance again. However, as soon as the figure spoke, "a crushing weight of responsibility seemed in an instant to be lifted." That cold, incisive, ironical voice could belong to but one man in all the world:

"It's a lovely evening, my dear Watson. I really think that you will be more comfortable outside than in."

Watson's happiness at discovering Holmes on the moor was overwhelming, and Holmes too was repressing his emotion at meeting his friend so unexpectedly. They had grown accustomed to seeing one another every day since Watson had moved back to Baker Street. They didn't realize how much their separation during this investigation had bothered them until they were joyfully reunited again. The transcript we have is so sweet it's nearly sickening, like a child who's gotten into the sugar and doesn't know when to stop. It is too much, certainly, for me, and it was almost too much for them.

Watson is a visual creature, as is evidenced by the way he feasts on the image of women he meets. The same applies here, to Holmes.

When Watson stepped out of the hut, his eyes roved over Holmes, picking out the details, deducing less than Holmes might have, but learning things about Holmes's stay out on the moors all the same. Holmes was roughed up a bit by this ascetic living, a little brown and wind-worn, but still with the "cat-like love of personal cleanliness which was one of his characteristics." His face was neatly shaven, his clothes well cared for. You could take the dandy out of the city, but you simply could not take the dandy out of Holmes.

"I never was more glad to see anyone in my life," Watson wrote of the moment. He went straight up to Holmes and grasped him by the hand.

The pleasure was mutual. Holmes's gray eyes "danced with amusement." He swore to Watson that he had no idea someone had found him, let alone who, until he was within twenty paces of the door. Watson guessed it was his footprint that gave him away, but Holmes assured him that, dear as the doctor was to him, he couldn't pick his foot out of all the prints in the world. But he could identify his cigarette, and he could guess Watson's behavior with such accuracy that he predicted Watson was armed within the hut. A man of action such as himself would not wait with his hands folded in his lap.

And yet, love as raw and open as this reunion occasioned is easily injured. When Watson discovered that Holmes had been using him and manipulating his ignorance, he was hurt, and even more so when he thought back to the careful letters he had written for his friend supposedly back in London: "My reports have all been wasted!"

Holmes was aghast at Watson's emotion. Imagine someone who dislikes being lied to and tricked! For some reason Holmes can know Watson's actions in advance, but not his feelings. It is Holmes's most significant blind spot, not just in relation to Watson, but in his work as a detective as well. The question of motive that the officers of Scotland Yard rely on so heavily is not altogether useless—an intuitive understanding of human nature serves them nearly as well as Holmes's deductions.

Holmes worked to rectify his mistake quickly. He produced Watson's reports from a pocket over his heart. He *had* been reading them, and they were helpful! Secrecy seemed necessary to Holmes, because not only could he keep an eye on the principle players without them feeling his scrutiny, he could also guard over Watson's safety, and not vex him with the worry which someone of his kindness would naturally feel if their friend was sleeping outdoors on the inclement moors. Couldn't Watson see that it was only consideration for him that made Holmes appear so inconsiderate?

Holmes's beseeching softened Watson towards him, and the relief Holmes felt at winning him back after such a sudden breech pushed him to a place of boldness. Watson's forgiveness showed on his face (every one of his emotions may be read plainly there), and for the first time in over a year and a half, Holmes hooked Watson by the collar, and gave him a kiss.

"That's better," said Sherlock Holmes. And it was. At the time, it certainly was. Holmes had broken first, and my eyebrows shot up when I realized it, because I thought for sure Watson would have been the one. Holmes was a fisher of men, very catch and release. I thought Watson would grow desperate first, seeing as Holmes was his only source of masculine converse, but apparently there is no replacing Watson.

Watson's narrative in the official canon suddenly loses daylight, as though the men were so carried away discussing the details of the case that they lost track of the time. But I have the truth from Watson. He gave me as many details as he could bring himself to speak, one day about a year into our marriage, when he realized that he and I had never had an argument.

"Darling," I told him. "We're too old for arguments." He smiled and took my hand. We were at the seaside on an anniversary trip.

"Mary and I fought," he told me. "Horrible, long, silent stand-offs." The sun was just beginning to set, and it felt as if it was falling down on us, so thick did the sunlight seem by the sea. A breeze disturbed Watson's mustache, or maybe his mouth twitched in agitation. He said softly in addition, "Holmes and I fought too."

But, so the story went, they always made up spectacularly. On the moors, after all their dissonance and Watson's marriage and their hesitant resumption of courtship in the past few months, they found themselves alone at last, in the twilight, in a place far from Baker Street and the scene of their old troubles.

Holmes ducked back into his ancient dwelling, and he pulled Watson in after him, finger still hooked under the neck of his shirt. The hut was too low to stand in, so Holmes sunk straight to his knees and brought Watson down with him.

Watson and I, and Holmes as well, we're from a modest generation. Our mothers might have never been fully naked past the age of infancy, and we have all inherited that shyness. In my experiences making love with Watson, some bit of clothing always remained in place, and such was true, as far as I can gather, with Sherlock Holmes. I would be surprised if in this particular instance they even unbuttoned their shirts all the way. It wasn't strictly necessary.

The air would have been clammy as the evening fog rolled in, but the chill would have been kept at bay by their breaths, their bodies. Sherlock Holmes, his muscles as tight as the strings on his violin, pushed and pulled Watson as he pleased. They had each been a long time wanting this connection; they quivered on the edge of it, fearful lest it should escape them once again.

They kissed savagely, Watson's mustache in complete disrepair, Holmes's usually thin, pale lips flushed with passion. They loved each other forcefully for only a few moments, their stamina at a significant low after so long apart, but it was enough to sate them. They sat back on the packed dirt floor of the hut to catch their breaths.

They did get around to talking about the case eventually, just as Watson has written down, but it was mixed in with a kind of intimate chatter, the likes of which is usually found shared over bedroom pillows. At first they began by laughing about Dr. Mortimer's strange fixation with skulls, and Watson relayed the trick he used in distracting Mortimer from asking too much about the case.

"I am certainly developing the wisdom of the serpent, for when Mortimer pressed his questions to an inconvenient extent I asked him casually to what type Frankland's skull belonged, and so heard nothing but craniology for the rest of our drive!" He had not lived for years with Sherlock Holmes for nothing. It is a tactic that works on any obsessive personality.

"Has the good doctor asked after your skull as he has after mine?" Holmes said, his words taking solid shape with the smoke from a cigarette. He sat on an outcropping of rock, having allowed Watson the stone slab of the bed. There was much amusement in his voice.

"He hasn't. I suppose I'm a much less interesting subject." Holmes made a gesture waving away Watson's modesty. Watson continued to speak cautiously. "Dr. Mortimer is a peculiar fellow, is he not? So much so that when he first asked to examine your skull, I...well I thought he was after something else."

"He wasn't, Watson. He is just a scientist. We are locked away in laboratories for so long we forget how to talk to people. Besides which, though he is a curious person, he is of absolutely no interest to me."

"Why is that?" Watson asked, beginning to right his buttons and smooth his hair.

"Most men pale in comparison to you, Watson."

Watson opened his mouth to speak, but it was rather too much for him to process. Holmes was in a most loving mood lately, relative to his usual behavior. It was, and still is, very flattering to experience praise from such a Caesar.

They lapsed into a discussion of the case, and by the time Holmes suggested that Watson had best get back to Sir Henry, his endangered charge, they were put together once again as though nothing had happened. A question was thick in the air between them about what would occur once they returned home, but no one was going to speak of it just then, and in any case they were interrupted by a blood-chilling cry from outside.

Both men rushed into the darkness assuming their client had fallen prey to the legendary hound of his forefathers, both sick in their hearts at the sound of it. Holmes was in an absolute state, furious with himself and with Watson for allowing their client to be killed when they knew enough to have stopped it.

Guilt welled up in Watson even as hysteria seemed to consume Holmes when, after much stomping and shouting, he started to dance and laugh.

"Good heavens, have you gone mad?" Watson asked. I cannot think of a more useless question to ask of someone who might be mad, but Sherlock Holmes was not mad, he was merely ecstatic. Setting aside how disturbing it is to ever be so enthused beside the body of a man you just heard die in terror, even Watson felt lighter when they both realized: this was not Sir Henry, but the unfortunate convict, in Sir Henry's old coat.

Holmes was in a fit of joy that did not end until Stapleton arrived and he was required to control himself. The murderous naturalist was just as cold as Holmes was hot over these proceedings. Strolling up to the man he'd just killed by design, he was also able to conceal his surprise at finding the wrong man in the right coat.

Holmes can never truly mask himself like that, for he is not a cold man, no matter how often he aspires to be machine-like. A steam engine is a machine too, and Holmes was positively stoked with the excitement of this problem. He often trembled with the effort to hide his exhilaration; it shivers through him when he must swallow it down, like a nasty medicine, and it's never far from coming back up. When he and Watson parted ways from Stapleton, it was all on his surface again. Holmes was breathing deeply the moist air like it was the sweetest incense. Watson kept his eyes sliced sideways, watching him.

"Could this be my stern, self-contained friend?" Watson wondered. "These were hidden fires, indeed!"

Yes, indeed.

1919: Retreat

I clear the table myself, stacking the dishes noisily and escaping into the hall outside the kitchen. My Watson makes an effort to be discreet, but Holmes is going out of his way to make me uncomfortable. Eyeing Watson and all but licking his chops, I think he may have even winked… It's making me feel rather ill.

I could probably tolerate it from any other man, but then I know there isn't any other man when it comes to Watson; there is only this one.

I won't pretend that it doesn't break my heart a little. The knowledge that my husband's love is divided, that his loyalty lies sometimes elsewhere. He loves me, but he loves Holmes too, and he has known Holmes longer, and stuck with him through worse. The biggest difference is that I have never betrayed Watson, I have never taken from him more than I've given, I have never hurt him. But perhaps I do not have the capacity? Perhaps only Sherlock Holmes could truly injure him.

But I am letting the world-famous detective get to me. He is not so untouchable. Sure, I am stifling tears in the hallway while he is making love in the dining room, but whose house is he in? Who has Watson chosen, and made vows to, and stuck by? Who puts him back together when he returns from Holmes's seaside house in agony?

It is easy to be intimidated by thoughts of them at their best. Watson and Holmes; they were golden, they were unstoppable, but it's balanced out by their worst. Mathematically I should have nothing to worry about, but I can think of a way to be positively sure.

I compose myself in the hall mirror, then grasp it by its heavy frame, and remove it from the wall. I know that if I can angle it properly, I'll be able to see the men's reflection in the china cabinet. I look like a madwoman sitting on the floor with a mirror bigger than my torso, tipping it this way and that, but I need to get a glance at them alone. When I finally find their pale likenesses in the glass, what I see actually helps.

They are grasped together at the table, hands squeezed firm on each other's arms, heads leaned close together. But Watson's head is shaking back and forth, and he looks upset, and Sherlock Holmes has lost the superior look he has for me and now seems concerned, conciliatory, as if he is begging for something that's being refused to him.

I am soothed by this tableau. I replace the mirror on the wall and prepare myself to take dessert out into the dining room. I pop into the kitchen for the tray and avert my face from Maurice so he won't see that I have been upset. Watson would notice, and Holmes too I assume, but right now they are probably too wrapped up in each other to consider me at all. Still: better to hide myself.

I walk into the dining room with the tray in front of my face and start polite conversation about where the cake and the coffee came from before setting it down on the table. My words die on my lips when I realize the room is empty.

They're gone.

1889: The Hound of the Baskervilles (continued)

Sherlock Holmes may have been excited about the death of the convict on the moor, but the poor man's sister was not. He was hated by all the citizenry in the county for his horrid crimes, but still the man's sister loved him. "Evil indeed is the man who has not one woman to mourn him," Watson noted. That is true enough.

Pleased as he was to find the convict dead, Holmes wondered aloud if he shouldn't arrest the whole household for aiding him in the first place, but he said it with a smile. As if he had never ignored the law himself, and encouraged Watson to do the same! But then he spotted the line of portraits of past Baskervilles and realized something that made him ecstatic all over again. Holmes was required to suppress this emotion while in front of Sir Henry, but when Watson came to his room later that night (sometimes discretion in these narratives is entirely left wanting—Watson was not quite accustomed to being guilty), Holmes seized him by the arm and took a candle down with them to look at the portraits alone.

It was the one of Sir Hugo, the Baskerville who allegedly conjured the devilish hound and inadvertently set it upon his whole family. Holmes quizzed Watson on it, and then covered the hat and hair of the painted man to reveal a remarkable family resemblance to...Stapleton.

Watson was astonished, and Holmes nearly lost himself in a fit of laughter. For some reason, among my friends, I find people are under the assumption that Holmes is a stoic figure; reasonable, rational, and always in the right. I have read these stories quite closely, and if one isolates his objective behavior from all the trappings of admiration that Watson surrounds them with, Holmes easily appears insane. Not just the strange circumstances of his depressions, but these wild upswings as well! The way he goes gibbering off on the obscure threads of a case, the way he receives a charge from the mere figuring out of a problem… He never loses his reason—for it is his reason alone, once he has proven himself right, that saves him from the asylum—but at times he almost cannot harness himself. At any rate, he could not hold his madness down indefinitely, and it usually exploded in front Watson, who never appeared to judge him harshly.

This fit was brought on by the idea of catching Stapleton and adding him to their Baker Street collection, the image of pinning him under glass like a specimen. "I have not heard him laugh often," Watson wrote, "and it has always boded ill to somebody." What a disturbing sort man whose laughter means danger and whose pleasure is violence. There is nothing so happy that Sherlock Holmes cannot make it seem sinister.

Holmes was rather partial to the image of catching Stapleton like one of the naturalist's own butterflies, and metaphorically refers to nets all during the case, though usually he is resistant to such literary speech. But he liked Stapleton as an adversary, liked all the hoops and troubles he had to go through to trap him. It was one of the more elaborate and taxing cases Watson recorded, but Holmes enjoyed it all the more for the energy he expended. He put a few more things into place, but still noted, "Even now we have no clear case against this very wily man. But I shall be very much surprised if it is not clear enough before we go to bed this night."

Watson snorted into his mustache as they stood waiting for Lestrade to arrive from London and dared not look at Holmes lest he be crippled by the subtext in those words.

Lestrade was much more disposed towards Holmes here than we've seen him previously; he had become a more experienced detective himself, and as such recognized Holmes's greatness at the profession. But that does not mean Lestrade understood Holmes any better, for he and Watson were both frustrated by Holmes's habit of fostering mystery. During dinner and on the long drive out to Baskerville Hall, they were left to stew in their own anxieties as Holmes retained all his knowledge for himself. Watson hazarded a couple guesses at why:

"Partly it came no doubt from his own masterful nature, which loved to dominate and surprise those who were around him." This is my guess! The need to reinforce his assumed superiority, to constantly reassure himself that he is better by keeping everyone else in the dark. Watson gives him more credit, as though Holmes has ever truly felt humble: "Partly also from his professional caution, which urged him never to take any chances."

Holmes was anything but professional. The thrill of the case caused him such reckless giddiness that it affected those around him. He manages to pull Lestrade into some suggestive banter about whether he's armed and where. I'm surprised Watson could transcribe it all without blushing, but something about a hunt turns men into boys again, and it was all ribaldry and singing nerves as they approached the Stapleton house in the dark.

They waited for Sir Henry to emerge, and then for the hound to attack. At the moment of approach, Watson glanced at Holmes, and his face "was pale and exultant, his eyes shining brightly in the moonlight." He was serene thinking he knew exactly what was waiting for him in the misty night, but he did not expect the hound to be breathing fire, or phosphorus, as it turned out to be. *That* rattled Holmes for the barest moment, and Sir Henry got the scare of his life in that slim second of hesitation. I suppose it is a blessing that Holmes is so vain he takes it as a personal failing to overlook anything; with the precarious way he plays with people, setting them up as if he is directing a play where the deaths are only temporary, he cannot afford to be wrong. People don't get back up in real life unless they are saved in time, which is thankfully what happened here. With greater intellect comes greater responsibility—I would not thank my maker for giving me that sort of burden.

Sir Henry thanked Holmes for saving his life, even though Holmes admitted to him that he had endangered it in the first place. It is well of him to be honest in that, for I hate him least when he is honest.

The mystery was solved and Stapleton was lost upon the moor, presumed dead. Holmes almost drowned himself in the mire fetching back Sir Henry's missing boot. Watson often compares him to a bloodhound, but even the massive beast who lived on the moor before it was gunned down never brought itself to run full-long into a sink hole like that, the rash child. Though his reason remains intact on a case, his sense of self-preservation absolutely vanishes.

But once the case was done, Watson and Holmes returned to Baker Street alive and renewed in one another. They exited from the crawling air of the moor and left the menacing mood of the place behind. On the long journey back to London the atmosphere transmuted, and the horrible dread of the Baskerville estate yielded to an emotion opposite but similar, the other hand of expectation: hope. It was an excited sort of charge shared between the two of them, the knowledge that something had changed, and that more alterations would follow suit. They were not going back to what they were before, they were moving on.

1890: The Yellow Face

The year is out before Watson's narrative resumes. Was it a second giggling honeymoon that he was as reluctant to share as the first? Or was it a time too honest, too awkward, too tempestuous to reveal? These men would have needed to renegotiate their boundaries, their new terms for one another.

But they were so happy to be back together, regardless of what might be in their way now; they were young again, for a time. They got so sweet with one another that Holmes even admitted he was mistaken, a rare and precious occurrence more infrequent than blue moons. Watson writes gently of him in this case, explaining with a peculiar affection how Holmes's supreme laziness is mixed with freakish bursts of energy, and even mentioning his use of cocaine passingly, saying that it was his one and only "occasional" vice, because that was how Watson chose to perceive it at the time. Holmes had put the drug away for a season, for the purpose of winning Watson back.

On the first warm day of spring, they went for a walk together, repeating the behavior of their initial courtship: "For two hours we rambled about together, in silence for the most part, as befits two men who know each other intimately." I imagine they walked past the alley where they first kissed and smiled at one another. They knew more about each other than either one would ever speak aloud.

Holmes was being extra cautious here, trying to lure Watson back to him for good. Sure he was sleeping at Baker Street once again, but he still went to work every day, spoke to his wife, helped manage that household. Here was a creature with one foot in the ocean and one on dry land, and ultimately he would have to choose. Holmes wanted to have him permanently back, so much so that he managed to bite his tongue when he discovered their walk had caused a potential client to wait so long he finally left. Life without Watson was worse than life without puzzles. He had learned that the hard way.

The client returned soon after they got home anyway. Holmes said to him, "I can see that you have not slept for a night or two. That tries a man's nerves more than work, and more even than pleasure." He winked at Watson over the poor man's head, and kept on with the cheeky double remarks, telling him not to worry, that "my friend and I have listened to many strange secrets in this room."

They were soon distracted by the peculiar circumstances of the case, one in which Holmes assumed the blackmail of a former husband when it was instead the concealment of a mix-race child. The client mostly solved his own case, bursting into a neighboring house and embracing his wife's daughter with a kind of acceptance that was rare in those days. Watson found it very touching, and Holmes capitalized on his tender mood. He tugged Watson away from the happy family, back to London, where he lit a candle and gestured Watson to follow him to his bedroom.

What I wouldn't give to have been a fly on the wall as Holmes made his concession, telling Watson that, "if it should ever strike you that I am getting a little over-confident in my powers," to knock him down a peg by reminding him of this case. And what I wouldn't give after that to be a fly with the ability to buzz out an open window, because it was then that Sherlock Holmes asked Watson to come back to him. In his way.

"So how shall your wife be dealt with?" Holmes asked cheerfully, setting his candle down and beginning to change for sleep.

"Pardon?" asked Watson, frozen in the act of unbuttoning.

"Well, this arrangement seems less than ideal, you splitting your time between two households. Perhaps you might divorce," he suggested breezily. "Have any proof of adultery?" Holmes joked.

But Watson did not think it was funny. He frowned at Holmes as he said, "There will be no divorce, Holmes. What an unthinkable thing! I made my vows to Mary, I promised her the rest of my life."

Holmes had ceased his chuckling. "It'll be a very long life if it's an unhappy one, Watson. The same will be true for her as well. I've seen so many people torture themselves by staying together for outdated morals, for public approval, for nothing."

"Who said we were unhappy?" Watson shrugged him off. "I never said that."

It was a moment, I gather, even rarer than Holmes admitting a mistake: it was Holmes speechless. His lip quivered, his mouth opened, but nothing came out. What must have been going through his head... Should he scold Watson? If his vows were so meaningful to him, then why was he here in his friend's room instead of at home with his wife? What about a threat? Leave your wife or I'll give her reason enough to leave you? Perhaps he even thought about pleading with Watson, about exposing his own need?

But if he was about to reveal his true longing, he waited too long. Watson couldn't tolerate the sight of his gaping face anymore and removed himself to his own former bedroom, where he slept for the first night since they'd returned from Baskerville Hall, like a guest in someone else's house. They had run into their first snag on this second try.

I honestly wonder at Holmes's reaction after Watson left the room. Did he sink to the bed limply, wondering helplessly what he had just done? Did he grit his teeth and get on with the business of undressing as if nothing was the matter? Or did he, as I speculate, overcome his stony nature for once and resolve to work harder at persuading Watson to his way of thinking. He would put forth his best effort in the early warm months of 1889, and it would be promising for a time, until the temperature turned on him.

1890: The Greek Interpreter

Watson reports this story as taking place in the summer, though it was just another warm day of spring. The cold would snap back in the next weeks, and by the time summer really arrived, their attempt at reconciling would be finished despite some of Holmes's best efforts. It just wasn't meant to be for another painful handful of years.

I'll admit that sometimes I find Holmes fascinating too, much the way a hideous, newly-discovered life form is fascinating, or the way disasters are fascinating. Watson said, in beginning to tell this warm-weather case, "During my long and intimate acquaintance with Mr. Sherlock Holmes I had never heard him refer to his relations. This reticence upon his part had increased the somewhat inhuman effect which he produced upon me, until sometimes I found myself regarding him as an isolated phenomenon, a brain without a heart." That is how Holmes comes across, even to a most "intimate" friend like Watson. And though disinclined to form new friendships, Holmes did want to hold onto the one he had, a thing harder and harder to do ever since Watson married. Yes, they had renewed their physical relationship, but Holmes knew he had to do more than resume his old tactics if he wanted to maintain Watson now. The introduction of Watson to his brother Mycroft was a way of binding his friend closer to him, of investing himself ever so slightly, at last.

Holmes took Watson down to the Diogenes Club, where his brother sat all day amongst "the most unsociable and unclubbable men in town." Imagine Sherlock Holmes without his bursts of energy, without his dogged persistence to prove himself right, and you are nearer to imagining his brother. Imagine Sherlock Holmes conceding another's superiority and listening like a pupil, and that is Sherlock Holmes in the presence of Mycroft. It was the closest to humble that he had ever come in Watson's presence, and it was a very charming move on the part of Holmes.

Knowing all that, it is no wonder to me why Holmes neglected to mention his brother for all those years previous. Watson gathered obliquely that the detective was an orphan, but for a long time he believed that Holmes had no living relatives at all. I feel safe in speculating that the Holmes boys lost their parents at a young age, though Mycroft was old enough to take charge of his younger brother. With seven years difference between them, I would guess that Mr. and Mrs. Holmes expired when Sherlock Holmes was around ten or eleven, and from thence forward Mycroft became somewhat of a father-figure to Sherlock. It explains why Holmes is so quick to assure Watson that Mycroft's mental powers were greater than his own (he felt he had not yet surpassed his teacher), and it explains the rather endearing way he worked to impress Mycroft by guessing the history, task, and occupation of men who passed in the street below. I also deduce that Mycroft, as unenergetic as he appeared here, was a rather uninvolved guardian, which accounts for how Holmes would have developed his almost pathological independence.

Holmes is a more intriguing study than the majority of his cases, with his hidden history and his muted lawless streak. For example: when trying to gain access to a house in the pursuit of this Greek mystery, Holmes coerces a locked window open right in front of Inspector Gregson! The Inspector chose to let it slide with only this comment: "It is a mercy that you are on the side of the force, and not against it, Mr. Holmes." How brazen he was, how unique, how hypnotizing. How lucky indeed that he is on our side.

I am less interested in the mystery here than in the personal details, and in what this trip to the Diogenes Club signaled for Holmes's newfound but ultimately fruitless maturity. Holmes had done his best for Watson, making a genuine effort to share himself, and it did occur to Watson that *maybe* something pleasant would work out despite his inability to meet Holmes even halfway this time.

1890: Silver Blaze

The Adventure of Silver Blaze begins with Holmes and Watson sharing breakfast in Baker Street. Watson, who had been waiting for this case to come to Holmes, or for Holmes to go to it, had got a fellow physician to cover his patients, knowing he would be headed out to the country to find a missing horse, and looking forward to it. I have a suspicion that Watson was being…not *unfair* to Holmes considering all that Holmes had done to him in the past, but perhaps he was taking advantage of being the one with all the power, the one who could stay or go at any moment, the one who was being solicited, at last. I think it might have gone to his head a bit. He let Holmes believe he would never change his mind about his sacred marriage vows.

Holmes was in rare form during this case, cerebral, much more controlled; he was getting into a veritable habit of civilized behavior. He sat quietly and in deep concentration as they rode out with the local inspector and the owner of the horse, and Watson had to rouse him when they stopped. How different from the wild excitement Watson was used to, and yet Holmes did not seem to be depressed—the case was exciting him, but it wasn't crippling him with energy. At thirty-seven years of age, it was as if Holmes was finally growing up.

He was still his own self, however; as he and Watson strolled across the moor looking for where the horse might have fled to after its coach was killed, Watson noted: "The sun was beginning to sink behind the stables of Mapleton, and the long sloping plain in front of us was tinged with gold, deepening into rich, ruddy brown where the faded ferns and brambles caught the evening light. But the glories of the landscape were all wasted upon my companion."

An artist but not a poet was Sherlock Holmes, not a romantic. In fact he left Watson to watch the glorious sunset on his own. Watson stood stranded outside a horse faker's home and waited until "the reds had all faded to greys," but he was in a forgiving mood towards his friend at this time. Being away from Holmes does make his heart grow fonder.

Holmes reemerged having thoroughly cowed the blustering man who lived there, and he was in cheerful spirits still. He had already solved the case and was now just shading in the picture. This was the artist in him, the need to render the whole case in loving detail. Once he realized that the horse's coach had been intending to injure the creature, Holmes thought to ask if any of the sheep had gone lame; the man would have needed to practice, after all. He was so pleased at predicting this answer that he pinched Watson's arm in excitement. After a whole careful day of muted discovery, a kind of innocent impishness overwhelmed him. He had even decided to protect the horse faker from Silver Blaze's owner, a bit of retaliation on the man who had been too "cavalier" towards Holmes for his own taste.

The recovery of Silver Blaze would not occur for four more days, on the occasion of the race. There was still the little problem of an apparent murder, but the problem was slumbering for the time, since Holmes was rather suspicious that the man had brought death upon himself. In the meantime Holmes and Watson took the train back to London. Sitting across from each other in a smoking cabin, Holmes leaned back and studied Watson minutely.

With the mystery of Silver Blaze solved, Watson was once again the most intriguing thing in the vicinity. He dared to discuss their predicament again, their impasse.

"Are you still under the impression that you love her?" Holmes asked, referring to Mary.

"Of course, Holmes. You never cease loving someone if the love is true. I am merely...learning to love who she really is, rather than the idea I had constructed of her. It was the same with you, actually."

Holmes smiled a little, just the barest twitch at the corner of his mouth as he kept his penetrating eyes fixed on Watson. "And have you ever ceased loving me?" asked Holmes.

"No," Watson said in all plainness and honesty.

Holmes drew his thin fingers over his even thinner lips and chose his words carefully.

"There are ways to...annul the marriage, you know. Legal ways of ignoring it, of practically dissolving the union without officially ending it. You wouldn't have to damage her, Watson. It wouldn't even embarrass her overmuch. But you would be free all the same."

Watson nodded and answered cryptically, "That's an idea." He didn't want to rock the boat; he was enjoying himself.

The conversation wouldn't come to a head until the case did. Something about the expansiveness of the countryside opened Holmes up, though this time they were all the way back to Victoria Station before they were able to shake off their clients. Holmes decided they'd walk a ways before getting a cab if indeed they felt a need for one. He wanted to be in the air for a bit longer, even if it was only the London fog.

"So Watson, what shall it be, then? Do you think Mary would prefer to be free or kept? Last I really knew her she seemed an independent sort, but marriage does change a woman in ways entirely unpredictable to men."

"Holmes..." Watson sighed, and then trailed off into watching his footsteps. He'd have to explain now, wouldn't he? That he was not prepared to simply throw over Mary. It wasn't so much a consideration for her as it was for himself. So Sherlock Holmes had been acting properly for several months, so what? How about all those years of irascibility, the cocaine bottles, bullet holes in the wall, disreputable men and boys tramping in at all hours on some obscure mission for him... It's all well and good to associate with Sherlock Holmes when he is acting properly and one has an escape route, but what if he should become displeased and revert to his bad habits? Watson did not want to burn any of his bridges. Better to keep both wife and friend engaged, and move according to his own convenience.

"It isn't kind to her, Watson," Holmes said sharply, reading at least half of Watson's thoughts. "To hang a woman on like this, it isn't noble. I thought your morals were higher."

"As if you're such a great champion of women, Holmes," Watson whined in meager defense. "Or conventional morals, for that matter. Don't misrepresent yourself, it's ridiculous."

"Can you really pretend you aren't being dishonest?" Holmes asked, picking up his pace and forcing Watson to catch up with him, an assertion of power.

"Perhaps I am," Watson admitted, following at Holmes's heel. "But it's your side you're on in the whole mess and not Mary's, and I'd thank you not to pretend otherwise. My God we might as well be speaking gibberish to one another for all the truth we're saying right now."

Holmes led them back the rest of the way in silence and slammed his way into his own quarters, locking the door pointedly. Watson held his ear next to the keyhole, guessing at where the morocco case had got to in his long absence, trying to hear if Holmes was using the drug again. Turning to it in a time of frustration would be the first real sign of the addict. This was why he didn't want to go all in with Holmes! This never-ending distrust.

After a while Watson asked himself just what cocaine injections were supposed to sound like, shook his head at himself for acting foolish, and stepped away from the door. He wondered if Holmes could tell that he stood outside the door for a time. Probably. It was not the first time Watson had found that sort of thing annoying, but this night it somehow felt more significant.

1890: The Copper Beeches

The next day became cold again, a last mean-spirited whip-crack from winter, but the atmosphere was colder by far inside the rooms of 221B Baker Street. Watson did not even know the full extent of the chill he had caused; one night sleeping alone was enough to put him in a forgiving mood, but Holmes was a much more stubborn being.

Watson may not have realized at the time, but what he had confessed to Holmes the night before was crushing. His marriage, though still very new and untested, was a more permanent relationship to Watson than his nearly ten years of friendship with Holmes. The added impetus from the law and society made this woman, about whom Watson knew relatively little and was still striving to understand, equal if not greater than Holmes in his consideration. How absolutely vile and unfair, but what could ever be done about it? Their union was bedrock while Holmes and Watson were merely…bedfellows. They were nothing in comparison.

Holmes was stung by this realization, angry with both himself and Watson. How could he have missed what an unalterable situation this was at the very start of it? Why didn't he stop Watson before the ceremony? And how could Watson, apparently knowing full well what his wedding meant, have ever gone through with it? To truly leave! How could he? It was a painful thing to finally come to terms with, and even though Watson sat directly across from him, Holmes at last felt the full agony of what he had lost.

But he wouldn't say any of that aloud. Nor would he allow his behavior to reflect the brimming sadness he felt. Instead Holmes snipped at Watson until they were both miserable.

"To the man who loves art for its own sake, it is frequently in its lowliest manifestations that the keenest pleasure is to be derived." Thus began a condescending lecture on how Watson failed to accurately characterize the only important aspect of each case in his writings: Holmes's "severe reasoning" and the remarkable talents he has developed in himself.

Watson took up the same argumentative tone of the night before, telling Holmes, "It seems to me that I have done you full justice in the matter," and indeed he had been more than fair in his writings, positively gilding Holmes with praise and admiration, downplaying every flaw. But that wasn't really what Holmes was upset about that day anyway. He might have argued with Watson just as vehemently over the weather for all it mattered to him.

In his recounting, Watson laments "the egotism which I had more than once observed to be a strong factor in my friend's singular character," not realizing somehow that Holmes's swollen ego had nothing to do with it. This was about his shriveled, desiccated heart.

They were distracted from what might have boiled into a real fight by the arrival of a client, a freckled, down-to-earth young woman seeking advice about a curious job offer. The details of the case were so incomplete that Holmes could only get a vague idea of potential danger before sending the woman off to the Copper Beeches estate and warning her to be on her guard.

It was two rather uncomfortable weeks before they would hear from her again, both men putting themselves to distraction over her situation so as to avoid thinking about their own. Holmes kept concluding that no sister of his should ever take such a position, and nevermind that he didn't have a sister, as Watson kept mumbling after him.

When at last they got an emergency communication from Miss Hunter, Holmes threw it at Watson and said, "Just look up the trains in Bradshaw."

Watson read the panicked note, but made no move to see about the trains. Holmes looked up at him from his chemistry experiment.

He sighed profoundly and asked, "Will you come with me?"

"I should wish to," Watson said tightly.

"Just look it up, then."

It was a brisk day when they made off, and Watson could not help but default to a cheerful disposition, beaming around at the charming country houses. He was happy to be out of London, but Holmes would have preferred the city. He said to Watson, "The pressure of public opinion can do in the town what the law cannot accomplish. There is no lane so vile that the scream of a child, or the thud of a drunkard's blow, does not beget sympathy and indignation among the neighbours, and the whole machinery of justice is ever so close that a word of complaint can set it going, and there is but a step between the crime and the dock." Essentially, London forces one to check one's impulses if for nothing more than the urge to avoid judgment; the open air of the country can be rather too freeing.

On that tiresome note, Watson disembarked from the train to listen to Miss Hunter's continued story. Her employer was an absolute monster, imprisoning his own daughter so as to have use of her money, terrorizing the whole household with a large mastiff hound that he kept half-starved for viciousness. In the end the beast turned on its owner, and Watson had to fire upon the creature, killing it instantly. The case was explained thoroughly by the maid, and Holmes immediately ceased to care. And yet it continued to bother Watson, and I have yet to hear a satisfactory answer as to why.

My theories are that either he was hoping Holmes would find some sort of romantic affection towards this lady, which would have been idealistic in the extreme, since he knew Holmes's nature better than anyone, and could readily attest to how indelible it was. More likely he was just exasperated that Holmes couldn't seem to care about anything: "As to Miss Violet Hunter, my friend Holmes, rather to my disappointment, manifested no further interest in her when once she had ceased to be the centre of one of his problems." No care at all for this noble woman's fate, no care at all (it seemed) for his lifetime friend, and that had always been the problem with Holmes. His tin heart.

When they returned home from their adventure, Watson was done. "I shall sleep at home tonight, I think," he said. "With the missus."

"Do whatever you must, Watson. I have no claim on you, do I?"

"No, Holmes," Watson said soberly. "Not really."

Watson thought that would be the worst of it, but as Holmes turned to go to bed and Watson turned towards the door, something came flying across the room and crashed just above his head. He looked around to see Holmes disappear into his room, and then bent to pick up the shattered chemical tube that had been thrown at him.

Watson dropped the shard with a sigh and put on his hat. Things were over once again.

1890: The Dying Detective

A long memory has Sherlock Holmes. Almost the whole year goes by before he wounds Watson back, a touch for a touch. They had seen each other a few times since the spring, exclusively when Watson would stop by here and there to keep their acquaintance up. It was not a mutual maintenance. Holmes still felt rather bruised I imagine, and wouldn't have pulled this stunt if he was not in pain himself. This was not a purely malicious plot anyway, per se; Mrs. Hudson was caught up in the ruse too, and he *was* trying to catch a very clever man, a poisoner, and a patient one. He was a puckish sort of enemy, though not as smart as Holmes usually likes them, and rather too full of himself. A man should not have to talk up his achievements so much; his art should speak for itself.

This man Culverton Smith sent Holmes a little trinket box, spring loaded with a deadly powder. Holmes took the opportunity to fake sick and worry the only two people who could stand him if it meant finally solving a case. He pretended to resist all medical treatment until Mrs. Hudson insisted, and then he acquiesced to having Watson over. I find this story a rather painful one to read, for what I know it put Watson's emotions through.

Watson ran to him, of course, in an absolute state. Rushing through his head was the horrible thought that Holmes would die and that their last times spent together would have been those stiff, horrible visits, and that Watson would have to live the rest of his life wishing he had stayed with Holmes just a little while longer, wishing he had known in advance how little time there really was.

He rushed towards the supposed sickbed upon entering Holmes's bedroom, but Holmes held him back.

"If you approach me, Watson, I shall order you out of the house."

"But why?" Watson whimpered.

"Because it is my desire. Is that not enough?"

Watson nodded. He marked that Holmes was as masterful as ever, even when physically weak. And though he was not really dying, I imagine the day he does actually perish he will be just the same, ordering people about as if his authority could live on forever. Watson was certainly of that opinion. He wrote: "To the last gasp he would always be the master."

"I only wished to help," Watson said. He felt absolutely crushed. He thought the greatest man he had ever known was dying before his eyes.

Holmes told him that it was his desire to lay unattended. He looked the part of a dying man, all his wasted theatrical talent at work in makeup and acting. Watson acquiesced. He'd do anything for Holmes, even if it meant doing nothing.

"You are not angry?" Holmes asked him.

Poor devil, Watson thought. *How could I be angry when I saw him lying in such a plight before me?*

Holmes spewed some nonsense about it being a Sumatran disease, communicable only by touch, so Watson must stay away. Watson, the quiet hero, again resolved that he would treat Holmes even if it killed him. Holmes was far from a mere stranger to him, after all. Watson would lay down his life for him.

Holmes refused, again and again, and it pierced Watson every time, until at last Holmes finally got his revenge for being abandoned, and took pity. Of a sort, that is.

He said: "If I am to have a doctor whether I will or not, let me at least have someone in whom I have confidence."

"Then you have none in me?"

"In your friendship, certainly." But not in his professional qualifications. Watson withstood the blow like a true soldier.

"Such a remark is unworthy of you, Holmes." It is just the sort of thing *I* have come to expect from Holmes, but that man never truly falls from the pedestal Watson has placed him on.

Holmes told Watson that he would accept another physician, but it must be the man of his choosing, and it must not be until two hours hence. Watson was faithful, but restless. He wandered around the room and nearly opened the lethal trinket that Holmes was sent. To his credit, Holmes did seem to be seriously disturbed by Watson's proximity to the deathly little box.

"Put it down this instant, Watson!" he yelled, effectively saving Watson's life. But then he excused the outburst by saying, "You fidget me beyond endurance. Sit down, man, and let me have my rest."

When at last Holmes allowed Watson to fetch Mr. Smith, he gave him specific instructions intermixed with some babble about oysters to make his illness convincing (to Watson at least; I bet I might have seen through such shamming after a lifetime of hearing school children try to fake ill). Watson fetched the crooked, irritable Culverton Smith and returned to Baker Street before him. Holmes told Watson to hide in the room and hear what Smith had to say. Watson tried to protest these further strange instructions, but when Holmes heard Smith approach the door, he insisted at Watson:

"There is just room behind the head of my bed, Watson. Quick, man, if you love me! Don't speak! Don't move! Just listen with all your ears."

Startled, Watson did what he was told. If it was a matter of love, then what else could he do?

Smith came in and began to gloat over Holmes, chastising him for suspecting Smith in his nephew's death, of which he was naturally guilty. Watson had to seriously restrain himself from jumping out at Smith and stopping him taunting Holmes. The way he treated the supposedly dying man was rough, shaking Holmes as he revealed the attempt on his life and confessed to murdering his nephew the same way. Holmes, having heard what he most needed, asked Smith to turn up the lamp, a signal to Inspector Morton who waited on the street below. When Smith tried to deny his confession, Holmes at last remembered Watson, and called him out of hiding.

Watson was so happy, so relieved to hear Holmes's voice return to strength, to hear the amusement in it, that he forgot to be mad at him for a time. He stayed with Holmes as Smith was carted off to the station, for Holmes had indeed given up food, drink, and tobacco to help make himself convincing. Watson doctored him as he dressed.

"You won't be offended, Watson?" Holmes asked him casually at last. He was feeling all better after exacting his own little revenge, and really he was not so unlike Culverton Smith in pettiness here. "You will realize that among your many talents dissimulation finds no place."

Holmes was fixing himself in the glass, nearly humming, satisfied with all that he had accomplished that night. Watson gazed at Holmes through the mirror, his face wide open and honest, injured by the violent joy he had just felt as much as the remnants of fear and sorrow. Holmes smiled gently at him. He was finally feeling forgiving.

"But your appearance, Holmes?" Watson asked with trembling emotion. "Your ghastly face?"

Holmes revealed his methods at malingering, the starvation, the lack of water and tobacco, the makeup around the eyes. But Watson still had questions.

"But why would you not let me near you, since there was in truth no infection?"

"Can you ask, my dear Watson? Do you imagine that I have no respect for your medical talents? Could I fancy that your astute judgment would pass a dying man who, however weak, had no rise of pulse or temperature?"

Watson tried to smile at the confidence Holmes had in him, but he didn't really feel it. He picked up Holmes's coat to help his friend into it, but while he stood behind Holmes, hands on his shoulders, his grip betrayed how he truly felt. Holmes was right about one thing; Watson is a horrible liar.

Holmes turned around and took both of Watson's hands in his own.

"You're upset, friend Watson."

"I thought you were dying, Holmes," he pleaded, as if for understanding. "How would you feel if you honestly believed I was dying, and then found out it was all an elaborate trick?"

"I'd be very impressed with your new acting abilities," Holmes tried to kid. "Come, we'll sup at Simpson's after giving our reports." He stepped towards the door, but Watson sank onto what—mere moments before—he had considered a death bed. Holmes returned quietly and sat beside him.

"You'll forgive me, Watson?"

Watson put his head in his hands and wondered if he would. He thought establishing his own life with a wife and a practice would stop Holmes from taking advantage of him, but it was not so. It crossed Watson's mind that perhaps Holmes enjoyed this power, the ability to summon Watson at a moment's notice, to manipulate him, to punish him almost… It felt like Holmes was retaliating against him, and it occurred to him that they each resented the hold the other man had over them. Watson sighed in exhaustion, feeling defeated and drained…but there was still so much left to do before he could be done.

Watson leapt up and led the way down to the police station. He didn't talk to Holmes the whole way, and ignored his invitations to dinner. They were separated to provide individual statements, and Watson tried to hurry out ahead of Holmes, but he wasn't wily enough. In the street a few blocks from the station, Holmes caught up with him, and they finally had it out.

Watson stopped in his relentless trudge home and finally addressed his friend: "It's horrible to care about you, Holmes. It's the very worst thing that ever happened to me."

Holmes stood in the darkest area between two lamps and had the decency to lower his face. Watson waited for his reaction, defiant in the face of Holmes's shame, rare as it was to encounter.

"I cannot help that, Watson. We're in the same boat."

"You don't seem to be all that affected!" Watson shouted.

Holmes strode up to him and grasped his arm, somewhat to keep him quiet, but mostly to convey his authenticity.

"Are you serious, man? I'm in agony."

Watson could see it was true, but it took an act of powerful deliberation from Holmes to show it, and even then it was only visible in his eyes, in the tension around them, almost like someone had a knife in his back, but he was trying to take it manfully.

"Good," Watson told him gently. "That at least is fair."

Holmes sighed tempestuously and linked his arm with Watson's to continue the walk home. They were much like family in their ability to snarl at each other one moment and forgive each other the next. I watched my brothers interact with the same sort of dynamic for years while they were alive.

"I promise to never die on you again, Watson," Holmes said as they neared Baker Street, their feet echoing off the cobbles, their merged shadows cast faintly in the moonlight.

"Don't make promises you can't keep, Holmes. No one lives forever."

Watson could feel Holmes smile in the dark. "You don't know that, Doctor. There might be a discovery any moment of some life-extending property. Even now some alchemist might be developing the elixir of eternal life from a substance hitherto underappreciated. I suspect the secret may be hidden in beeswax," Holmes said while inclining his head. "I have a few ideas for experimentation should I ever give up detecting. And of course there is no ruling out some unexpected magic, skeptical though I remain of such wondrous things. You know, I read a story in *Lippencott's* just the other day about a young man who manages to put off aging entirely by wishing it onto his portrait."

"I know the one you mean, Holmes! I'm surprised that you could stand to read anything so fantastical. You've always preferred fact over fiction, crime over wordcraft."

"Ah, well, this work was an exception since it was a bit of both."

"How do you mean?" Watson was engaged enough in the conversation that he forgot to turn towards his own house where his wife was waiting up to hear the bad news of Holmes's sudden recovery. She was always waiting around for her husband at the leisure of Sherlock Holmes.

"Did you read the story very closely, Watson?" Watson shook his head, mystified. What truth could there be in such a fairy tale as what Oscar Wilde had written? "It was a confession, my dear, from a man whose affections are very much like our own. Someone ought to warn him not to tell the truth so often; the public won't allow it if they ever notice."

"You mean to claim the man is guilty based solely on his work?"

"No more guilty than dozens of good men, Watson, and his work is plain enough. I wouldn't be surprised if it was brought against him in court someday."

"What about my stories, Holmes? Have I given us away as well?"

Holmes smiled and let himself back into his house where Mrs. Hudson had laid out food for him, most likely in anger, though she would not be getting such an apology as Watson had. Holmes treated Mrs. Hudson relatively well considering how he "disliked and distrusted the sex," and Mrs. Hudson was fond of him in a way as well, but everyone has a limit, and leave it to Sherlock Holmes to discover that limit in each and every one of us.

"Not knowingly, my friend. It's the brazen way this Wilde man has that will rankle the public most. They'd like to hang someone for cheek in this country."

"You had better hope that isn't really so, Holmes. You'd break your promise to me."

Holmes's smile deepened in the firelight. "Nothing could make me do that, Watson. No power on earth, and no man alive." But of course, that would prove untrue soon enough as well.

1890: The Blue Carbuncle

Life got away from them for a few weeks, and Watson didn't come around to see Holmes until a few days after Christmas. They had left each other last on civil terms, but the deeper wounds were still healing. Watson wasn't purposefully avoiding Holmes, at least not consciously, but it wasn't an easy thing to simply drop by. However, something about the holidays put Watson in a sentimental mood, and he wanted to put a patch on the last few months of parrying and find a little peace.

Holmes gave him a standoffish reception, not rising from his seat and providing Watson with a very matter-of-fact account of how a rough-looking hat had come to his attention (dropped during a kerfuffle in the street, along with a holiday goose that some good Samaritan was attempting to return to its rightful owner through our detective). He challenged Watson to deduce something from it and chucked his magnifying glass into Watson's lap. Watson sighed heavily and looked it over, but told Holmes he saw nothing.

"On the contrary, Watson, you can see everything. You fail, however to reason from what you see."

"Pray tell me what it is that you can infer from this hat?" Watson asked, regretting that he had made the trip already. Perhaps enough time had not yet passed; Holmes was obviously still raw over having been left again, but really, what could he expect if he behaved this way?

Holmes lifted the hat from Watson and concluded, among other things, that its owner was a drunk whose wife had ceased to love him.

"My dear Holmes!" Watson ejaculated in disbelief, but he was ignored. When Holmes had made all of his conclusions, Watson protested again.

"Is it possible that even now," Holmes condescended, "when I give you these results, you are unable to see how they are attained?"

"I have no doubt that I am very stupid," Watson said, finally getting agitated by Holmes's rudeness. "For example, how did you deduce that this man was an intellectual?"

Holmes banged the hat on his head and it fell straight to his nose. He tipped the brim up and looked at Watson as if he were an utter simpleton. Big head, big brain. They went through his conclusions point by point, coming at last to the question of how Holmes knew the man's wife no longer loved him.

"This hat has not been brushed for weeks. When I see you, my dear Watson, with a week's accumulation of dust upon your hat, and when your wife allows you to go out in such a state, I shall fear that you also have been unfortunate enough to lose your wife's affection."

Watson got the distinct impression that Holmes was hoping for just such a thing to happen, and he decided to sting him back. Laughing, Watson asked Holmes the purpose of knowing all this, since there was no crime connected to the hat, but no sooner than he had spoken when it was revealed that the goose found beside the hat concealed a valuable missing blue gem.

It was turned over to Holmes by the honest man who'd found the bird on the street, and Holmes softened just to look at it. He could be quite fond of trinkets if they were connected with some particularly enjoyable crime, like the small box from Culverton Smith that might have killed him and now rested—gutted of its deadly powder which Holmes had taken it upon himself to chemically neutralize—on his mantle. Holmes told Watson that every good stone is a nucleus of crime, that people will die, murder, and maim over them. He got such a fond look on his face that Watson warmed towards him again. He informed Holmes that he would be stopping by later when the case was a bit further along. It was not a question.

He arrived back just when the owner of the hat came to reclaim his property. He was unaware of the blue carbuncle, and was sent on his merry way. Still on the case, Holmes and Watson struck out in the cold to chase down the source of the bird. Holmes played a neat trick to get a belligerent bird seller to show him his books, and this deception at last put Holmes in a perfectly tolerable mood.

"I daresay that if I had put one hundred pounds down in front of him, that man would not have given me such complete information as was drawn from him by the idea that he was doing me on a wager." He finally smiled at Watson and thumped him kindly on the shoulder. He had been injured by Watson, but oh…the scars were so mutual. They were in this thing together.

"Well, Watson, we are, I fancy, nearing the end of our quest." But they were much nearer than he knew. They apprehended the pathetic culprit there in the street and took him back by force of personality to Baker Street. The poor fool tried to give Holmes a fake name, but he was not allowed.

"No, no; the real name," said Holmes sweetly. "It is always awkward doing business with an alias."

Watson snorted as they piled into a four-wheeler, and it was a silent ride back with Holmes and Watson largely ignoring their nervous friend, and instead considering each other with a sort of wry surrender, an amusement at the way they never seemed to learn from their own mistakes, and only returned for more of the same.

Back at Baker Street however, all eyes were on James Ryder, the head attendant at the Hotel Cosmopolitan, from whence the jewel went missing. Holmes told the man that his goose had come to this very place, and that it had laid the "bonniest, brightest blue egg" they had ever seen. Holmes held up the radiant stone, and Ryder nearly fainted into the fire for fear of being caught.

Holmes was not impressed with this man. He was an amateur and a rat, recklessly losing his stolen treasure, but being wise enough to make sure there was another man to pin its theft on in the first place. He had the nerve to ask for mercy, and Sherlock Holmes had the nerve to grant it to him. Ordering the man from his sight in disgust, he sat down with Watson and was required to explain himself. Holmes, though forgiving, was still in the mood to jab at someone. I doubt he ever feels truly content enough to keep his *bons mots* to himself.

"After all, Watson, I am not retained by the police to supply their deficiencies," Holmes shrugged. "Besides, it is the season of forgiveness."

Holmes invited his friend to stay for dinner. Watson rolled his eyes and accepted and they shared a quiet meal together. But Holmes was not altogether done retaliating. He couldn't really help himself.

1891: The Final Problem

The pain evident in this next story makes me absolutely despise Holmes—his hollow vows, his hollow heart. Less than six months after he had promised Watson to never deceive him with something so serious as death again, it became "necessary" to do so, and not just for an evening, but for three excruciating years.

Watson was shredded as he sat down two years after the events and wrote: "It may be remembered that after my marriage, and my subsequent start in private practice, the very intimate relations which had existed between Holmes and myself became to some extent modified." He wanted to do all that he could in his friend's memory to be honest about what they were to one another, as well as what they had ceased to be. Watson was saddened by the distance that had kept them apart for most of 1890—apparently to him the last year they would ever have—but in a way he was thankful for that space as well; if Holmes had been destined to leave this world, then thank God he had never given up Mary! Thank God he was not completely alone.

On April twenty-fourth of 1891, the problem began to unfold. Holmes showed up at Watson's house looking ragged and pale, guarding himself from the windows, and telling Watson that he would have to leave soon over the back fence.

"Are you afraid of something?" Watson asked innocently.

"Well, I am," Holmes told him. "Of air-guns."

This at least was true; unlike the last incident of The Dying Detective, this time Holmes believed that he was dying too, and the trick that would soon be played on Watson, well...it was not his intention, certainly not at first. Holmes was being dogged to the fraying ends of his nerves, and in his beleaguered state, he turned to his kind and solid friend Watson. He had a haunted look on his face, pale, strained, but he smiled as he showed Watson his bloody knuckles, putting on a brave face.

"It is not an airy nothing, you see. On the contrary, it is solid enough for a man to break his hand over. Is Mrs. Watson in?"

She was not, and Holmes's smile got bigger, his eyes a little less tense. "It makes it the easier for me to propose that you should come away with me for a week to the Continent," Holmes said in explanation for his perk up. If his life was in danger, he would want to spend his last days with Watson. His dear Watson.

"Where?" Watson asked.

"Oh," Holmes said softly. "Anywhere."

This was highly out-of-character for Holmes, and he soon sat back to explain to Watson what was so different about this case.

"You have probably never heard of Professor Moriarty?" he quizzed.

"Never," Watson answered quickly, so eager to please. I trap him up like this all the time.

"Yes, you have Watson, from me," he said, smiling truly. "But most of the citizenry and even the police have no notion of him. That's what puts him on a pinnacle in the records of crime. I tell you, Watson, in all seriousness, that if I could beat that man, if I could free society of him, I should feel that my own career had reached its summit. I would be prepared to turn to some more placid line in life, perhaps a house on the shore," he said, and added wistfully, "where I can study alchemy."

Watson grinned at him, and the conversation returned to the topic of Moriarty. Watson left out this small touch of gentleness from Holmes in his account. It was at once too private and too profoundly sad for him to write it down at the time.

Holmes, though afraid for his life, could not help but gush copiously over James Moriarty. Gifted at mathematics, educated, from a good family, but infected with "hereditary tendencies of the most diabolical kind" which undermined his golden potential. For all their opposition, Holmes could see himself in Moriarty, could understand how the "criminal strain which ran in his blood was increased and rendered infinitely more dangerous by his extraordinary mental powers." What of Holmes's "scarlet thread of murder" which makes this dull world a breathtaking mystery for him? How hard did Holmes struggle every day against his own restless nature, his own commanding brain? Did he not drug himself to keep his hands clean from that fascinating underworld in which Moriarty reigned?

"For years I have endeavored to break through the veil which shrouded it, and at last the time came when I seized my thread and followed it, until it led me, after a thousand cunning windings, to ex-Professor Moriarty of mathematical celebrity."

Watson listened to Holmes admire this evil man, a feverish light breaking out in his eyes. "He is the Napoleon of crime, Watson. He is a genius, a philosopher, an abstract thinker. He has a brain of the first order. I had at last met an antagonist who was my intellectual equal. My horror at his crimes was lost in my admiration at his skill. Never have I risen to such a height."

Watson was disturbed to hear all this; it had always upset him to see how Holmes lusted for his prey, how he thrilled in their hideous deeds. And then Holmes told him the most startling news at all: Professor Moriarty had paid Holmes a visit.

Holmes had a cold shock when he looked up and saw the mathematician standing in his doorway, his heart leapt but his hand stayed steady, and he looked over his opponent for the very first time, his eyes feasting almost without his consent, roving lasciviously.

Moriarty's slow, reptilian gaze was taking in Holmes as well. They found each other irresistibly fascinating.

"It is a dangerous habit to finger loaded firearms in the pocket of one's dressing-gown," Moriarty said archly. Holmes didn't see the point of standing on ceremony, and brought the weapon out, laying it cocked upon the table at which he sat. Moriarty, his own hands clasped behind his back, began to rock back and forth on his feet, and explain himself.

Moriarty had done Sherlock Holmes the compliment of coming to see him in person, to warn him away from this chase. It was almost pointless to say anything, but he could not stay away any more than Holmes: the detective should steer wide of Moriarty, but he knew that already; Holmes would make a great asset to Moriarty, but he would never switch sides; Holmes would kill himself in this pursuit, but so be it. Everyone's death is inevitable.

"All that I have to say has already crossed your mind," Moriarty said with a sort of sigh in his voice.

"Then possibly my answer has crossed yours," Holmes replied somberly.

They were synchronized, in utter harmony. Moriarty had tolerated being hunted as long as he cared to, but it was fast becoming clear that this persecution would have to cease. Moriarty, though he knew the request was futile, asked Holmes to end his pursuit. He did not want to see it all end badly.

"It has been an intellectual treat to me to see the way in which you have grappled with this affair, and I say, unaffectedly, that it would be a grief to me to be forced to take any extreme measure."

Holmes smiled at the flattery, but Moriarty assured Holmes that he was being genuine. Holmes was unafraid of danger, but it was not just danger that Moriarty saw before them, "it is inevitable destruction. If you are clever enough to bring destruction upon me, rest assured that I shall do as much to you."

"You have paid me several compliments," Holmes told Moriarty. "Let me pay you one in return when I say that if I were assured of the former eventuality I would, in the interests of the public, cheerfully accept the latter."

It was the highest praise either of them could give, the admission that their lives, and their minds, were equal.

Holmes was hounded all day before coming to see Watson, not just by physical assaults, but by the memory of the "soft, precise speech" of the professor, as insinuating as a snake's hiss. But as Holmes explained the attacks he had suffered, Watson forgot all about the allure that Moriarty held for Holmes:

"I had often admired my friend's courage, but never more than now, as he sat quietly checking off a series of incidents which must have combined to make up a day of horror." Watson felt a surge of love for Holmes as he watched the steely way Holmes withstood the pressure. I cannot say that he was not impressive.

"You will spend the night here?" Watson asked Holmes. Obviously he wanted him to stay. Obviously he was overcome with love once again.

Staying would have been too dangerous for Watson, so Holmes told him carefully where to meet him the next day. He needed to disappear for just the next few days, just until the web he'd woven around Moriarty and his gang could be closed by the police. Watson, filled with an unreasonable sense of safety around Holmes that still afflicts him to this day, entreated Holmes to stay with him. Holmes, to his credit, would not risk his friend.

With the help of Mycroft and some well-timed vehicles, they make it onto the train alive, Holmes dressed like an old Italian priest with very little grasp of the language. Moriarty chased them to the station but managed to miss them. Watson wondered aloud what Moriarty would have done if he had overtaken them.

"There cannot be the least doubt that he would have made a murderous attack on me," Holmes told him brightly. And a few days later, when it turned out that Moriarty had not been caught up along with his gang, Holmes was all the more sure that he was a marked man. He told Watson to leave him and go home.

"You will find me a dangerous companion now," Holmes said. Moriarty had nothing to do except exact revenge; he could not go back to England, and all his business prospects were shot full of holes. Holmes realized he would have to face Moriarty now, or else look over his shoulder for the rest of his life. He urged Watson to leave, but it is not in Watson's nature to cut and run. Holmes was required to trick him, yet again, using the man's kindness against him.

And yet...he lingered with Watson for at least a week. He knew that soon he would face a death match, and that he would have to remove Watson for his own safety eventually, but they honeymooned again among quaint Alpine villages, ignoring the strain of fear that followed them everywhere, just enjoying each other's company as if they were on the deck of a slowly sinking ship. Inevitably finished, yes, but still not quite done yet.

I believe that Holmes handled the anxiety well, even smiling after a large stone nearly fell on him as they moved through a mountain pass, always knowing what was coming, that it was getting closer all the time.

He stayed in high spirits as best as he could, not least to keep Watson at ease, but also as he described, because "the air of London was sweeter for his presence." If he had to run himself through on a case and a criminal, then let it be this one, for it was worthy of his sacrifice.

At last, on the fourth of May, it was time. It was Moriarty who finally lured Watson away, since Holmes was having a difficult time doing it himself. A ruse arrived in the form of a letter that summoned Watson back to the hotel from Reichenbach Falls. Watson went away, totally convinced that a patient was waiting for him, and Holmes stayed behind to meet his fate. It was a noble move at the time to knowingly stay behind, but it is still rather marred for me by how he lied to Watson afterward. However: the image of Holmes, tall and thin and resolute, standing beside the roaring, crashing, hellish falls is a powerful one.

Watson glanced back at him once, and saw another figure hurrying towards him on the dead end outlook path towards Holmes. Watson thought nothing of it until he arrived at the hotel and realized that he had been tricked. His heart sank, and he rushed back, but he was wildly too late. All that remained were Holmes's walking stick, a shuffle of footprints, and a cigarette case weighing down a note, addressed to Watson.

Watson took up the note and his eyes started to fill with tears, blurring the handwriting that was as neat as ever, even though it must have been written under great duress. Holmes would have known that he was about to kill, be killed, or both. He wrote to Watson saying that he was ready for the end of this case, however it might manifest, "though I fear that it is a cost which will give pain to my friends, and especially, my dear Watson, to you." It warmed Watson to know that Holmes counted himself as having friends, because so often during his depressions he claimed he had none. And in the end, Holmes even conceded to Mrs. Watson, like a gentleman.

Watson had never felt more alone. Everything he had experienced, everything he'd done, it was as if none of it could possibly matter. What was the use of paying attention, of keeping any sort of record, if Holmes was not around to criticize it? If Watson would not be contributing to his public figure? On the journey back to England he had decided to give up his writings, to relegate himself to being a doctor and a husband, no longer a scribe. He only told the story of Holmes's demise when the public started to get the wrong impression of it. It was one last story to gild the monument he had built. After that he thought he would set down his pen forever.

This was a wretched time in Watson's life, entirely on par with the time just after he'd come home from Afghanistan to find himself friendless, homeless, poor, and alone. Holmes was gone and Mary...well, Mary was not the comfort he needed her to be.

She did her best to disguise the relief she felt at knowing Sherlock Holmes would never darken her door again, but Watson could perceive *that* at least, since she was no better at lying than he was. What he failed to notice, and it was the end of his marriage in more ways than one, was how thin and pale Mary had become. She carried herself gingerly, she flinched at every move she made, and she watched Watson with sunken eyes—waiting, vainly, for him to notice. Or care.

The day she finally could not wait any longer, Mary went next door for her diagnosis. It was a uterine tumor; a happy woman might have thought the growth and symptoms were a baby, but Mary was not so young as to jump immediately to the idea of pregnancy, and she knew that she did not glow so much as burn. She wanted Watson to forget about Sherlock Holmes long enough to worry about her health, but he never did. She finally had the news that she was dying from Watson's colleague, and when she told Watson, he wondered why she had kept it from him.

"Why?" Mary asked him loudly. "You really cannot think why?"

Watson could not—Moriarty's brother had just started publishing memories of the professor, painting him better than he deserved, and tarnishing Sherlock Holmes in the process. Watson was all wrapped up in the man, even though he had been presumed dead for more than a year, and he could hardly muster any grief at hearing about Mary's condition. It was another painful loss, but so what? It was only salt on an already open wound.

Mary died with a clergyman at her bedside, but Watson stayed downstairs as word of her death spread through the neighborhood and mourners gathered in the house. He looked grieved, but those who were close to Mary at the end of her life had to wonder who he was grieving for; was he sad for her unlived life, for his empty one, or was he still, as ever, missing Sherlock Holmes?

A few ladies who had been friendly with his wife abandoned Watson as their physician after her death. The man next door was less inclined to help out his neighbor by taking on patients. Not that this mattered much to Watson—where did he need to go if Holmes was not around to summon him away to some thrilling adventure? Watson found his whole life barely filled the rooms of his home, as if he had died at some point too, unnoticed, and now spent his time in a very roomy coffin. He relocated to a smaller practice in Kensington. He kept his profile low.

Though he thought the memories of Holmes would be too painful to ever revisit, Watson could not help but relive them all. He compiled every note he had on their cases, together and apart, and he even brought himself to start setting down the narrative of the circumstances surrounding Henry Baskerville's troubles, lingering quite a bit over his memory of the time, thinking back with a kind of bitter joy at what he thought had been their last reunion. Should he have stayed with Holmes in the first place? Should he have returned to Holmes then? Would it possibly hurt any less now if he had done either? These unanswerable questions plagued him every day.

It was not hard to idealize the dead, especially since Watson had gotten into the habit of idealizing Holmes when he was still alive, but when he looked back, he honestly could not see what should have been done differently. He remembered how difficult Holmes had been, how miserable they had made each other at times, but he still wished it had somehow been otherwise. The ache of his impotence was just as bad as his grief.

He thought about speaking to Mycroft, but didn't. He thought about bringing flowers to Mrs. Hudson, but couldn't. He thought about taking some time to visit Colonel Hayter again, but this interaction he was unable to avoid, because Colonel Hayter came to him.

He was not the only man to stop by and wish Watson condolences. Watson lost track of how many inspectors, how many clients, how many street arabs had stopped by after the demise of Holmes. It seemed that no matter how long dead the man was, people remembered him…because of Watson.

The Colonel did not send word ahead announcing himself, probably because he had heard the rumors about Watson becoming reclusive and unsocial. He merely knocked on Watson's door, his face sad but smiling. Watson let him right in; an old friend, and also an old friend who knew Holmes uniquely, and who understood what Watson had lost.

"Not feeling too terribly today I hope, Watson," the Colonel said gently.

"I've been worse," Watson told him, stepping aside to allow him in. His house was a shambles of case notes and cigarette ashes. In truth, Watson left it a little messy because it made it look as if Holmes resided there.

"I have heard as much. Tongues are wagging about you, but most of them not unkindly. You've suffered quite a few losses, my good man. I am sorry."

Watson nodded and cleared a spot for the Colonel to sit down. Watson poured them drinks, and quite unlike women or even civilian men, they sat in a military silence.

At last Watson said, "He was the greatest man I ever knew." He was thankful for the way his mustache helped disguise his trembling bottom lip.

Hayter grasped Watson's knee. "He was remarkable. I can't even imagine… To have known him, as well as you knew him…" the Colonel tried to speak carefully, but he ran out of words for what he wanted to say. Hayter was trying to convey the sort of sympathy most people gave to Watson on behalf of Mary. He alone of Watson's friends knew the true nature of the love he had shared with Holmes, for he had shared in it himself, hadn't he? But he was still hesitant to speak of it.

"To mourn him…the way you do…but to have to do it in secret…" Hayter stammered off, shaking his head. Watson covered the hand on his knee with his own, very much appreciative that someone, even if it was only one man, knew just how he suffered.

Hayter and Watson gazed at each other, and Hayter began to lean forward slowly, almost imperceptibly, in case Watson should be offended by what he wanted to do. But Colonel Hayter had always been rather fond of Watson, and though it was Holmes he connected with on the occasion of their visit to his country house, it had not been Holmes he was hoping for. Holmes was amusing for a time, enthusiastic, perfect for a brief encounter, but it was Watson whom people fell in love with, present company included.

Hayter bent his head and kissed Watson on his cheek, the way someone might kiss a recently widowed aunt. But when Watson inclined towards him, Hayter kissed Watson on his lips, slowly.

Holmes was the only man he had ever kissed until that moment. A thousand things assaulted his mind: it was so unlike the kiss of a woman that it couldn't help but recall every kiss with Holmes, but the beard brushing his face just as quickly proved it was not Holmes, and yet these lips had also kissed Holmes. Was it a betrayal? Was it an abomination? Or was it merely the closest comfort he would ever be able to find?

Watson did not make love with Hayter; he couldn't bring himself to go any further than being petted and soothed. They used their mouths, but not their words. Any more than that would have felt unfaithful to him, and to this day, Holmes is still the only man Watson has ever had any conversation with. He remains, for Watson, the one and only Him.

Life was settling down and becoming gray for Watson. He still had dreams where he imagined Holmes alive—somehow magically, mercifully alive—but they were becoming less frequent. It was three years before his dreams would come true.

1919: Walk

I surmise pretty rapidly where my husband has disappeared to, leaving me with a tray of softening cake slices, each one falling to gelatinous pieces. I spot him and Holmes through the window, walking arm-in-arm across our field. The neighbors are far enough away from us in the country that they wouldn't see more than two human figures, unless of course they had binoculars for bird-watching, as I do.

They've walked out towards the horse fence that lines the perimeter of the next property, hands stretched out to brush the tall grass. Sherlock Holmes throws his head back in laughter, and a sickening self-consciousness rolls through my body, wondering if Watson is telling tales about me. I'm sure in the next moment that I'm being silly; why would they leave just to talk about me? Probably neither one of them even thinks about me when they are alone together. I don't know which thought makes me feel worse.

I keep the binoculars pressed to my face hard enough to leave little marks. Holmes will know what I have been up to, but to hell with him and what he knows! I have a right to see this if I want to.

Holmes snatches a weed bloom from the grass with his skeletal fingers and hands it to Watson like a suitor. It's just a little scraggly bunch of yellow flowers that pop up every spring, spreading further and further each year. Watson smiles at the gesture and tosses it over his shoulder for luck. Watson and I do that on our walks. That makes Holmes laugh too. When did he get so damn merry? I was under the impression that laughter in him was rare.

For a moment they grow still, and Holmes touches Watson's face, tracing the lines coming from his eyes, smile lines made by a lifetime of mostly happiness. He has a couple of stress lines between his eyes from all the horrible things Holmes has done to him over the years, but still he lets Holmes stroke his cheek and pat his chest and kiss him on the lips.

I tear the binoculars away from my eyes and fling them away from me. One of the scopes lands in a piece of cake. I turn to stare at it, trying to obliterate what I have just seen and replace it with something else. I've imagined them together, pictured it in my head as Watson told me his stories, but it's very different than witnessing it myself. Having never met Holmes, it was easy to talk about him in regards to Watson; it was just like speaking of Mary, like imagining his relationship with someone long dead. But now this man is in my house, in my time, and somehow I just never thought he would be.

Staring at the slaughtered dessert, I don't notice Maurice standing in the doorway until he clears his throat. I haven't said much to him about all this, but he knows it anyway. No one ever keeps secrets from their servants; all you can hope is that they're loyal to you.

"And what have you been doing?" Maurice asks with sympathy.

"Bird watching," I say stiffly.

"What have we got today, then?" he asks, moving to look out the window himself. "Ah, a cock and a swallow."

"Oh, shut it, Maurice!" I tell him, but I can't help but laugh. It's best to keep light about these things, since there is bung all I can do about them. I hand Maurice the demolished cake on its saucer so it won't be seen and ask him to bring another in replacement. I have to fetch back our guest and finishing hosting him. It's the only way to have him out of here.

1894: The Empty House

Watson had taken to reading about crime and horror incessantly in his bereavement, wallowing in his memories of Holmes. It filled him with sorrow every time he came across a case, like the murder of the Honorable Ronald Adair, that Holmes would have liked and which could not be solved without him. But he kept at his research with the compulsion of an addict. He couldn't stop thinking of Holmes anyway, even if he kept his nose out of the papers. Outside of his control, he kept having dreams of Holmes. Sweet, awful dreams…

Watson even tried to solve a few cases on his own, with absolutely no success. It became a bit of a habit for him in the three years that Holmes was thought to be dead to examine scenes of crime and collect the details from the papers as though Holmes might ask him for a summary at any moment. That is why he walked past Ronald Adair's rooms and, upon hearing someone more out of touch with crime-solving than even himself spout his theories on the street, Watson backed away in disgust and misery, wishing Holmes were around to put such a fool in his place. He backed away so quickly that he trod over an old man who cursed him roundly and took off around the corner.

Watson went to his house in an absolute fog of Sherlock Holmes, and sat in his study wistfully for only a moment before that same old man was let in to apologize for his rude outburst. How many times had Holmes pulled this trick, disguising himself and sneaking up on Watson, just to have the pleasure of that look of childish wonder on his face? If he'd done it once he'd done a dozen times, but at no time was Watson more unprepared for it than this.

Watson fainted at the sight of him. It wouldn't have taken half the power of that shock to tip him off his feet. He'd been horribly depressed for months, off his food most of the time, deriving very little joy from life. Holmes could have kicked himself, I'm sure, for revealing himself like such a prat. Watson came around to the sensation of Holmes tugging at his collar and the taste of brandy with just a hint of Holmes's mouth where it had pulled from the flask before him. It was a feeling of such bliss he nearly feared to open his eyes. He was sure he was only dreaming.

But as his vision cleared and Holmes remained solid flesh before him, the truth began to dawn bright and happy in his heart. Holmes smiled at him and bit his lip, looking amazingly sheepish.

"My dear Watson," he said kindly. "I owe you a thousand apologies. I had no idea that you would be so affected." In truth, Holmes was quietly delighted by Watson's reaction; so Watson *had* missed him, terribly it seemed. And Watson was beside himself to find Holmes returned.

"Holmes! Is it really you?" Watson was so desperate that this not be some sort of trick of his brain that he demanded an explanation about how it could be possible. Holmes hesitated, thinking he might have shocked Watson too harshly and shouldn't overburden him with information, but Watson insisted.

"I am all right," he said, "but indeed, Holmes I can hardly believe my eyes." He was more willing to believe his hands. He gripped Holmes forcefully by the arm and kept handling him, palms pressing to be sure he was real, and warm with life. This was his arm, his thin, sinewy arm! Watson thought he would never feel it again.

As Holmes lifted him from his slump, Watson put an arm across Holmes's shoulder and pressed his face beneath Holmes's unmistakable jaw. Watson's lips grazed the light stubble on his neck.

"Well, you're not a spirit, anyhow," Watson said as Holmes righted him and stepped back. A spasm of desire flexed over Holmes's face, but now was not the time. They had a long night before them still.

Holmes removed himself to the other side of Watson's desk and put himself in order. He lit a cigarette and started to tell of his escape from Reichenbach Falls as though it were nothing, though his body gave up more of the truth. Watson could at least make accurate medical deductions, noting that the usually thin Holmes was even thinner than usual, and pale, and rough. He had a sharper look in his eye, like a man has when they snatch him off a deserted island where he has had to fend for himself, trying to stave off beasts and madness alike.

Holmes moved subtly to stretch himself after stepping out of his hunched character. Watson watched every movement closely, as if enchanted by them. The slight crick of the neck, the way he bunched and relaxed his shoulders or extended his legs. He was magnificent to see.

"It is no joke when a tall man has to take a foot off his stature for several hours on end," Holmes told him apologetically. "Now, my dear fellow, perhaps it would be better if I gave you an account of the whole situation when tonight's work is finished."

"I should much prefer to hear now," Watson said dreamily. He didn't really care what he heard or when, he only wanted to keep Holmes in front of him for as long as possible.

"So you'll come with me tonight?" Holmes asked him, almost like he was requesting a dance.

"When you like and where you like," Watson vowed to him.

Holmes smiled deeply. "This is indeed like the old days," he said with great relief. He was afraid that Watson might have altered in his absence, that he would no longer be his man. But of course there was never any chance of that. Even in death Sherlock Holmes held his ground.

Holmes gave the quick details of his struggle with Moriarty. After all the emotion he'd felt leading up to the struggle, that heartfelt note he had left for Watson, the shadow that had hung over his head for weeks making him feel sure he would come to his end, it all amounted to a very short climax indeed. Moriarty meant to take them both over the falls, but Holmes slipped away from him as easily as any other opponent, and left Moriarty at the edge to fall or recover on his own. Moriarty naturally fell, and Holmes was wiped of all his own sentiment and adrenaline when he stuck his face out over the edge to watch his nemesis plummet. The scientist in Holmes knows how to elbow his way to the front, and he couldn't resist the urge to observe the horrible drop that Moriarty experienced before banging off a rock and being lost beneath the water.

And all the while he was watching the Professor die, he was taking stock of his unique opportunity; to fake his death at that moment meant he might avoid a select few more assassins all together. Not only might he walk away from this place alive, but ever after he might live without that stifling pall of worry, like the Sword of Damocles twirling above his head. He would prefer not to live at all if it meant existing within that constant cloud—his own Valley of Fear. At long last he truly knew what John Douglas had been talking about it. It was a horrible way to live.

And so, like Douglas before him, Holmes faked his own death. By scaling the side of the cliff he was able to leave no track for Watson to find, though he might have simply walked backwards, as was his first idea, for all that Watson would have been able to deduce from it all.

"I watched you, my dear Watson, investigating in the most sympathetic and inefficient manner the circumstances of my death." Watson covered his mouth with his hand to hide his smile. How long had it been since Holmes had told him he was a wretched detective? Too long to be sure! Of all the things to miss about Sherlock Holmes, this criticism Watson treasured to have back.

Holmes had lain on a thin ledge above the falls and from there watched Watson make all the wrong conclusions, hardly thinking to care at all for the agony that Watson was in, only noting every wrong assumption and watching Watson weave together his own ending. When Watson published the account of The Final Problem, Holmes had snapped it up with keen interest. It's not every man who gets to read his own eulogy. A right Tom Sawyer there is in Sherlock Holmes.

The terrifying side of the cliff had its unnerving effect on Holmes, both as he climbed up and then back down, though going down he had more than that to worry about, namely a confederate of Moriarty's who had seen Holmes live and was now trying to murder him with falling rocks. Holmes escaped from him and travelled by night for more than a week before reaching Florence and contacting his brother. Though it would have been kind to let Watson know he was still alive, it would not have been practical, because (as has been established before) for Watson to play a part correctly he must not know he is acting.

"I owe you many apologies," Holmes said again. He never did speak any of his apologies outright, though Watson found a way to forgive him anyway. Probably because of this: "Several times during the last three years I have taken up my pen to write to you, but always I feared lest your affectionate regard for me should tempt you to some indiscretion which would betray my secret." He was upon the Tor again, careful not to provoke Watson's human kindness.

"I would have suddenly grown undeniably happy," Watson agreed with him. "I would have dropped every last thing in my life and come to you at once."

"I suspected as much," Holmes said quietly.

Holmes travelled and amused himself as he waited for his enemies to stick their necks out, and he even published under the name Sigerson some few narratives about his explorations. He couldn't help himself. Holmes had grown used to being heard about and could not give that up as easily as he abandoned everything else. He went through Tibet, Persia, the Sudan, back to France, and then finally to London.

Watson had been right about the murder of Ronald Adair—it had proved irresistible to Holmes, who hurried back not just because the case was so interesting, but because Colonel Sebastian Moran was involved. Holmes came home, gave Mrs. Hudson the same sort of shock he was then giving to Watson, and found his rooms just as he had left them to Mycroft. The only thing missing was Watson. It did pang Holmes occasionally during his solitary travels to be without Watson, but it was especially apparent how much he was missed once Holmes was back in their old rooms. Watson's chair was poignantly covered with dust.

Watson wouldn't have believed the story of Holmes's escape from anyone else's lips, but there sat Holmes: spare, spritely, unsinkable Holmes. He seemed an absolute miracle.

A moment passed as the story of Holmes's resurrection faded into their past. Holmes then looked around at their present, and he deduced something.

"These are smaller digs than you had before, Watson," Holmes suggested carefully.

"You have learned somehow of my other sad bereavement," Watson said. He waited to see if Holmes had any remark to that. He did, naturally.

"I told you that women are never to be entirely trusted, didn't I?"

"Don't be unfair, Holmes. She couldn't help dying on me."

Holmes waited a beat before saying softly, "I could."

Watson should have been offended (I certainly am) that Holmes had such a choice in whether or not to abandon him and *always* did it anyway. But Watson only continued bursting with happiness—here was this incredible man who could resurrect himself from the dead! He was maybe second only to Jesus Christ, but with at least one very important difference: he needed Watson for his own salvation as much as Watson needed him.

At last Watson could detain Holmes no longer, and it was time for another adventure. He almost laughed out loud in the cab on the way over, feeling himself in his old life again, armed and ignorant at the side of

Sherlock Holmes. All he knew about where they were headed was what he could glean from Holmes's face: that a grave mission lay before them, but that Holmes still had some reason to smile sardonically from time to time as he directed the cab through a maze of byways and alleys, trying to avoid being traced. Watson knew that such a smile boded ill for whoever they were chasing that night.

At their final destination, they made their way through the back door of an empty house. It was too dark to really see, but Watson could feel that the rooms they entered were empty, and using the walls to guide him he could feel that the wallpaper was in tatters. Watson was stepping around timidly, blind to where his feet were setting down, when Holmes took his wrist and led him confidently, if quietly, into the front room of the house. There he could dimly see Holmes's shape in the light that filtered through the dirty window. Holmes brought him very close and whispered in his ear.

"Do you know where we are?" he asked. Watson did; they were just opposite the old rooms in Baker Street, but he took a moment to answer this, because the feel of Holmes's breath across his face nearly put him into a swoon.

"But why are we here?" Watson asked, shaking himself out of his daze.

Holmes smiled. Watson could tell by the way what little yellow light there was in the room gleamed on his teeth, and he nearly lost his head again to think that he might have a whole lifetime of seeing that grin in the night.

Instead of answering, Holmes instructed Watson to the window, to look up and see for the second time that night, the impossible yet unmistakable shape of Sherlock Holmes.

Watson was so astonished by this trick he threw out his hand to grasp Holmes in the dark, just to be sure he had not truly transferred himself to the window across the street. He could feel Holmes being wracked with a silent fit of laughter.

"Well?" Holmes managed to ask.

"It's marvelous!" Watson told him.

Holmes was proud to tell Watson all of this bust, who made it, out of what medium, where it was done, and how long it took. Watson could hear the joy of the artist in his companion's voice. "It really is rather like me, is it not?" Holmes asked.

"I should be prepared to swear it was you."

Not that Watson was so much of a skeptic; if he could have seen the outline of the Queen in that window, he'd swear that she was up there too, but Holmes was still tickled to hear that his idea was so convincing. It had to fool Colonel Moran, who had already failed to kill Holmes at Reichenbach, into trying the murder one more time.

Holmes, practically overcome with excitement over his first real case in years, was in no mood for anything but hunting. When Watson thought he observed two men in the street, Holmes shushed him, for naturally he had seen them long before, and they were police plants anyway. When Watson noticed the dummy's shadow had moved in the window, Holmes snapped that of course it had moved! It had to look realistic. To sit still now, so close to the first capture of his revised career, was painful to Holmes, and he was preparing to make it painful for Watson too when Moran finally arrived after two hours of waiting.

Holmes's screed against Watson's idiocy was cut short with a gasp, and Watson heard the detective all but choke on his excitement, trying with all his might to keep hold of himself. It also came to pass that he had need to take hold of Watson as well. Holmes dragged him into the darkest corner of the room with that disturbing strength he becomes possessed of when his solution depends on it. Holmes put his hand over Watson's mouth, warning him not to make a sound, his hand quivering so that he could not feel the way Watson's lips puckered beneath them, sneaking him a kiss.

Then at last Watson heard what Holmes could hear, the movement of someone else in the house. He clasped his revolver as he and Holmes both flattened themselves into the shadows, and from there they watched Moran creep in, assemble a gun, and aim it at the figure in the window.

In Moran's eyes was the same shimmering look that Holmes would get when he was about to close in on a target, and Moran sighed before he pressed the trigger of his gun, the same sigh Holmes used to give before pressing the plunger on a cocaine syringe. These were men of the same feral breed, snapping at each other's heels in the jungles of the city.

After the shot rang out, Holmes sprang upon Moran. He got his neck squeezed a bit before Watson ran in to help, and then Holmes blew a whistle summoning a plainclothesman from the street and Inspector Lestrade, who greeted Holmes cordially, saying it was good to see him back in London.

Holmes tried to reciprocate the kind sentiment, and almost managed it: "I think you want a little unofficial help. Three undetected murders in one year won't do, Lestrade. But you handled the Molesey Mystery with less than your usual—that's to say, you handled it fairly well."

Lestrade and Watson raised eyebrows at each other and tried to pinch the smiles off their faces. This was serious business and all, but how fun to have Sherlock Holmes returned and seemingly improved. He must have missed them as well to come home so complimentary.

With more light in the room, Watson got a solid look at Moran: "With the brow of a philosopher above and the jaw of a sensualist below, the man must have started with great capacities for good or for evil." Who else does that sound like, then?

Holmes recognized the kindred connection, as did the prisoner. Moran kept muttering "You fiend! You clever, clever fiend!" as if he was only just understanding the caliber of the prey he'd been after. What was this man Holmes doing working for the police if he was going to be so horribly, horribly clever? He should have been their new commander after Moriarty, the wretched creature!

Holmes was happy to have his captive's esteem. "Ah, Colonel! 'Journeys end in lovers' meetings,' as the old play says." Holmes tweaked the Colonel a bit even as he put his own collar back in place from where this man had recently tried to throttle him to death. "Colonel Sebastian Moran, once of Her Majesty's Indian Army, and the best heavy-game shot that our Eastern Empire has ever produced. I believe I am correct, Colonel, in saying that your bag of tigers still remains unrivalled?"

The Colonel could say nothing, and Watson described his as being in almost a trance, and so smoldering with restrained power that he looked like a tiger himself. Holmes certainly thought so.

"You are my tiger," Holmes said to him, and pointing around at Watson and Lestrade he added, "and these are my reserve guns." He taunted Moran by telling him that, with the exception of him using the same house that Holmes had thought to use, everything had gone according to plan. Moran had acted just as Holmes knew he would. Like knows like.

Moran could hardly tolerate it. He all but begged Lestrade to take him away to jail. He may have been caught in the act of trying to pull off a murder, but he shouldn't have to listen to this unbearable gloating!

He was not however charged with trying to murder Sherlock Holmes, but instead with the murder of the Honorable Ronald Adair. His unique gun would prove his guilt, and Holmes handed Lestrade the prize prisoner with no strings attached to him, congratulating the Inspector on his singular capture. For once it really was the game he was after, and not the credit. It was so good just to be back at it, and free for a time from assassins, that he didn't care a whit who knew how impressive he had been.

Walking into the Baker Street rooms after three years was incredible for Watson. The dust and clutter showed that no one had truly lived in these rooms for a while, but that was thankfully about to change. Here were Holmes's chemical glasses, his violin, his mess of papers, his jack-knife stuck in the mantle just like it ever was. Mrs. Hudson was perfectly safe and had even found the bullet that was meant for Holmes. She gave it to him and departed.

Holmes held out the flattened bullet to show Watson.

"A soft revolver bullet, as you perceive, Watson. There's genius in that, for who would expect to find such a thing fired from an air-gun?" Holmes would hold onto that small piece of genius all his life, a rather morbid bit of memorabilia. Watson took the bullet and shook his head. Imagine something so small obliterating such a fine man as stood before him? Liquefying his brilliant thoughts with the simple force of its momentum? What a horrifying little thing it was.

"Plum in the middle of the back of the head and smack through the brain," Holmes said, holding up the bust of himself with its forehead blown out, and yet talking just as pleasantly as if he was having tea. He spoke of Colonel Moran's crack shot with pride, even pulling down his entry in the catalogue to read Watson the man's impressive biography. He explained his logic behind capturing Moran, and then concluded that the man was no longer a threat to them.

"Once again Mr. Sherlock Holmes is free to devote his life to examining those interesting little problems which the complex life of London so plentifully presents," Holmes said, lighting a cigarette with relish and pleasure at the very thought of it. He and Watson sat in silence for a bit, but they couldn't take their eyes off one another. Holmes was smiling and swinging his crossed leg happily, like a schoolboy. Watson had to blink forcefully every few seconds so that he would not spoil their reunion with a bunch of weeping. There was a strange ache in his heart, the opposite of when it had been broken, but painful all the same—it was the ache of healing.

Holmes finished his cigarette, crushed it out in the eye of his bust like he was adding the last smudge of paint onto a masterpiece, and then simply let the thing roll from his hands onto the floor. With his foot Holmes tucked the shattered thing under his chair and away. He sighed and then beckoned Watson over to him. Watson rose to obey.

"You look just as I left you, Watson," Holmes said, taking his hand and looking up at him. "A little sadder, perhaps. I hear it's been a hard time for you."

Watson said nothing. These were not questions.

"You'll stay with me tonight," Holmes said. This too was not a question, but Watson nodded anyway. They removed themselves to Holmes's bedchamber, and that's about all I care to know about that night.

When Watson awoke the next morning he kept his eyes shut. He had of late taken to imagining himself back at Baker Street in those malleable moments after sleep, when the world was not yet real again, and a man had to remember it all. If Watson exerted himself he could almost hear the movement of Mrs. Hudson below, he could sense the dimensions of Holmes's room (for he always imagined himself there, and not in his own bed), and if he concentrated very hard he could even smell the ghost of Holmes's pipe smoke. This was the only time in his long dreary days that he felt happy, and hopeful, and safe. Each morning it crushed him to open his eyes and see his small, basic room in Kensington and remember that he was alone.

Watson prepared himself for the blow, for he knew beneath his thoughts that he had to be dreaming. He forced his eyes full open, withstanding the pain from the light, but his fantasy persisted. And then it rushed back to him; Holmes returned, Moran imprisoned, the night spent in each other's arms. Holmes was sitting in his robe beside Watson, the smoke from his pipe partially clouding his frowning face from view, one knee up and a small mountain of paper scraps that he was slowly turning over.

"Good morning, Watson," he said without looking over. On another day Watson might have asked how Holmes knew he had opened his eyes, but not on this one. At last Watson couldn't hold it in anymore, and tears began sliding rapidly down his face.

This Holmes took a bit longer to notice. When he didn't get a verbal response, he turned to his friend and found him crying with his hand over his eyes, trying to hide his weakness.

"What's the matter, man? You're not injured, are you?"

"No," Watson said, almost laughing, and trying to stop that at least, lest he become fully hysterical.

"Well, what is it then? Everything's set back to right now, there's no need to get upset."

"You don't understand, Holmes!" Watson groaned. "I've had so many dreams where you came back alive, that somehow I had missed your tracks or you'd been fished out of the Falls, or any number of impossible things that seemed so convincing in the dream…but then I'd wake up. And for a moment I would feel it as true as anything, and then remember that you were gone all over again."

Holmes was watching Watson curiously, but said nothing. He looked as if he was thinking of calling another doctor in, one who still had his sense.

"And now it's swapped round!" Watson said insistently. How to make Holmes understand what it was doing to him? "I keep thinking this isn't real, that you aren't real," he said, grasping Holmes's arm since the corporeal feel of it the previous night and brought him such reassurance. It helped, but only a little. This had all been waiting to come out for longer than either man could know.

Holmes at last seemed to realize Watson's trouble and tucked his pipe in the side of his mouth so that he could take both of Watson's hands and bring them to his heart. Watson likes pretty gestures like that.

"I don't want you to ever think so little of my powers again, Watson," Holmes lectured with amusement, one hand holding Watson's hands together and the other punctuating his words with little stabs of his pipe. "I promised you I would never die, and I mean to keep that promise. I shall be offended if you ever assume I've perished again. Have I made myself clear?"

Watson nodded and took back his hands to dry his face. "I love you, Holmes. It's positively indecent how much I love you."

"Of course it is. Do us a favor and just move breakfast in here after Mrs. Hudson brings it up, I don't want to upset these papers."

"Anything you like, my friend," Watson told him. And then Sherlock Holmes came the closest to blushing that I believe he ever got, and he stuffed his pipe back in his mouth to hide a very foolish smile.

1894: The Golden Pince-Nez

By November Watson had moved back to Baker Street. In truth, after that first night with Holmes, he never slept in Kensington again. Watson sold his practice for a healthy amount of money, and only later discovered that Holmes had financed every cent of it through a filter of people to make sure Watson would be able to come home and stay. He had his tragic flaws, but Holmes was not about to make the exact same mistake twice; Watson was finally available, and Holmes did not hesitate in securing him again. Even I must admit that it was a sweet thing to do. He may not have ever bothered to say it, but it was quite clear that he loved Watson too.

They had an easy time of it for that first year, and there is only one case on record in 1894 after *The Empty House* precisely because Watson was so happy once more. When he is content he tends to close around the feeling protectively, like an oyster with a pearl. Even I know very little of this period outside of what I have gleaned from this one case; Watson is quite secretive about it.

It was a sloshing night in November, and Holmes tried to pretend he was glad to have no case to run down, since the weather was so wretched. Of course when a client pulled up he was ready to dig out his foul weather gear with enthusiastic glee, the liar.

However they were not required out in the gale. Young Stanley Hopkins, a rising detective with the official force, came in plainly perplexed. He told the story of Willoughby Smith's murder, and of how he had tried to apply Holmes's methods in his investigation. But without a motive he was lost to even know where to start. Lucky for Holmes the motives of most people are obscure to him; that was the part he always needed explained to him in the end. Searching for a motive means guessing at people's emotions, and it's what often leads Scotland Yard to accuse and juries to convict the wrong man. It is another thing to know patterns of motivation—that is what Holmes studies the agony columns for—but the police begin by thinking that their suspect is either just like them in thought or else entirely monstrous and unknowable, and in both directions they tend to be wrong. For Holmes the facts must speak for themselves.

Of course, he must have all the facts first. Holmes was getting agitated with Hopkins by the lack of evidence until the young official handed him the pince-nez glasses that were found in the dead man's hand, presumably ripped from the murderer. *That* Holmes was satisfied to have. He examined them as Watson and Hopkins sat watching, and then tossed off an impressive list of features for their owner that deeply impressed Hopkins. The next day found Holmes and Watson at the scene of the crime.

I think Watson set down this case alone of that year because it displayed some of Holmes's prettiest tricks. The way a painter might sketch his sweetheart in a hurry if he'd seen her turn just the right way or be in exquisite light, Watson wanted an image of Holmes at this time. Finally, he thought, they had worked through all their personal failings. Surely after three years apart neither one would ever take the other for granted again. At last he had a Holmes who seemed mature and respectful and settled, and this story put him on record as such. It was good of Watson to preserve the moment, because of course it wouldn't last very long. Watson had no inkling at the time. He thought that by writing this story he was marking a new beginning. He would look back on this time later and wonder at how brief it truly was.

Holmes deduced their woman murderer must still be hiding in the house, since her exit was blocked and only one room could be concealing her, the bedroom of Professor Coram. Holmes could find her out by sounding the walls, but he much preferred to save himself the work, and so had his criminal reveal herself by dropping ash all over the floor and then observing where it had been smudged. He did the same thing when he needed the location of the stolen Naval Treaty in 1888. He'll go climbing around if he absolutely has to, but it's so much more artful to coax his prey into the net. "I take a short cut when I can get it," he told Watson. And don't we all.

Watson and the Professor were both surprised to see Holmes tearing through cigarette after cigarette, oblivious to his plotting. Watson even spotted Holmes being friendly with the housekeeper, and thought how nice that he really could be charming to a woman if only he wanted to (or if only he needed something from her, like information on the Professor's eating habits). It seemed that Holmes really had altered himself, and for the better: "We loitered the morning away in the garden… As to my friend, all his usual energy seemed to have deserted him. I had never known him handle a case in such a half-hearted fashion." To Watson it seemed a kind of calming, a good omen for their future. He is a terminal optimist.

That sort of creeping mildness had gotten the better of Holmes once before, but even Holmes thought he had thrown it off for good this time. Wasn't there such a thing as too much excitement? And didn't he have all he could handle in fighting Moriarty? But here he was beginning to miss it already. And just like any drug it became less and less effective in regular doses.

When Holmes had seen the hiding place of their murderer in the ashes, he rose up with his cheeks aflame. Watson noted: "Only at a crisis have I seen those battle-signals flying." Here was his moment, but it was so fleeting, it hardly propped him up for an hour. By the time they had been to the Russian embassy and dropped off the papers to secure a man's release from prison, Holmes was utterly deflated. He tried to hide it from Watson, and had he not been so miserable he could have managed to easily. It was a question of energy, and Holmes just couldn't make the effort.

"That was an interesting one, eh?" Watson asked him in their hansom ride home. "One for the public I should think, it was quite singular."

Holmes fluttered his eyes slowly in response. He could feel himself being pulled down; it was only important to get inside before he was overtaken by paralysis. As a young man these fits of malaise had caught him unawares once or twice and it had been very awkward. He once lay across a study table in the university library for an entire day, not just sun up to sun down, but for a full twenty-four hours at least. People worried he'd had a stroke over his exams, and at last someone dared to shake his shoulder and roused him enough to send him away. They looked at him so strangely after that.

"You were not energized by the mystery, Holmes? I thought it seemed just to your taste."

Holmes opened his mouth but could not speak. It had gone as far as his voice already. He grasped Watson's arm to reassure him, but the gesture only made our doctor more concerned. Where was the man's strength? Watson had had invalids hold him more tightly.

When they arrived home, Watson brought him inside and put him straight to bed. He wanted to give Holmes something for his malady, but the only treatment he knew was what Holmes chose for it, the cocaine solution, and it was no cure, but only a new disease in itself. They would do without it.

And without it they did. Holmes snapped back from his misery in a few days, just like always, but the problem remained lurking, building, underneath.

1895: Wisteria Lodge

The next story begins thusly: "I find it recorded in my notebook that it was a bleak and windy day towards the end of March in the year 1892." I did tell you that Watson's notes held errors, didn't I? Sherlock Holmes was dead in 1892. I've examined his original papers, and you should see this sad wiggle that he took for a *2* and in which I see a very weak and confused *5*. Certainly Watson was absolutely wrong with his number, and so I shall use mine instead.

Holmes got a note asking for a consultation, and took to it right away because of the client's use of the word "grotesque" in relation to his troubles. What a marvelous word to Sherlock Holmes, and how he mulled it in his mouth like something savory. Here are the moments that Watson calls artistic, when the connoisseur Holmes comes out and kisses his fingers in enthusiasm. There was a certain *je ne sais quoi* in that word, something rich and scarlet and gold. Made merely of letters arranged just so on a telegram, that word was enough to start his heart racing faster. He never knew how very much of his life was spent feeling half-dead except in these small moments when a true zest for living would seize him. It was an exquisite sensation.

That is when Watson thoughtlessly asked if Holmes would see the man who had written to him.

"My dear Watson," Holmes said to him, his voice like that of someone offended or injured. "You know how bored I have been since we locked up Colonel Carruthers. My mind is like a racing engine, tearing itself to pieces because it is not connected up with the work for which it was built." He began to get upset, an emotional state very rare for someone like Holmes, who is more prone to throwing tantrums should he ever lose control of himself; this was an inward versus an outward expression of hot frustration. It *was* tearing him up. "Life is commonplace, the papers are sterile; audacity and romance seem to have passed forever from the criminal world. Can you ask me, then, whether I am ready to look into any new problem, however trivial it may prove?"

Watson gaped at his friend, shocked by the sudden outpouring of such obviously well-formed and unhappy thoughts. He wanted to ask Holmes if he was all right, for God's sake, but before he could speak there was a step upon the stair, and their client was before them. Holmes returned in an instant to his old, guarded self.

Mr. Scott Eccles was a bachelor—he had met an attractive, lively man named Garcia and went for a stay at his household, Wisteria Lodge. Garcia received a note that unsettled him during dinner, and when Eccles woke the next day, Garcia and all his people were gone. Holmes was already interested before Inspectors Gregson and Baynes arrived and said that Garcia had been found dead. Grotesque, indeed.

Holmes was impressed with Baynes's talent for observation, but he was not as perfectly trained in the art of deduction. He had gotten a wealth of data from the note (recovered from the fire), but from it he concluded nothing except that since a woman had written it, a woman must be at the bottom of the whole mess. Holmes doubted that to Watson: "There is, on the face of it, something unnatural about this strange and sudden friendship between the young Spaniard and Scott Eccles." He might understand it from Eccles's end—for no man may be a "bachelor" around Sherlock Holmes without him knowing why—but it was Garcia who had pushed the friendship, and that did not add up at all.

"What did he want with Eccles?" Holmes wondered. "What could Eccles possibly supply? I see no charm in the man. He is not particularly intelligent—not a man likely to be congenial to a quick-witted Latin." Holmes concluded that Garcia must have valued Eccles for something else. "Eccles is the very type of conventional British respectability." He would be believed by police whatever he said. Holmes and Watson had watched him go out with the inspectors still unsuspected, despite how badly his own story implicated him. Perhaps that was the value he held for Garcia; he would have been an unassailable alibi.

Holmes conceded that there might be some kind of tryst. The lady in question might have a jealous husband who would beat a man to death over such a note as they had read, but Holmes doubted it, and it was all speculation at best. "We can only possess our souls in patience until this excellent inspector comes back for us. Meanwhile we can thank our lucky fate which has rescued us for a few short hours from the insufferable fatigues of idleness."

He said it in a light way, but he wasn't being funny. His eyes already had that haunted look in them. It wasn't enough; it was absolutely never enough.

The case brought Holmes and Watson out to Wisteria Lodge the next day, and there they found some gruesome items, blood and bones and the like, and Holmes was left to his own investigation since Inspector Baynes was anxious to prove himself independently. Watson was encouraged to see Holmes enlivened by the case, but even he had to watch closely to see it: "I could tell by numerous subtle signs, which might have been lost upon anyone but myself, that Holmes was on a hot scent. As impassive as ever to the casual observer, there were nonetheless a subdued eagerness and suggestion of tension in his brightened eyes and a brisker manner which assured me that the game was afoot. After his habit he said nothing, and after mine I asked no questions."

He may not have seen all that he imagined, for the days went on in the country and Sherlock Holmes was actually *not* acting like himself. He was muted, taking long walks, chatting with the village folks and looking in on some local plants. He was still on the case, covering his investigation by posing as an amateur botanist, but he did it all so quietly, as if only out of habit.

The only rise Watson got from him was the day Holmes thought Inspector Baynes might have scooped him by making an arrest, but even that Holmes did with an air of sighing. Baynes was so very promising, but so very wrong in his arrest of the cook, and Holmes merely warned him against acting rashly. Not that he was prepared to take his own advice, as we shall see shortly.

Holmes brought Watson back to their room to convince him that they must break the law to find a missing woman—the author of the note, Miss Burnet. I wonder if Holmes wasn't hoping to make the case more thrilling for himself by forcing the point. He could talk himself into anything, just as easily as he could convince Watson: "There was something in the ice-cold reasoning of Holmes which made it impossible to shrink from any adventure which he might recommend." It ended up not being necessary to break out Miss Burnet, and also that Baynes was on the same trail as Holmes after all, and using his arrest of Garcia's cook as a trap for their suspect. In the end, they did not even capture their man; they had to solve their case through news out of Madrid by matching the description of a dead man to the one whom they had chased. He was Don Murillo, The Tiger of San Pedro.

Inspector Baynes brought the news and they all agreed their case was concluded. After his departure, Holmes sat with his pipe and listlessly asked Watson if there remained anything he didn't understand. A few questions about the bizarre voodoo items found in the house were all he voiced, and Holmes explained what he had learned about such practices.

"As I have had occasion to remark," Holmes said as he slowly closed up his notebook, "there is but one step from the grotesque to the horrible." He let the book slide out of his lap and onto the floor as if he didn't have the energy to lift it again.

1895: The Solitary Cyclist

The string of curiously unsatisfactory cases continued for poor Holmes. He was waiting for a problem to save him from himself, from making the same mistakes with Watson all over again. He couldn't rely on his old syringe to get him over the rough patches anymore, but things were different now. Ever since the struggle with Moriarty, he no longer trekked over peaks and valleys in his quest, but plodded through a dry, flat desert of dull happenings and commonplace mysteries. The cases just didn't seize him like they used to, and perhaps the drug would be a failure too, even if he did go back to it. He tried to hold onto this idea to keep himself out of the substance, but a chemist knows better; of course a drug would do what it always did, so long as the variables were the same. Was he the same? Something was changed, either physical or mental. If it were mental, the cocaine would help him once more; so had his brain altered, or was it only his mind?

One experiment would be all it would take to test the question, but should the drug lift him even the slightest bit out of his miserable trudge, he would take it up again with a vengeance. His arms would be covered in small scars like the old days, and Watson would find out, and what would happen then? Watson had already left Holmes once before; would he do it again? Or had the death of Sherlock Holmes affected Watson as well, made him more tolerant of all his friend's faults, if only he might have him alive?

Holmes's problem was the work—if only the work would be good again. That could sustain him, but it was not to be so.

"It is true," Watson begins the story of The Solitary Cyclist, "that the circumstance did not admit of any striking illustration of those powers for which my friend was famous." I really feel like Holmes was making his best effort to keep his hands busy, but to no avail. Watson said in this and at least one other story (the case of Black Peter, in July of the same year) that 1895 was the start of an unprecedented busy time for Holmes. In fact he was interrupted from some other work by the story of this cycling woman, and he let it disturb the business he was already pursuing, hoping that it might draw his passion better. This is how his busyness began that year, with Holmes reaching desperately for any case that might enrapture him, any problem at all, letting them all stack upon him, and yet still he could feel no great excitement. Later it would be the unnatural frenzy of the drug which kept him so active, and not much later at all; he would be back on the substance before the summer was out.

Watson found this case very exciting indeed, and even I sit on the edge of my seat, the way he tells of their chase after the abducted girl, and a brief shoot-out around her forced marriage to a wretched man who was after the inheritance she didn't even know she was due yet. The only pleasure Holmes got out of the whole thing was the day the horrible bridegroom surprised him as he was making inquiries and tried Holmes at a little impromptu boxing. Holmes got off with a cut on his lip and a bruised face while the other man had to be carted home. It is so infrequently that Holmes is ever taken unawares so abruptly that for half the day he felt a lovely tingling throughout his body, a whisper of the roaring sensation he once felt when he struggled for a solution. His lip throbbed in time with a hard-beating heart, and he was nearly optimistic. But it was a short-lived thrill, and the tedious business of rescuing people and learning of their insipid and uninspired motivations... Well, all that only made him *miss* Moriarty. Terrifying as he was, the man was at least an artist and a gentleman. He took pride in his work.

This case was completed in late April, just when the papers were exploding with a criminal and social scandal: the trials of Oscar Wilde. Holmes had pointed to the paper on April third, when the whole mess started, and had said to Watson, "I told you they'd find him out." Wilde's conviction absolutely terrified the homosexual men of London—there was a mass exodus of Uranians to France while the trial was under way. Wilde's case proved to them that no one was safe from the law passed in 1886, the amendment to the Offenses Against the Person Act that turned them all into criminals, and named them in the public square at last as a race apart. It would unsettle Watson and Holmes as well, though in totally different ways, exciting sympathetic concern and destructive action respectively. It would snap the string of their tenuous reunion, and trigger an event that would affect both of them profoundly, and adversely, for longer than either man realized.

1895: The Three Students

Holmes was, and still is, unmatched in the field of detection. He had been approached by both sides of the Wilde scandal and declined to contribute to either; one side because they were right, and the other because they were so provably wrong. He would not help the Marquess of Queensberry in his personal vendettas against the people who influenced his sons—the man had wanted Holmes's services in regards to his eldest son's relations with Lord Roseberry, and he had requested Holmes, much more vociferously, to investigate his younger son's relationship with Oscar Wilde. Holmes had declined both times. Not only was he honorable enough not to persecute others for what he did himself, he didn't care for Lord Queensberry; the Ninth Marquess was a violent and unstable man. Holmes knew his rules for boxing quite well, but Queensberry himself fought men in the street and carried a horsewhip with him everywhere he went to threaten and cow people. He did not keep to the spirit of fair sportsmanship that his own rules promoted, so why should Sherlock Holmes promote the spirit of laws which he found unjust and unfair on the man's behalf?

He did however put forth some effort, in May of 1895, to make some inquiries on Wilde's behalf; not only as a member of the club himself, but for the hideous precedence Wilde's conviction would set for all of them. But there was nothing to be done. Of what they accused him, Wilde was guilty. Holmes certainly couldn't risk himself and Watson coming under suspicion for a case so hopelessly lost already. He could only shake his head and sink lower into the hopeless mood he'd found himself in since coming back to life.

But that is why they were in Oxford in May of 1895—Holmes had an idea he might start with Wilde's university days and systematically cast doubt on all the accusations against him, but Wilde seemed dead set to be his own worst enemy, and no one could or would speak for him anyway. The climate was too vicious for even kindness to be bestowed on Wilde. Only the bravest of his closest friends ever dared to help him, and their efforts were always thankless.

Publishing this story to the masses in 1904, Watson was secure enough to say only this: "It was in the year '95 that a combination of events, into which I need not enter, caused Mr. Sherlock Holmes and myself to spend some weeks in one of our great university towns, and it was during this time that the small but instructive adventure which I am about to relate befell us." It was rather a danger to say even this; I have figured it out, and so others might as well, but it was the least he could do to acknowledge it. It was not nothing, after all, and he was not uninvolved.

After their true mission turned out to be such a sad failure, they endeavored to cover the trip with some legitimate purpose, should they themselves be brought up about the intent of the questions Holmes had asked several of the old professors and staff—those questions would be put down to idle gossip, unrelated to their business in the area, if only they could come up with another story. Such was their fear of persecution, the lengths which had to be gone to, only to exist as they were made and love how they chose.

They secured temporary rooms and Holmes went to bury himself in the nearest library. He set himself to work on a project of some importance, Watson reports, having to do with early English charters. Watson said that Holmes was "uncomfortable" away from Baker Street and all his belongings, that he was in bad temper. This is a bit of an understatement; Holmes was coming to a personal crisis that would put them both through agony. His impressive will was about to be thoroughly broken.

But first this case would be sorted through. It was a bit of a logical treat, something he would have enjoyed much more in earlier years. In fact, it reminded him a bit of the first few unofficial problems he ever solved, back in school when people would come to him with their little "perplexions," a word he invented to describe the puzzled faces his classmates would make when they were out of their depths. He could always discover, just from talking with those boys, where they had lost their possessions or if their mates had borrowed their clothes, their girlfriends, even their answers on a test.

In 1885 a professor's office has been broken into and an exam had been…examined. It must have been one of the three students who were getting ready to take it, and Holmes got to figure out which one. "Quite a little parlor game—sort of three-card trick, is it not?" he asked Watson. It was a nice way to display his talents, but recalling to him his younger days was not exactly healthy for Holmes, I don't think—they were not his best times.

He got to turn out a few nice deductions while he was at it; he knew the order the papers were found in, marked the direction of a scratch, and tied an odd substance to one student: the guilty party. Holmes was even well enough at one moment to joke with Watson when he realized that he himself had made them miss dinner: "What with your eternal tobacco, Watson, and your irregularity at meals, I expect that you will get notice to quit, and that I shall share your downfall." They smiled at each other secretly; they were just as married as I am, really. They were not so different at all.

The decision had been threatening Sherlock Holmes for months, but something about this case, the terrible priorities of society and law that had brought him out to the university, finished his resolve. I believe it might have been nostalgia—for those heady days when he was at school, the hope he had once known, the ambition that had once driven him. Seeing young Gilchrist confess his crime, and what a tiny thing it seemed! To sneak on an exam, but resolve to be a better man thereafter… Holmes sprung from the room with forgiveness in his heart, for the boy himself, for the servant who had covered for him since he'd known him as a child, and for the professor as well. They just didn't know the horrors of the world, they were so darling and innocent. Holmes had once been that way himself, silly and young. He missed it. He was only forty-one years old, and yet he missed his youth terribly. Life was both too long and too short to spend it as fearfully sad as he had recently been.

When they returned to Baker Street the following week, Holmes brought home with him a bottle of the seven percent solution. He could have gotten it at any pharmacy, at any time when he was out of Watson's sight. I would wager he did it while Watson was asleep. He was disappointed in himself, but he was finally decided. It might not work like it used to, he kept reminding himself—this was an experiment, and nothing more. But he was smart enough to know when he was lying to himself.

He waited until they got back to Baker Street. He needed his morocco case anyway, and if this was to be an experiment, then he would treat it as such. He would sit as his chemical table after Watson had gone trustingly to bed, and he would know once and for all.

Arriving home they found that the newspapers had stacked up on the table. Holmes saw that Wilde had been convicted and sentenced to two years of hard labor, the worst he could have gotten, and yet the judge had said it was not enough. Even Mrs. Hudson gossiped to them about the case, saying, "Can you believe it? For someone as famous as that to stoop to such lowness?" Watson's face had broken out in emotion, and Holmes had hurried him upstairs before she noticed, and he shooed Mrs. Hudson away to her own business. Holmes had had quite enough of the dreary world at that point, the dun-colored, commonplace world.

Watson was tired from their journey home. He had a cigarette and went to bed, but not before wondering aloud about Mrs. Hudson—to think of how much she loved them, he said, how much she loved Holmes especially; would she feel the same way if she knew? Would she gain sympathy for Wilde, or would she be revolted by them as well? Would she report them to the police and tell the next tenants: "Can you believe it? For someone as famous as Sherlock Holmes to stoop to such lowness?" Holmes didn't want to talk about it. He waited for Watson to retire and threw the newspapers straight into the fire.

It was time for him to know. Wilde had been a man of passion, of flame. He had a whole philosophy around it. Did he regret anything at this moment? Would he regret it in the future, or on his death bed, or when he met his maker? Holmes had never gone in for their preening ways—the Decadents, as they fancied themselves, claiming the insult that critics threw at them as their regal title. A lazy crew, Holmes had always felt, but not without interest. There was something to the notion of creating oneself like a work of art. Had not Holmes crafted his mind in much the same way? Didn't he choose to live recklessly, and with a hard, gem-like flame?

"To get back one's youth, one has merely to repeat one's follies."

It was time now for Sherlock Holmes to rekindle himself, or to at least try and rescue his mind from stagnation. Watson might understand, or he might not, but this was no way to let a life go by, with one tedious day after another. Sherlock Holmes, for all his faults, did not take his life for granted. At least, not after he'd nearly lost it, or when he was in his right mind.

Holmes cleared a space on his chemical table. He laid out the syringe, the bottle, and he rolled up his sleeve. He loaded the solution in; how near this was to loading a bullet into a gun! It felt just as deadly I imagine, but it felt necessary as well. It was time to know, and even I can hardly blame him this time, because he did deserve a life he could enjoy. Each of us should only have to die once, after all.

He put the needle on his skin, slid it in just the slightest bit. That sensation had stopped hurting him years ago, it felt less like a pinch and more like a kiss. He held it for a long moment, knowing that he could stop, and yet still knowing that he would not. He hung his head for a moment, made a soft, strangled noise of both agony and expectation, and he pushed the plunger. He knew the results in an instant.

It had worked! But of course it had worked! It zinged through him just like it always did, it made his heart race at long last. Holmes was so relieved, so ecstatic! There was the ghost of an idea in his head about how really horrible this was, how unhealthy, but what did that matter now? He was only thankful that he had his solution once again, the solution to his greatest problem.

He gathered up the morocco case quickly and smuggled it to his room. He would lock it in his safe when not in use so that Watson would never suspect. Watson! He would go to him now to celebrate. Wasn't the air clearer? The news of the day so fittingly ironic? Holmes went to Watson's room that night and stayed with him until morning, though neither slept. Holmes finally felt alive again.

Watson was reassured that Holmes was fine, that the past few months had only been his peculiar nature at work, a customary low point in someone who could reach so high. Here he was back to normal, the same old full-blooded, energetic Holmes. It would be months before Watson noticed a disturbance, and even then the real cause would have to be pointed out to him by someone else. His trusting nature is at once the most attractive and unfortunate feature he has, and it has very rarely done him any favors.

1919: Dessert

"I would like to give my compliments to the chef," Holmes says when I request he and Watson come back inside. I acquiesce, since at least he will not be able to charm Maurice with his lies after what we just witnessed. Let him swan around as if he did not kiss other people's husbands! We are not fooled.

Watson sits down to his dessert as if nothing is amiss, tucking his napkin into his shirt and smiling like someone very feeble-minded indeed. I feel a powerful urge to smash my cake into his happy face. What is he smiling about, exactly? What makes him so bloody happy?

"You know," I tell my husband, "if Maurice and I could see you through the windows, I feel quite sure that the neighbors could as well."

Watson looks up at me, concerned. "You didn't see us, did you darling?" He really wouldn't want to hurt me by making me a witness. Holmes had done it to him too many times to count, flirted with others right in front of his face. Watson knows it feels awful. I have my own nosy self to thank for grabbing the binoculars. It's not as if when I let Watson visit Holmes by the sea that I delude myself that they aren't...up to their old business. But it's different somehow when it's so far removed from me, when he comes back exactly the same as when he left, and never brings anyone home with him.

"It won't be long until he leaves," Watson says, taking my hand kindly. "You know I'll never move him to come here again. Even if I wanted him to, he refuses to be flexible. And then it will just be you and I."

"Yes, of course," I say. "Husband and wife." Can't I feel sure of that? Isn't that something sturdy to lean on?

Holmes returns from the kitchen. Is he holding himself a little more stiffly I wonder? Has Maurice done that servant's trick of implying all he knows while very carefully never speaking of it? It could just be my wishful thinking, until Holmes refuses his dessert over Watson's insistence that he try some. Food, it now seems, is disagreeable to him. I wish him nothing but the most profound discomfort. I hope he's off his food forever more.

I can see Holmes's eyes darting all over the house, learning all manner of things he has no business knowing, about me and my family, my past and present. Knowing him from afar, thinking of him almost like a character that Watson had made up for his stories, I do find that I have some measure of sympathy for him, and more than enough understanding of his motives and thoughts. Perhaps it is my woman's intuition, or perhaps we are somewhat alike in ways that have nothing to do with our professions in life, nor the contents of our heads. I was a harder woman than most of my peers, even before the war put a little toughness into us all, and Sherlock Holmes is an uncrackable soul indeed. We are kiln-fired kin, he and I.

He notices me staring at him and twitches half his mouth in a smile at me. He might have been sneering, I can't be sure. Maybe he's developed a facial tic in his old age, from all the cocaine that once buffeted his brain.

"Are you deducing anything, Mrs. Watson?" he asks me quietly. Watson looks up a bit, trying to catch up on what is passing between the two of us.

"I'm only thinking that we have quite a bit in common, Mr. Holmes. Probably too much to ever be very friendly."

"Don't be so sure!" Watson says optimistically, looking between Holmes and I with bright and hopeful eyes. "The two of you could really enjoy each other's company if you chose to! You're both very intellectual and very much concerned with the fate of the world. You might even make a better team with each other than I can make with either of you."

"Yes," said Holmes. "But neither of us would choose it, my friend. There is too much pride in the way, isn't that your point, Mrs. Watson?"

"Quite so," I tell him pleasantly. He does *understand,* this Sherlock Holmes. He doesn't need things explained to him at least.

We both turn to see Watson throw up his hands and tell us, "So be it! What a strange person I must be for wanting everyone to get along. I suppose I brought it on myself by throwing in with you obstinate lot." He goes grumpily back to his cake.

Holmes and I look at each other again, and at last I find him smiling with me, and not at me. How funny Watson is! And how rare that anyone else appreciates him as much as I do.

1895: Black Peter

"I have never known my friend to be in better form, both mental and physical, than in the year '95," Watson wrote. It was July, and Holmes had gotten into a comfortable habit with his drug again, and he was for a time very happy. Watson was none the wiser: "Holmes, like all great artists, lived for his art's sake." Was that not Oscar Wilde's own philosophy? Art for art's sake? Sherlock Holmes had taken up his torch, and it was burning brightly once again.

At the beginning of July Holmes was out of Baker Street all of the time, energized, active again. Watson thought it was only wonderful, that it proved Holmes was at last engaged in a case which challenged him. It was, in reality, the drug that made it seem so. Holmes made himself ridiculously busy, dressing up in disguise, inhabiting all manner of strange places throughout the city, and telling Watson nothing of it. Watson allowed him his secrets, thinking they were harmless, and really rather charming. Holmes came home one morning with a sinister spear under his arm and a flush in his face, like a schoolboy just returned from playing cricket. When at last Holmes was prepared to speak of his new puzzle, he was all a dither over it.

"If you could have looked into the butcher's back shop you would have seen a dead pig swung from a hook in the ceiling," Holmes said, leaning roguishly across the table at Watson. "And a gentleman in his shirt-sleeves furiously stabbing at it with this weapon. I was that energetic person."

Some man had been harpooned at home, and Inspector Hopkins had wired to Holmes for help on the case just the night before. Where Sherlock Holmes borrowed a harpoon from in so short a time is beyond me. He knows enough sailors I suppose, or maybe he just happened to have the thing lying around in his room, a remnant of some man he had known in earlier years. He went to make sure that only a great show of strength could propel a harpoon through flesh in an enclosed area. I'd wager that he might have known that without going to the butcher's himself, but when else would he have a sane excuse to toss a harpoon around at hanging pigs? He took up the job with vigor, and was fresh from his activity when Hopkins arrived at Baker Street full of dejection. Holmes chastised Hopkins for not bringing him into the matter sooner, but was delighted to be invited now. They went to the scene immediately.

They realized that someone had tried to break into the cabin where Black Peter died, but ultimately failed to do so. Holmes would set up an ambush for whoever that was, but it would be several hours before the burglar was likely to return, and so Holmes, in his charming mood, suggested that he and Watson go for a walk. "Let us walk in these beautiful woods, Watson, and give a few hours to the birds and the flowers," he said suggestively.

Holmes linked their arms together and told Hopkins they would see him later in the night. Watson smiled as Holmes led him through the trees. This would be unlike their walks together in London, but not altogether different—on this too Holmes would snatch Watson into dark places to show him some hot affection. They had plenty of time before they would stake out their man, and Holmes was in a sparkling mood over it. He kissed Watson against at least half a dozen trees, he took him by the hand and told him massive amounts of dull information regarding the types of trees, what kinds of debris they drop on the ground, and how the knowledge of seeds and leaves could aid in the detection of crime.

"You pick things up wherever you go, Watson. Much like you leave things behind," Holmes said, his grand profile against the forest backdrop. He cut his eyes sideways at Watson as he spoke.

It seems to me that we pick up people as we go along as well, and if we're lucky, we don't lose them at all.

The man they found breaking into the crime scene that night was not their killer, or at least Holmes did not think he was. He was on the right track from the beginning, looking for an expert harpooner, and a man of considerable strength. He lured that man to him by placing an advertisement for a sea job in the newspaper, sent word for Hopkins to come and be taught a lesson, and then found himself bored right away once it was all finally apparent. Well there's the killer, and no need to even chase him around; so what? How dull it all became.

After neatly cuffing Patrick Cairns, Hopkins admitted his mistake, and told Holmes that he forgot who was the master, and who the student.

"We all learn by experience," Holmes told him. "Your lesson this time is that you should never lose sight of the alternative." Holmes of course was speaking from experience. One should never forget that there are alternatives.

Holmes banished the case from his mind after Hopkins left, whereupon he disappeared to his room for a secret injection, and came back out to spend the night at his chemical table. In the morning he had the sort of dazed serene look that Watson might have recognized from the early days of Holmes's use of cocaine, except that he attributed it to a sleepless night, and ignored it unwisely. Holmes's was the face of someone who was busy on the inside of himself, documenting the minute workings of his body, almost researching his own sensations. Any kind of drug-user might look like that, whether the drug is meant to sharpen or dull the world, whether it is meant to give one clarity or dreams. But Watson was no expert on all that, and he was never suspicious of his friend if he could help it.

No matter—the problem would soon become undeniable.

1895: The Norwood Builder

Cocaine was always second prize to Sherlock Holmes, it was only a bandage on his wound. It got him through the long, lightless days in a city full of dullards and idiots. Sick as it was, he still missed Moriarty; he met the fiendish man only twice, but he felt as if no one had ever known him better, not even Watson, the dear man. He was not stupid—Holmes could not abide people who were very simple, and even the working men he used to go about with had a clever spark about them, though they were not well read—but Watson was never as observant as Holmes deserved. Surely Watson tried, no one ever *tried* harder to know Sherlock Holmes, but it takes one to know one, as the saying goes, and Moriarty was a man after his own fashion. He knew Holmes without having to guess about him. He knew him like a brother.

"From the point of view of the criminal expert, London has become a singularly uninteresting city since the death of the late lamented Professor Moriarty."

Watson thought Holmes was kidding, and joked back with him that the decent citizens of London would disagree. Holmes smiled painfully. Alexander the Great wept when there were no more lands to conquer, no more wars to fight; Sherlock Holmes went back to cocaine.

"Well," he said to Watson. "I must not be selfish." He got up from his breakfast, leaving it nearly untouched. He could hardly taste it anyway. He said London used to be the one place in the world where someone like himself found true purpose, but that was all gone now, and London was like any other city—dreary and teeming with useless hoards of people.

Watson was not aware of all that was being said to him. He was only curious because their "months of partnership had not been so uneventful as Holmes stated" and this was only a "whimsical protest." He should have known better by then that Holmes's whims were more powerful than an average man's hard-thought decisions.

As Holmes opened the paper sadly, a panicked man burst mercifully through the door. He was afraid of being arrested for murder. The news nearly made Holmes happy at last.

Watson saw it. "My companion's expressive face showed a sympathy which was not, I am afraid, entirely unmixed with satisfaction."

Holmes had a pleasant time with this case, while it lasted. Certainly the cantankerous old Oldacre was more interesting than most, and it was an absolute treat to remind Inspector Lestrade that he had not yet surpassed his master either, and could stand a few more lessons. Throughout the whole investigation Lestrade had been boastful and proud, and it was quite gratifying for Holmes to smoke out Mr. Oldacre, and wipe the smug look of superiority off Lestrade's face. He was not at all as conciliatory as Hopkins; he had been at it longer and thought himself better, and was proved wrong once again. Lestrade went home to his family at night; he didn't live and breathe for his work like Holmes did, and therefore he would never overtake him at this game. Until Lestrade did nothing but live and die by the chase, he would never outrun Sherlock Holmes.

Well, this case pleased Holmes in the sense that it was better than sitting at home and contriving reasons to disappear into his room every half an hour for another injection. Lestrade was of the opinion that this case was the biggest thing Holmes had ever done, but it was not by half. He didn't even care to put his name on it, the solution meant so little to him. What did it matter, indeed, that one old man had tried to revenge himself on a woman who had spurned him? What petty nonsense people filled their lives with, and yet still thought them full.

Instead of making his cases better, the drug was replacing them as the source of his excitement. Holmes kept studying Watson to see if he suspected, but unless Watson had become an expert at deception, he saw nothing, and was perfectly happy. He was pleased that Holmes no longer exhausted himself on cases, not realizing that this was the only way Holmes had learned to keep his hands clean, and his pursuits honest. The cocaine only kept him afloat; it could not bring him to shore.

The next case would be the last we the public would hear about for a while. Sherlock Holmes would have his own personal problems to solve after that.

1895: The Bruce-Partington Plans

The weather did not help Holmes that November when a dense yellow fog settled over London and would not let up for days. He tried to set himself something useful, cross-indexing his books and studying music, and only going for the cocaine bottle when he felt himself descending to a place from which he could not return at will.

Watson did not see the strain until the fourth day, when Holmes's will was crumbling under his want, when he was using the drug and letting it crawl through his veins unexpressed. Holmes was agitated to such a pitch that he could not stay seated; he paced and carried on and couldn't have given a damn what Watson noticed. It was nearly making him mad. He could feel the force that must have driven Moriarty to horrendous and complicated crimes, the same impulse as an artist before a blank canvas who feels the need to fill it from his own over-brimming mind. Holmes called Watson to the window to try and make him see it.

"Look out of this window, Watson. See how the figures loom up, are dimly seen, and then blend once more into the cloud-bank. The thief or the murderer could roam London on such a day as the tiger does the jungle, unseen until he pounces, and then evident only to his victim." It disgusted Sherlock Holmes that no one else could see the potential, and yet he was not a thief or a killer! Where were they all, the useless class of criminals he was supposed to hunt? Why would they pass up such a golden opportunity as this yellow, awful fog?

"There have been numerous petty thefts," Watson told him, but Holmes only snorted in contempt. Nearly six months of daily use of cocaine had built up in him, and he was feeling the effects, though he was ill-equipped to know it. He thought he was only sinking again when he was actually plateauing. The difference was the way his body acted, the way he twitched and itched and moved without ceasing, rather than the corpse-like catatonia he knew in his natural state. He could have clawed his own skin with his restless mania. He could have clawed someone else's.

"This great and somber stage is set for something more worthy than that," Holmes said of the robberies. He sneered out the window at the roiling smog. "It is fortunate for this community that I am not a criminal."

"It is indeed!" Watson told him heartily. What was all this talk? What was wrong with Holmes?

Holmes knew of several men who wanted him dead. He thought back to August, to Mr. Oldacre's empty, impotent threat. "I have you to thank for a good deal," he'd said. "Perhaps I'll pay my debt someday." How many pathetic creatures had sworn their revenge on him, and yet here he was! Standing in front of a perfect day for murder, and standing unmolested. Holmes wondered if he was his own assassin, how long would it take him to accomplish the deed? He scoffed that a day like this would never pass without a serious attempt.

This talk sounded almost as if Holmes *wanted* to kill himself, as if he wanted to put himself out of his misery.

It was all unnerving to Watson. The weather had dampened him too, but not so much as all that. He was at last feeling the rumblings of Holmes's turmoil, and it was not that he was blind to it, more that he was not looking. For six months Holmes had been lying to him, and he was an expert liar. Anyone would be fooled if Sherlock Holmes meant to fool them, but Watson especially did not go searching for betrayals that should not be there in the first place.

The uncomfortable moment was relieved by a telegram from Mycroft, announcing that he would soon be coming by Baker Street. Holmes was stirred with a feeling like hope; Mycroft never moved out of his regular way. What treat might await him if it could disturb Mycroft in his recumbence? If anyone could save him, it would be his brother; after all, Mycroft had done as much for him once before, when their parents were lost, even though it was not in his lethargic nature. In fact it was not for either of them to go out of his way for the other. A family trait if there ever was one, along with their remarkable minds. Did Watson have the capacity to even grasp what it all meant? How would he like to know what Mycroft truly did for a living? He had alluded to Watson during

The Greek Interpreter that Mycroft was a part of the British government, but by God it was much more than that.

"I did not know you quite so well in those days," Holmes told Watson. "You would also be right in a sense if you said that occasionally he is the British government." Holmes really was filled with a childishness around his bigger brother. To impress Mycroft, knowing that his mental capacity was more massive than his frame, was a reward rivaled by nothing else in the world. And to have Mycroft come to him at last! Why, it was like Mycroft knew his baby brother was in need.

It did not look like a warm, familial relationship from the outside, but that is the way of things with men named Holmes. Mycroft demanded that Holmes drop his petty problems and concentrate on this irritating problem that had landed in his lap. Holmes was nevertheless anxious to please him, reassuring him that he cared little for recognition, less even than Mycroft himself cared (an utter lie), but that it was only the love of the game he was after. Watson smiled to see Holmes acting like such a puppy, but the smile was brief on his face. Before they departed from Mycroft, as Holmes dressed and he and Lestrade busily bounced ideas between one another about the solution of the mystery, Mycroft waved Watson nearer to him and leaned his impressive head close to Watson's ear.

"My brother is not well," he said to Watson. "What do you know of it?"

"Oh," Watson said in surprise at Mycroft's blunt question. "He has been down lately because of the smog..."

Mycroft shook his head. "Sherlock isn't so capricious as to let the air disturb him. He looks ill, and his eyes seem feverish. What does he take into his body? Is he eating well? Does he drink much? Smoke? I don't recall many vices or imagine him prone to them."

Watson pulled on his mustache nervously, feeling like a nanny being grilled by the mother. Had he been slacking on the health of his charge?

"Well," Watson said. "I wrote of his use of cocaine a few years back, but he hasn't touched it since..." Watson trailed off, before saying too much.

"In your stories, you mean?" Mycroft asked lazily. "I don't read them, they're positive rot. But cocaine, you say?" Mycroft arched his eyebrow, and then began to nod heavily. "I might see him at that. Be sure to check him for it!" After that brief order he was gone, lumbering back to his customary orbit, without even saying goodbye to his brother.

Watson turned around to find Holmes and Lestrade impatient with him. It was time to go, on with his coat! He tried to watch Holmes, tried to see into his eyes, but what was the difference between "cocaine and ambition" as he had phrased it years before? It had been a long time since Watson had seen them in contrast. He was keen to remember it now.

Standing on the rails where the dead government worker was found, Holmes was struck with the hard, quivering stance of a hunting dog. Watson frowned while watching his friend. He took in every detail. Holmes "was a different man from the limp and lounging figure in the mouse-colored dressing-gown who had prowled so restlessly only a few hours before round the fog-girt room." Holmes was alive, but was it only the case that had revived him?

"There is material here," Holmes said. "There is scope. I am dull indeed not to have understood its possibilities." Was that an indication that his mind was compromised? That in his normal state he might have known better? Watson was no good at this; he was no detective.

After pulling out a map of London, Holmes took to the streets on his own, telling Watson to wait for him, and confident enough to say that Watson may even now begin his story about how they saved the State. Watson was at last thoroughly suspicious: "I felt some reflection of his elation in my own mind, for I knew well that he would not depart so far from his usual austerity of demeanor unless there was a good cause for exultation." What was that cause? Which case had him so pleased, the criminal case or the morocco one? Watson resolved to find out for sure.

Watson spent his hours at home that evening cleaning and straightening, a thin excuse to search their rooms thoroughly. But all that he was able to find was what Holmes asked him to bring to dinner: a jemmy, a dark lantern, a chisel, and a revolver. He met Holmes to hear his theory of how their murdered body got on top of a train, and his excuses for his own behavior: "When I found that the leading international agent, who had just left London, lived in a row of houses which abutted upon the Underground, I was so pleased that you were a little astonished at my sudden frivolity."

"Oh, that was it, was it?"

"Yes," said Holmes seriously. "That was it."

At last Watson was suspicious in his own right. Once again, just like during the Wisteria Lodge murder, Holmes told Watson that the case demanded they break the law. Or not "they" really—Watson would stand guard in the street and watch Holmes commit the actual crime. It started to dawn on Watson just how long he had been oblivious to Holmes's shifts, and just how dangerous it was to let Holmes get a taste of lawlessness, especially if he was (as Watson had almost entirely despaired of) injecting cocaine again. But what could he do right then? Holmes always told him he was a man of action, and it was the truth. He would not derail progress so important. He agreed to do whatever Holmes asked. He would follow him into hell if that was where Sherlock Holmes was headed, and it just so happened…

Watson's heart was sinking as Holmes stood to shake his hand. "I knew you would not shrink at the last," Holmes told him, his gaze softening almost imperceptibly. "For a moment I saw something in his eyes which was nearer to tenderness than I had ever seen before," Watson wrote. What he did not record was that this look nearly broke his heart.

What did such emotion even mean if it was artificially stimulated? Watson would make sure before he absolutely despaired, but… Could Mycroft really be mistaken? And wasn't Watson totting up enough circumstantial evidence to convince the average English jury? His answer would have to wait for the night, for he had a case to assist in, but my husband was greatly troubled by the investigations he would soon have to make himself.

Watson ended up going along with Holmes in the burglary, following him upstairs to where their victim had been transferred through his own window onto the roof of a train car and left to pitch and sway as the machine would. The smudges on the window sill were enough to confirm it.

"So far we are justified. What do you think of it, Watson?" Holmes asked breathlessly in the dark.

"A masterpiece," Watson said grimly. "You have never risen to a greater height."

"I cannot agree with you there," said Holmes, also grim. Still nothing could reach him the way that Moriarty did, nothing could ever make him so grand. Like a chilly finger down his spine, that is how Moriarty touched him; the only man who ever made Holmes look over his shoulder.

Holmes made a full confession to Lestrade about breaking into the dead man's house. Lestrade could hardly believe it, and Watson too was aghast—what was all the secrecy about, if he was just going to blurt it out to the nearest official? Mycroft too, in his own languid way, was also surprised. He shot up an eyebrow, aimed at Watson, and returned his attention to his sizzling brother.

Lestrade was the first to speak of it. "No wonder you get results that are beyond us in the force. But some of these days you'll go too far, and you'll find yourself and your friend in trouble," Lestrade warned, also glancing at Watson, as if he were worried for him too.

"For England, home and beauty—eh, Watson?" My husband moved his mouth like a guppy, unable to really answer Holmes's extreme excitement. "Martyrs on the altar of our country. But what do you think of it, Mycroft?" Holmes asked anxiously.

"Excellent, Sherlock!" Mycroft boomed loudly, his face serious. He would not disappoint his brother in this moment. They made an appointment to catch up with their suspect that night (the man had been dispatching cryptic messages through the paper), and Lestrade and Mycroft left, both uneasily. Watson remained behind.

It was painful for Watson to talk around these events when he wrote this story, but the case was too important to leave out of the fullness of his record. He did his best to disguise the events in the background, but I can see them plainly. Once you know where to look, it's all there quite clearly. Holmes threw himself into work of a different sort, every few hours going to his room, and coming back with skipping steps. It disturbed Watson to a terrific degree.

"For my own part," Watson wrote, "I had none of this power of detachment, and the day, in consequence, appeared to be interminable." At last it was time for the conclusion of their investigation. They met with Mycroft and Lestrade, went to the meeting place, and laid in wait. Holmes was on a preternatural plane of perception and heard their man approaching long before anyone else. When at last the subject was revealed, it was the very unfraternal brother of another man who met his death in the whole mess, from the stress of it all. Watson could sympathize.

Holmes was taken aback by the identity of their man, and he told Watson to write him down as an ass for not realizing it before. The man was put away and would eventually die quickly into his prison sentence. Mycroft patted Watson heavily on the shoulder as they all departed, warning him with a last look to keep after Sherlock, to take care of him properly. He was a doctor after all, and someone had to do it. Mycroft had put in his time already, when Sherlock was a boy, and it was now Watson's responsibility.

Watson kept his mouth shut for a while, trying to figure it out on his own, using Holmes's own methods. But Watson could not confirm one way or the other whether Holmes was truly back on the drug. At one moment it would be all but obvious that he was on the brink of destruction from it, exhausted to the point of collapse, on the edge of a breakdown. But the next moment Holmes would seem well and calm, like he had been getting regular exercise and eating healthy portions since the day he was born. Watson knew the way to find out for sure; get a look at Holmes's arm, see if there were fresh marks from the needle. But Watson couldn't bring himself to do it for weeks. Even messages from Mycroft every half-month with nothing more than an annoyed question mark upon them were not enough to force a confrontation.

However, when Holmes came back home with an emerald tie-pin from the dead man's fiancée, gay as ever, as if the whole case had been nothing but fun and gain, Watson at last broke. He asked Holmes closer, saying that he wanted to see the ornament on his neck, and then he clasped Holmes by the wrist and pushed back his sleeve in one rough motion.

And there were the marks.

Holmes slapped Watson as he ripped his arm back. He started to breathe in a ragged sort of way, pacing up and down the room, shooting dark glances at Watson, who only stayed still, trying not to lose himself to his emotions. Holmes's face burned red with embarrassment and outrage, but it was Watson who eventually spoke first.

"Mycroft told me I should check," he said. Holmes halted in his tracks and his face blanched to white.

"Mycroft knows?"

Watson's lips twisted like he'd just bitten something bitter. Was Mycroft the only one he worried about disappointing then? No one else in all the world who he should be ashamed in front of?

"Apparently it was perfectly obvious to him," Watson said from his chair by the fire. "Me, I saw nothing amiss, even though it's been going on for months, hasn't it?"

"I didn't want to worry you," Holmes said, sitting down at last across from Watson. The light from the fire cast half of his face in darkness. He looked like a man with two faces, a man divided.

"How long?" Watson asked him.

"It's been since May," Holmes said. He had been deceiving Watson for some time. At least he admitted it.

"It's starting to tell on you," Watson said. "I only saw it after your brother pointed it out to me, but you can't deny that you're acting rashly, that your body has become dependent on the drug. Shall I tell you what your symptoms are? What they will become? Are you not restless enough without cocaine? Do you not tax your body enough already? My God, Holmes, I cannot think of a worse drug for a man like you! I'm surprised that your heart hasn't burst already!"

"Don't be so dramatic, Watson, I've used it longer than this before and not dropped dead."

"Yes, but that was ten years ago, Holmes! You aren't a young man anymore! And with the strain you put on yourself I'd wager your heart's even older than you are!"

"Keep your voice down!" Holmes hissed. "You'll disturb Mrs. Hudson."

"You don't care about her," Watson said, shaking his head sadly. "You're only ashamed, Holmes, and well you should be. It's weak of you."

"Weak?" Holmes asked, his eyes flashing dangerously. "You think this is what weakness looks like? It isn't an easy balance to strike, Doctor. Maybe the drug is killing me, but it'll do it slower than a bullet."

"You…you don't mean to suggest you'd harm yourself?" Watson asked. The suggestion of death again was all it took to douse Watson's anger, but it only inflamed Holmes.

"I might save a lot of men a great deal of trouble if I did," Holmes said, getting up to pace again, his hands clenching and unclenching as he went. "You're a simple man, Watson, very painfully simple sometimes, and you don't understand what this is like. It's something wrong with me, it's a sickness that cannot go untreated."

"This isn't a cure, Holmes!" Watson said emphatically, though he was now keeping his voice down. "It's poison!"

"It works, Watson. It's the only thing that does." Holmes moved without ceasing, some part of him was wringing or twitching even when he stood still. It was a terrible thing for Watson to see a man as extraordinary as Sherlock Holmes so sadly afflicted.

"I won't watch you destroy yourself, Holmes," Watson said seriously. "I care entirely too much about you. If you can't stop, I…" Watson trailed off. He could not imagine going back to their early days, of keeping his mouth shut while Holmes corrupted himself in tiny measurements. He'd rather never set eyes on Holmes again than see his powers wither away.

But no, that wasn't true. Watson would much rather alleviate Holmes of this addiction, to save *him* for once, to be *his* hero. He stood up resolutely.

"Not to worry, my friend, we'll get this fiend off your back." Holmes was quite a bit less enthused by the prospect, only holding his head in his hand and rubbing his face like he is trying to erase himself. "Where are you keeping the stuff, Holmes? We'll start right away."

Holmes made no motion to fetch the drug for Watson. The silence got longer, it was horribly awkward, and the only sound in the room was the impatient movement of Holmes's foot under the table and the crackling of the fire.

"Don't you want to be rid of the habit?" Watson asked finally.

Holmes stood up wearily and beckoned Watson closer, put an arm over his shoulders, led him into his bedroom. He sat Watson down on the bed and opened his safe. Several spent bottles of cocaine were lying next to quite a few more full ones. Holmes dragged his fingernails across the bottles, making a pretty tinkling sound. He pulled one empty and one full bottle out and brought them over to Watson.

"Can it really mean so much to you, Watson?" he asked, rolling the bottles gently in his hand.

"Is it really that much to you?" Watson countered. "You are not a man of moderation, Holmes, this will consume you entirely if you let it."

Holmes handed Watson the empty bottle and said, "I don't want to stop doing it here. Find another place, a hospital perhaps, but private. And don't bother me about this," he held up the full bottle, "until you've found it. Those are my conditions."

"I know the very place," Watson said immediately, for indeed he had been looking for a reason to take Holmes out to Colonel Hayter's country estate since he had come back to life. He reached for the bottle in Holmes's hand.

Holmes squeezed down on it and would not relinquish. "You can have them when we're disembarking from the train," he said, and then ushered Watson out of his room. He shut the door and locked it against his friend. Watson started to make the plans immediately, before Holmes could change his prodigious mind.

1896: The Veiled Lodger

This is the first of my husband's stories I reference that has not yet been published. A great many of Holmes's later stories (post-resurrection) were drafted before the war and will indeed be published very soon, but Watson is particular now that I have been catching his errors that there not be any more mistakes in the stories, and so they languish here in our house as he and I both pore over them. Not that most of what I know about Holmes's movements in 1896 will ever be written. In fact, the Veiled Lodger incident is the only one I see during this year, and that is because Holmes was rather indisposed for the majority of it. Truly most of these documents are ready to go before the public, but the public is not desirous of them yet. It has been a long few years of hardship, and people need a break from the never-ending talk of horror and misery. People, that is, who are not Sherlock Holmes.

It was a joke between Watson and Colonel Hayter while they rehabilitated Holmes that one of them should go out and murder someone so their charge would have something to do. Not that they joked much, because Holmes was really a pitiable sight, petulant at first, but then dreadfully struck down by his own malfunctions. The first day he arrived, Colonel Hayter greeted both men with a bracing hug each. He was unique in his relation to the pair of them, and as a group all three men found a strangely easy way to coexist, until of course Holmes had to be quarantined. They put him on the second floor so that he could not easily escape, but also so that if he did fling himself from the window, he wouldn't cause himself permanent injury. For all his experience as a doctor, Watson knew very little about weaning a man from cocaine. He treated Holmes as if he might go mad at any moment. He had seen the effects of opium, as had Colonel Hayter, who had pulled his own head out of that magical cloud of smoke after returning to England from war abroad, but opium was not cocaine.

Holmes tolerated their dramatics like a man with bigger concerns. He would quit again to keep Watson, and because he *had* noticed disturbing changes in himself. He overlooked things every now and then, only little details, but his whole career relied on little details and his ability to know them for what they were. It absolutely terrified Holmes to think of losing his one true talent. He did not want to ruin all of his careful construction, the monolith he had built of his mind. Watson was probably right about that at least—Holmes's vanity, his artistic integrity, his commitment to himself—even if he was wrong about what withdrawal would do to him. Holmes had dragged himself out of this hole once before, he knew he could do it again. It was only tiresome having to do it in front of an audience.

It was his unique psychology that made Holmes so susceptible to cocaine; someone else might use it every day and give it up at a moment's notice with only the barest discomfort. The hold it had over Holmes was more powerful than the way it made his heart race, or the way it made the world around him sharpen into focus; it let him touch the breathless hope that used to drive him, the feeling that he was searching for something beyond all the answers to his cases, and the expectation that he would one day find it. That sensation had gone away from Holmes, and he missed it dearly.

But he felt like he might be able to stand the yearning for a while again. Certainly losing Watson would not help him, and Watson wouldn't tolerate the drug at all. Holmes had stopped his use once before, he was sure he could do it again, and he prepared for his stay at Colonel Hayter's like it was a second tour of war. It isn't a pretty fight, but he'd waged it before and come out alive. Of course, it was easy to be brave while the drug was still in his body.

Only one day after giving it up, Holmes felt uncomfortable in his skin. Nausea kept him from attempting to eat dinner, though he did sit at the table with Watson and Hayter, and every word they spoke to each other bit him like an insect. They were chatting about some kind of political move that Holmes was unaware of since it had absolutely no impact on the criminal class, and even though Watson and Hayter disagreed, they did so amiably. How irritating! Holmes was quite in the mood for a shouting match to break out, but he wasn't so far gone that he couldn't contain his aggravation; Holmes pressed the tines of his fork into his wrist to keep from flipping the table over on their pleasant little debate.

Food disgusted him, daylight exhausted him, and he took to his room after a few days to get away from the revolting, happy world. It disappointed him more and more as the drug left his system. It seemed to reject him as much as he rejected it. Holmes lay prostrate on his bed in an agony of nothingness. Pain would have been preferable to him then. Pain would at least have been something to reckon with.

Watson bent to his friend's fluctuating moods as best he knew how. When Holmes was desultory, Watson tried to engage him; when Holmes was hateful, Watson was patient with him; when Holmes lay in the midst of a seizure of nihilism, Watson held his unfeeling hand. When Holmes smarted off, Watson reminded him of why it was important to quit this drug. When Holmes complained that his mind was putrefying around such non-academic company, Watson brought him a book.

Watson had read *The Strange Case of Doctor Jekyll and Mr. Hyde* during his hard times, and thought Holmes might get as much from it as he did. Something about Jekyll's responsibility for Hyde, the way the man gave into his desires to be someone who cared not for consequence, who cared not for society, nor for his own best interests—Holmes could surely relate to that, and understand that destruction was the only inevitability if he did not stop in time? Well, Holmes must have grasped the analogy, because when next Watson returned to the room, he found the book being thrown at him in contempt. Holmes never was one for literature.

"I'm supposed to learn my lesson from that?" Holmes asked from a bed he hadn't left in days, damp with sweat and tangled in frustration.

"I thought it echoed your struggle, yes," Watson told him enduringly. You had to be strong with Holmes; only unwavering consistency would have any effect on him at all.

"Idiot," Holmes spat, and it was unclear ultimately whether he meant Dr. Watson or Dr. Jekyll. "Hyde is naturally the better choice—what is the use of position and wealth if you're sick with longing for a life unlived?"

Watson retrieved his rather battered copy of the story and returned it to the bedside table. Holmes had written angrily in all the margins, the way he had done with his Bible, filling every free space with criticism, skepticism, and scorn. Watson leafed through the Stevenson book, and hoped that he would soon see a day when he could show it to Holmes and they would both laugh heartily at it. Remember our hardships! How distant they become.

"You aren't sympathetic with the way Doctor Jekyll feels?" Watson asked as he flipped through the pages. "How about when he says, 'To cast in my lot with Jekyll, was to die to those appetites which I had long secretly indulged and had of late begun to pamper.' That's like you and your crimes, Holmes, you and your cocaine. 'To cast in with Hyde, was to die a thousand interests and aspirations, and to become, at a blow and for ever, despised and friendless.' Does that not do you justice?"

Watson had consistently held his breath at this point in the narrative, the moment when Jekyll acknowledged that the bargain was unequal—anyone should naturally choose to be the socially esteemed and wealthy doctor, to be kind and liked and healthy, except for one problem: Hyde never pined to be Doctor Jekyll, but Jekyll longed always to be the selfish, uncaring Hyde. Jekyll would "suffer smartingly" his loss, and Hyde would feel no loss at all. It made Watson shudder for the nature of man. It made him worry for Sherlock Holmes.

"Jekyll's a coward," Holmes told him. "A real man would be able to accept his nature, not work to split it in half. I don't pass the years lying to myself, at the very least," Holmes said with disgust.

"'The fires of abstinence,'" Watson said. "That is what you feel now."

"Shut up, Watson!" Holmes said as he snatched the book from Watson's hands and threw it out the door once more. He was doing enough for Watson without having to hear all his ignorant thoughts about it, apparently. Watson left in an injured hurry, slamming the door behind him and kicking the book through the railings of the balustrade where it fell a full story and clattered onto the first floor.

Colonel Hayter was more than tolerant of these small scenes. He loved Watson, he desired Holmes, but he was a man of ascetic training, and he controlled himself all the while. As a host to Holmes's rehabilitation, he managed to be a friend to both him and Watson, a thing perfectly impossible for most of mankind to accomplish. Hayter was not only a friend, but in some respects a mending wall; when Holmes complained that Watson was a small-minded simpleton, Hayter told him the stories behind his scars, and of how Watson had patiently saved him from injury, infection, and despair as his doctor in the field. Likewise when Watson grew dejected at Holmes's wretched attitude, Hayter reminded him of Holmes's brilliance, of his magnificence; could anyone be so great without paying a price for it? Well: here was the debt collector. If the State would be continually saved, someone would have to gather the fragments of Holmes and hold them together. Holmes and Watson both suffered for the greater good, so Colonel Hayter would do his part as well. For Queen and country and the love that is unspeakable. He was an honorable man.

At last it was possible to bring an ill-tempered Holmes back to Baker Street. Watson stayed in a hotel for a few weeks, thinking it best to let Holmes find his own independence in their rooms, and because they were pretty well sick of each other by then. Holmes called Watson in on the *Veiled Lodger* case because it was one they had found together, during the time of Watson's first marriage when he was back in his bachelor rooms, waffling between wife and Life, between domesticity and danger.

They went together out to see a woman who mentioned Abbas Parva, the place where a man named Ronder had been killed rather suspiciously by a lion in 1889. The woman they met was his disgruntled wife, a woman whose face was mutilated in the same attack. She wanted to make a clean breast of the old incident, and she did, saying that she would die soon and wanted the truth to be known.

Sherlock Holmes was at this time on his own, staying clean of cocaine but wildly unhappy about it. He was not in a patient mood at all. When he suspected Mrs. Ronder of suicidal intentions, he snapped at her, "Your life is not your own. Keep your hands off it."

Had Holmes not just been through months of distasteful withdrawal to make him realize that very thing? Had he not only himself just realized that his life was not merely his own, but that others relied on him as well? Mrs. Ronder defied him to name someone she was of use to, and even showed him her mutilated face, asking if Holmes would bear such a burden. Holmes did not flinch. He told her, "The example of patient suffering is in itself the most precious of all lessons to an impatient world." He knew it well enough himself. He could admire her for continuing on, even though it pained her terribly. He was called to do the same thing, and it was comforting to meet a fellow sufferer.

When Mrs. Ronder sent Holmes her poison with a note saying she would take his advice and carry on, Watson decided to come back home. If Holmes could now inspire others with his temperance and control, then he must be in a place of remission and health. Holmes welcomed his one friend back with as much enthusiasm as he could find. He was dampened, it seemed, permanently. He was damaged by too much awareness, by the heights he'd reached with Moriarty, by the furthest extremities of life. He knew too much, but he tried to forget. For Watson, he did try.

Holmes would in the end suffer a great deal of monotony to have Watson back in his rooms, and he really did keep clean of his solution for a while, for the sake of someone else. But even his best efforts in this area were not sufficient. It would take some time for both he and Watson to discover that fact, and in the meantime there would be more cases, more adventures, and just enough happiness to sustain them fondly towards one another in their subsequent years apart.

1897: The Missing Three-Quarter

Holmes had stopped using the drug, but he had only just begun complaining about it. Should a few days go by without a case, and if Holmes was not unconscious due to one of his strange fits, he would make little nasty comments about how glad he was to be saved from the ravages of cocaine so that he could die from boredom instead. Even when he received a note promising some "terrible misfortune" that February morning, he still had something sneering to say about it: "Even the most insignificant problem would be welcome in these stagnant days." Watson kept a close scrutiny on Holmes when work was scarce. It was hard to know when Holmes was only letting off his frustration and when he was teetering near a fateful decision. Perhaps he was always seriously contemplating going back to the drug. Perhaps he always would.

"Things had indeed been very slow with us," Watson wrote, and he meant both the business of detection and their careful rebuilding now that Holmes was recovered. Watson was willing to put in the work, however, because he hoped this was the last of it. "For years I had gradually weaned him from that drug mania which had threatened once to check his remarkable career." He knew that if Holmes could have it his way, he wouldn't ever want the drug again; it was not like in the early days when he used the substance for fun—he would much rather feel the thrill of a challenge and the natural sparks of his own brain. "I knew that under ordinary conditions he no longer craved for this artificial stimulus," Watson said, "but I was well aware that the fiend was not dead but sleeping, and I have known that the sleep was a light one and the waking near when in periods of idleness I have seen the drawn look upon Holmes's face, and the brooding of his deep-set and inscrutable eyes."

Watson blessed this man Overton and whatever tragedy had befallen him, for he would help lift Holmes out of his perilous doldrums, even it was only for an hour. Overton was missing a rugby player on the eve of an important game. Holmes laughed when the man asked him in astonishment where he had been living if he didn't know about sports—who could not have heard of Godfrey Staunton, the young athlete that could not be found?

"You live in a different world to me, Mr. Overton," Holmes told him. "A sweeter and healthier one." Watson nodded to their client, trying to reassure him. He looked like he thought they might be making fun of him, but it was only the honest truth.

The case was good enough if there were no other prospects, and they found Staunton's hotel room with very little in it besides his hysterically miserly uncle. That amused Holmes for a bit, as did having the opportunity to lie to the girl at the telegram office, though some people are so gullible that to Holmes it seems a waste to be creative towards them. And yet he kept on with the case as long as it was able to keep him out of his stifling rooms, his stifling thoughts.

Their next point of contact with the missing man was a Dr. Armstrong. They'd found a receipt from him in the hotel room, and it proved that Staunton had need of a medical man. Watson did not know Armstrong's name. Since selling his practice essentially to Holmes, Watson had been living a life of relative leisure (his only obligation being to occasionally act as Holmes's nursemaid and scratching post). However, Dr. Armstrong had heard of Holmes already, and told the detective right away that he did not approve of his profession.

Holmes found himself liking the man's quick honesty, his deep eyes, his clear intelligence, despite the look of frowning disapproval on his face. Holmes went to tease him: "In that, Doctor, you will find yourself in agreement with every criminal in the country."

Armstrong would not be toyed with. He thought Holmes was an agent of his friend's penny-pinching uncle and had already made up his mind to let slip no secrets. He told Holmes, "Where your calling is more open to criticism is when you pry into the secrets of private individuals, and when you incidentally waste the time of men who are more busy than yourself."

Holmes nearly smiled. What a fine thrust! How good of him to know at a glance that Holmes wished to be a busy man, a man of purpose, and that this area was where his pride might be wounded. He questioned Armstrong by tiny steps until at last he got a fiery reaction out of him. Armstrong threw them out of his house and would not hear them any further.

Holmes was chipper on the street outside, and Watson was very happy to see him like that until he understood the reason why. "Dr. Leslie Armstrong is certainly a man of energy and character," Holmes said. "I have not seen a man who if he turns his talents that way, was more calculated to fill the gap left by the illustrious Moriarty." Watson didn't know if he should be more offended by the clear sparkle of attraction in Holmes's eyes or by the admiration for Moriarty and criminal potential in his voice; both were disturbing to him, and not exactly what he would wish for Holmes to find pleasure in during this precarious time.

But even this mood, as much as Holmes was enjoying its archness, did not last the day. Holmes went off on his own and came back late, pale and tired and having made an enemy of Armstrong's coachman as well by poking around and trying to shadow the doctor's movements. He took out his frustration on Watson, as per his usual, disdaining every suggestion the man put forth. He was getting fixated on Armstrong—how long had it been since anyone had given him the slip?—and the preoccupation was mutual.

The next morning at breakfast Armstrong sent Holmes a pert little note saying that Holmes would never follow him anywhere. Holmes smiled wanly.

"An outspoken, honest antagonist is the doctor. Well, well, he excites my curiosity, and I must really know before I leave him."

Holmes left Watson the next day as well, and once again returned dismayed by his lack of success in trying to pursue Armstrong's movements. Overton and Cambridge lost their rugby match without their star three-quarter, and the day after that, Watson got a shock of disappointment too. He woke up to see Holmes by the fire with his syringe in his hand. He let out a groan of sadness. His face must have looked tragic.

"No, no, my dear fellow, there is no cause for alarm," Holmes said, setting the needle down like he had been caught with stolen property. "It is not upon this occasion the instrument of evil."

Watson believed Holmes that it might have some legitimate use in the investigation, but it was disturbing nonetheless to see the expression that Holmes had on his face as he contemplated the syringe. It was a quiet, dark storm in his eyes of hatred and desire. Why would he even keep the thing? Why bring it with him? God, he must keep his morocco case on him all the time like some morbid talisman.

Holmes told Watson to eat while he himself did not, though he warned Watson they would not stop or sup until they found where Dr. Armstrong went each day in his carriage. The syringe was full of aniseed, and he meant to transfer the pungent substance to Armstrong's vehicle so that a dog named Pompey might follow it. Almost any vessel might have served this purpose, but Holmes had out his syringe anyway. He could not help but nip after a dangerous game, after all; he was as much a hunting creature as the mongrel he held leashed in his hand.

Soon enough they were able to follow Dr. Armstrong, and they found poor Staunton weeping at the deathbed of his secret, consumptive young wife. All that Watson could see positive in the whole mess was that Armstrong finally saw that Holmes would not expose Staunton's marriage to his uncle, and grasped his hand and called him a good man. And yet for all that, as they left "that house of grief" for the winter day outside, the look in Holmes's eyes was almost as blank as the dead girl's. Contentment in his heart was like water through a sieve.

1897: The Devil's Foot

I am amused by how Watson's narrative changes to fit Holmes's preferences; though he claimed to never approve of the stories, the stories still bend to please him. Where in the beginning Holmes had been angry that he got no notoriety and all his talent went to the credit of the police, in later years his fame was portrayed as a grand burden to him, apparently one he bore in protest. It was true when Watson said that Holmes liked to sit and smirk at all the misplaced credit that was heaped on his Scotland Yard inspectors, but I doubt very much the purity of his motivations. He may have loved the work above all else, but he didn't hate that his name preceded him wherever he went.

By 1910 when this story was compiled and published, Watson was away from Baker Street, and married to me. He got a note from Holmes (I don't know what kind of game it was for him—those whimsical telegrams that could disturb Watson for up to a week obsessing about just what Holmes might be thinking); the note told him to write about "the Cornish horror" because the case was so strange. I am skeptical that was the reason behind it, knowing the story as I do now. Watson wondered what could have possibly brought the case back to his mind, but it is easily seen: he was missing his Watson, and he was remembering one of their most tender moments, and he wanted Watson to remember it too.

"It was, then, in the spring of the 1897 that Holmes's iron constitution showed some symptoms of giving way in the face of constant hard work of a most exacting kind, aggravated, perhaps, by occasional indiscretions of his own."

It had been hard for Holmes giving up his chemical comfort, not as hard as what drove him back to it, but he and Watson both knew that Holmes's bad moods tended to compound with one another. He was doing tolerably well, but how to keep him getting better? A month after the Missing Three-Quarter, Watson and Holmes consulted with a practicing physician who advised Holmes to "surrender himself to complete rest" if he wanted to avoid absolute breakdown.

"I find a good breakdown refreshing every now and again," Holmes told him flippantly.

Dr. Agar threatened to bar Holmes from practice all together, and Holmes snorted at the idea, as if anyone could hold such power over him. The doctor who shared his bed could hardly get him to stop killing himself, so a consulting physician had almost no chance at all.

"We could go out to the country, Holmes," Watson said. "It worked out all right for you last year." He was alluding to the recovery at Colonel Hayter's estate. He shouldn't have.

"And how well did a vacation serve me the first time we visited Colonel Hayter?" Watson had not forgotten about it, but he thought enough had changed in ten years for a vacation to produce different results. He wouldn't take Holmes to see any of his old army companions this time; better to isolate him and find him some true rest. "You may actually enjoy a rest now, you know. You aren't the same man you were back then, Holmes."

"I've been the same man all my life," he grumbled miserably, but at last he relented. He was too tired to really fight about it, and Watson was resolute.

They went out to the Cornish peninsula, a nice bleak, dreary part of the coast that even Watson couldn't help thinking of as a death trap, for Mounts Bay was no place for ships, and the shores were barren and uninviting. An evil place he called it, where countless sailors had met a smashing death on the rocks. And that was just the sea! Surrounding them were deserted moors and the remnants of an ancient village that was nothing but stone slabs and burial mounds. Hideous.

It made Holmes smile, as Watson thought it might. He knew better than to take him anywhere pleasant, and at first Holmes responded well to the "sinister glamour" of the atmosphere. They had fond memories attached to moors after all, and Holmes had ordered some books thinking he'd compile a very dry thesis on the origin of the Cornish language. Watson was glad for a moment, imagining a peaceful retirement for them both someday, thinking wouldn't it be nice if they could be like this always.

But the world would never leave them alone. They made some slim few acquaintances out there, the vicar and his lodger Mr. Tregennis. Watson was highly annoyed that their provincial little mysteries should come and burst his happy bubble, but there was no taking a case away from Holmes once he had it; easier to pry a fox's throat from a hound's jaw. He must be satisfied that he has rattled all the life out of it before you may take it from him.

Watson gave up any hope of a peaceful time; how could he expect Holmes to return to his studies when two men were laughing with mad terror at a card game with their dead sister? Their one surviving brother, Mr. Tregennis, thought it must be some demonic power that caused it. Watson shook his head as they walked to the house, thinking that he must have met more devils on the moors than any sane man in all of England. It was getting to be quite tiresome, really.

Watson sighed all through their tour of the house. The brothers had been carted off and the sister's body was laid out, her face still looking horrified. Holmes looked all around, but was not struck by any lightning realizations of truth. At last he had mercy on Watson, took him by the arm, and led them back to their cottage where Watson could resume picking on him about his smoking habits.

They sat for a time in a cloud of Holmes's thinking until he himself found it so stifling he suggested a walk. "To let the brain work without sufficient material is like racing an engine. It racks itself to pieces." He liked that image of a machine working itself apart, he used it a lot. Watson knew it well enough to record it twice in his stories; moreover he himself had watched Holmes come undone on several occasions, and found the metaphor just as apt.

"The sea air, sunshine, and patience, Watson," Holmes lectured to his companion. "All else will come." They smiled at each other as they walked outside. Yes, it was always Watson surely who would not let them have any quietude; why couldn't he learn to sit back and appreciate the surroundings?

Holmes bored Watson all day with his nattering on all the local history he has learned. His thoughts jumped back and forth from that project and his case, waiting for the facts to finally mature. It took the inclusion of Dr. Leon Sterndale and the death of Tregennis from the same strange horror that killed his sister to at last give Holmes a pattern to trace. He disappeared for long solitary walks and, without explaining any of his movements to Watson, who watched him come and go without question, only glad to see him busy.

Until of course he set up a little experiment with whatever poison he'd discovered at use on this family. He told Watson that he didn't have to participate, but what kind of talk was that? Watson only waved away the suggestion without a word. If he was willing to live with Holmes, he would certainly die with him for one of his fool experiments. Where was there even a question?

"I thought I knew my Watson," Holmes said with an endearingly satisfied glint in his eye. They would face each other across the table, poison between, door and window open in the hope that some ventilation would keep them from its full effects. Watson remembered one of the first things he ever learned about Sherlock Holmes, when their mutual acquaintance Stamford had said, "Holmes is a little too scientific for my tastes—it approaches to cold-bloodedness. I could imagine his giving a friend a little pinch of the latest vegetable alkaloid, not out of malevolence, you understand, but simply out of a spirit of inquiry in order to have an accurate idea of the effects. To do him justice, I think that he would take it himself with the same readiness."

And here finally was proof of that. How funny Watson found it! They'd known each other for sixteen years at this point, lived more than enough together for several lifetimes, so Watson would not begrudge Holmes getting them both killed if it would only drag him out of his sad mood. What is the point of a long life if it is a daily misery, after all?

It is odd how Watson could see the point of risking this dangerous substance for Holmes's happiness, but not the cocaine. Perhaps his problem was the way cocaine altered the personality he loved, made Holmes rabid and fragile at the same time. He would rather see Holmes dead than changed it seems, but I doubt Watson would ever put it quite that way. I guess we all have blind spots, don't we?

Holmes assumed they would be able to stop the experiment in time should it become too overwhelming, but the symptoms were strong and immediate. Watson was almost consumed by the poison, but in a last moment of clarity he caught sight of Holmes's face, rigid with horror, and in a heroic moment he managed to lunge them both through the open door, saving their lives.

Outside the air was clear, and their bleak surroundings turned heavenly. Both men gasped at the air, trying to replace the noxious smoke as quickly as possible. The sky seemed dizzying, high and huge after escaping from such a dark place. It was minutes before either one spoke.

"I owe you both my thanks and my apology," Holmes said to Watson in a shaken voice. "It was an unjustifiable experiment even for one's self, and doubly so for a friend." He reached for Watson's hand across the grass and their clammy fingers clasped together. "I really am very sorry." Holmes put himself in that kind of danger all the time, but he was never so careless with Watson's life, at least not when he was well. Everything was an unfair trade with Sherlock Holmes; with or without the drug he became reckless, in one direction because he felt too much, and in the other because he felt too little. But he was trying, the tragic man, only the game was rigged against him.

Watson nearly died a second time to see Holmes so raw, so open to him. "You know that it is my greatest joy and privilege to help you," Watson told him gently, bringing Holmes's shivering fingers to his lips. The moment didn't last long, but it was worth a thousand near-deaths to experience it for Watson. He wrote that this was the most he had seen of Holmes's heart, and my only surprise is that it was ever enough to sustain him through all the other times.

In the next second Holmes was already making dark jokes about how they must have been mad before ever inhaling the smoke, and he was desperate to discuss the case. His one lingering sign of tenderness was to link arms with Watson and lead him into the arbor to clear their lungs of the smoke. There Holmes broke down his suspicions, his mind sparking as the flint chips of all his observations went striking against one another. And yet even as his brain sped away from what had already happened into what it meant for the case's conclusion, his body seemed to be under someone else's control, someone who wanted to linger and remember what had just been survived. It was a testament to how distressed he had been by their ordeal, for Holmes's hands moved almost without his notice to smooth and check Watson. It was only when Dr. Sterndale came upon them early that Holmes snatched his hands back and beckoned for the explorer to come and approach them. It was time to accuse him of the murder of Tregennis, whom Holmes had deduced to be the poisoner of his family.

Sterndale nearly attacked Holmes, but held himself back. "I have lived so long among savages and beyond the law that I have got into the way of being a law unto myself," he said as he gathered himself. Watson could feel Holmes suppressing a laugh, probably because he had said the same thing himself, though in reference to the beasts of London instead of the jungle. That made two of them, didn't it? In fact Holmes was rather coming around to like the idea of taking the law fully into his own hands; mightn't he like the sensation of doing whatever he pleased, not just in support of the law, but also in spite of it? He had always had a notion that he would be a superior criminal, after all.

Just look at the way he was able to cow Dr. Sterndale who had stalked and killed lions in the jungles of Africa. What a fearsome presence Holmes would be as the leader of a criminal organization, perhaps better than Moriarty himself, since Holmes was so perfectly prepared to thwart the police after working alongside them his whole life (excepting a toe or two out of line of course).

But that was not the issue here, while law-abiding Holmes still had a case to complete. Holmes told Sterndale of all his own movements, saying that he had followed him everywhere he went.

"I saw no one," Sterndale protested.

"That is what you may expect to see when I follow you," Holmes told him. The fear of never knowing which of your secrets he had discovered could convert a great many people to do as he instructed them, should Holmes ever choose to bend himself that way. Even Sterndale believed he was the devil himself, and Holmes smiled to hear such a kind compliment. Holmes would not have to miss Moriarty if he became him, would he? It was starting to cross his mind in those days.

Sterndale told a very sad tale about how he had to remain estranged from the deceased Tregennis sister, about how the outdated laws of England would not grant him a divorce from his first wife so that he might marry his true love. And so when she was killed for money by her own brother, Sterndale avenged her with the same fate, locking up the brother Tregennis with the deathly powder that Sterndale himself had accidentally supplied.

"Perhaps, if you loved a woman, you would have done as much yourself," Sterndale concluded. Holmes asked him what his plans were if the murder had gone undetected, and Sterndale said he would finish his work in Africa. Holmes sent him off to do it, letting him leave their presence a free man. Sterndale was not the first person Holmes would let escape from the laws of the land, but he was much further from being the last. It gets to be a bit of a habit with Holmes for a time here, a measure of control that he exercised when he found his own body exempt from his mastery.

He started smoking and made some smart comment about the fumes. He and Watson remained where they sat for a time, only enjoying the air, and the sanity in their minds, and the life in their bodies. At least that was what occupied Watson's thoughts; Holmes was still lingering over the case. He asked if Watson agreed that the man should be released, and Watson did. And then Holmes told him, "I have never loved, Watson, but if I did and if the woman I loved had met such an end, I might act even as our lawless lion-hunter has done. Who knows?"

I know. While I don't believe he was mis-speaking when he said that he had never loved, since how the rest of us know that word is quite unlike any emotion Holmes has ever had, I do know that he would avenge Watson if anyone should ever harm him. He would prove it himself soon enough, and even show himself to be selfless and sacrificing for Watson's sake. So what does he call that, I wonder? And what would anyone else call it either, if not love? Perhaps there simply isn't a word for what he feels towards Watson.

1897: Abbey Grange

They returned home in autumn when Holmes at last seemed stable, and once again Holmes tried to lose himself in his work. All that year he went from case to case, from papers to projects to potions on his chemistry table. Watson didn't know if Holmes would ever be happier without the drug, but if he could only learn to be content with a life unthreatened by poison… How long would it take for him to stop missing it?

By winter of that year Holmes was in a dark mood most days, less lethargic than he was before their vacation on the coast, but all the more worrisome when one considered what he was busy with. Watson had wandered by his desk on several occasions and, based on glances at the papers Holmes kept doodling on, he had a suspicion that Holmes was planning a perfect crime, one that he himself would not be able to detect. It was only an intellectual exercise, of course, but Watson still didn't like it. It was only a matter of time before that attitude bled into his work and his relationship with the law. What had Professor Moriarty been if not an intellect unconnected to a sense of morality? That poor man Wilde had once said of his evil character that he was "a face without a heart," and hadn't Watson once thought something similar of Holmes? "A brain without a heart," he'd written during The Greek Interpreter case. Someday the slim connection between Holmes's thoughts and his conscience might shrivel from disuse, and then who would be the detective to stop *him*? There was no one else.

Holmes woke Watson early one winter morning, telling him to dress and come, because the game was afoot. Hopkins had sent him a note proclaiming a most remarkable case, and so Holmes hurried out to Abbey Grange to see it. Hopkins had never called him in on any problem that was not worthy of his attention before, and so he was buzzing with the promise of it. Even Watson found something to like about the cases Hopkins brought, for he had included every one in his stories.

"I must admit, Watson, that you do have some power of selection, which atones for much which I deplore in your narratives. Your fatal habit of looking at everything from the point of view of a story instead of as a scientific exercise has ruined what might have been an instructive and even classical series of demonstrations. You slur over work of the utmost finesse and delicacy, in order to dwell upon sensational details which may excite, but cannot possibly instruct, the reader."

"Why do you not write them yourself?" Watson said sharply. It is quite a bit more fatal, Watson could see, to think of everything in units and figures, and Holmes was quite a one to talk about sensational details as if he was above being drawn in by them. If Watson had ever watched Holmes purr once over a salacious plot or a grizzly murder, he'd seen him do it a hundred times. Holmes promised Watson that he would write a textbook someday (he is working on it now I believe), in his declining years. Watson thought about digging Holmes over his bad habits, telling him he might not live as long as he thought, but that would be a hateful thing to say. Besides, there was always a chance that Holmes was more vulnerable than he appeared, and it isn't fair to shove a man when he's near a ledge, no matter how shamelessly he bluffs that he would never lose his balance.

At first Holmes despaired of the case, thinking that Hopkins (like everyone else) had at last disappointed him. It appeared to be an obvious story of robbery and violence. A drunkard had been happily murdered, his poor young wife roughed up but probably better off without her husband. It was perhaps a sign that he was already in his declining years that Holmes did not realize until he was on a train home all the inconsistencies he had failed to add up properly: a blood stain on a chair that was supposedly covered by a restrained victim, the knots in the repurposed bell cord, the dregs of wine left by the killers. Holmes was not at all intuitive about human nature, but he knew the observable pattern of its expression; murderers would have surely finished their drinks.

Even the most finely made timepiece cannot function if it is not wound up. Holmes could be slow to start in those days, with neither his old youthful impatience nor the artificial kick-start of cocaine to engage his mind's machinery. It seized him on the train, and Holmes leapt outside as it was pulling out of the next station, yanking Watson with him.

"Excuse me, my dear fellow," Holmes told him, patting back down his collar and staring around at where they had alighted. His thoughts were firing quickly now, and he told Watson that if he had not let the very convincing account of the wife fill him with complacency, he would have known it to be wrong by the evidence right away. It was the hazard of narrative to science once again, I fear; the facts were being clouded by the story.

Watson returned with him to Abbey Grange and for two hours sat with Holmes in the dining room, like a maid with an overactive child, as Holmes darted to and fro, climbing half the furniture and crawling beneath the rest.

"Dear me, how slow-witted I have been, and how nearly I have committed the blunder of my lifetime!" Holmes said happily when he had finished his inspection. He was now looking for a single suspect, not a gang of men, and his was a sailor of higher class than an average crewman—a captain it turned out to be. And since the dead man was such a brute and the captain apparently an unstained gentleman, Holmes stayed his hand until he could speak to this quick, strong person who had so nearly tricked him. Something about so thoroughly obstructing a case rather tickled him; it was like being guilty by proxy.

"I had rather play tricks with the law of England than with my own conscience," he said carefully. Watson was partly relieved that Holmes considered his conscience in his cases at all, though he was just as bothered that Holmes so easily disregarded the law as being inconsistent with his values. Lestrade had been right; Holmes might someday put them both into trouble.

Such as when Holmes kept his developing theories to himself, giving Hopkins only physical hints, like the location of the supposedly robbed silverware, sunk in a lake near Abbey Grange. "I believe that you are a wizard, Mr. Holmes," Hopkins had told him when the silverware was indeed uncovered. "I really do think that you have powers that are not human."

Holmes let Hopkins leave while biting his tongue. Wizardry! The silly man. He would have liked to explain it all, but instead he deliberately neglected to tell the whole truth, keeping the secrets of the murderers and going a long way in making himself an accomplice in the concealment of their crime. If he had only raised a finger to aid them he would have been guilty, but Sherlock Holmes knew very well the line he must walk.

"What I know is unofficial," he explained to Watson. "I have the right to private judgment, but Hopkins has none. He must disclose all, or he is a traitor to his service." Holmes however had long grown accustomed to serving only himself. His unique powers gave him the privilege (which he quite enjoyed exercising at times) to withhold information he deduced in his own mind and which any discerning man might realize if he cared to apply the proper methods. He did it even to Captain Crocker, who arrived in a nervous state moments after Hopkins had left, and said to Holmes, "Speak out, man! You can't sit there and play with me like a cat with a mouse." But he really, truly could.

Holmes told the captain to calm down, to have a cigar, and assured him that he did not smoke with just any common criminal off the street. Watson rolled his eyes discreetly; probably Captain Crocker would be surprised at how many uncommon criminals there were, since Holmes had unearthed plenty that he liked to sit and linger with.

Crocker told his tale; he had loved this recent widow, Mary, from before she had wed, though when he heard of her nuptials he did not grieve. "I was not such a selfish hound as that," Crocker said, and Watson wanted to nudge Holmes teasingly about their own Mary and his jealous reaction, but he saw the signal of Holmes's hand that said jokes should wait. Holmes was on the edge of his seat, waiting to hear the details of his crime scene. He would not tolerate interruption well at this moment.

Crocker made a full confession, and after testing him to see if he really was devoted to the lady and her happiness above his own, Holmes declared himself a judge and Watson a jury and they set the man free. Holmes had absolutely taken the law into his own hands, and it was a pleasing, powerful sort of feeling. He would do it more often in the future.

1897: Charles Augustus Milverton

Before the year was out, on a day when the winter chill had calmed enough to make the weather pleasant, Holmes and Watson were out on a walk. He couldn't be cranky every day, and this was one of the better ones. They went walking like they did in their younger days, a long, meandering route that Holmes kept perfectly in his head, knowing exactly where they were at all times. They managed to walk past their alley, which never happened by accident, and they lingered just at the entrance while Holmes lit a cigarette and reminisced.

His long history with Watson being in his mind as they returned home, that is why Holmes reacted with such vehement disgust when he saw the card that had arrived in their absence. Charles Augustus Milverton was, according to Holmes, the worst man in London. He was due to come around that evening.

"Do you feel a creeping, shrinking sensation, Watson, when you stand before the serpents in the Zoo and see the slithery, gliding, venomous creatures?" Holmes asked as he stretched out before the fire, probably trying to rid that very tightening from his skin. "Well, that's how Milverton impresses me." He would prefer to deal with murderers over Milverton, and I will tell you why.

The Labouchère Amendment that became official law in 1886 was known as the Blackmailer's Charter. It made homosexual acts a crime, and it made being a homosexual criminal. Should a letter or a photograph of a compromising nature fall into the wrong hands, the man whom the evidence concerned could be blackmailed without recourse. Even a married man, if his mistress should be discovered or his gambling debts exposed might not have to go to jail for his shame, but for a man like Holmes…

He had been careful and lucky all his life, either engaging with gentlemen or with those who would not be believed against Holmes anyway; mostly his judge of male character saved him from anyone who would sell his secrets to a blackmailer, but then he had other precautions too. He knew better than most not to put such things in his correspondence, not even a passing reference, not a single hint. He was never one for love letters anyway, Sherlock Holmes. No one knowing Holmes ever got a sweet, anonymous card and attributed it to him.

Moreover, it isn't exactly easy to rob a thief. You would discover Sherlock Holmes's secrets and use them against him? You had better pray you don't have any secrets of your own. If it meant his reputation, I don't imagine Holmes would spare any avenue of deception, and might go so far as to frame a man who had it out for him. He certainly, at the end of this case, had no problem seeing a threat killed, though it was not by his own hand. But how guilty is the hand that doesn't rise to prevent such an act? Holmes's answer is probably different from ours:

"I have said that he is the worst man in London," he told Watson of Milverton, "and I would ask you how could one compare the ruffian who in hot blood bludgeons his mate with this man, who methodically and at his leisure tortures the soul and wrings the nerves in order to add to his already swollen money-bags?" But what about the man who declines to act, in cold blood, like Sherlock Holmes? Of that he has never really given his opinion, but we might venture to guess.

Watson, always a man of trust and naïveté, wondered if Milverton was entirely beyond the reach of the law.

"His victims dare not hit back," Holmes said as if the words were foul in his mouth. It filled him to the brim with a gentlemanly disgust to think of a leech like Milverton. It was so frightfully unsportsmanlike, so very unmanly, to wheedle money from people in the dark. "If ever he blackmailed an innocent person, then, indeed, we should have him; but he is as cunning as the Evil One." And where would he find an innocent person anyway? Everyone has secrets.

Holmes was meeting with Milverton that evening on behalf of a client who was to be married in a fortnight, unless of course some of her unwise and youthful letters were to be mailed to her fiancé. Holmes could not bring himself to be civil with Milverton, a rare thing indeed. This whole topic was a matter of one of his few (but firm) principles. Holmes wouldn't even shake Milverton's hand, regardless of the pleasure it gave Milverton to receive the snub. Men like this parasite loved to be under another man's skin.

Milverton gestured to Watson asking, "This gentleman? Is it discreet? Is it right?"

Watson swears those were his questions, not asking whether Watson was discreet, but if it were discreet, that is the situation in the room. Holmes was not unclear as to his meaning, and his lip curled in a sneer. He told Milverton defiantly, "Dr. Watson is my friend and partner."

"Very good, Mr. Holmes," Milverton said in an oily voice. He deflected the implied threat by turning the conversation to Holmes's unfortunate client. Milverton could not be bargained down, he was not in the business of negotiations. Holmes was rash in his uncommon anger. He told Watson to block the exit, but Milverton showed a weapon, and even worse told Holmes that he was disappointed in this lack of originality. So many people have tried to trap and rob him; he expected more from Sherlock Holmes.

Milverton was allowed to leave unmolested. It really was highly unlikely that he kept his ill-gotten letters on his person, but Holmes followed after Milverton quickly, dressed like a rakish young workman (Watson's words—Holmes was almost forty-four years old, and I'd never call him rakish). He was off to wage his assault against Milverton.

Holmes left for hours each day, several days in a row, and he seemed to really absorb his character, for he had a smug youthful look on his face whenever he returned each night. And then one day he came back with his cheeks flushed from the wind, laughing like a man fit to burst from the pleasure he felt.

"You would not call me a marrying man, Watson?" he asked archly.

"No, indeed!" Watson said. Good heavens, the unfortunate woman it would take to marry Sherlock Holmes…

"You'll be interested to hear that I am engaged." To Milverton's housemaid. And very pleased he was to prove he could manage it. He had never been engaged before, and it was a hilarious thing to do! Watson was offended that he would trick the girl so terribly, but Holmes has always cared little for the feelings of women, and of course young people would get engaged here and there with no harm done.

"I rejoice to say that I have a hated rival who will certainly cut me out the instant that my back is turned," Holmes told Watson, to reassure him that the girl would not be left in the lurch. "What a splendid night it is!" Holmes exclaimed. He meant to use the weather to cover his robbery of Milverton's house. He only wanted the layout of the house from the maid, and he didn't care who he had to lie to, for he rather enjoyed doing it, as I have already documented. His own small crimes were getting bolder.

Watson didn't like it one bit. He could just see Holmes getting caught. Scotland Yard would be called. Lestrade or Gregson would have to come for him. Milverton would be smiling, obsequious, only too happy to give evidence against the formerly magnificent Sherlock Holmes. The inspectors would shake their heads at him, but they would say they knew it all along. Sensed it really, that the man had never been quite right. Oh, it would be an agony. Watson's own name would go down foolishly. His own words in every story would serve to make him a mockery for eternity.

"For heaven's sake, Holmes, think what you are doing," he said pleadingly. But Holmes was already decided. He believed he could pull it off, after all, and the chance of such a victory absolutely outweighed the risk. He could taste his satisfaction in besting Milverton. It, much more than his costume, made him feel young again. This was what he had been searching to find, this feeling again.

It is not hard to talk Watson into any task he finds displeasing, you only have to strike the right tone; one that says you too are torn by the decision, but also bound to act for some noble reason. Earning his trust initially is no easy feat, but once he has vetted you and found you sound, you might convince him of anything using your own fine character as collateral. Holmes would commit his crime that very night, with or without Watson, but knowing full well that Watson would not let him seek any sort of peril alone, nevermind what petty reasons really lay at the bottom of Holmes's motivation. Such as pride:

"Milverton had, as you saw, the best of the first exchanges; but my self-respect and my reputation are concerned to fight it to a finish."

The arrogant man. His reputation certainly was on the line, not that he appeared to care overmuch about it. But Watson did care, and he insisted on going with him—it is very much in his nature to risk himself unnecessarily. Holmes said he could serve little purpose in tagging along, but Watson was now resolute. He would take a cab straight to the police station if Holmes refused his company. "Other people beside you have self-respect and even reputations."

Holmes smiled, but twisted it so that he might appear annoyed. "Well, well, my dear fellow, be it so. We have shared the same room for some years, and it would be amusing if we ended by sharing the same cell." Watson would not have minded it, though Holmes would be a terrible friend to have in a gaol full of men he'd helped convict. But: when Holmes breaks the law he shatters it into pieces, and let those pieces fall where they may.

"You know, Watson," Holmes told him as they prepared. "I don't mind confessing to you that I have always had an idea that I would have made a highly efficient criminal." Watson nodded distractedly. Yes, he had heard this all before, even said it himself once or twice, but he had never known Holmes to be so enthused by the idea. "This is the chance of my lifetime in that direction!" Just a chance, too, that he happened to have a full burglar's kit on him, with the most updated picks and a diamond-tipped glass cutter? Not at all; he'd thought this out for quite a while.

Perhaps a few daring instances of breaking the law instead of defending it, perhaps that would make the world interesting again? He didn't want to go too over the top, at least not at first; no murders (so he thought), no beatings, though he'd be adept at either one. Just another toe in the waters of theft, where the skill was in causing no damage and meeting no people, only the deft removal of the intended object. A nice, clean, intellectual sort of crime. The sort of thing a man of letters could be proud of.

Between releasing Captain Crocker and planning to rob Milverton, Holmes hadn't felt the overwhelming impulse for cocaine in weeks. He was in a paroxysm of excitement for this burglary. He told Watson to secure some silent shoes. He wanted masks for the adventure so that he would really feel the part. Of course he planned not to be seen at all, but why resist the urge to dress up?

Watson amused his little vanities, though I would say that was unwise. In his middle age, with all the time spent beside Holmes, he had learned to follow that man everywhere, to bolster him in all of his endeavors. When had Holmes ever put him into a perilous place that he could not just as quickly rescue him from? The day that happened (and it would not be a far-off day), well…then things would be different, wouldn't they?

Watson offered to make masks for the both of them, out of silk. Why not? If one had to ruin oneself for someone else, Sherlock Holmes was clearly worthy. And a cell together, would it really be so different than

Baker Street? Surely on the day of his death, Watson would look back and only be amused by it all, no matter how it ended up. He could just as easily imagine someone like Lestrade neglecting to prosecute, or going out of his way to believe Holmes was only on an innocent walk. Through Milverton's heavily guarded house. In a mask. That is the ultimate test for any choice Watson makes: how will he wish he had chosen on the last day of his life? And the answer is: he would always choose to follow Holmes, to attempt to earn his rare approval.

"I can see you have a strong natural turn for this sort of thing," Holmes said approvingly to Watson as they readied themselves for the assault. It was such a treat to see him so energized; Watson might do a great many unlawful things just to please him so thoroughly.

They put on fancy dress so that they would blend into the neighborhood. It felt like a childhood caper—a fake fiancé, creeping through someone else's yard all got up in roguish costumes. Watson is of the opinion that they looked truculent, hostile—I'm sure they looked perfectly adorable, the silly boys. The night started off so playfully that, despite how it ended, they both remember fondly standing in Milverton's laurels, breathless beside one another.

They broke in through the conservatory. Holmes took Watson's hand in the dark, in the thick air of the flowers and plants. According to Watson, Holmes can see very well in the dark, better than most mortal men, etc. At any rate, he held Watson's hand all through the treacherous roots and delicate blooms, and he kissed Watson's hand before they passed into the house, a secret act Holmes might not remember now himself, so jumped up on his own daring like he was. He kept Watson's hand pressed to his chest as they entered the house, where Watson could feel his heart beating like a humming bird. As they went through a hall, Watson was lost in the dark, as Holmes had made sure he himself would not be. They froze bravely as a cat rushed by them. They entered Milverton's bedroom.

Bright and warm, a fire still burning, smoke in the air as if someone had just left. Holmes went straight to Milverton's tall safe, still pulling Watson with him. He passed one hand over the safe as the other roamed up Watson's arm and grasped his neck in excitement. Regardless of the way he was being squeezed, Watson inspected their escape route and noticed it was unlocked. Pointing this out to Holmes, he got the thrill of his life: Holmes's lips wet against his ear: "I don't like it," he said about the door being curiously unlocked, unbolted. "I can't quite make it out.

Anyhow we have no time to lose." But he spared the barest second to kiss Watson's face, the tiny space of skin between his ear and the mask. And Watson asked him if he could do anything? Because of course he would do anything in the world.

He was not required, however, to do anything but stand watch. As he waited, the atmosphere around Holmes finally got to him, and Holmes's exhilaration infected Watson's brain as well: "My first feeling of fear had passed away, and I thrilled now with a keener zest than I had ever enjoyed when we were the defenders of the law instead of its defiers." A terrible influence, Sherlock Holmes, like a virus with no cure. "Far from feeling guilty," Watson wrote, "I rejoiced and exulted in our dangers."

Watson stood guard and watched Holmes with the sort of admiration he could only dream of deserving. For half an hour Holmes worked quietly to open the safe, a trick he had practiced before then, for interest's sake. And yet as soon as he had it open and had a parcel of letters in his hand, Holmes heard a sound approaching the room. He closed back up the safe (not perfectly though), tucked himself in the curtains, and gestured for Watson to do the same. Milverton entered moments later, using his very modern electric light to see, pacing and smoking like an agitated man. Watson and Holmes observed the back of his head from a slit in the curtains. Holmes had his silent, spidery hands all over Watson in that precarious situation. He grasped his fingers to reassure him, held their shoulders tight together, pressed his lips to Watson's face for a long interval. It was less like a kiss and more like being branded. This state Holmes was in was quite unique. He had never so forcefully broken the rules before, and he was in an ecstasy of rebellion.

But then a woman entered. Watson saw how beautiful and resolute she was, how vengeful. And even Holmes would later admit admiration for her. Next to Irene Adler, she was an exquisite soul only accidently placed into a female body, for she had the flint and daring of a man, and had them in greater quantity than most men you will find in the street.

The woman revealed her face. She had come to Milverton under false pretenses to avenge her husband, who had broken his heart when he read some letters that were never meant for his eyes. She was righteous and resolute in her purpose. The lady told Milverton that he would ruin no more lives, and she shot him to death before fleeing into the night.

Watson insists, to me, to this very day, that there was never a thing they could have done to save Milverton. The woman was too quick, the situation so unexpected, but still he made a move to leap out, my man of action. He wrote: "As the woman poured bullet after bullet into Milverton's shrinking body I was about to spring out, when I felt Holmes's cold, strong grasp upon my wrist. I understood the whole argument of that firm, restraining grip—that it was no affair of ours; that justice had overtaken a villain." When Sherlock Holmes broke the law, it did not heal afterwards.

Holmes kept his icy head all the while. As soon as the assassin left, he locked the door to the rest of the household, dumped the safe's evil contents into the fire, and led the way to their escape. Watson was almost caught as he flung himself over the garden wall, but once on the other side, Holmes picked him up and they ran until the trail behind them was silent. They had escaped. Holmes was dizzy with the thrill of it. Milverton dead, and himself escaped and free! He kissed Watson fiercely while their faces were still covered, then tore off and threw away their disguises. He rushed Watson back to Baker Street to take him to bed. Finally, finally, here it was! He could feel life rushing through him.

Lestrade came by the next morning. He walked in on a breakfast that was nearly numb with the buzzing thrill of the previous night. Watson let Holmes's intoxicated mood get the better of him. He was having fun.

To think that just the night before he imagined not only Lestrade, but Gregson, MacDonald, and Hopkins storming in here to haul them both to prison. How ridiculous! Here was Lestrade, perfectly unsuspecting, asking Holmes to consult on a murder that he himself had witnessed. In fact, he probably thought that Holmes would really enjoy the case, not just because the murder was so brazen, but because the men seen fleeing from the scene (presumed to be the killers) had burned all of Milverton's incriminating papers.

"It is probable that the criminals were men of good position, whose sole object was to prevent social exposure," Lestrade said. He was not ignorant, after all those years, of just what bound Watson to Baker Street, or Holmes to Watson. He thought that Holmes might be able to understand the couple of men who were surely being blackmailed by Milverton together. He would understand them and bring them to justice.

Holmes pretended to be surprised by all this, not very well, but Watson was amused by how little Lestrade noticed it. This must be how Holmes felt all the time, knowing full well all the details of the crimes before his eyes, and marveling at how everyone else could miss the obvious.

Lestrade described the man who was nearly caught as he scaled the wall around Milverton's property. Holmes could not resist being smart:

"That's rather vague. Why, it might be a description of Watson!"

He burst out laughing at Watson, and Lestrade, who was used to this sort of treatment by now, only tolerated it and tried to take the joke in good sport.

"It's true," he said smiling tolerantly. "It might be a description of Watson."

Watson suppressed a chill that wanted to creep up his spine, and he made himself laugh along with the others. In the end, Holmes refused the case. Obviously.

"I think there are certain crimes which the law cannot touch, and which therefore, to some extent, justify private revenge." He looked Lestrade in the eyes as he made this excuse, and Lestrade nodded grimly. "I have made up my mind," Holmes concluded. "My sympathies are with the criminals rather than with the victim."

"I thought they might be," said Lestrade fairly. You cannot expect a man to betray his own kind, after all.

Once the inspector left, the room lapsed into silence. Watson wondered if it was the gravity of death that weighed on Holmes's forehead, but at last Holmes sprang up and led Watson outside, down Baker Street and along Oxford until he found the picture of the woman they had seen transform into a murderess. Watson was shocked to know her avenged husband's identity (though he still will not tell me who it was), and Holmes's eyes sparkled as he saw the knowledge spring brightly into Watson's as well. He put a hushing finger over his lips and took Watson back home again.

They passed the rest of the winter quite happily, but certainly that could not last. Holmes would need to either escalate or relapse, because he lacked the ability to be still or content. I suppose he is like a shark in that respect; Holmes must move always or die.

1898: The Retired Colourman

I must ask that my irregular spelling be forgiven. There is more than distance separating England and America; Oscar Wilde once said that they were two peoples divided by a common language. Anyone spotting inconsistencies may attribute them to my dual citizenship and my uneven education which took place in both countries over many years and was never standardized.

Summer 1898 found Sherlock Holmes back in his usual mood, sort of despondent and sharp-edged, treating Watson like the furniture. Watson could not even pleasantly discuss the events of the day with him, everything had to be a production.

For example: a man had just left 221B as Watson was returning. Watson thought he looked rather pathetic and futile. Holmes seized upon this.

"But is not all life pathetic and futile?" Holmes asked. "We reach. We grasp. And what is left in our hands at the end? A shadow. Or worse than a shadow—misery."

"Is he one of your clients?" Watson asked brightly. He had learned at last not to indulge every one of Holmes's moods, for the man would only take advantage of the attention. It is the same when a toddler is at a whiny bent, you'll do yourself no favors to encourage them by reacting.

But Holmes knew how to prod his own bad tempers—he started by assuming Scotland Yard had sent this client along "just as medical men occasionally send their incurables to a quack." Then it was all, "life is a ceaseless grind," and so forth, until Watson asked Holmes what he was going to do about it. He planned to do nothing. He was just complaining to hear the sound of his own voice. He sent Watson out in his stead.

Watson was such a constant, comfortable creature that he did what he was told without feeling the slightest inconvenience. Even when he was giving his report to Holmes and getting picked at for the poetic way he had learned to talk since he took up the pen, he was not upset. He only stared at Holmes's sharp eyes, "bright and keen as rapiers," and forgave him for his foul little turn. This was not the slow sinking into the mire of depression, this was only the usual impatience of his temperament, and Watson withstood it firmly.

Holmes knew how to reign himself in too, however. There was only so long he could insult Watson before he would offend him, and Holmes had learned the limit. He told Watson that his research was insufficient, but he caught himself being unkind, and made room for Watson's feelings.

"Don't be hurt, my dear fellow. You know that I am quite impersonal. No one else would have done better," he shrugged, offering the observation up as a consolation prize. He was better at saving Watson's opinion of him now than he was in earlier years, but only barely. He had learned to lay it on quite a bit too thick.

"With your natural advantages, Watson, every lady is your helper and accomplice. What about the girl at the post-office, or the wife of the green-grocer?" Holmes asked, starting to tease Watson, though it was against his best interests in an apology. "I can picture you whispering soft nothings with the young lady at the Blue Anchor, and receiving hard somethings in exchange." He nudged Watson with the toe of his shoe until he could see Watson forgive him for being so short, and then he returned to criticizing him. "All this you have left undone."

It turned out that Watson needn't have bothered anyway, since Holmes had gotten the information he wanted on his own, and once again was only complaining to pass the time. As the case became more interesting, and another detective arrived trying to rival Holmes, he got into better spirits. The teasing of Watson continued when Holmes sent him on a false clue to take the client out of the way. He fooled Watson, sending him out to Little Purlington knowing that both he and client Amberley would be stuck there.

"I much fear, my dear Watson, that there is no return train tonight. I have unwittingly condemned you to the horrors of a country inn," he lied. "However," Holmes added rakishly over the telephone, "there is always Nature, Watson—Nature and Josiah Amberley—you can be in close commune with both." Watson could hear him laughing even over the bad connection. He took it in stride, with the patience of his profession.

While they were gone, Holmes took up his recent side-hobby once more: burglary. He confessed it himself to Inspector MacKinnon, who was assigned to the case, "Burglary has always been an alternative profession had I cared to adopt it, and I have little doubt that I should have come to the front." He was apprehended on his way out of the house by the other detective, a man named Barker, and after having a laugh together they decided to surprise Amberley with the question of where he had hidden the bodies. It is unwise to bring a lie to Sherlock Holmes and present it as the truth; this man's wife did not run away with her lover. He was a cruel husband and a cold man, and he had murdered them both. The evidence bore it out.

Holmes was in a better mood at the end of this case, even tweaking MacKinnon a bit while letting him take all the credit. It was just like Watson remembered things, back before the drug, the Falls, back when things were easy. He often remembers things quite a bit rosier than they actually were, my dear husband, but he was right in thinking that this was one of Holmes's better periods. He had his little ups and downs, and right then he was in an elevated place.

It wouldn't last a month.

1898: The Dancing Men

I believe that one of the great sympathetic relationships of Holmes's life was with a man he had never met. Something was so suggestive about Oscar Wilde's life, almost as if it was the life that Holmes could have but never did live out himself. Seeing his name in the paper was, to Holmes, like seeing the name of an illegitimate brother; sure you did not share the same title nor the same fate, but you were, at least in part, the same blood. Wilde probably said it best in his only novel: "He felt that he had known them all, those strange, terrible figures that had passed across the stage of the world and made sin so marvelous and evil so full of subtlety. It seemed to him that in some mysterious way their lives had been his own." It was a question of influence, of conscious influence, and Sherlock Holmes felt a very strong kinship to this man, though the whole world thought them so different. Wilde was like a benevolent Moriarty; one of a few great man among a rabble of simpletons.

In 1898 there was published a long poem, "The Ballad of Reading Gaol," by a prisoner identified only by his cell number: C.3.3. Holmes made it a habit to consume all information relating to crime or criminals, and he was not curious, like most everyone else, as to who the author really was. He might not have been an overly literary man, but he knew two similar fingerprints when he saw them. This was Wilde's hand at work or he would eat his own hat. He pointed it out to Watson in the early spring of that year when he finally got around to reading the poem and sniffing out its source. He asked Watson if he could disagree about the origins.

"Well, surely there is some doubt. I mean, it could have been any man who'd passed through that prison with the unfortunate condemned man, this C.T.W."

"Charles Thomas Wooldridge," Holmes said. "Undoubtedly. He was a member of the Royal Horse Guards, and hanged two years ago today for the murder of his wife. I remember the crime and the execution."

"But are you really so sure about the author of this work, Holmes?" Watson asked him. "You aren't particularly well-versed in literature."

"It isn't a matter literature," Holmes told him cryptically, and turned back to poring over the poem. The line that choruses started to echo in his mind: Each man kills the thing he loves. What did Sherlock Holmes love?

The question consumed him for the bulk of June, since he felt quite sure that it was true that every man murdered what he loved best, so it was only a matter of learning what that thing was. It seemed for him that it was a toss between two things: his own mind and his dear Watson. Would he not know which he loved most until one or the other was destroyed?

He invented experiments for himself—often working on one puzzle helps him solve another, as it trained his mind to function within a pattern of logical thought. The only problem was that one of his problems was not a logical one. He had to try and question his own heart.

It was during one of these projects in late June that he felt Watson idly staring at him, and decided to have a little fun with him. Holmes broke in on his thoughts about South African securities the same way someone might delight his sweetheart by contriving to pull a flower or a coin from behind her ear. Watson is always astonished when anyone can guess at his thoughts, apparently not realizing how expressive his face is, or how predictable his mind. It's very fun when I manage to do it, and Holmes was no less amused than I.

"Now, Watson, confess yourself utterly taken aback," he said.

He was of course, until Holmes explained his process, and then Holmes was annoyed with himself that he had told. Like summer lightning, the way his moods flashed so suddenly out of a clear blue sky. In one instance he was showing Watson a childish trick, and then in the next he was berating him for being childish in enjoying it. The hypocrisy of the man! How exhausting.

Before he could really hit his stride with complaining however, a case was brought to him with a tantalizing little cipher of dancing men who apparently belied something sinister. Holmes spent a cheerful few hours figuring it out and then got some lovely activity when he had to apprehend a murderer, and yet still he had a fog about him that he could not break through.

"The way of paradoxes is the way of truth," Wilde knew. Life was undoubtedly always too short, but it was also too long to spend suffering. To be bored, for Sherlock Holmes, was to suffer. It used to be that his work was enough to sustain him, but since Moriarty made all his other cases pale in comparison, he had found a new way to give his life a little pep. Those small crimes he committed in uncovering bigger ones, they helped. But this ballad by Wilde…it was doing a serious turn on him. At the outset it reminded him how horrible prison must be, and just because Holmes had made friends with some few official inspectors did not mean there weren't many more jealous rivals who would put him away at the slightest infraction if they could. But more than that was the plaintive tone of sorrowful ownership for a life lived all the way to the hilt. It was less cautionary perhaps, and more prophetic; not a message of "don't do as I have done" but rather a reminder not to judge too harshly, for we will all want forgiveness in the end. A *memento mori*: as you are now, so once was I, etc.

Holmes felt, the longer he thought about it, a very contradictory impulse. He was not usually much taken with the notion of paradoxes. Things for Holmes either were or they weren't. His whole career and often citizens' lives depended on the truth being absolutely pure and relatively simple. And yet he felt a self-destructive urge to do with conviction what he knew could only end him, to follow his nature wheresoever it would it would lead.

But he was not a criminal, and he would henceforth cease to pose as one. Holmes would turn back to his one real vice and take it up again deliberately, because it was the only way to be true to himself.

Regrets were for the end of a life, not the thick of it. Now was the time for mistakes. "To get back one's youth, one has merely to repeat one's follies. Nowadays most people die of a sort of creeping common sense, and discover when it is too late that the only things one never regrets are one's mistakes." Holmes had been reading fiction again, but was any of it untrue?

It looked to Holmes as if he must love his own mind the best, for in the next few years he would all but pickle his brain in that seven percent solution. It was his cross to bear, and he was taking it up again, quietly; he knew he would be able to answer for it if he found himself in a spiritual dock someday, but for now it was his own private matter. This was the only life he'd been guaranteed, and if Watson could live without wanting to touch the outer edges of experience, well…so much the worse for him. Holmes would keep it a secret as long as he could, but…*quod scripsi, scripsi.* He washed his hands of it.

1919: Music

After dessert we move back into the sitting room where Watson has prepared a gift for Holmes, a recording of German music that they'd once heard together at St. James's Hall. It's a fascinating thing to sit and watch Holmes listen to music. Watson gives me a look asking me to be quiet, but he needn't have bothered. As Holmes is enraptured by the music, so am I entranced by him. His eyes lose their usual sharp focus and a dreamy film comes over them. He leans back like he's lost in an abstraction. I like music too, but it doesn't seize me by the scruff quite like this.

Beside him Watson also seems distracted by watching Holmes, but his face does not have the happy reverie of the detective's. His face is showing signs of strain and sadness, the same look from before the war when he would return from visits with Holmes, like he'd left something precious behind and didn't know if he would ever see it again. The evening is drawing to a close, and he knows it. This music, which seemed like such a fun treat when he first planned it, is only reminding him of a past he hardly knows anymore, and misses very much.

The thing with music is that it may only be heard in the present; it must move to exist, and in moving it ends all too quickly. I can see Watson becoming maudlin, worrying about the inevitable moment when Holmes will have to leave. He was always under a burden of sadness when he came back from visiting Holmes before the war, as if he had drawn from a well of grief, and it would be days before the contents of his pail would evaporate away. It was hard enough departing from Holmes, how much harder will it be to let Holmes walk away from him?

When the record ends, Holmes snaps up to peruse the rest of our collection, pulling several that he would like to hear. Watson thinks he is glad to have their goodbye put off for that much longer, but he shouldn't be. It only makes his anxious misery last a few hours longer.

1899: Thor Bridge

Watson might have seen it, if he'd been paying attention. By October when the narrative is next picked up, Sherlock Holmes had turned mysteriously chipper when he should not have been happy at all. On a whipping cold morning Watson said, "I descended to breakfast prepared to find my companion in depressed spirits, for, like all great artists, he was easily impressed by his surroundings." His mood instead was "particularly bright and joyous," which never happened with Holmes by accident, and Watson even called it a "somewhat sinister cheefulness." I don't know how he didn't see what was really going on.

Holmes was better now at hiding his resumed habit than he had been before, when he had turned to it in desperation and frenzy. At last he was trying to use the substance as it was meant to be administered: as medication, as maintenance. He measured out a single dose a day as if it were a beneficial vitamin. It sustained him through September, which he called "a month of trivialities and stagnation," and when at last a worthy case came to him he was ready to meet it.

A woman was dead, her children's governess seemed the obvious culprit, but her husband was a hot-tempered fellow, and drew suspicion to himself as well. He even threatened Holmes, though he did it in so impotent a fashion that it only seemed quaint. "You've done yourself no good this morning, Mr. Holmes, for I have broken stronger men than you. No man ever crossed me and was the better for it."

"So many have said so, and yet here I am," said Holmes with a smile. Promises, promises, they're all he ever heard!

In this case, Holmes demonstrated to Watson the art of bluffing. Less of a legal problem than lying (and he had become very careful about that sort of thing since June), but also a different sort of craft. Not pure theater; it was the difference between disguise and impersonation. One is pure creation, and the other adaptation; there must be a seed of truth in it.

If Holmes seems more moral and strident here, that is why; he was only bluffing. As if he cared more for this mistreated girl than any number of others he had helped or hampered based on his own selfish whims. "It is only for the young lady's sake that I touch your case at all," Holmes told his client. I sincerely doubt the truth of that; let the case be boring and see how chivalrous he stays.

The emphasis of the drug is apparent to me. Instead of a Holmes impatient for details that would make his life less of a misery, grasping at wisps and finding them horribly insufficient, his new subtle use of the substance and a greater understanding of himself allowed the cocaine to underscore his pleasure; it provided him the solid foundation for a very thrilling experience. Even people unfamiliar with his strange behavior could see the way he was "vibrating with nervous energy" as the events surrounding the dead woman started to bloom in his mind. It was always a golden period of grace when he first began his habit again; with all that he had learned the last few times, he knew how to extend this state to its absolute limits. It would be more than a year before the symptoms of the drug would finally catch up to him. In the past it had been his own intemperance that had done him in first.

It was a good time for Watson as well. Holmes was harboring a deep flame over what he suspected about the chipped stone on Thor Bridge, and in his sweet agitation over it, he was quite warm towards Watson. Watson reports that on the train ride from where the governess was being held back to the scene of the crime, Holmes was in a very sensitive condition of restlessness. "Suddenly, however, as we neared our destination he seated himself opposite to me—we had a first-class carriage to ourselves—and laying a hand upon each of my knees he looked into my eyes with the peculiarly mischievous gaze which was characteristic of his more imp-like moods." He touched Watson firmly as if to discharge some of his excessive energy into his friend; Watson was always being used to ground him.

"Watson," he said breathlessly. "I have some recollection that you go armed upon these excursions of ours."

Watson innocently said that of course he must, since Holmes so rarely had regard for his own safety.

"Yes, yes, I am a little absent-minded in such matters," Holmes answered quietly. "But have you your revolver on you?" he asked. His hands started to slide up Watson's thighs, feeling for his weapon. Watson, still easily flustered by amorous attention no matter how old or experienced he'd become, stopped Holmes's hands before they got too familiar. Private car or not, they were on the train! He pulled his gun out hurriedly and handed it to Holmes, who was able to think of many things at once, and spoke with a sly double meaning to Watson.

"It's heavy—remarkably heavy," he said. Watson agreed that it was so, not exactly sure what Holmes was implying. Holmes hefted it for a minute, dumped the cartridges into his hand, replaced all but one, and said, "Do you know, Watson, I believe your revolver is going to have a very intimate connection with the mystery which we are investigating."

"My dear Holmes, you are joking," Watson murmured suspiciously.

Holmes handed back the single remaining bullet to Watson; it was warm with body heat from rolling around in Holmes's palm. Upon looking up, Watson could see Holmes stroking the gun with his fine, long fingers. He put my poor husband in a flush for the rest of the night.

Holmes got to do a pretty trick, standing in the place of the dead woman's body, holding Watson's gun to his head, and then letting it go with a weight attached. It struck the bridge making the same mark as the one already left by their conniving "victim" and sunk into the mere. It was a neat victory for Holmes, but it was obvious from his conversation with Watson afterwards that he was still in a contemplative place in regards to himself:

"I have been sluggish in mind and wanting in that mixture of imagination and reality which is the basis of my art," he told Watson. Where was the Holmes of his twenties and thirties? Those young decades when all he needed was within his own reserves, and he was an exquisite machine which produced more than it took in? Now the conversion of energy was slowed, and he was not optimal. It was the way of all flesh, perhaps. He was doing his best to manage it.

In the end Holmes concluded that their client would probably join forces with his formerly accused governess and do quite well. They had "learned something in that schoolroom of sorrow where our earthly lessons are taught." Of sorrow Holmes was too familiar; that exquisite, purifying emotion which reveals one's true character.

Wilde had lost his freedom, Holmes had lost his fire, and I have lost my family, but: what does not kill us makes us stronger.

1900: The Six Napoleons

The only case recorded for this year, the year of Oscar Wilde's death which would not occur until late November, was one of significance for Holmes. It was not so much the problem of someone cracking up Napoleon busts in order to find a rare stolen pearl that had been hidden in one of six. What made this case special was the credit he received. His fame, by 1900 was untouchable. For years its importance had been declining, until it finally mattered very little to Holmes what "everyone" thought of him. His circle of esteemed opinions was rather small indeed, including about the top one percent of criminals in all the world, and the few men he knew to be personally worthy, such as his handful of friendly inspectors, and of course, my dear Watson.

In this particular case, Holmes was able to acquire the black pearl of the Borgias in such a remarkable, inscrutable way that it caused Watson and Lestrade, both old veterans of Holmes's queer methods, to burst into wonder-filled applause. Holmes blushed like one of us mere mortals, and took a grateful bow in his own sitting room. Watson said, "It was at such moments that for an instant he ceased to be a reasoning machine, and betrayed his human love for admiration and applause. The same singularly proud and reserved nature which turned away with disdain from popular notoriety was capable of being moved to its depths by spontaneous wonder and praise from a friend."

This case was the one instance where Inspector Lestrade, a stoic man himself, revealed to Holmes just what he had meant to him and the officials at Scotland Yard: "We're not jealous of you at Scotland Yard. No, sir, we are very proud of you, and if you come down tomorrow, there's not a man, from the oldest inspector to the youngest constable, who wouldn't be glad to shake you by the hand."

Holmes thanked him with as much earnestness as he had ever felt, even turning away to hide his small display of emotion. He wouldn't have been so touchable, you can be sure, if there had not been cocaine in his veins, but the emotion was at its base his own true one. He was not, regardless of how he acted or seemed, anything but human.

1901: The Priory School

Sherlock Holmes does not make mistakes like you or I. First of all, his mistakes are never one hundred percent wrong, he is always right somewhere. Second, his mistakes matter more. When I commit a mistake I need a new sheaf of paper or I have a simple apology to make; Holmes has people's lives in his hands. He enjoys being so much smarter than everyone else, but he has a responsibility to be just as right as he always thinks he is. Cocaine, after a period of extended use especially, will compromise anyone's mind. That's all fine for some rough on the street, but Sherlock Holmes had finally earned the stature of a man whose word was above question. He wagered more than himself when he bet on cocaine.

He had kept his discipline for over a year, never allowing himself to get into a frenzy of use, but the dosage had by necessity increased. He couldn't rely on Watson to be his physician here, and so it was the chemist in Holmes who administered the substance. I am surprised he did so well for long. He must have had an iron constitution indeed, but even iron will rust.

The small oversight in this case was negligible, not unlike the matter of The Yellow Face. It was a missed inference due to missing information, a hazard of his trade to be sure, but not one he ever used to suffer so often or so easily.

The apparently kidnapped child of a wealthy former statesman managed to draw Holmes out of London though his plate was overflowing with work. It ended up being a very lucrative case to Holmes, since he neatly acquired a reward from the boy's father before telling him that he was the man suspected in his son's kidnapping. That was not, needless to say, an act of greed on Holmes's part, but an act of poetry. He might have had double the sum if he wanted to help conceal the case, but he rather enjoyed taking this respected man's cheque and then informing him of his own complacent guilt. The only thing was, it wasn't the father's plot, but a thing cooked up by his older illegitimate son, whom he was only covering for to avoid a scandal.

It was otherwise a pleasurable and successful case, for Watson as well, who got to enjoy the Holmes who emerges only on our English moors, "a very different Holmes from the introspective and pallid dreamer of Baker Street." In his maturity Holmes shifted not only from the love of fame to the love of informed credit, but also from the exhilaration of the city to the thrill of open air. He got to fake a sprained ankle, drag Watson into the dirt and across the morass, and hoist himself on Watson's shoulders to spy at his suspects. He had a good time all around, but he was not the pistoning machine he used to be; he could not engage every last bit of himself. Little bits of his mind held themselves aloof.

Upon learning who all was involved in the crime, and pointing out that all those who willingly take part in the committing of a crime are morally guilty of all that results from it, he still let it largely go. "I am not in an official position, and there is no reason so long as the ends of justice are served, why I should disclose all that I know." It was enough for him to catch the murderer, and let the rest of the schemers go with a shrug. The drug was dulling small parts of him, vital parts of him, even while it gave him the energy he thought he needed to keep himself in operation. Before the autumn of the year, he would finally come to the full realization of what he was losing, and it would scare him.

1901: Lady Frances Carfax

Holmes began this summer mystery in artificially high spirits, teasing Watson for having gone to the Turkish baths, knowing that Watson went only for legitimate, healthful purposes, unlike himself. His mind was darting around talking of Watson's boots, of the hazards presented by independent women, of one in particular who had gone missing, the Lady Frances Carfax. He gave this French assignment to Watson, pleading extreme busyness and the fact that his absence from England "causes an unhealthy excitement among the criminal classes." I mean all this to illustrate that he was busy indeed since the cocaine made his hands restless—this he thought he could maintain forever.

His symptoms had not escaped him, but Holmes thought they were minor. When I say his hands were restless, I mean that even Watson had seen (and recognized in hindsight) the way Holmes's fingers trembled and clenched like he was developing a nervous condition. He had gained some restless habits like rubbing his face and arranging his cigarette ashes in little piles. He would stand or sit as if in trances, in a numb fog of distraction, but these were never worrisome things in Holmes—his natural state was so like that of a drug-user that it was hard to know the difference until he was more than a little afflicted.

Holmes had found himself too active for even London to occupy him though, and so he followed Watson out to France to head him off, and managed to keep him from getting killed before roundly criticizing everything he'd done.

"A singularly consistent investigation you have made, my dear Watson. I cannot at the moment recall any possible blunder which you have omitted," he said in his annoyingly brisk manner, as if he were only telling you of his itinerary. In his later years he had grown better at not scolding

Watson so, but the drug certainly caused a regression in him, so that he hardly noticed Watson's hurt feelings.

At any rate, they returned together to London to seek out a vicious man with a bitten ear and his accomplice wife. Lady Frances was in a great deal of danger from this pair, but eh…there was only so much Holmes could do about all that until they began to pawn some of her jewelry. And even when the lady's suitor saw these villains purchasing a coffin, Holmes hardly cared until he realized he might be justified in breaking into their rooms.

"We simply can't afford to wait for the police or to keep within the four corners of the law," he told Watson in a sudden notion. "We'll just take our luck together, as we have occasionally in the past." So much for trying to avoid prison, but when one contains such multitudes as Sherlock Holmes, one can act in several different directions at once and barely feel the pull.

Watson, to his sometime credit, would follow a friend anywhere, even into the embarrassing scene that Holmes rushed into. He forced his way into the house, only to be confronted by a cool criminal and a convincing story as to Lady Frances's disappearance. Holmes let go his own name, but it did nothing to intimidate the villain. He promised to search the house until he found Lady Frances, and brought out a revolver so that no one would stop him. He had the police called on him, since he was making a circus of the entire siege. This was not the subtle, sure, and gentlemanly detective that Watson had always admired, this was like being partnered with a drunk.

"Why, you're a common burglar," Holy Peters told him, seeming to enjoy being for once in good standing with the law against another man, especially if that man could be an internationally respected detective.

Holmes only smiled back at him, hardly knowing how badly he was being lured. "So you might describe me!" he said. "My companion is also a dangerous ruffian. And together we are going through your house." The man looked Watson up and down contemptuously, and Watson found himself in a rather surreal position, feeling the need to make polite excuses to a man he suspected of murder and theft. His friend was acting strangely, crazily, even more so than usual. Watson stuck by him though, remembering that he had been fooled before; how many fake seizures, trick disguises, and dramatic scenes had he had to take up his cues on and support? Hoping that Holmes was just pulling an extended ruse, Watson set his features and tried to appear as confident as Holmes did.

Holmes demanded to see the contents of the coffin, and since Peters would not give his consent, Holmes ran in and lifted the lid without it. Inside was not Lady Frances, it was some elderly woman they had pulled out of the workhouse infirmary and brought to die in their house, "as Christian folk should." A shiver of sickening rage shuddered through Holmes. It was hard to see, but Watson standing just beside him, could feel the tremor.

"I'd give something for a photograph of your gaping, staring face when you pulled aside that lid," Peters jeered at Holmes. He even got the satisfaction of having the police force Holmes from his house, though the young sergeants wouldn't put their hands out to arrest Holmes, having heard of his legendary skills. They only asked him to leave, since it was the law, and they could not bend it for him.

Holmes's hands once again betrayed him, clenched in tight annoyance at being mocked, though he kept his voice clipped and pleasant for the officers. Watson was burning with embarrassment, and as they went off to confirm the story behind this elderly body, he watched Holmes with a wondering eye. What was all of this, then? Could Holmes have really been so mistaken?

They had to wait for the warrant until the next day, and Watson left Holmes alone that night since he was "too irritable for conversation and too restless for sleep." Watson could tell he had not slept at all when, on the next morning, Holmes tore into his room with his eyes sunken and his face haggard.

"Good heavens, Watson, what has become of any brains that God has given me? Quick, man, quick! It's life or death!" They went to find Lady Frances very nearly dead, but not past the point of resuscitation. The lady was saved but the criminals were lost, and as such this case was a failure. Holmes certainly knew why, but he didn't dare admit to it explicitly; Watson was aware of something uncharacteristic rumbling around them, but it was one thing to have him frowning, silently curious, and quite another to have him know. Holmes was at least aware of his own culpability:

"Should you care to add the case to your annals, my dear Watson, it can only be as an example of that temporary eclipse to which even the best-balanced mind may be exposed," he told Watson as humbly as could.

"Such slips are common to all mortals, and the greatest is he who can recognize and repair them." This comment is the best inkling that I have that he was going to attempt to be his own doctor for once. He was very disinterested in his physical health, but what does he have, after all, without his mind? He had come to this conclusion before, and yet here he was again. Was he not ashamed?

"It had all been so clear," he told Watson about this case, "if only my own sight had not been dimmed."

He would attempt to cleanse himself again. It would end…differently than the other times. It would end in my favor.

1901: The Sussex Vampire

It was too bad for him at first to be handed a case of whimsical fancy. He wanted to gently wean himself down, but vampires? Such a silly question could drive him to much worse than cocaine. He despaired of the whole topic, wondering what he and Watson had to do with "walking corpses who can only be held in their grave by stakes driven through their hearts." But it was more than just simple superstition; a curious accumulation of morbid evidence really did seem to point to a blood-sucking Peruvian mother.

The man recommending the case to Holmes gave Watson as a personal introduction: they had played one another at rugby years and years previously. Watson remembered the man—what he lacks in dates and numbers, he makes up for in faces and personalities—he recalled him as being "a good-natured chap. It's quite like him to be so concerned over a friend's case."

It almost made Holmes smile, but he was a bit pulled from missing his drug, and so he only shook his head at Watson, wondering at his blindness. This man Ferguson, he was not so privy to another man's marriage, it was his own that he wrote for help on.

"I never get your limits, Watson. There are unexplored possibilities about you," Holmes said wearily.

Watson truly was rediscovering himself however, for when his old rugby mate walked in, Watson realized just how old they both were, and sighed at his lost vigor. He was not the only one feeling so worn.

When Ferguson beseeched Holmes to come at once and advise him on his troubles, he agreed to go see about the matter: "There is a lull at present. I can give you my undivided energies." Vampires; Holmes was obviously desperate for a distraction.

But he already had an idea what would motivate a woman to suck blood from her own baby. Arriving at the household, Holmes started collecting confirmation of a unique sibling rivalry. The older boy, a sickly teenager from Ferguson's previous marriage, was a remarkable little monster. The moment he ran in to hug his father with "the abandon of a loving girl," Holmes could have laughed. This was a type far more interesting than vampires, a boy with a viciously sharp mind inside of an insufficient body. He had learned of a way he might murder his young half brother, and therefore keep all of the affection he unnaturally craved from his father. After revealing the culprit and recommending they send the boy to sea for a year to set him right. He and Watson left Ferguson to make up with his wife.

"Well that was an ugly business!" Watson exclaimed as they got outside and began walking back to their luggage, not wanting to bother the family for a ride. Holmes laughed deeply in his throat, and Watson asked him just what he could find so funny.

"Oh it's just not as uncommon as you might think," he said. "The majority of evils in the world are committed by bright young men with a jealous fixation. Most of the time it's over beautiful young women, is all. Then it doesn't look so strange."

"Well, yes, I imagine that's so," Watson said agreeably.

"Did you never notice that expression on Billy?" Holmes asked, cutting his eyes sideways at Watson.

"Our Billy? Why of course not! He'd never do anything so gruesome."

"Oh probably not so extreme, no," Holmes said. "But he refuses to leave our employ and seek his own fortune. He won't see himself replaced."

"You must admit we run a rather exciting household, though," Watson conjectured happily. "Perhaps it's the thrill that keeps him with us."

"Perhaps," Holmes said noncommittally. They had taken on Billy as a page when he was only eleven years old, just three years younger than Ferguson's own boy. An orphaned thing, taken in at a tender age, and he grew up taking his orders from Holmes and Mrs. Hudson. He was loyal to them both, almost as if they were his parents, but still not quite. Holmes knew that look of jealousy on the Ferguson boy because he had seen it before, when he caught Billy looking at Watson. Holmes was monitoring the situation for any trouble, but Billy was a much older, much more controlled being than this nasty little boy they'd met tonight.

This strange case had hardly taken up a single night. Holmes would need more, so very much more, if he was going to get himself well again.

1902: The Red Circle

It's easy for me to see that Holmes was having an unpleasant winter. As far as it appears, he had measured his use of cocaine down to nothing, and was in a touchy, snotty mood without it. A landlady came to him with concern about her odd new tenant, and Holmes's answer was to tell her, "I do not understand why I, whose time is of some value, should interfere in the matter."

He was only compiling his reference books, rolling his eyes behind his scraps of paper, wondering why he was forced to suffer fools. But the lady talked him into it with his own reputation, saying she was referred by a friend who said he was so kind, so smart, etc. Watson smiled to see this flattery work. Holmes seemed to get up in spite of himself. He was very weary of his client's unease, and where Watson saw him soothing her, he was really just trying to keep her from babbling pitiful facts about her personal situation. Indeed, when the woman had told her story and left, he took down his large book of agony columns and was still unsympathetic.

"Dear me! What a chorus of groans, cries, and bleatings!" he said as he searched through the columns for any message to the lodger. He was in an uncharitable mood, which naturally changed when the case got interesting.

Finding messages he thought pertained, Holmes took up the case with at last a small bit of enthusiasm. It managed to get him out of the house, and that reminded him of what was good for him. "It is art for art's sake, Watson," he told my husband. "I suppose when you doctored you found yourself studying cases without thought of a fee?"

"For my education, Holmes," Watson said.

"Education never ends," Holmes answered. Certainly he was learning something new about himself every day, about the person he was growing into. Watson didn't know it all at the time (he learned it later, from Holmes's own lips, which is how the knowledge comes to me), but Holmes was nearing a pocket of very strange years in his life. The same was true for all of us.

In crawling around on this case, Holmes and Watson uncovered a couple of fearful Italian witnesses, and a rather thrillingly dangerous case that Inspector Gregson was working from the other end. They met in the middle.

"Journeys end with lovers' meetings," Holmes exclaimed when he spotted the official. It was a favorite flirt of his, Watson says. A little bit of cheek ever since he was respectable enough to chance it. His longtime inspectors, those who had become better investigators because of Holmes's influence, also became that much less rigid. Gregson, and Lestrade too, could not have failed to notice his nature, but they took it upon themselves not to care. His little asides didn't help, especially in front of the other officers, the young ones who were still zealous, still being trained, but usually they played it off as an irregular's eccentricity. Just Holmes speaking above everyone's heads, business as usual.

Of course, the Pinkerton man from America wasn't as concerned with that, though he did blush deeply when Holmes recognized his name and complimented him on a case he'd worked. Still had a few glittering charms hanging off him, Holmes did. He wasn't all the way past his prime.

The case ended up in the happy death of a vicious criminal, and Holmes was pleased enough after finding his case so worthy that he took Watson out to a Wagner concert. There he sat, content and distracted, hopeful that his most trying personal times were behind him, that the only challenges in the future would be those he received from puzzles, but...that was not exactly the way of things. Before the year was out, he and Watson would be separated again, and it wouldn't be over a woman (I would come along quite later) or over cocaine. It would be at once simpler and more complicated than that. It would be a surprise to them both.

1902: Shoscombe Old Place

The year progressed normally enough; cases in, cases out. Another horse-racing problem came upon them. Watson at last knew more about the situation than Holmes since he gambles on the races (I know absolutely *nothing* about horse-racing and still don't care to—Watson feels the same way about bird-watching, so it's an even situation). Debts, horses, a family only just holding on to some married-into wealth, bones in a furnace. Why wouldn't Holmes get excited? These criminals, these weird crimes, they were doing him a kindness. They gave him a bit of a challenge.

Watson called it a "bright May evening" that found them traveling out to Shoscombe in a first-class carriage by themselves. Holmes had his feet up on Watson's knee, happy to be pretending with Watson that they were fishermen, and that they were in the country for nothing more than leisure. Lying was a quick way to feel superior; present people with a simple picture, and they never suspect you again.

The case turned out to be very little trouble, all told. The nature of a dog, so much more consistent and logical than the nature of thinking man, proved to Holmes that the lady at the center of this case was somehow altered, since a dog did not change its loyalty for no reason. She had died of disease and was being impersonated by her brother to maintain her widow's property until the brother could pay off his debts. No large crime, and nothing to get too excited about, though Holmes did relish the opportunity to break into a crypt over it. It was just the concealment of a death, but the mystery had given Holmes some pleasure to solve, and that was enough to be getting on with.

Holmes had vacillated between testing his theories and actually expending some leisure with a fishing pole during their stay. They caught dinner one night, and had some lovely private moments that Watson has never detailed. I'm sure they were quaint and pastoral and vomit-inducing, but I guess they deserved to be, while the sun still somewhat shined on them.

1902: The Three Garridebs

I don't like Sherlock Holmes, and I think I have made that perfectly clear. I could criticize him all day; his self-love, his vanity, his insanity, his addiction, his obsessions, his egotism, his cold and flinty devil's logic… But I cannot hate him for one thing, and it is the love of my dear Watson. Consistently, and no matter what kind of sour mood he was in, he has never failed my husband on a mission of importance. If it meant getting in the way of an attack, if it meant sacrificing his own life, if it meant botching the evidence for a case, so be it: he would not allow harm to befall his partner. And if an injury did ever arrive, he felt sick about it, no matter how minor it was.

In this case we have another simple client who is tricked out of his house with an unlikely story about an eccentric American millionaire who wanted to fund men with similarities to himself. Something like this is in the case of The Red-Headed League, and now here we have a man who claims his name is Garrideb who says he must find two more to make them all wealthy. I don't know why it is so easy for some Englishmen to believe that America is full of rich loons who love to bequeath their wealth to strangers. I suppose I've heard crazier things about America, but it is still surprising that so many have been so thoroughly fooled. It isn't *that* foreign a place, really.

Watson begins the case by acknowledging that its events might be either a comedy or a tragedy, depending on where one concentrated. Sure the swindle was amusing, but as Watson foreshadowed, a lot would be lost over it: one man's freedom, another's reason, Watson a bit of blood, and Holmes too would pay a price in the end. That part did not make it into the public account.

In the summer of 1902 Holmes was in one of his funks. After the Shoscombe case in May he languished during the week that crossed into June and had "spent several days in bed" according to Watson, only emerging from his room when this case came to him.

The facts of the case helped pull him out of his emotional pit, hand over struggling hand. First there was an American man with London clothes and an inoffensive accent. How suspicious! After catching the man out on several tiny lies, Holmes started stacking the facts he knew, the little inconsistencies told by the American man who claimed his name was Garrideb. As he investigated further, a sinister flavor turned up; the man they were dealing with was (predictably) an imposter, but his real identity was "Killer" Evans. He killed the man who used to live in the real British Garrideb's house, and he needed access to a hidden area beneath the floor which contained money forging equipment.

Holmes warned Watson of the danger, that their "Wild West friend" might live up to his nickname. I wonder if they felt a sense of foreboding about it, though of course I can only speculate. They had walked into lion's dens before and come out unscathed. Maybe they felt no fear at all because they thought themselves invincible.

They waited for Evans to break into the house, and tried to creep up to capture him, but he was alert to them. In another convincing ruse, he rose as if he would give himself up to capture, but then pulled out a fast revolver and fired into the room towards Holmes and Watson.

Watson was hit, grazed really. In the same old leg that always gets shot. I've seen the scar on his thigh. I've kissed that scar. It's a uniting mark that ties Watson to both Holmes and myself, but it's a dividing line as well, as I will soon explain.

Holmes cracked Evans on the head with the butt of his gun and searched him for weapons in a flash. Then he was at Watson's side, arms around him, lifting him into a chair.

"You're not hurt, Watson? For God's sake, say that you are not hurt!" He knelt at my husband's knees and cut open his clothes over the wound to see that it was as Watson said, only "a mere scratch." And though the wound stung at first, Watson said he could hardly feel it when he realized what was happening to Holmes, the overwhelming emotions (imagine emotions on Sherlock Holmes!) that were swarming his face.

"It was worth a wound," Watson wrote, "it was worth many wounds to know the depth of loyalty and love which lay behind that cold mask. The clear, hard eyes were dimmed for a moment, and the firm lips were shaking. For the one and only time I caught a glimpse of a great heart as well as of a great brain. All my years of humble but single-minded service culminated in that moment of revelation." This was the peak of them, right in that very instant! Watson might have guessed, with his literary flair, what would happen from here, but I doubt he would take the moment back. In fact, I'm sure that if he were being honest, he would want the whole case and all its outcomes exactly as they happened. Ends are all inevitable anyway, one might as well appreciate a nice one.

When Holmes realized that Watson would live, he mastered himself once again. One profound sigh of relief, and then he turned on Evans with a cold look.

"If you had killed Watson, you would not have got out of this room alive," Holmes told the man simply. What, if not love, could make Sherlock Holmes a murderer? Though he would flirt with crime on his own, he would never dare take a life with his own hand, not for any reason. Only his dear Watson could force him to that extreme, and without hesitation, without a single regret. It would not have even been a question.

Their prisoner, bloodied and dazed, explained what he had done and his motivation. He asked Holmes whom he had hurt, what he had done to Garrideb that was criminal? He had paid his debt in full for the shooting death of his former partner, and Garrideb was fine!

Yes, but Watson was injured. "It's only attempted murder, so far as I can see," Holmes told him briskly. Evans would absolutely not be allowed to go free.

After placing a call to Scotland Yard and handing over Evans, Holmes and Watson returned to Baker Street. Leaving Watson beside the fire, Holmes went to knock up a pharmacy for bandages, ointments, and… something else. He came back as the sun rose, and sat nervously as Watson bandaged himself. Holmes left one hand in his pocket, the other rubbing his lips the whole time, chewing on his fingernails. Once Watson declared to him that he was as good as new, Holmes brought him over to their breakfast table to talk. He had something serious to say.

"Tonight has been a revelation, my dear Watson," he began. "It has reminded me how much…how very much you mean to me." Holmes struggled to be able to say all of what he meant. Watson smiled fondly at him before Holmes took his hand out of his pocket and set something on the table between them. It was a small glass bottle. It was a liquid cocaine solution.

"Holmes," Watson said slowly. "You don't have to—"

"I believe this is what is best for me," Holmes said carefully. "But I know that it's the right thing for you."

Watson's mouth hung open; what was all this? He was all right, everything was all right before tonight! There was no reason to be so drastic!

Holmes held up his long-fingered hand to Watson's stuttering. "This isn't a rash decision," he said.

"I don't see how not! Holmes you've been clear of this drug for five years, you've been doing so well! Please don't sacrifice that progress because of such a small injury," Watson pleaded, gesturing at his leg.

Holmes smiled patiently. "I've only been away from it less than a year," Holmes confessed. "I took it up again without you ever noticing, and used it successfully for quite some time. I lied to you."

Watson, frowning, shook his head in disbelief. Holmes had a look on his face of sorrowful resignation. Each man kills the thing he loves, and Holmes had finally realized what (or who) it was that he loved. His mind was safe, but his Watson was wounded—it had almost happened right under his nose! How to save Watson from the danger that Holmes could not help but put him in? Better to drive him away and save him. Better to kill the thing he loved second best.

"I know you won't tolerate this," Holmes said, pointing to the drug. "And I know equally that I must use it, as I see fit, if I am to be what I must be. I hope we can still be great friends, dear Watson, great partners, but…" he trailed off with a flutter of his hand, and then allowed it to reach for Watson across the table. Their fingers clutched together tightly. "You'll be safer this way." He was saving Watson by sacrificing himself.

Watson had become so comfortable, he had become so accustomed to their life together; it just didn't occur to him that anything could upset it. And yet, his leg throbbed, shot through by a bullet again, and just like the last time he had felt that sting, his life was at a precipice. Holmes was serious. Things larger than himself were moving him once again.

"You'll be all right," Holmes said, rising and leaning over the table to press his cheek to Watson's forehead. "You'll be much better off."

He left to go to his room, leaving the cocaine bottle where it stood on the table, staring at Watson like a tiny being that *wanted* to give him some privacy, but obviously could not. Watson grabbed the bottle and stared at it, aghast that it could make such a drastic impact on his life, but he set it right back down again. If this was what Holmes wanted, again and still, then what could he do about it? Did he really want to wage that fight forever?

That summer Watson moved out of Baker Street. The separation was amicable, almost as if they really were just fellow lodgers and not so much more. Watson set up his medical practice once again, he struck out on his own with a renewed purpose to establish himself as an individual, not as Sherlock Holmes's scribe.

He became aware in the process of reestablishing himself of just how stagnant he had become living in the shadow of Holmes, how much he had been complacent with a life of leisure and disconnect. He wouldn't knowingly live with a drug user, and since clearly Holmes was making the choice to be one, he was ending their cohabitation. The way it was presented, he was telling Watson that his decision, however strangely it was motivated, was a firm one. Watson loved Holmes enough to leave when he was asked. And might some distance not be a renewal for them both? There was no reason not to think so.

1919: Departure

At last it is time for Holmes to take his leave. I am glad to see the back of him, and yet…what do I really hate him for? Ultimately it was he who released Watson back into the world for me to find. Perhaps he regretted it later (who wouldn't?), but in 1902 Watson moved out again. He kept involved with Holmes for quite a long while, but within two years he was moving on from the steady role Holmes had cast him in; he was his own man again! And as a man alone he was, as per his nature, on the look-out for a woman.

I was that woman. I met Watson when he came to treat my father for his heart—I remember my first sight of him. I didn't know who he was at first, and after I learned of him I was skeptical about this literary and crime-fighting doctor. What all did he know about medicine, about my father's health, when he frittered away half his time writing stories and solving mysteries?

But when I saw him I took him in right away as a military man; with seven brothers—three of whom were joined up at the time, the rest of whom went when the war required them—I could spot all the signs. The regulation mustache, the stiff walk, the language. I said to him moodily as soon as he walked in, "Oh just what we need, another soldier!" And he told me that I was highly observant, and that I reminded him of a very close friend of his. How unsettling.

Watson gifts Holmes the Wagner recording as he is heading towards the door, forces it into his hands as we all stand awkwardly shifting. My heart is…undecided. It's fluttering in excitement and anxiety as our party comes to a close, as Holmes picks up his hat and coat, and pulls his serpentine pipe out of the pocket. He has already been nearly five hours without it, the deprived man.

I step up to say goodbye first. Holmes reaches out and starts to stoop towards me, as if he will kiss my hand. I grasp him in a handshake however, and look him in his steely gray eyes, and he winks at me on the side that Watson cannot see, and it does make me smile. I see his wager by kissing his cheek and telling him, "Good-night, Mister Sherlock Holmes," as Irene Adler did before me. Holmes knows what I mean by it. We part from each other, each looking lemon-faced, but I know it is only to hide our amusement. We have grown tolerant of each other over this visit, somehow. Perhaps it is all our common ground.

I touch Watson's elbow and tell him, "I'll be in the dining room," which is on the other side of our central stairs, and as far as I can be from him without stepping into the kitchen or going up stairs. I'm telling him that I will give them some privacy. I'm tempted to actually do it, too.

I comprise my morals; I move out of the foyer, go through the sitting room, and tuck myself behind the wall in the dining room. I cannot see them, but if I press myself tightly to the wall and shut my eyes, I can channel all my focus into hearing what they are saying. I can only pick up some few sweet murmurings.

"Well," Holmes says. "Journeys end in lovers' parting, my dear Watson."

"I'll see you again soon, though, shall I? I might travel to the coast before the weather turns frigid. And of course you're always welcome to come see us here."

Holmes's response is indecipherable, but I think I know the sounds that follow: a rustling of cloth, a sighing of breath, a low sound from Watson like he makes when he is holding in a flood of tears—the same noise he made the day we went to war, and the same noise he made when we were all called home again. My heart breaks to think of them embracing, but I'm more hurt to think of Watson's pain. He hates goodbyes, however temporary they may be. He always has.

1902: The Illustrious Client

Twenty years is not so easily set aside, however. Watson had moved out to Queen Anne Street to resume practicing medicine, and a prestigious list of patients he had too, being at last in some upscale premises and with his own bit of fame due to his stories. Holmes had forced some distance between them (very selflessly I think—he realized that, sober or soused, his company was a threat to Watson), but it wasn't a clean break. A bit of backsliding was necessary perhaps, a period of gradual lessening, a more casual redefinition of their friendship. Watson acquired new rooms over the summer and autumn, but still in September he and Holmes saw each other regularly. When Watson first learned of this illustrious client in fact, he and Holmes were enjoying each other's company at the Turkish baths. This, hopefully needless to say, is before Watson ever met me. I wouldn't be in his life until December.

They maintained flirtations, and as far as it appears to me, carnal relations as well, but by Holmes's choosing they established themselves independently once more. Whenever he felt the desire to take up with Watson thoroughly again, something like this very case would come along and remind him why distance was necessary. The uncommon violence of what should have been a simple matter of disillusioning a young lady over her fiancé underlined for Holmes what a perilous life he led. He needed the reminding, and he took it quite to heart; his whole aim of depriving himself of Watson was to keep Watson from injury, and yet old habits die terribly hard. Not three months after divorcing himself from Watson he was asking him back as if he didn't know how not to. After explaining the details of his latest matter to Watson, he concluded:

"I am bound, therefore, to hope that it is not a false scent and that he has some real need for our assistance."

"Our?" Watson asked, surprised.

"Well," Holmes fumbled. "If you will be so good."

"I shall be honored," Watson told him. And so it went on between them as if neither one knew better.

Their illustrious client's illustrious representative was a man of rather flamboyant fashion, maybe "posing as a somdomite" as Lord Queensberry would put, maybe a fully fledged member of the club. One would hope a man who had his sexuality to conceal would not go around in lavender spats and winking and such, but who knows. People have been known to act more recklessly than that.

"Of course, I was prepared to find Dr. Watson," he said with a raised eyebrow and lowered head. Holmes and Watson shot glances at one another, but let the remark slide. How is it any business of his where anyone was living or why?

Colonel Sir James Damery gave them the details of the problem: a promising young woman named Violet was in all ways devoted to an absolute scoundrel. Adelbert Gruner was a convicted murderer, but he still managed to talk his way into an engagement with Violet, and the man who was being represented by this flouncing Colonel Damery wanted the girl disabused of her illusions. It was nearly impossible, for her heart was resolute.

Holmes first went to intimidate Gruner, then to attempt to reason with Violet. He found her "indescribably annoying in the calm aloofness and supreme self-complaisance" she displayed, which is only fitting medicine, since he is just as irritating to everyone who speaks with him, and more so since he is almost never wrong. Violet at least had the redeeming quality of being totally deluded and pitiable. Holmes repels pity.

He provoked an attack on himself, knowingly, and then let the papers play it up that he was within inches of death. Didn't tell Watson either, again. The poor man's showed me the placard that he stood on between the Grand Hotel and Charing Cross Station when he saw the news. "Murderous Attack Upon Sherlock Holmes," the paper blared. Watson hurried to Baker Street with what was by then a familiar feeling of nauseous fear. How many times had Holmes done this to him? How many times had he promised that it would never happen again?

Watson met a surgeon in the hall who told him as soon as he spotted Watson's stricken face, "No immediate danger. Two lacerated scalp wounds and some considerable bruises. Several stitches have been necessary. Morphine has been injected and quiet is essential, but...an interview of a few minutes would not be absolutely forbidden."There could be no telling Watson to leave now.

Holmes was in mostly darkness, seeping through his bandages, whispering roughly. "Don't look so scared, Watson. It's not as bad as it seems." At some point he complained to Watson about the morphine, upset that at first it made him itch and hallucinate, and eventually that it made him so complacent and dull. Not his drug at all, but not to worry the medical man in the room! He would quit the cocaine while he was on morphine. Heaven knows what they'd do in combination. He disliked the thick, molten sensation of morphine so much that before he was fully healed he gave it up. He chose to feel the pain of his injury over the suffocating lethargy that morphine brought. Something about that numbness scared him more than his cracked brow, more than the idea of death itself.

At least during this case, for all the damage it inflicted, he told Watson to act as if his friend were dying, and did not require him to believe it was true all the while. Holmes decided he would fool his surgeon instead, and that Watson's playacting abilities, such as they weren't, would be sufficient. What a mercy! If only he'd thought to extend it before the papers caught the story.

He was still malingering though, for sympathy, and for fun. "There was a curious secretive streak in the man which led to many dramatic effects, but left even his closest friend guessing as to what his exact plans might be." Watson didn't mind it, he was just happy to have his infuriating friend alive and in good spirits. "He pushed to an extreme the axiom that the only safe plotter was he who plotted alone. I was nearer him than anyone else, and yet I was always conscious of the gap between." I think, perhaps, that this is why he didn't have much of a turn when Holmes asked him to leave in the first place. It seemed...unavoidable, but more than that, it seemed right. Holmes belonged on a pedestal. Watson did not.

Holmes took his lumps over this case, but once out of commission and pretending to be at death's door, he sent Watson to try and distract Gruner, a feat he would never have successfully accomplished, since lying is not in his nature and being tricked was not in Gruner's. Holmes had to burst in, injured though he truly was, to stop Watson being murdered. During the upheaval a spurned lover threw vitriol into Gruner's face, destroying its European good looks in a second.

It was, in the end, an ugly matter. A triumphant case objectively, but still leaving a horrible disfigurement, a wronged woman charged with vitriol-throwing, a marriage cancelled, and very nearly Holmes standing in the dock for burglary (which he was in the habit of committing yet again—it appears to go with the territory of cocaine confidence). But they needed Gruner's diary to win Violet to the side of reason; it was only his client's standing, and not Holmes's own, that saved him from the law in the end. It may have seemed like only another notch in his belt, but this case and all its risks reminded Holmes first that Watson was still not safe with him, and second that he was still not immune from the law. His worst torments were dogging him still. More distance was necessary, even more distance.

The next case would not be told by Watson at all. It is one of only two that are written by Holmes himself, and it is solved without Watson at his side. It was what Holmes needed to do, for the good of both himself and Watson, a true severance. In that time apart they both moved on to new companions; Watson to me, and Holmes to a short string of men who could distract him from the curious loneliness he never thought himself capable of: the loneliness of a love lost.

1903: The Blanched Soldier

Not that Holmes could really go anywhere without Watson; they had each formed the other, changed him, affected him irrevocably. Holmes, working always to be more like a machine and less like a man, couldn't shake off the presence of knowing what Watson would think, or the mistakes that Watson would have made, had he come along. It even helped to know Watson's human nature, to understand the nature of army men and the bond between soldier friends...that helped him with this case. It was almost like a bereavement to Holmes, to be so close to his memories of Watson without including him. It was almost as if his friend had died. Why else shouldn't he be called in to assist?

But Holmes's resolution was strong, and Watson's singular devotion to him was migrating. Holmes says in introduction to this case that Watson had left him for a wife, a single selfish act that Holmes could not hold against him, since Holmes had taken more that he could ever repay from Watson. We were not, as yet, married, and would not even be engaged until 1904 after he had met all of my family and secured their approval, but Holmes knew the writing on the wall, he knew the trajectory of my presence. Once Watson had mentioned me to Holmes, it had gone quite far enough, and there was only one way it could end. That ending would be a beautiful beginning, a wedding that would happen in November of 1904, on Guy Fawkes' day. It was the last temperate autumn Saturday of the year. It was perfect.

So Holmes was doubly disingenuous when he wrote, "The good Watson had at that time deserted me for a wife," since it was Holmes who had left, and I was not yet officially Watson's wife. This story has not gone to print at this time, but Holmes refuses to change a word of it now. I have seen it in several different forms: Holmes's original all marked over with notes from Watson, a second draft where Holmes took absolutely none of Watson's advice, and what appears to be a penultimate version which I copied out for Watson's literary agent. I believe Holmes wants this to be his effort alone, and that he has his own reasons for putting things the way that he has.

He missed Watson on this soldier case, and I think that emotion more than anything else is what prompted him to write it down and at last appease Watson's requests that Holmes take up the pen himself. Chief among the things that reminded him of Watson was the military man who secured Holmes to find out what had happened to his old army friend. Holmes could relate to this client, since he was missing an honorable old soldier himself. Mr. James Dodd was very frank with his feelings, saying plainly that he loved his friend Godfrey and only wished to find out what had happened to him. Holmes took up the case not least because he found the figure of a hidden, white-faced former solider interesting, but also because he genuinely wanted to help Mr. Dodd.

More than the army aspect of the case, it reminded him of Watson in its medical elements; Godfrey, it turned out, was suffering from leprosy (or as it happily turned out to be, pseudo-leprosy), and it panged Holmes to think that he did not have Watson to simply turn to and ask for advice. Even in the writing of this narrative he felt the overwhelming emptiness that Watson left. We never stop realizing all that someone was to us once they are gone—those surprising pockets of vacancy persist forever.

"And here it is that I miss my Watson," Holmes wrote. "By cunning questions and ejaculations of wonder he could elevate my simple art, which is but systematized common sense, into a prodigy." More than simply missing the man himself, Holmes missed the way Watson's eyes saw him; I too know that feeling of elevation and esteem from Watson. His admiring gaze is like the light of the sun, warm and nurturing and very sorely missed when it is gone.

1903: The Mazarin Stone

They still, of course, saw something of each other while Holmes remained in London and before Watson and I were officially wed. Watson continued to visit Baker Street and occasionally got mixed up in cases despite being busy in his own profession once more. I know for sure that they engaged in the Three Gables case in the spring, though I have little more to say about that one. Holmes was in a real mood the whole time, threatening people, insulting their racial features, extorting money...essentially finding an amusing way to pass the time. Being apart was starting to become commonplace, comfortable. They cooled as they separated, like the precipitate that results from a chemical reaction; it was a volatile concoction once, but it was settling now.

Both of them moved on from one another, not in their deepest hearts, but still they added new lovers to their lives. I myself was Watson's addition; while we were courting I knew little of how he spent his time away from me, but I did not require his full faith and fidelity until we were vowed to one another. He didn't see Holmes for some few years after we were first married. We were rather wrapped up in ourselves then.

But in 1903, Holmes had found someone else too, someone who had been right under his nose for nearly fifteen years—Billy, their page. He was twenty-six now, and with Watson gone he was promoted from mere page to somewhat of a secretary, apprentice, and companion. Watson was visiting Baker Street after several months away, and he looked around at everything fondly, including Billy, "the young but very wise and tactful"—an important requirement—"page, who had helped a little to fill the gap of loneliness and isolation which surrounded the saturnine figure of the great detective." Billy however did not return Watson's kind feelings; he smiled, but it was as if the ends of his mouth had been riveted into place.

"It all seems very unchanged, Billy," Watson said as he rocked pleasantly back and forth on his feet. "You don't change either. I hope the same can be said of him?"

Billy, in fact, *had* changed from the child he used to be. He had a bit of Holmes in him I suspect, that icy part, except untempered by any of Holmes's human connections—his brother Mycroft and friend Watson. Billy was much more alone, and his concern with Holmes was more possessive than it was affectionate. He was jealous seeing Watson returned. They found room enough between one another to talk about Holmes, with Billy commenting that Holmes was sleeping all day and refusing food. "You know his way when he is keen on a case," Billy said.

"Yes, I know."

Billy's lips pursed slightly. I think he was making fun of Watson as he told of Holmes's exploits: "He's following someone. Yesterday he was out as a workman looking for a job. Today he was an old woman. Fairly took me in, he did!" He went on to tell Watson that he liked who Holmes liked, and did what Holmes asked him to. "Mr. Holmes always knows whatever there is to know," he said. He was really quite taken with the man.

Watson noticed something that was unfamiliar, a curtain drawn across the window. "We've got something funny behind it," Billy said with a small smirk on his face. It was a dummy of Holmes. Billy detached the head to show it to Watson, explaining that there were men staked out across the street bent on assassination. Watson remembered the adventure of The Empty House and told Billy, "We used something of the sort once before!"

"Before my time," Billy told him crisply. He was around back then but at only fourteen, he wasn't involved with Holmes in quite the same way. Now he was in the thick of it, in danger right alongside his mentor. Billy peaked out the window to look at the men who were menacing them. Holmes came charging out of his room to snatch the curtains closed again.

"That will do, Billy," he said darkly. "You were in danger of your life then, my boy, and I can't do without you just yet."

Watson, bless his sweet soul, hadn't thought of what might be going on between them. Billy's face was still quite young and boyish, but his eyes displayed a cunning age. He had turned out to be handsome, and very devoted to Holmes. The circumstances started to dawn on Watson once Billy was out of the room.

"That boy is a problem, Watson," Holmes said seriously. "How far am I justified in allowing him to be in danger?"

It was the same problem with Watson, obviously, but to Holmes it must have felt different, since he didn't force Billy to leave, but rather let him hang around as much as he liked. It is risky to stand so close to Sherlock Holmes, but it was a risk that Holmes, in the end, would not let Watson take. Watson got pushed away, a selfless act to help preserve his precious life. But Billy was something else—he could make his own choices, and take his own chances. Holmes felt somehow less culpable of any fate that might befall Billy. He wasn't in love with the boy, after all, so the stakes and the rules were different; Billy could still leave at any time, and Holmes wasn't making any great effort to have him stay. With Watson, Holmes had lied and cajoled and even paid to keep him in Baker Street, for his own sake and regardless of what Watson would do if left uninfluenced and told the whole truth. Theirs hadn't been a fair partnership; Holmes had stacked the deck against Watson with his ability to act and mislead. Indeed, this very case reminded everyone how flawlessly Holmes pretended to be someone he was not, a workman, an old woman, any disguise he chose. With such talent comes a greater responsibility to use it well and to know its power. If he lies to people he absolutely becomes responsible for them. Billy wasn't being lied to.

But Watson still was, in little ways. Holmes downplayed the danger he was in (hard to do after already admitting that a magnificent hunter was planning to murder him) and sent him out to fetch the police, through the back so the potential murderer would not be suspicious. Watson insisted upon staying to help protect Holmes, but he was not allowed.

"I can't possibly leave you," Watson told Holmes.

"Yes, you can, Watson," Holmes said with a small, twisted smile. "And you will, for you have never failed to play the game. I am sure you will play it to the end." Even Watson's stalwart insistence was nothing to Sherlock Holmes. No man's will is his own if Holmes has decided to manipulate it. He even told Watson that this villain he was about to host would not be immune: "This man has come for his own purpose, but he may stay for mine," Holmes said.

The suspect arrived, Count Sylvius, and was cheerfully stopped from murdering Holmes's likeness. The Count was informed that he himself would tell Holmes where the missing Mazarin stone was hidden. The man was skeptical of this assertion; Holmes was not. Holmes intimated to his would-be attacker that it had been his own "play-acting, busybody self" who had been following the Count for some days, and that the only fact which he did not know already was the location of the stone. *That* remained for Count Sylvius to reveal, and Holmes told him that he would confess it before he left those very rooms. This did not sit well with our criminal.

"You won't die in your bed, Holmes," Sylvius told him menacingly. Holmes shrugged; he already suspected that he would not.

After having Billy usher up this man's muscular companion, Holmes swapped himself for his own dummy and was able to snatch the stone right out of Count Sylvius's hand. They gave up the game without much of a struggle after that, since fighting had just become so pointless.

"I believe you are the devil himself," the Count said.

"Not far from him, at any rate," Holmes answered with a polite smile, and I'm sure some amount of pride. He had a few more tricks to keep the pleasure of his capture going—a bit of nothing-up-my-sleeve, slipping the stone into his client's pocket and then insisting jocularly that he was an accomplice. When the joke on Lord Cantlemere failed to amuse anyone but Holmes (Watson was mostly embarrassed, Cantlemere irritated and harassed by Holmes's "perverted" sense of humor), it became clear to Watson that Holmes was indeed still using his drug. Something about all of Holmes's actions seemed caricatured and over-exaggerated, and Watson even wrote the account of the case rather strangely, using an unprecedented third-person narration. I don't know why, unless the whole circumstances simply made him uncomfortable enough to want to distance himself.

Billy was called back up to usher Lord Cantlemere out again, and as he left behind their rather nonplussed visitor, he lingered just inside the door.

"That was a very deft capture, Mr. Holmes," Billy said softly, leaning as close to the detective's ear as decency would permit. Billy continued on downstairs after saying this, and Holmes merely shrugged his eyebrows at Watson and threw his long form into a chair.

Watson could not say nothing. He sat across from Holmes in his old chair and shook his head slowly, letting the truth sink in.

"He's young enough to be your son, Holmes."

"So what if he is?" Holmes said lightly. "I haven't got any sons, and he hasn't got a father, and you know that I am much more concerned with the letter of the law, not always the moral spirit behind it. You paint me gray enough in your stories."

"I'm not asking about the law's morals, I'm asking about your own."

"Well, I wish you wouldn't, Watson," said Holmes as he leaned to reach beneath his chair and pulled out a familiar case. "You won't like the answers."

Watson watched as Holmes extracted cocaine into his syringe and rolled up his sleeve. There were the marks, fresh and numerous, that made Watson recall their earlier years together. No, he did not like this at all.

"Is Billy aware of your habit?" Watson asked.

"He is," Holmes said. "He even likes to inject me himself when I'll permit it." Holmes injected himself right then, and Watson nearly shuddered to think of anyone but a doctor doing something so intimate. A scarlet thread of blood bloomed into the glass like a tendril. Holmes looked at it fondly before he pressed the plunger down. The liquid sped into his arm. His eyes closed down to slits. He brought the needle to his mouth to get any residual fluid off of it, and at last Watson could not stand it anymore.

"For God's sake, Holmes, at least have enough care to be sanitary. The last thing you need is an infected vein." He snatched the syringe out of Holmes's hand.

"Don't take it too far, Watson. And don't think I don't have more if you're planning to damage it," he said, slumped in his chair with his head hung strangely to the side. Watson set the tools down on the table beside Holmes's dangling arm. He says that he thought of me in that moment, gratefully, glad that this was not his life anymore, and that he would soon begin a new one. Probably he was not the only one thinking rather happily on the changes that had occurred at Baker Street, for in the next moment Billy arrived with dinner from Mrs. Hudson. It was food for two, but Watson knew he would not be staying. Holmes too appeared less than uninterested in the meal. Billy set it down and smiled tenderly at Holmes, an almost motherly look that did not belong on his handsome, boyish face.

"There he's having a good time, then," Billy said, though he was not directing himself to Watson, but more to the room and himself.

Billy walked over to the chair where Holmes lay like a rag doll. When he was not on a case, he let the energy of the drug build within him instead of expending it. He had the most unparalleled chemistry, reacting in ways no one else would to the same stimulus. Anyone else would be abuzz, but Holmes could contain that power, concentrate it. He was a very peculiar creature.

Billy raked his hands through Holmes's thin hair, and the sensation seemed to give Holmes some kind of charge. His eyes contracted quickly and he encouraged Billy to keep at it by a flaring gesture from his hand. Watson decided it was time to leave.

He put on his hat and left the room without any notice being taken of his movements. He was halfway down the stairs when Billy called out, "Visit us again soon, Doctor," in a questionable tone. Watson froze in the stair well and heard Holmes say in a low voice, "Be nice, Billy."

Watson wouldn't see Holmes again until September, for one of the last cases of his career. If Watson was feeling tired and in need of a change, it was nothing to how Holmes felt. London just wasn't what it used to be. Neither was fame, neither was cocaine, neither was crime. He was planning, very quietly, with only Mrs. Hudson knowing the full details because he wanted her to go with him, to retire to the coast. Though he was only forty-nine years old, it was time for Sherlock Holmes to wind down. To stop.

1903: The Creeping Man

Holmes had to keep his hands busy in the meantime however, and it was to his old reliable pastimes that he turned. Watson writes, "The relations between us in those latter days were peculiar. He was a man of habits, narrow and concentrated habits, and I had become one of them." Like the violin, the tobacco, and the cocaine, Holmes would reach for Watson as a matter of course, and Watson would almost always move to meet him.

Not that it was necessarily a request, in this case. A note arrived from Holmes: "Come at once if convenient—if inconvenient come all the same." Not exactly an easy summons to ignore.

Holmes was one of his dearest friends, no one else like him in all the world or all the men that Watson had known. Writing had taught him to be even more sentimental than he already was, and even though half the time with Holmes was spent rolling his eyes or getting nagged at, he returned out of a sense of duty and friendship and hope that this would be one of those other, happier times.

Upon walking in, Watson found Holmes curled up in silence, and he waited until Holmes came pleasantly out of his thoughts and welcomed him to his former home. He seemed a tad too cheerful, and then asked a seemingly ridiculous question about dog behavior, and Watson started to wish he'd not come at all. It showed in his face, of course.

"The same old Watson!" Holmes said. "You never learn that the gravest issues may depend upon the smallest things." He went on to explain about one dog in particular who had started treating its owner strangely, attacking him on one or two isolated occasions, but with a viciousness that did not make sense, as the creature used to be very devoted. It was all to do with the case that a Mr. Bennett was bringing to him.

"Young Mr. Bennett is before his time if that is his ring," Holmes said after they heard the bell. "I had hoped to have a longer chat with you before he came." Holmes had some news to break to Watson. He finally knew his date of departure from the city. He would be leaving hardly a week before our wedding. I do believe he was officially invited, but no one ever expected him to attend, and Holmes naturally met that lack of expectation. I had never set eyes on him until he walked into my house after the armistice.

Well, so: their client's future father-in-law, employer, and landlord was acting strangely and being bitten by his own dog. He had just returned from traveling abroad in Germany and had with him a locked box that he guarded passionately. During the telling of his story the client became agitated when he felt that Holmes had quit listening to him. He was only doing a little calculating in his head, however. The incidents of the dog's attacks happened at regular intervals, and between those facts, the foreign box, and secret correspondence between the professor (for the man they were focused on was an eminent scientist), and what turned out to be a rather unorthodox doctor, Holmes formed a theory. He still wanted more evidence, and he invited Watson to come out with him: "There is, if I remember right, an inn called the Chequers where the port used to be above mediocrity and the linen was above reproach. I think, Watson, that our lot for the next few days might lie in less pleasant places."

I allowed Watson to go, since I was not his wife as yet, and because every man needs a last bachelor's hurrah before he's married. I believe Holmes meant to inform Watson of his retirement that weekend, but he was caught accidentally by this case and the pleasant time he was having with Watson; he didn't want to sour it just then, and they would need to return in a week anyway to see its conclusion, so instead of his own affairs, Holmes talked of his theories all through dinner.

Holmes thought the professor was nursing a drug addiction (he would think that), and the man was in a way, though of a more Jekyll and Hyde variety than even Holmes's habit. A week later Watson went off with Holmes again, to catch the professor in the act. They enlisted their client to follow him, and they staked out the house. It was here, and the narrative we have from Watson glazes over the moment, that Holmes told Watson he was leaving.

"It was a fine night," Watson did write, "but chilly, and we were glad of our warm overcoats. There was a breeze, and clouds were scudding across the sky, obscuring from time to time the half-moon. It would have been a dismal vigil were it not for the expectation and excitement which carried us along." Holmes, being as he was emotionally immature, could bring out the child in anyone. They were boys on an adventure, always.

"Remember I once had a notion, Watson," Holmes said, huddling close, "to retire to the seaside spend the rest of my life in scholarly pursuits?" Watson did remember. A few times Holmes had joked about it in all their long years, moving out of the city for a quiet, respectable life. Watson chuckled to remember how Holmes said he would study alchemy, try to live forever! What had he wanted to study? Ants? No, bees! Watson's chuckle quieted however when he remembered the dark days of Moriarty, and the night Holmes came to him to talk about retirement as if he'd never live to see it. He thought he would die young, be murdered. But here he was still, right beside Watson. Holmes said to him: "I leave for Sussex at the end of October."

"Permanently?" Watson asked. Holmes nodded. The news was numbing. "Will Billy be going with you?"

"Oh, no," Holmes drawled. "He doesn't like me that much. A young man like Billy wouldn't give up London unless he had to. Mrs. Hudson has consented to look after me though." Holmes glanced at Watson during a patch of moonlight. "You'll come to visit me?"

"Of course, Holmes, of course!" Watson said with whispered vigor. "Don't be ridiculous old chap, it's you who will never come to me. I bet you never even meet my new bride."

"Probably not, my friend." He touched the side of Watson's face then, his cool fingers feeling the smile lines that crinkled from Watson's eyes, and at that moment their prey for the night emerged, and they were sucked into the game again.

The old professor had found a younger woman to marry and was taking shots of monkey extract to rejuvenate himself, the main side effect however was to make him more volatile and ape-like, a state which greatly concerned those closest to him. They found a letter in his locked box from a dubious doctor named Lowenstein, whom Watson recalled being "an obscure scientist who was striving in some unknown way for the secret of rejuvenescence and the elixir of life."

Holmes, on the brink of his retirement, rather mused over what this case revealed. How fateful it seemed; he *had* established bee hives for himself in Sussex. It began as a joke and then became like a promise he had made to himself, an artful ending. He certainly didn't expect to find some ambrosia through them, but now it seemed not so funny to even try or pretend.

"There is danger there—a very real danger to humanity. Consider, Watson, that the material, the sensual, the worldly would all prolong their worthless lives. The spiritual would not avoid the call to something higher. It would be the survival of the least fit." How disgusting the mere idea should seem to any scientist. Holmes judged Professor Presbury harshly. He decided he would do something else with the bees, because the immortality of Sherlock Holmes? Well, that was already assured. Watson with his stories had seen to that. They would both live on, after a fashion, forever.

1907: The Lion's Mane

At last here is the Holmes I have known and heard of throughout the decade of my marriage to Watson, the one who has lived a dull little life in the Sussex Downs. Watson left our house maybe three or four times a year to go visit Holmes. I brooded during those long weekends, wondering what they were doing, and wondering would I consider my husband unfaithful if he were with another man. Would he mind if I took up relations with one of the girls I knew at university? Does gender make a difference? Should it? It all gave me a terrible nauseous headache. I just assumed each of his visits were no more than he told me about after each return, and enjoyed being alone in the house. Good weekends those, after I decided to see them as mine and not his. I hosted husbandless parties. I didn't have a problem with Sherlock Holmes back then, or at least not much of one.

It did concern me for a while that Watson would come back from his visits with a painful smile that wouldn't fade for days. The weekends he spent with Holmes were very occasional because they filled him with a sort of wistful sadness, they made him miss things he could not have back: the way London used to be, the way Holmes used to be, the way he used to be.

It also was not enjoyable—just as Holmes didn't like the thought of me nor I of him—for Watson to meet Holmes's most recent companion after Billy: Harold Stackhurst, a nearby schoolmaster. He and Holmes took to each other quickly, both intellectuals, and both with athletic interests (Stackhurst was a rowing Blue in his day). Mrs. Hudson confirmed what kind of friend Mr. Stackhurst really was, by accident, for on one of these visits she remarked that it was surprising to her that Holmes should find another friend as good as the doctor in a place so remote.

All those years in London, all those people in and out of her house, and Holmes had managed to find only Dr. Watson to get along with before. And now Stackhurst.

The story I have before me, another still unpublished, as quite of few of these later narratives are, is the only mystery Holmes solved in retirement, aside from the gossiping questions about who was having an affair with the inkeeper's wife, and which boy had vandalized one of Stackhurst's classrooms. It's a rather nasty little mystery, surrounding a man who appeared to have been whipped to death, but was actually attacked by a horrible great jellyfish with fiery colors called the Lion's Mane. In writing up the account, Holmes (playing the author for the second and so-far final time) completely lost the rest of his discretion when it came to his relationships. Truly he might have been right not to care; how could the law really touch him anymore, so far from the city, and so respected as he was?

Holmes wrote of his companionship with Mr. Stackhurst thusly: "He and I were always friendly from the day I came to the coast, and he was the one man who was on such terms with me that we could drop in on each other in the evenings without an invitation." This is a fact that Watson was able to ascertain during a visit a little time before this gruesome mystery, since Stackhurst came walking into Holmes's little villa unconcernedly one evening as they sat talking of the social habits of Holmes's bees.

"Well, I think I know who this is!" Stackhurst exclaimed when he realized that Holmes was not alone. "Could it be Dr. Watson? An honor and a pleasure to meet you!"

Watson liked him right away; he was a very cheerful fellow. Watson even had an idea to get him alone to talk about their mutual acquaintance—the reason I have been told all about Holmes in recent years is most likely due to Watson's overwhelming need to discuss the man and all the impact their friendship has made on his life. But though I am unique in my understanding of them, there are many points which I cannot rise to meet; the fact that I am a woman, and that I don't even like Sherlock Holmes, and that I have never known a love that was perilous—all this keeps me at some distance that I cannot overcome. Stackhurst filled in those spaces, but Watson would not be able to speak with him until some time after the events of the Lion's Mane case occurred and were written down.

Throughout that mystery, Stackhurst stepped into Watson's roll as they tried to find out who (though it turned out to be what) killed his science master. Holmes described Stackhurst as "a willing collaborator" in the investigation against the math master who was the dead man's rival in love. The woman impressed Holmes, a sure sign of his maturity: "Women have seldom been an attraction to me, for my brain has always governed my heart," he wrote. "But I could not look upon her perfect clear-cut face, with all the soft freshness of the downlands in her delicate coloring, without realizing that no young man would cross her path unscathed." A kinder man, a calmer one; retirement, against all odds, seemed to agree with Sherlock Holmes.

Holmes was finally becoming a reasonable sort of person, with some of his worst spikes being dulled down by the wind and sea. He was mostly sober—he knew better than to try and "give up" the drug definitively since there was never any predicting when he would need it again, but he seldom used it anymore. Boredom was now to be expected, and he had chosen a life of quiet uniformity, and the choice seems to have made the difference to him. Before he had been workless without his wish or consent, and now he accepted it. Watson was proud of him, in a way, but a Holmes without that maddening passion was not really the one he knew. He couldn't exactly be jealous of Stackhurst because they did not share the same man. Stackhurst had seen only a small exercise of Holmes's power and was absolutely staggered at its brilliance. He hardly knew that power! But he did know this quiet new Holmes, and Watson had questions about how he was doing now. Stackhurst had some questions too, and they finally got asked during one of Watson's visits after the Lion's Mane was killed.

"You've known him well," the headmaster said. "Is it really usual for him to, after a case has ended, for him to..." He struggled for the words. "He said it was a normal occurrence, but it seemed so..."

"Was he disconsolate for a few days?" Watson asked knowingly.

"Longer than that! He was in a wretched state for over half a month. He shrugged it off when he could bring himself to move, but how could such a thing be usual?"

"His talents come at a price," Watson said sagely. "But you've said that this was unusual to you? That is a positive sign. Holmes needs either ever-challenging cases or consistent hobbies."

"Hobbies he has here," said Stackhurst. "He studies more than even my professors, and he never seems to tire of taking notes on those bees, watching their every minute behavior. Heaven knows what use it all is to him, but he records it all the same."

Watson smiled; yes, still gathering obscure and apparently useless knowledge, always for his own secret purposes. This conversation with Stackhurst had been had while Holmes instructed Mrs. Hudson on the dinner he wanted prepared for his friends. Holmes returned from the kitchen, took one look at his two guests, and knew in an instant.

"Talking about me, I see. I hope you have not been telling tales out of school, Stackhurst."

"How could you know we spoke of you?" Stackhurst burst out wonderingly.

Holmes looked Watson over affectionately and said, "I can tell by my old friend's smile." That trip was the last they would see of each other for some time; life got away with them for a while, and soon after that, international conflict would get away with life for all of us. And yet circumstances would throw them together one last time.

1914: His Last Bow

Rumblings of war called all those able and honorable into service for the country. Everyone's plans, the natural trajectory of our lives, were interrupted. Watson thought he'd be a comfortable old man for the rest of his days, when he had to leave our house and return to active duty. We spent most of the war apart—Watson abroad and myself working domestically to help the newly orphaned, widowed, and childless cope with their circumstances. I received as much help as I gave, for I lost my family one by one, everyone except for Watson. I worried that he would find me too changed when he returned, that we wouldn't fit one another anymore, but somehow we had grown together, even as we lived apart.

Between Watson leaving our house and taking up with his regiment, Sherlock Holmes managed to find him. He needed someone upon whom he could thoroughly rely, and as Mycroft was absolutely indispensible from the government for even a moment, it fell to Watson. God knows how he tracked him down, or if he'd kept tabs on Watson all the while, waiting to snag him for this job when he knew there was no chance of meeting me (seems a bit too much of a coincidence otherwise, if you'll excuse my flattering myself). However it was done, they were off on a mission to stop a spy returning to Germany before they could even shake hands, Watson acting as a chauffer, and Holmes as an Irish-American turncoat, a roll he'd been building for two years.

Now, they hired a detective to do a spy's job, and a vain detective at that, one who prided himself on always getting his man. He was reluctant to start this job, and eager to finish it, and so once Von Bork the German agent was secure, Holmes blew his own cover. He would continue to make himself useful during the war, naturally, but not as the creatively talkative Altamont. Apparently he gave the impression of having "declared war on the King's English as well as on the English king." All an act, of course, and a fine one at that. The stage surely wept at losing him all over again.

Watson's prose expands for this story, full of love towards the country he has fought for over and over again. He has departed again from his standard narrative format to allow the story to be bigger than himself, bigger than even Holmes, encapsulating the whole darkening landscape and the specter hanging over the entire civilized world. Here more than ever before did Watson become something beyond a mere chronicler, but an artist unto himself; and though it may annoy Holmes to have liberty taken with his deeds, here it was only too valuable. At last it was a bit of a collaboration between himself and Holmes. They made history together.

Holmes was sixty, but still devilishly spry, still full of nerve. While in character he prodded Von Bork about the five agents they'd lost to the British police since he joined, knowing full well that the latter is what caused the former. Even after Von Bork was subdued he continued to be smart, sharing the man's wine with Watson, needling him with how terribly he had been fooled. Von Bork swore he would revenge himself on Holmes.

"The old sweet song," he said, turning sentimentally towards Watson and laying a hand on his heart. "How often have I heard it in days gone by. It was a favorite ditty of the late lamented Professor Moriarty. Colonel Sebastian Moran has also been known to warble it. And yet I live and keep bees upon the South Downs." He even had his book with him, a small joke on his part, wrapping it up as a prop for Von Bork. *Practical Handbook of Bee Culture, with Some Observations upon the Segregation of the Queen*. It amused him how human in organization those insects were, how British in their devotion to their Queen. England was greatly on his mind in those days, as it was for all of us.

"You are a sportsman," Holmes said to his prisoner, "and you will bear me no ill-will. You have done your best for your country, and I have done my best for mine, and what could be more natural?" Don't we all owe a debt? Who we are, our characters, whatever freedoms we're able to find—each one of us has something to give back to wherever we call home.

At last, with Von Bork trussed up and quietly contemplating his wretched luck, Holmes finally remembered who he hadn't seen in a couple of years, and paid him some due attention.

"But you, Watson!" He grasped my husband by his shoulders and turned him towards the light. "How have the years used you? You seem the same blithe boy as ever." And he was; a little portlier, a little gray, but with a face like a child, still full of sparkling hope and awe.

"I feel twenty years younger, Holmes." He had been expecting a soldier's life again, dreary and bloody and coarse, when Holmes had pulled him out for another adventure. How thrilling! How like the old days. "But you, Holmes—you have changed very little—save for that horrible goatee." He reached forward to stroke Holmes's face and chin. Von Bork was so past caring what they did that it was as if they were alone.

At last they put Von Bork in the car. Holmes prodded him further by offering to light a cigar and stick it in his mouth, and the man struggled furiously to get out of his bonds, but Holmes was as good at knot-tying as anything else, and it was all a vain effort. Holmes lit a cigar anyway and passed it to Watson, the end damp with his own mouth.

"Watson," he said as he prepared a cigar for himself. "You are joining up with your old service, as I understand. Stand with me here upon the terrace, for it may be the last quiet talk that we shall ever have."

They walked a bit, always keeping the car in sight, in case Von Bork should somehow manage to escape. They were by the sea, with tall grasses whispering all around them, and a moon high and bright in the sky. They walked arm-in-arm, laughing over things remembered and teasing one another fondly. Everything was so new, so strange. Watson says he had never seen Holmes so nostalgic, so romantic. He told Holmes that night that it seemed like the last moment of peace in all the world.

"There's an east wind coming, Watson," Holmes had said somberly, looking out at the bright, serrated sea. It flashed like knives as far as his eye could see, and it worried him greatly. He was not without a sense of crown and country; he did not ever want the sun to set permanently on the empire, even if it did get dark every now and again.

"I think not, Holmes," Watson answered, noticing the direction the grass was leaning, feeling the air. What was Holmes talking about with the wind? "It is very warm."

"Good old Watson!" For once it seemed that Holmes was the sappy one, Watson the man of concrete observation. It made Holmes smile and kiss his friend's lightly wrinkled cheek. "You are the one fixed point in a changing age," he told Watson. "There's an east wind coming all the same, such a wind that never blew on England yet. It will be cold and bitter,

Watson, and a good many of us may wither before its blast. But it's God's own wind none the less, and a cleaner, better, stronger land will lie in the sunshine when the storm has cleared." It brings tears to my eyes to even transcribe this, and if they were Holmes's own true words and sentiment, well... I guess I like him more than I thought.

They drove back to London, deposited their prisoner, and parted company. Holmes was off to shave his face, change his clothes, and try to purify his well of English since it was allegedly "permanently defiled" by his time in America, though he sounds perfectly British to me now. Holmes and Watson didn't see each other again until this very day in 1919. And now they are parting again.

1919: Dear Holmes, Dear Watson

Watson looks devastated when the door clicks shut behind Sherlock Holmes. He watches through the small glass panes beside the door as Holmes descends our front steps and gets into the car which was brought round for him by Maurice. Watson stands and gazes until the dust from the tires settles and the rear lights are not even pinpricks in the night. We agreed before Holmes ever arrived that it wouldn't be right to have him stay the night, but my Watson looks so sad now that I almost wish I had ignored my own discomfort and had Holmes placed in the guest room for as long as he'd consent to stay. I feel like I've done Watson an unkindness.

This feeling only redoubles as I go to put my arms around my husband and he cringes away from me. Not as if I have become repellent to him, mind, but as if he thinks himself unworthy of comfort. Maybe he thinks he should be hard enough to withstand what he feels alone, or maybe he thinks that Sherlock Holmes would not crumble so and wishes to emulate his exalted friend; I would say he is wrong on both counts.

"I only want to be alone now, darling," he says thickly. His face is turned away from me, but I'm sure his tears are flowing. He reaches blindly out behind him for the stair rail, and I direct his hand to it. "I shall go to bed early, I think," he says as he drags himself heavily up the stairs. Every one of his footsteps feels like a blow to my heart. I feel his pain as if it were my own, and who's to say this isn't my pain as well? We are one union of man and wife, after all, and this visit has impacted me too.

There is no real way to resolve the situation; the story is too long, too old for revision. It is finished.

And yet... I feel the need to have my say, to do something about it all, to put my unique position in use. What good is all my knowledge and all the evidence I have collected if I cannot be, in a sense, a man of action. If there is one thing that comes across clearly throughout Watson's three decades of stories, it is that all the information in the world may yet be useless if it is not properly, practically applied.

And so: I go to the writing desk and lay down a piece of paper. On the top it has embossed *From the Home of Dr. and Mrs. Watson,* which might well be unfortunate for what I am about to create, but it is what it is, and well it would be if we all learned to deal with it. I take up a pen and write:

Dear Sherlock Holmes,

I never would have thought the words, nor expected myself to write them in earnest, but there they are. After finally meeting Holmes, who would I be kidding if I were to act as if I am not somewhat sympathetic, if I made believe that he is a man totally without my ken? We are not so different, he and I, we never have been. Watson, with a wisdom he hardly ever gets credited for, has known it all along.

For that wisdom there should be at last some form of thanks. I must do something if I can—and I do think I can—to make sure that my husband never goes crawling to bed with a hurt so unbearable again. A little gratitude is warranted, from Holmes and myself, for all that we have been privileged to receive from Watson. I steady my hand, and I compose my letter thusly:

I have a horrible suspicion that you can read handwriting as though it were a crystal ball, but I write in my own hand even knowing that I must be revealing myself. You may have an idea of how thoroughly I see you, of how well I am versed in your life with my husband. I feel that I could show you no more of myself than I already understand about you, and there are many reasons for this belief.

It is not only that Watson holds no secrets from me that he does not first hold from himself, and that being his wife and a woman, I can see plenty more that he is unaware of even in his own mind. He assures me, for example, that though his life has been full of those he has loved, he no longer pines for anyone but me. He would believe this with all his heart, but you and I both know that it is not true, and why. Certainly that alone brings us into intimate understanding with one another, and we should not pretend otherwise.

With that established, and knowing as I'm sure you do that I am an honest and honorable woman, I must insist that you not let the waning years go by without visiting our home again. Though it may be uncomfortable for you and I, it gives pain to Watson that he does not deserve to have a life so divided between two people. While someone like yourself might be accustomed to wearing many hats, it is not and never has been Watson's talent. We must not keep him apart like this.

I hear a sound behind me, and thinking it is Maurice I cover the letter with my hand, ignoring the wet ink on the page. I may have to write it again if it is too horribly smudged, or else Holmes will probably deduce I was interrupted while writing something I could not trust to just anyone.

But it is not Maurice who moves in the house, it is Watson. Red-eyed, but refreshed and smiling, he comes to put his hands on my shoulders. He kisses my forehead and I discover that he has rinsed his face, for his mustache is wet. I ask him how he is doing just as he asks me the same question. We both start laughing, and in the outburst I turn my letter over casually, so that he will not see.

"I suppose I am too vulnerable these days, nerves still jangled, but I've pulled myself together now."

"I'm all right as well, darling," I tell him. "I really did manage to have a satisfying evening."

Watson smiles. "Perhaps this should be the end of it though, don't you think?" I nod my agreement, and Watson suggests we go up to sleep.

"I will follow you, I only want to finish a small bit of personal business."

Watson nods unsuspectingly, pats both of my shoulders, and goes creaking up the stairs again. Of course he'll be all right, but I want better than that for him. I want him to have an ideal balance. I want us both to have all that we can of our pasts in a place where the memories live and breathe. I turn back to finish my letter.

We owe enough to Watson in appreciation for his kind acceptance, his nurturing hands, his unceasing faith, to make an effort on his behalf. I am calling on you to do your part for him, to come to him when he wants, and I in turn will do all I can to receive you. If it is the least we ever accomplish, to achieve these barest standards of civility and tolerance, it will yet be enough to bring a smile to the face of our dear Watson.

L.A. Fields is the author of *The Disorder Series*, published by Rebel Satori Press. Her work has been featured in *Wilde Stories 2009*, *Best Gay Romance 2010* and the Bram Stoker Award-winning *Unspeakable Horror: From the Shadows of the Closet*. She lives in Chicago, IL.

CPSIA information can be obtained
at www.ICGtesting.com
Printed in the USA
FSOW02n0748160916
25087FS

9 781590 213681